No Known Grave

No Known Grave

A Detective Inspector Tom Tyler Mystery

MAUREEN JENNINGS

McCLELLAND & STEWART

McClelland & Stewart and colophon are registered trademarks of McClelland
& Stewart, a division of Random House of Canada Limited, a Penguin Random
House Company

Library and Archives Canada Cataloguing in Publication

Jennings, Maureen, author
No known grave / Maureen Jennings.

Issued in print and electronic formats.
ISBN 978-0-7710-4329-1 (pbk.).—ISBN 978-0-7710-4341-3 (html)
I. Title.
PS8569.E562N65 2014   C813'.54   C2013-903012-3
                                                C2013-903013-1

Published simultaneously in the United States of America by
McClelland & Stewart, a division of Random House of Canada Limited

Library of Congress Control Number: 2014944149

Cover art: © Bert Hardy/Picture Post/Getty Images
Printed and bound in USA

McClelland & Stewart,
a division of Random House of Canada Limited,
a Penguin Random House Company
www.randomhouse.ca

1   2   3   4   5   18   17   16   15   14

To Iden. Of course and forever.
And to the town of Ludlow, our second home.

There is no moon, no light showing at all. It takes a few moments to become accustomed to the darkness, but the pigeons are easy to locate, cooing softly, rustling in the straw of the coop. They are used to being handled so it is easy to pick one out, a sleek, brown-speckled male. It doesn't protest when the capsule is fastened to its leg. Death comes swiftly and painlessly with a hard twist of the neck. Then the soft, warm body is removed.

St. Anne's Convalescent
Hospital, Ludlow,
Shropshire

July 15, 1942

1.

SHE WAS RUNNING. SHE WAS ALWAYS RUNNING. THIS time it was along the bank of the river. She was late for something, but she didn't know what it was. Then she saw a dense cloud of moths coming towards her. They were big and grey and seemed to click and clatter as they flew. She swerved to avoid them but it was too late, and one of them went straight into her eye, where it got stuck, frantically flapping its hard and scratchy wings. Try as she might she couldn't pull it out.

Daisy awoke at once. There had been a knock on the door.

"Ten past six, Miss Stevens."

She sat up.

"Thank you, Mr. Hughes. I'll be right there."

She swung her legs over the side of the bed, waiting for a moment to steady herself. She'd opened the blackout curtains when she went to bed, and the reassuring light of early morning was seeping in through the narrow window. She licked her dry lips, trying to shake off the anxiety of her dream. It didn't take a head doctor to interpret this latest nightmare. She didn't think she'd even bother reporting it to Dr. Beck. He'd said he wanted to hear her dreams, but what good would that do? He was a nice-enough bloke for a foreigner, but talking to him once a week couldn't really change anything.

She glanced over at the woman in the other bed. Barbara Oakshutt was the complete opposite of Daisy. Sleep was a place she escaped to, and nothing disturbed her. Daisy didn't even try to wake her. Babs wasn't in the early morning massage class and didn't have to get up until it was time for breakfast. One of the sisters always came to fetch her.

Daisy stood and padded over to the washstand, curling her toes against the cold surface of the uncarpeted floor. She poured water into the bowl and washed her face, drying herself gingerly. The new skin on her cheek was still tender. Then she sat down at the dresser, examined the row of lipsticks courtesy of the Yank packages, and selected one. This was definitely a day for "Tru-Crimson." She felt in need of a boost. She took a deep breath, pulled off the towel that she'd draped over the mirror, and leaned in close to apply the lipstick properly. She had well-shaped, full lips that she was secretly rather proud of. At least *they* were untouched by the accident. That's how she referred to it in her mind, although strictly speaking the bombing raid was not an accident at all. It was premeditated and quite intentional. The only "accidental" part was that she'd been caught by flying shrapnel.

Her twenty-second birthday was this weekend. Her mother had sent a card with a picture of a big-eyed puppy on the front. Inside was a scrawled note. *Sorry we can't come to visit this week, but Dad's lumbago is acting up. We'll try next fortnight.*

Daisy wasn't really that disappointed. Visits with her family were always tense: too many awkward silences that her mother tried to fill with silly gossip from the neighbourhood. Daisy knew her mother blamed her for what had happened. She'd been dead set against her daughter enlisting from the beginning. She considered that Daisy had put herself into the line of fire, as it were.

Daisy replaced the cap on the lipstick tube and studied the effect as best she could. It would have to do. There was a moan from Barbara, followed by a series of whimpers.

Daisy went over to the bed. "Buck up, Babs. You've got to keep going."

There was no response and Daisy gave a little shrug. "I'll see you later then."

Moving more quickly now, she went to the wardrobe that was shoved into a corner of the room and took out her clothes. The patients were allowed to wear civvies if they wanted to, but Daisy preferred to dress in her WREN outfit. Putting on the familiar uniform gave her a feeling of purpose. Crisp white blouse, navy skirt, black stockings and sensible shoes, plain tie. She had just got it right when she heard the stairs creak and another soft tap on the door.

"I'm coming," Daisy called.

"There's a nice cup of tea waiting. You don't want it getting cold, look you."

"Two minutes."

Daisy went to the dresser, where the wig sat on its wooden form. Her mother had insisted they invest in top-quality hair, and it was thick and glossy brown, slightly longer than she'd been used to before. She pulled it on, gave a final check in the mirror to see that it was sitting properly, then reached into the drawer and took out the black eye patch. As a joke, an act of defiance, she'd had one of the sisters paint a dainty white flower on the surface. "I'd rather look like a walking work of art than a bloody pirate. Besides, it takes people's minds off the rest of my face."

She tied on the patch.

The orderly was waiting for her on the landing.

"Pretty as a picture as always, Miss Stevens."

"If you were an Irishman, Mr. Hughes, I'd say you were full of blarney."

"Good thing I'm Welsh then. We always tell the truth, look you."

Daisy managed to smile.

—

When Nigel Melrose felt his sheet being pulled away from his face, he said, loud and angry, "For God's sake. It's still bloody nighttime." He tried to tug the cover back up, but the other man had a firm hold. "Have a heart, Vic," spluttered Melrose. "I need my sleep. It knits the ravelled sleeve of care, as the Scottish thane so brilliantly put it."

For an answer, Victor Clark lifted his cane and poked him hard in the ribs.

Melrose yelped. "All right. All right. I'm up." He sat upright and squinted at his tormentor. "Lord help us, Vic. Do you look especially bad this morning or is it me?"

Clark pointed at Melrose. Then he lurched over to the windows and opened the curtains.

The third man, Eddie Prescott, now stirred and Clark went to him. This one he approached more cautiously. A more gentle poke and a step backward, out of range. Prescott sat up at once, his arms flailing as if to throw a punch.

"'Oo's there? Speak up, you sod. Speak up or I'll knock your block off."

Melrose answered for the mute Clark. "How beautifully poetic as usual, Eddie. But you can relax. It's just Vic making sure you're up. Rub-a-dub class this morning."

Prescott lowered his fists. "Sorry."

Vic grunted.

"That was his way of saying, 'Don't worry, old chap,'" murmured Melrose. "He takes no offence. As the call girl said to the bishop when they collided in the fog."

Eddie got out of bed, his foot feeling for his slippers. Surreptitiously, Melrose kicked one out of reach. Clark saw him and wagged his finger reproachfully.

At that moment the door was pushed open and a man in a wheelchair appeared on the threshold. He was wearing a shirt and trousers in RAF blue. Heavy, dark glasses obscured his face.

"Morning, guys. Melly, I'm glad you're already in top form. I could hear the quotes falling out of your mouth."

"Morning, Jeremy," said Melrose. "It's good to know I can still reach the plebs in the balcony."

Prescott hooted. "'Ere we go again. 'E thinks 'e's bloody Laurence Olivier."

"Better that, old chap, than having no aspirations at all above the gutter," replied Melrose.

Before Prescott could respond, Clark thrust his cane between the two men. The rumblings in his throat were clear enough. He wasn't a big man, but even his inability to speak couldn't hide the fact that he meant business.

Melrose threw up his hands. "Don't worry, Vic. I won't be drawn. I have more important things to dwell on." He turned to the man in the wheelchair. "Come on, Jeremy, I'll take you down. Let me just garb myself more appropriately. Don't want to embarrass the sisters."

He removed a burgundy-coloured silk dressing gown from a hook on the door, slipped it on, then smoothed his hair with a pair of silver-backed brushes from the dresser.

"All right then, those of you who have eyes to see, speak up. Hmm. I suppose that means just you, Vic. Am I presentable? You nod? Good." He shoved the wheelchair around so he could take the handles. "We'd better get a move on, my friend. Sarge will have our hides if we're late again. And I will die if I don't get my morning cuppa char, paltry as it is."

"Oi, what about me? I'm not ready yet," Eddie called to him.

"I cannot take responsibility for mandragora heads," said Melrose with a flap of his hand. "Vic will help you, I'm sure."

"See you downstairs," called out Jeremy Bancroft as the door closed behind them.

Prescott felt for the clothes that were neatly folded on the chair beside the bed.

"One of these days, Vic, I'm going to clock that bloke. Bloody toffee-nosed snob."

Clark grunted.

"No, seriously," continued Prescott. "The only reason I haven't bashed his head in is 'cos he's older than me. I never beat up women, kiddies, or old men."

Clark handed him his shirt and stood by while Prescott struggled to get dressed. He got into a pair of baggy black-and-white-checked trousers, a brown-striped shirt, and a paisley waistcoat.

"Do I look all right?" he asked finally. "Yesterday, Melrose made some crack about me applying to join the circus. Sod him."

He reached for Clark's shoulder. "Lead on. The lame leading the blind. What a bloody joke."

2.

THE ROOM THAT THE HOSPITAL HAD MADE AVAILABLE
for the massage classes had once been the wine cellar of the
manor house. It was awkward for the disabled students to get
in and out of, there were no windows, and it tended to be too
cool for comfort, but they liked having it all to themselves.
Windows were irrelevant.

"Whose turn is it to be the body?" asked the orderly who
had accompanied them.

"Daisy's," said Prestcott and Bancroft in unison.

"Oh, no," she replied at once. "If you think I'm going to take
my clothes off and lie on that table without our teacher here,
you've got another think coming. I don't trust you blokes as far
as I could throw you. You're always making some excuse to
bump my bosoms. The tibia–fibula attachment isn't in the
middle of my chest, as you well know."

Clark made a sort of gurgling sound.

"Don't make poor Vic laugh, he could break his wires," said
Melrose.

"Come on now," said Hughes. "Mr. McHattie won't be
happy, look you, if he finds you sitting around idle when he gets
here. Mr. Clark, how about you being the victim . . . I mean, the
subject? You're the only one who will keep his mouth shut."

"Ouch, that was unkind," said Melrose. "I'm sure Vic will be
as chatty as any of us when the doctor applies the tin opener to
his jaw."

Vic Clark waved his hand energetically at the orderly, indicating he didn't want to volunteer.

"All right," said Hughes. "By the authority invested in me by this hospital, I nominate you, Mr. Bancroft."

The Canadian moaned. "Must I? I hate being the one they practise on. It's like having four orchestras all playing different tunes at the same time. Eddie, you are far too tentative, and Melly, you and Vic act like you're trying to scrub paint off of a piece of wood. Daisy's the only one of you with any kind of decent touch."

"It's all a pile of shite, if you ask me," said Prescott. "They just want us to keep busy. We could as easily take up bloody basket-weaving."

"Get on the table, for God's sake, Jeremy," said Melrose. "I can't take Eddie's bellyaching this early in the morning."

"Do I have to strip? It's freezing in here."

Melrose's voice was scornful. "I thought all Canuck children were rolled in snow and ice from the moment of birth. Makes them tough as seals."

"I was born in Victoria, I'll have you know," snorted Bancroft. "It's a little England in more ways than one. It's never cold there."

"They'll warm you up once they get going," said Hughes.

"I'll help you, Jeremy," said Daisy. "Here. Give me your jersey. Can you manage your trousers yourself?"

Melrose whistled. "I'd say no if I were you, Bancroft."

"Oh for goodness' sake, do you have to dirty everything?" Daisy's voice was angry.

"Thank you, Daisy," said Bancroft. "I just need a shoulder to lean on for balance."

"Here," said the orderly. "Allow me."

Politely, Daisy turned away as Bancroft stripped down to his underwear, but Melrose whistled again.

"Quite awe-inspiring," he muttered. "Better than the Rockies, I'd say."

Daisy frowned but pretended not to know what he meant.

Hughes helped Bancroft to get onto the gurney, where he stretched out on his back.

"Hurry up, won't you, I'm freezing."

Daisy took a blanket from one of the shelves and covered him. "We can work around it. No sense in catching your death."

The other three moved in closer. Vic tentatively lifted Bancroft's leg. Eddie reached for one arm, Melrose took the other.

"I have to say," chuckled Hughes, "a less inspiring bunch I've yet to see. Lord help the poor patients if you ever get any. Ladies and Mr. Melrose excepted, naturally."

"What on earth has happened to our illustrious leader?" asked Bancroft. "It's so utterly unlike him to be late."

"I hope he's not been taken ill," said Daisy. "Come to think of it, I didn't hear his bagpipes this morning."

"Speaking of being ill . . ." said Melrose. "In the interests of our mental health, can we get him to cease and desist his serenades?"

"Not a chance," said the orderly, grinning. "It makes him very happy. And we all want the sergeant to be happy, don't we?"

"By the way, Hughes," continued the actor, "I do rather resent the implication that I am some sort of effeminate poufter. Not all thespians are that way, don't you know. I'm as red-blooded as the next chap. I've already asked Daisy to marry me. Not to mention all our chaste sisters."

Prescott guffawed. "That's not what I've 'eard. Queer as a box of frogs, you theatre lot."

Before Melrose could retaliate, Daisy said, "Shouldn't you go and check up on Sarge, Mr. Hughes? He really might have been taken ill."

"More likely he's gone on strike so he won't have to deal with such a sorry bunch of cripples. But I'd better pop over and see what's keeping him. Miss Stevens, I'm leaving you in charge."

He left.

Daisy spoke up. "Come on, chaps. We've got a job to do, and the faster we learn the better. Idle hands are only going to help Hitler in the long run."

"Well put," said Bancroft.

"As always," added Melrose, "our Daisy is a veritable treasure trove of pithy sayings."

3.

SERGEANT MCHATTIE AND HIS FAMILY OCCUPIED one of two cottages that were nestled into a gentle slope about a hundred yards behind the main building. As Hughes approached, he felt a sharp twinge of uneasiness. He could see that the blackout curtains were still drawn in all of the front windows. He knew that Mrs. McHattie and her daughter always visited her family in Wem on Tuesday nights and therefore wouldn't be at home, but where was Jock? It was so unlike him to be sleeping in. The two young laddies, perhaps, now that it was the school holidays, but not the sergeant. Hughes glanced over at the other cottage nearby, where Mrs. Fuller, the cook, lived with her son. Hughes had seen her earlier serving breakfast in the dining room, and, as he would have expected, her curtains were all pulled back and the windows were wide open.

He stepped up to the front door of the McHattie cottage and knocked. No answer. Had the sarge indeed been taken ill? He knocked again. Silence. He tried the doorknob, which turned easily. He pushed open the door and went inside.

The place was in darkness.

"Sergeant McHattie? Jock? Are you home?"

There was no response.

Hughes switched on the overhead light.

"Anybody home? It's me, Hughes."

There was no wireless playing, no dishes on the kitchen table, no sign that anybody had been up and about. Jock's bagpipes drooped over a chair.

Suddenly, a cat yowled and ran out from the kitchen. "Shite," Hughes gasped. "Bloody hell, Blackie. You gave me a fright there."

The cat darted up the stairs and Hughes followed it to a small landing. There was a night light here, barely penetrating the gloom but sufficient for him to make out two partly open doors.

He sniffed. There was a sour smell in the air.

Cautiously, he peeked inside the first bedroom.

"Jock? Jock, you in here?"

The blackout curtains were closed here as well and it was pitch-dark. He snapped on the light.

Even though the orderly was used to the frailty of the human body, what he saw made bile rush up into his mouth. Sprawled on the floor between the door and the bed was the elder of Jock's young sons, Ben. He was lying on his back, his arms flung out to the sides. He was dressed in his pyjamas, the top stained with blood, which had also streaked his face in dark rivulets.

Jock McHattie was in the bed, still under the covers. He had a halo of blood around his head, and there was a large, ragged tear in his pillow. Bits of white substance had spread everywhere. Brains or feathers, it was hard to tell.

Although Hughes knew there was nothing he could do for either of them, he had to make sure. He stepped closer to the boy, crouched down, and touched Ben's hand. It was cool. There was a large, black-rimmed hole in the middle of the boy's forehead. He had been shot at close range.

Slowly, Hughes straightened up and went over to the bed. Like his son, Jock appeared to have been shot. There was an identical wound in his temple. His skin was also cold. Death for both of them must have occurred some hours earlier.

The cat was meowing loudly and rubbing itself against Ben's body.

Hughes backed away onto the landing, but just as he did so, he heard a sound, so soft he almost missed it, coming from the second bedroom. His knees were shaking, but he made himself go and look. Again he had to turn on the light. There was another whimper. It seemed to be coming from underneath the nearer of the two beds. He bent down. The terrified face of a young boy stared out at him. It was Charlie, the younger McHattie boy.

"Mr. Hughes," he whispered. "Please help me, Mr. Hughes."

4 .

Detective Inspector Tom Tyler was sitting in the kitchen, half listening to the wireless and swishing the last drop of tea around in his cup. He wished he could read tea leaves the way his gran had. She was good – uncannily accurate, although he suspected most of her predictions relied on her shrewd judgment of character and the fact that she was privy to a lot of talk from her friends and neighbours.

"Ask your question in good faith and you'll get good guidance," his gran would say.

On an impulse, Tyler turned the cup three times and upended it in the saucer. He righted the cup and stared at the clump of tea leaves. It didn't mean anything to him. Just looked like a black, shapeless mess, which was, come to think of it, how he was feeling about his life at the moment. "Fat lot of help you are," he said to the blameless china.

He gave the cup a bit of a shake, hoping that some of the tea leaves would settle into more of a pattern. Give him some sign. Maybe "What does the future hold?" was too broad a question. But what *did* it hold? The move to Ludlow was intended to be a new beginning. New town, new position. When the local inspector resigned for health reasons, Tyler had jumped at the chance to apply for his job.

"Don't be deceived by the quaint rural setting, Tyler," said Chief Constable Anderson during his interview. "It's true we've led a quiet, peaceful life up till now, but since the war, we've got no end of action. There's the RAF chaps from the base pulling drunk and disorderlies every weekend; constant complaints about evacuees with ringworm and light fingers; and to add to the mix, the ever-present problem of the black market. I'd say there's never a dull moment."

Tyler assured the chief that this suited him just fine and he was offered the position.

When he'd told the chief he'd been separated from his wife for more than a year, Anderson had suggested Tyler bunk with Sergeant Oliver Rowell. The sergeant, a widower, was occupying the house the local council provided for the senior officers of the constabulary. "He's got extra room, so it's simpler all round," were the chief constable's words, and Tyler had agreed willingly, happy at the thought of company.

So three days earlier he'd arrived with some basic possessions, ready to take up *this new phase*, which was how he described it to himself.

He'd put away his clothes and the books he'd brought with him but so far hadn't determined the best place for his two precious paintings. He hadn't even unwrapped the canvases yet. They were portraits of Clare Somerville, the woman he always thought of as his one true love. Beautiful Clare, unfortunately vanished into the maw of "war business" somewhere in Switzerland.

Tyler peered into the cup. Was there anything there to indicate he would see Clare soon? Ever see her again?

He heard Sergeant Rowell's heavy tread on the stairs and checked the clock. It was almost time to get over to the station. Rowell was well over six feet tall and automatically ducked his head as he came through the kitchen doorway. Old house, low ceilings.

"Good Lord, sir. If I didn't know better, I'd think you were reading your tea leaves."

Tyler pushed the cup and saucer away. "I'm just trying to judge if I have enough for another cup."

"I'm not a big tea drinker. If you run out, you can have some of my ration."

"Thank you, Oliver." Tyler felt a twinge of guilt at having been caught in his little fib.

He took out his cigarette case and tapped out a cigarette, his second of the morning. He was counting them these days. An allowance of ten maximum.

"Anything new on the African front?" Rowell asked.

"Nope. Rommel hasn't retaken El Alamein, which is a good thing. On the other hand, the U-boats are having a field day. Two more ships sunk in the Atlantic."

They heard the shrill ringing of the telephone coming from the hall.

"I'll get it," said Rowell.

Tyler leaned over and switched off the wireless, then he went to the sink to rinse out his cup. So much for fortune-telling. He could hear the sergeant's voice.

"Oh my Lord. I'll get the inspector. Just a minute."

Tyler could tell this was no ordinary call and his heart thudded. He was always half fearful something might happen to his daughter. Or to Clare.

Rowell came to the door. "It's the almoner from the convalescent hospital, sir. She says it's urgent. Seems there's been some sort of a fatality on the grounds."

Tyler was already heading for the hall. He picked up the receiver.

"Detective Inspector Tyler here."

The voice on the other end sounded far away. "Inspector, this is Sister Rebecca Meade. I am at St. Anne's hospital. Can you come right away? There has been an, er, an incident." Suddenly her voice got louder. She'd moved the mouthpiece closer. "There are two victims. One was a member of the staff, Sergeant Jock McHattie. The other is his son, Ben. They have been shot. Both of them fatally."

"Do you know the circumstances, Sister?"

"The bodies were discovered by one of our orderlies. They were in one of the bedrooms of their own cottage. There is a younger boy, Charlie, who was hiding in the other bedroom. He is unharmed." The almoner's voice was surprisingly steady. "I am a nurse and I myself have checked the bodies. I would say that death occurred at least three or four hours ago. This could not have been an accident. The shootings were deliberate."

"Is everybody else at the hospital accounted for?"

"Yes. I have had all the staff and the patients brought together. We're not that large a hospital and we have been able to gather in the common room."

"I presume there is no sign of the assailant?"

"None."

"Is there anybody else in the family?"

"Mrs. McHattie and her daughter. They are not here at the moment. They are known to be visiting relatives overnight in Wem."

"Can we reach them?" he asked.

"I'm afraid I don't know either the name of the relative or the address. But this is a regular visit and they are due back sometime this morning. They took the bus."

"I'll have somebody meet them at the depot."

There was another pause. Tyler thought for a moment that the almoner might be drawing on a cigarette, but perhaps she was just trying to get her breath.

"Has the surviving boy said anything?" he asked.

"No, he has not. He is in a state of shock. Mr. Evan Hughes, our orderly, is with him."

"I must ask you to make sure nobody leaves the premises."

"I have already given orders to that effect."

"Well done."

The almoner's voice faded out again. "There is one more thing, Inspector. In the event Mrs. McHattie arrives sooner than expected, what shall I tell her?"

Tyler winced. He knew what that meant. "Please don't say anything for now. You'll have to stall."

Another intake of breath. She *was* smoking.

"I can only pray she and her daughter are unharmed."

There was nothing Tyler could say to that.

"I'll leave at once."

They rang off.

Tyler snatched his hat and jacket from the peg in the hall and called out to Rowell, "Let's go."

The police station was tucked into the end of a laneway directly across the street from the house. Tyler gave the sergeant a quick précis of the telephone call as they went.

"St. Anne's used to be the home of an old county family," said Rowell. "It's been turned into a convalescent hospital where they've got the shell-shocked types. I've heard they've got some really bad nerve cases, who're disfigured as well as everything else. I've seen them myself in town and to tell the truth they are a bit of a shock until you get used to them."

"Poor sods," said Tyler.

"Maybe one of them went berserk," added Rowell.

They turned into the car park next to the station.

"Has the Austin been repaired yet?" Tyler asked.

"Bailey is supposed to deliver it later this morning," replied Rowell. "Can't get the parts, apparently."

"Bloody marvellous. We'd be better off keeping a horse and carriage."

"There's the motorcycle and sidecar in the shed, sir. That's in good working order."

"Damn it, I haven't been on a motorcycle since I was a lad. I don't think this is the time for a refresher course."

"The new WAPC is a qualified driver as I understand it. She's reporting for duty this morning. She could take you."

Tyler stared at him. "What the hell – I'm supposed to show up at a crime scene on a motorcycle? And with a woman rider."

"I'm sure the young lady will be highly competent." Rowell gave him an anxious smile. "These days, nobody is surprised at unorthodox travel arrangements."

"Maybe I can hire a tractor."

The sergeant grimaced. "Not sure you'd even get one these days."

5.

Tyler crossed to the shed where the motorcycle was kept while Rowell hurried to unlock the station, which was shut down at night. Tyler eyed the motorcycle, which looked like it dated from the last war. There was indeed a sidecar, also vintage. He sighed. Perhaps after this war, the constabulary would get up-to-date equipment.

Rowell returned, accompanied by a young woman in police uniform. She was almost as tall as the sergeant, and rail thin, her height and slenderness accentuated by the tight-fitting navy blue uniform.

"This is our new officer, sir. Constable Agnes Mortimer. I've apprised her of the situation. What little we know anyway."

Tyler nodded at her. "Looks like the only conveyance is this motorcycle. Are you able to handle the wretched thing, Constable?"

"I am, sir."

"Let's wheel it out then. I suppose I'll have to sit in the sidecar."

"I do think it is a bit more dignified than the pillion, sir."

She had a distinct county accent, clipped and, to his ears, supercilious.

"I'll ring the hospital and tell them you are on your way, shall I, Inspector?" said Rowell.

"Do that, Sergeant. How many constables have we got on the day roster?"

"Including Constable Mortimer, we have six. Two others are on their rest day."

"Not today they're not. Get them in. Have all constables get over to St. Anne's right away. They'll need the camera and finger-printing kit. And I want you to send one of them to the square to meet the morning bus from Wem. Emphasize he mustn't say a word about what has happened. Just bring Mrs. McHattie and her daughter immediately to the hospital."

Constable Mortimer had heard this exchange and she frowned at Tyler.

"Begging your pardon, sir, but the women will wonder what is going on. I recommend you tell the constable exactly what he should impart."

"You do, do you?"

She was quite right, but he was irritated nonetheless. If she hadn't been handling the motorcycle, Tyler would have sent her to meet the bus. Women were better at that sort of thing. He turned back to Rowell.

"All he needs to say is that there has been an accident and he isn't at liberty to talk about it."

"Yes, sir. I'll send Chase. He's a steady man."

"Good. Then please get hold of Dr. Murnaghan. He lives in Whitchurch. He's retired, but he's one of the best coroners there is. I'd like him at the scene. Tell him it's urgent. You stay at the helm here with one of the off-duty men. Send the other one to St. Anne's."

"I believe he is spending his rest day in Shrewsbury, sir."

"Damn. I know we're going to need all the help we can get. Round up all the reservists in the area. Get them kitted out as best you can and have them come over as soon as possible."

Tyler clambered awkwardly into the sidecar, and the constable swung her leg over the bike. Her skirt didn't seem to encumber her in the least. She stuffed her cap into her pocket and started the engine.

The motorbike sprang to life with a roar and they shot off down the laneway.

"I presume you know where to go," Tyler shouted.

"Yes, sir. I grew up in Ludlow. I used to visit my aunt, Lady Cooper, at St. Anne's before she turned the house over to the War Office. It's situated on the opposite side of the river from Ludlow castle. Just past the bridge."

Tyler wondered why on earth a young woman from a good family had signed on as an auxiliary police constable. Not only were a lot of the older members of the constabulary opposed to having women officers, but as far as he could tell, the work was hardly challenging and certainly not well paid.

They turned onto Broad Street. The pavement was crowded with women on their way to catch the special coaches waiting in the square that would take them to the outlying munitions factories. Many of them turned anxiously to watch the motorcycle pass. They could tell bad news was in the offing.

At the bottom of the hill, just as they were about to shoot through the tunnel under the old city gate and into certain collision with a knot of cyclists entering from the other side, they made a sharp right turn onto Old Silk Lane. High stone walls bounded the lane on either side. There was no room for any oncoming vehicle to pass them.

"Sorry, sir."

"What?" It was hard to hear.

"I took that turn a bit too fast."

Tyler realized he had been gripping the edges of the sidecar. He felt like a right old idiot. A feeling not helped by the fact that his knees were bent up tight to his chest. There were no springs in the seat and every bump in the road jolted his posterior.

They turned left at the next intersection without any appreciable slowing down and narrowly missed a lorry coming across the bridge, en route to taking Italian POWs out to local farms to work for the day. The men sitting in the open back gaped as the motorcycle raced by. The Italians were always a reminder of the current conflict. They appeared to be very young, and Tyler felt the usual fleeting moment of pity.

The motorcycle bounced across the stone bridge, skidded right, and then raced along the leafy lane. Within minutes, much to Tyler's relief, they slowed down, and Constable Mortimer guided them into a grassy space off the side of the road, slipping in beside an ancient Austin already parked there.

"This is St. Anne's, sir."

Tyler would hardly have known there was a house there at all. It was surrounded by a high stone wall that was itself topped by a dense thicket. The roof and uppermost windows of the house were only just visible.

"We have to enter by this side gate," said Mortimer.

Tyler unfolded himself from the sidecar while the constable went ahead and lifted the latch on the wooden gate.

The house behind the bristling hedge was rather elegant, with softly weathered red brick, bay windows, and a gracious arched entrance. A concession to its current use was a ramp built along one side of the stairs. What once must have been the front lawn was now given over to vegetables. However, because of the high wall, the whole area was in deep shade and the plants didn't exactly appear to be flourishing. A handful of iron picnic tables and striped deck chairs were scattered on the strip of gravel path that ran along the front facade of the house.

The front door opened immediately and a woman in a plain blue frock came out and hurried towards them. He'd thought the title "Sister" had referred to her being a nurse, but Rebecca Meade was clearly also a member of a religious order. A good-sized silver cross hung around her neck, and she was wearing a short, dark veil, which covered most of her hair.

"Inspector. I'm Sister Rebecca. Thank you for coming so quickly."

She was probably his age or slightly older. The brown hair not hidden by the veil was lightly streaked with grey. In normal circumstances, she probably would have had a pleasant face, with smile lines at the corners of her eyes and a fresh complexion. But these were not normal circumstances and her expression was shadowed with worry.

"How is the situation, Sister?"

"Stable. All of the patients and staff are assembled in the common room, except for our two orderlies. One is taking care of the boy, the other I asked to stand watch at the cottage until you arrived." Her voice was calm, as it had been on the telephone, but he could see her self-control was hard won.

"Good work. My constables should be arriving very soon."

"I assume you will want to go to the cottage first," she added.

He nodded and turned to Mortimer. "I want you to supervise the residents. Reassure as best you can, but don't give out any unnecessary information. None. I'll be coming to talk to everybody soon. Send one of the constables to the cottage when they get here. We need a guard on the gate, both front and rear entrances of the house. Nobody should leave and nobody should be let in who's not authorized. Just let's hope our killer isn't hiding on the grounds somewhere."

"There really aren't any good hiding places to speak of, sir. Just shrubbery."

"All right. Glad to know that. Thank you, Constable. Clear about what to do?"

"Quite."

"Off you go then."

She strode off.

"This way, Inspector," said the nun.

The gravel path followed along the side of the house towards the rear. As they went past a broad window, Tyler saw that some of the patients had gathered in the bay. Incongruously, one of them appeared to be in clown's attire. A young woman with a pirate-like eye patch was next to him and beside her, a man in an elegant dressing gown and cravat. There was a long cigarette holder in his extended hand.

Tyler could see their disfigurements. Frighten the kiddies indeed.

As they walked, he scanned the grounds. The surrounding wall was only about fifty feet away from the house, and the area in between was also given over to vegetables. Here, too, the growth was spindly from lack of sunlight. Just past the bay window, there was a metal fire escape, its presence jarring against the weathered brick of the Victorian house.

The cottage where the crime had occurred was easy to identify. The blackout curtains were all closed, giving the house an oddly sightless, forlorn appearance. Normally it would have been pretty, with its white-painted bricks and a front strip of a flowerbed filled with pink dahlias and purple lupins. The high wall of thicket and stone loomed behind it.

A stocky, dark-haired young man was standing by the front door. He wore a white hospital jacket over his regular clothes. A tin helmet was perched on his head. He drew himself to attention as Tyler approached and saluted awkwardly, as if he were trying to suggest he was a military man.

"This is Dai Hughes," said Sister Rebecca. "He is one of our orderlies and he's also in the Home Guard. Dai, this is Inspector Tyler."

"Thank you, Hughes," said Tyler with a nod. "All quiet?"

"Yes, sir. Nobody has approached the premises."

He moved out of the way so Tyler could take a look at the door.

"We have touched nothing," said Sister Rebecca. "As you can see, there is no sign of a break-in. Evan Hughes, our other orderly, was the man who first arrived. He says the door was not locked."

"Would it be, usually?"

"It should have been. We ask the staff who live on the grounds to lock their doors for safety reasons." She hesitated. "Some of our patients have been severely traumatized by their experiences. They have been known to wander. 'Trying to go home,' as they see it. There is always somebody on duty at night, but needless to say, such incidents are upsetting for all concerned."

Tyler crouched down and peered at the door jamb. No scratches, nothing untoward.

"In fact, the key was still in the lock on the other side," said the almoner. "I found it myself."

Tyler addressed the young orderly. "Stay here, will you, Hughes? A constable should be arriving shortly, but until then, I want you to keep guard. Call me at once if you need to."

He opened the door and stepped inside the cottage, followed by Sister Rebecca. The air was already permeated with the insidious, inevitable smell of deteriorating human flesh.

"As I said, we have touched nothing," murmured the almoner. "However, not knowing that a crime had occurred, Evan Hughes did switch on the lights when he entered."

"Why was he here?"

"Sergeant McHattie is one of our teachers. He had not shown up for his seven o'clock massage class and Hughes came to fetch him."

Tyler looked around. The kitchen was to his left, the sitting room to his right. A narrow staircase was directly in front. Everything was neat and tidy, the furnishings sparse. The only nod to luxury was an ornate grandfather clock tucked into the far corner.

"The bodies are upstairs," said Sister Rebecca.

"Would you prefer to stay down here?" he asked.

"As I said, Inspector, I am a trained nurse. I might be of help."

"Of course. Thank you, Sister."

She led the way up the stairs, which were uncarpeted and creaked quite loudly. The landing was dimly lit by a night light plugged into the skirting board.

"In here."

Tyler stood for a moment in the doorway. The blackout curtains were closed tightly and the overhead light was on. Like the downstairs, this room was uncluttered and there was no sign of any struggle having taken place. There were two bodies. One, a young boy, lying a few feet inside the room, the other, much larger, in the bed. The noxious smell was stronger here.

Tyler went to the boy first. "This is McHattie's son, I presume?"

The almoner nodded. "Yes, that's Ben."

Tyler crouched down and shooed away the flies. The glazed eyes were open. There was the faint shadow of an unshaved moustache on the boy's upper lip and he touched it gently. Not even mature enough for stubble. Poor lad. He'd had no life yet.

"He was just sixteen years of age," said the nun. "We actually celebrated his birthday last week." She bit her lip. "A good boy."

There was a cricket bat lying close to Ben's out-flung arm. Tyler surmised he had entered the room armed with his trusty bat. It didn't appear to be blood-stained, so he assumed Ben had had no chance to engage in combat.

Treading carefully, Tyler approached the bed. Then he felt his stomach clench. On the bedside table was a ceramic dish in which sat two eyeballs. Brown irises. Tyler could see that the corpse had two sockets where eyes had once been.

Sister Rebecca must have sensed his shock. "Jock used artificial eyes. He was blinded during the Great War. Mustard gas in the trenches. He thought the prostheses made him less unsightly."

In fact, McHattie looked to have been a rather handsome man: firm chin and jaw, straight nose. His hair was cropped short, soldier-fashion, peppered with grey. Like his son, he had a jagged wound in his head.

The pillow beside him was splattered with blood but undinted. Gingerly, Tyler pulled down the quilt. McHattie was wearing blue cotton pyjamas. His bare feet were deeply scarred and pitted. Three toes were missing from the right foot.

Tyler pointed. "Also a result of the mustard gas, I presume?"

Sister Rebecca nodded. "His entire body was scarred. It's a miracle he survived at all, given the extent of his injuries. He coped extremely well, considering."

"So what are we dealing with here? Any theories, Sister?"

"None. As for robbery, Jock McHattie was hardly wealthy. He supported his family on a soldier's pension and the wages he earned as a teacher here, which weren't much. He was liked and respected in the hospital. Not only that, I cannot understand how anybody got in."

"That's certainly a high wall you've got there."

"Quite so. It completely surrounds the grounds. There are only two gates – one at the west entrance where you came in, the other on the east side. The east gate isn't really used and is always kept barred. The west one is bolted at ten thirty every night. The doors to the main house are also locked at this time."

"Who is responsible for that?"

"The Hughes brothers, Evan and Dai. Whichever of them has the night shift does the lock-up."

"Do they both live in the house?"

"Yes. They have a bedsit on the ground floor."

Tyler picked up a framed photograph from the dresser. Obviously the McHattie family: Jock, his arm around a plump, pretty woman; on his other side, a young woman who resembled the older one; two boys kneeling in front of them.

He replaced the photograph. "Let's take a look at the boys' room."

Tyler went into the adjoining room. Two single beds, both unmade. In comparison with the rest of the house, this room was untidy. A pile of comic books on the chair, some wooden tanks and a train set on the floor, drawings of aeroplanes tacked to the walls. The dead boy, Ben, had sprawled his signature across his drawings. He preferred Spitfires; his brother, bombers.

Tyler glanced over his shoulder at Sister Rebecca.

"Shirley McHattie lives at home, I take it?"

"Yes, she does." The nun frowned. "I should tell you, Inspector, that Shirley is eight months pregnant."

Tyler raised his eyebrows. "That so? How old is she?"

"She has just turned eighteen."

"And the father?"

"She has not revealed his identity. At least not publicly, that is."

"Any guesses as to who it might be?"

Sister Rebecca shook her head. "She was already pregnant when the family arrived here."

"Gossip?"

"What you might expect. A soldier who's gone overseas."

"Caused a rift in the family, did it?"

"I believe it has. Martha has already approached me about making arrangements for Shirley to give the baby up for adoption. The McHatties are staunch Methodists and the situation is a matter of great shame for them."

"Marriage not in the cards?"

"Mrs. McHattie said they weren't prepared to wait until the man returned, as there was a good chance he might never come back."

"Unfortunately, that is an all too common story these days."

The almoner sighed. "So it is."

"Where is Shirley's room? I'd like to take a look," said Tyler.

"It's off the kitchen."

Softly, Tyler closed the door to the boys' room and followed Sister Rebecca downstairs.

Shirley's room had probably once served as a pantry. Tyler stepped inside. There was just enough space for a single bed, a tiny dresser, and a wooden chair.

The blackout curtains here were open, but the morning sunshine was blocked by the forbidding wall about twenty feet away. The only concession to personal taste was a framed photograph of what appeared to be the snow-capped mountains of Scotland and a cut-out picture of the handsome film star Michael Wilding on the wall. There was no evidence of preparation for the imminent arrival of a baby. No knitting on the single chair, no crib waiting beside the bed.

A puff of wind stirred the inner lace curtain and Tyler saw that the window sash had been pushed up a few inches. As he took a step closer to take a look, a handful of bluebottles flew into the air. They had been crawling all over a dead pigeon lying on the windowsill. The bird was already stiff, its red legs and feet stretched out as if in protest. Its beak was open and its head flopped to one side.

"Oh dear, that is probably one of Mr. McHattie's racing pigeons," said the nun. "How on earth did it get inside? It must have flown against the window."

The pigeon had a rubber band on each leg; one had a number printed on it, 220; the other was slightly wider, and there appeared to be a tiny metal tube tucked down one side. Carefully, Tyler pulled it out. He could see a piece of tightly rolled, thin paper inside, which he removed and carefully unrolled.

In small block letters were printed the words:

THEY HAVE NO KNOWN GRAVE.

6.

TYLER SHOWED THE NUN THE PIECE OF PAPER. "Do you have any idea what this is about, Sister?"

She drew in her breath. "No, I don't."

"You said the pigeon must be one of McHattie's?"

"Jock belonged to a club that raced homing pigeons. In spite of his handicap, he was very active. He was most proud of the fact that his birds had won many trophies over the years."

"Did anybody help him?"

"As a matter of fact, yes. Alfie Fuller, our cook's son. That is, he did until recently."

"Oh?"

Before Sister Rebecca could elaborate, there was a light tap on the door. Constable Mortimer hovered on the threshold.

"Excuse me, sir. Mrs. McHattie and her daughter have returned."

Tyler's first response was intense relief. At least they were alive. Whatever macabre vendetta might have been inflicted on the family, it had not included the two women.

"I told them you would come and speak with them."

Tyler regarded the young woman for a moment. "Get your breath," said Tyler. "You being all upset is only going to make matters worse."

"Yes, sir. Sorry, sir."

"You don't have to apologize. Nobody likes this aspect of the job, believe me. Where are they?"

"Waiting in the foyer."

"Have the constables arrived?"

"Yes, sir. I issued your directions. I asked Constable Mady to stay in the common room with the residents in my place. Constable Chase is with Mrs. McHattie. The others have taken up their posts at the gates."

Tyler closed the door to Shirley's room. "I need to talk to the other son before I do anything else. Constable, I'd like you to stay with Mrs. and Miss McHattie. They'll probably feel better with a woman officer."

"Yes, sir."

Tyler turned to the almoner. "Sister, is there anywhere they can be put where they won't have contact with the residents?"

She nodded. "The doctor's consulting room. It's next to the common room."

"I know it," said Mortimer. "It used to be the library."

"Right then," said Tyler. "Let's use that." He looked at the constable. "Hard as it might seem, we cannot allow anybody into the cottage just yet. Even if Mrs. McHattie insists." He paused. "If you need to, you'll have to get one of the staff to restrain her. Do you understand what I mean?"

"Yes, I do. And I myself have been trained."

Tyler thought he detected the merest hint of sharpness in her voice. But what the hell, women police officers were a whole new kettle of fish. People were going to trip over sensitivities initially. As he seemed to have already done.

"Please make use of my office, Inspector," said the almoner. "It's off the dining room. The telephone is in there."

"You took over the breakfast room, did you?" chipped in the constable. "Good move. It does get a little more light at least."

"Constable Mortimer's aunt used to live here," said Tyler.

The officer turned pink. "Sorry, sir. Didn't mean to speak out of turn."

"I was simply clarifying for the almoner," said Tyler.

Sister Rebecca smiled at Mortimer. "Perhaps your knowledge of the house will come in useful."

Not for the first time, Tyler felt like a clod.

"Quite true, Sister," he said. "Now, I'd better get to it."

"Do you know how long you'll be, sir?" asked Mortimer.

"Given what he's gone through, I doubt the laddie will be up to a long interview. I'll come as soon as I can."

He turned back to Sister Rebecca. "Where is the boy?"

"I had him taken to our sitting room. Our quarters are separate from the main house. I thought it would be easier for him there."

"Your presence at the interview would be much appreciated, Sister. I assume he knows you." Tyler also felt the nun's calm manner would help all concerned. Including him.

"Yes, he does."

"By the way, Sister, what is the name of your order?"

"The Community of Mary Magdalene. We are Anglican nuns."

Tyler didn't know much about Anglican nuns, but that was more his side of the divide, as it were. Perhaps that was why Sister Rebecca was allowed to smoke. Not as strict as the Catholics.

They went outside.

"Please remain at your post, Hughes. A police officer will take over shortly."

"Yes, sir." The man shuffled his feet. "Is there anything else I can do, sir?"

"Not at the moment. I'll be coming to talk to everybody soon."

Sister Rebecca led the way along another gravel path, past a second cottage, identical to the McHatties'.

"Who lives here?" asked Tyler.

"Mrs. Fuller and Alfie."

"The one who helped McHattie?"

"Yes."

"Is Alfie a child?"

She shook her head. "I apologize, Inspector, I'm not being of much help. Alfie is an adult. He is forty-six years old." She hesitated. "He served in the Great War and suffered brain damage. He performs at the mental level of a seven-year-old."

Tyler felt she was choosing her words carefully. He'd come back to that later.

She'd said sometimes the patients had been known to wander. *God, he hoped he wasn't going to find out some sad battle-stunned lunatic had committed this slaughter.*

7.

THE SISTERS' QUARTERS WERE IN A LONG, LOW BUILDING that looked as if it had once seen life as the stables and carriage house. Like the cottages, it appeared to have been renovated recently, and the trim and doors gleamed a dark green against the white brick. It stood about a hundred feet from the main house, on the eastern side of the grounds. The ubiquitous grim stone wall ran close behind.

"How many of you are there?" Tyler asked the almoner.

"Five here at St. Anne's."

"And is everybody accounted for last night?" He'd kept his voice as neutral as he could, but she flinched.

"There was a sister on night duty in the hospital, but the rest of us were in our quarters. We retire early, as we start early."

It was hard to imagine that a woman devoted to a life of religious service would viciously kill two people, one a child, but Tyler was determined not to make assumptions before the facts were clear. He knew how unpredictable human nature could be.

Sister Rebecca opened a single door and ushered him inside.

They entered a small, low-ceilinged space that was probably the former tack room. Even though the window opposite was open, the room was close and stuffy and there wasn't much light. Tyler thought he could smell the old leather and brass polish, but he might have been imagining that. A man was seated in an armchair near the window with a child in his lap. He turned his head when Tyler and the nun entered, but he didn't stand up, putting a finger to his lips to indicate the boy was sleeping. Sister

Rebecca had told him Charlie McHattie was ten years old, but curled up like that, he seemed much younger.

Tyler went closer and the boy immediately opened his eyes and gazed at him in fear.

Like Tyler himself, the lad was a redhead, and there was a smattering of freckles across his nose and cheeks. He was still in his pyjamas.

The orderly tightened his grip.

"'S all right, look you. No need to fear. This gentleman is a police officer."

Charlie shrank back and Tyler squatted down on his haunches so he could be at the child's level.

"Hello, son. I'm Inspector Tyler. I know you've had a nasty shock, but I need to ask you some questions. Do you think you can be a very brave lad and answer them?"

"Where's me mum?" the boy whispered.

"She's at the hospital. You'll see her soon, I promise."

"And Shirle? Me sister?"

"You'll see her too."

"They ain't killed, are they?"

Tyler reached over and squeezed the boy's shoulder. The bones felt as brittle as a bird's. "No, they're right as rain, son. They were in Wem, as I understand."

"Every Tuesday. They go every Tuesday to visit Auntie Ethel."

Tyler's knee was hurting and he straightened up. "My old bones are getting stiff from crouching down here. How about I pull this chair over and sit next to you? Do you want to stay in Mr. Hughes's lap?"

Charlie nodded. Over his head, Tyler's eyes met those of the orderly. Evan Hughes was dark-haired and resembled his brother, except that his face was rough-hewn and looked as if several cleated shoes had run across it. Nevertheless, his expression was full of compassion for his little charge. His muscular arms were a place of shelter.

Tyler placed himself where the boy could talk to him more easily. "Do you think you can tell me what happened last night, son?"

Charlie looked at him. "He killed me dad and Ben, didn't he?"

"Who did, son?"

"The man who came in the house."

"Did you see him?"

Charlie dropped his head. "Can I wait for me mum?"

"You know what, your mum is going to be upset herself. It would be better all round if you could tell me first what happened, don't you think?"

"So they are killed, me dad and Ben?"

Tyler was unsure whether to evade the question for the moment but decided the boy would have to know sooner or later. "I'm afraid so, Charlie." He waited, but the boy didn't react, other than to press himself harder into Hughes's chest.

"We're going to find out who hurt them, I promise. All right?"

"All right."

The boy's voice was so low, Tyler could hardly hear him. Hughes lifted his chin.

"Speak up a bit, there's a good little laddie. The officer has got to do his job. You can bellow with the best of them, I know. I've heard you plenty of times. Tell the inspector what happened."

Charlie raised his voice, but it was still a whisper. "Ben woke me up. He was getting out of bed. He says there's somebody in the house. I was scairt. I asks him if it was a Jerry parachutist, but he says he dunno. He's going to take a look. He says to stay where I am, but if anything happens I've got to get under the bed and not move." Charlie stopped.

"You're doing grand," said Tyler. "What happened then?"

"He gets his cricket bat out of the cupboard and he goes out."

"Was your door open or closed?"

"Closed. Blackie jumps on us in the night if we leave it open."

"Your parents' room as well?"

Charlie nodded.

"Go on, son. What happened after Ben went out? Did you hear anybody speak? Did Ben say anything, for instance?"

Charlie shook his head.

"What next?"

"I heard a funny noise."

"Can you describe it for me?"

"It was a *phuft, phuft* sound."

"Anything else?"

"There was a thud."

That must have been Ben falling to the ground, thought Tyler.

"Was the *phuft* sound loud?"

"No."

"After you heard the noise what happened?"

"Somebody came to my door. It wasn't Ben."

Charlie halted. Tyler thought that all three of the adults in the room were holding their breath.

"Could you see who it was?" he asked.

Charlie whimpered like a puppy and Hughes soothed him.

"There now, there now. Try to answer the inspector's question, there's my brave laddie."

"Could you see this person?" Tyler repeated. "Had Ben switched on the light before he left?"

The boy shook his head. "No, he didn't. And I couldn't see the man. It was too dark."

"There's a night light on the landing. I'd guess you could at least make out the person's shape in the doorway. Anything you can say about that will help. For instance, you referred to a man just now. Are you sure about that? It couldn't have been a lady in slacks, could it?"

Charlie puckered his forehead. "Don't think so."

"Good. If you were going to say how big he was, this man, would you say he was big and wide like Mr. Hughes or more like me, a bit above medium?"

"Like you."

"Did he come right into your room?"

"No."

"He stayed by the door then?"

"Yes."

Tyler paused. "Is there anything else you can say about him, son? I assume because you couldn't see him too well he was probably wearing dark clothes. Did you see any white skin where his face would be? Or his hands?"

"No . . . He had a gun," whispered the boy. "I could tell he had a gun. A rifle. I could smell it too. Ben and me has shot rabbits. I know what a gun smells like."

Charlie was starting to cry, a level of hysteria creeping into his voice. Tyler knew he'd lose him soon.

"Hang on, Charlie. Us carrot tops are made of strong stuff. I've just got a couple more questions. If you don't feel like speaking, you can just shake or nod your head. All right? Now, how long was it after you heard the funny noise that the man appeared in the doorway?"

"I dunno."

"Tell you what, I'll count under my breath. You stop me when it seems about right. Here goes. Here's the *phuft* sound."

Tyler began, one . . . two . . . three . . . He had reached twelve by the time the boy held up his finger.

"Good. Well done. That gives me the idea." Tyler leaned forward a little. "Did he aim the gun at you, Charlie?"

A hard shake of his head.

"Do you think he knew you were awake?"

A nod. "I was sitting up in bed."

"Did you say anything to him, or he to you?"

The boy shook his head.

Tyler patted Charlie's hand. "And the man just looked at you but didn't stay for more than a couple of seconds?"

Another nod.

"When he left, you got underneath the bed, where you thought you'd be safe, didn't you?"

A nod.

"Clever lad. Did you call out to your pa at all?"

Charlie shook his head.

"You didn't want the bad man to come back, I'm sure. Did you hear him leave?"

"No. He was sitting on the landing the whole time."

Tyler met Hughes's look over the boy's head and the orderly shook his head slightly.

"You were right to stay where you were," said Tyler. "And you didn't move until Mr. Hughes found you?"

"No." Charlie was trembling violently now, and not even Hughes could comfort him. "I want to see me mum."

Tyler reached out and put his hand on the boy's head. "Hang on. We're almost done. You said the man had a rifle. Why did you think it was a rifle?"

"I saw the shape. It had a long barrel like Pa's shotgun."

Tyler could see that the boy had reached his limit.

"Absolutely last question, Charlie. Can you tell me what time this happened? I noticed there was a grandfather clock downstairs. Is it the kind that chimes on the hour?"

Charlie nodded.

"How many chimes did you hear when you were hiding under the bed?"

The boy was quiet for a moment, then he said softly, "Four. Then five. Then six. Mr. Hughes came after I'd counted seven."

Tyler could feel his own shoulders tensing at the realization of what the boy had endured.

"That is very helpful, Charlie. You are a trouper through and through. I'm going to have to leave you with Mr. Hughes for a bit. You look done in."

"When will me mum be here?"

"Won't be long, I promise."

The boy leaned his head against the orderly's chest. "All right."

8.

ONCE OUTSIDE, TYLER PAUSED TO GATHER HIMSELF together. Sister Rebecca stood beside him. Neither spoke for a moment.

"All right, Sister. Let's get this over with."

"Do you think the assailant did stay all that time in the cottage?"

"Not likely. I believe that's coming out of the laddie's fear. I saw men react like that when I was on the front. Previous war, same enemy. The expression 'frozen with fear' can be quite literal."

They headed back to the main house. "We can enter from the side," said the almoner, pausing at a set of French doors. Tyler could see inside. The room was intended to be cosy and intimate, accommodating two or three people. There were a couple of overfilled bookcases, two armchairs in front of a fireplace, an old-fashioned desk.

Tyler would have preferred to have met in a vast hall that could absorb the unimaginable extent of the shock he knew the McHatties were going to experience.

A young woman, presumably Shirley McHattie, was slumped in one of the armchairs. Her mother was standing by the fireplace. Like Charlie, Martha McHattie had bright red hair, hers smoothed back into a victory roll.

As soon as Tyler and Sister Rebecca entered the room, she spun around to face them.

"What is going on? A copper met us off the bus but wouldna say a word other than there'd been an accident at the hospital.

He hurried us here like the devil was on his tail. Now some slip of a lassie with marbles in her mouth has told me I can't go to my own house." Her accent was heavily Scottish, her tone belligerent. "The entire hospital is locked up in the common room, an' I just saw a constable running down the path. Is my husband all right? And my boys? I demand to know what's happened." She glared at Tyler. "Are you the one in charge?"

Tyler could see how much of her posture was bravado. She was very frightened.

"I'm Detective Inspector Tyler, Mrs. McHattie, and, yes, I am in charge. I'm afraid I have some very bad news. I—"

She interrupted him. "Maybe you'd better tell me in private then. My daughter here is expecting, and it's no good to have a shock at this stage."

The young woman was puffy with pregnancy, but she didn't seem particularly delicate. She frowned at her mother. "I'll be all right, Ma. If the news is that bad, we're better off to hear it together."

Mrs. McHattie went over and put her hand on her daughter's shoulder.

"Go on then. What's happened?"

He felt almost ill. Sister Rebecca was standing behind him and she moved forward slightly so that he could feel her presence. Steadying.

"Early this morning, the bodies of your husband, Jock, and your elder son, Ben, were discovered in your cottage. They had both been shot by an unknown assailant. I must tell you immediately that your younger son, Charlie, is unharmed. He is being cared for."

He had expected incomprehension. Most people could not assimilate such shocking news immediately. Shirley gave a little gasp and pressed her hands to her mouth, but Mrs. McHattie was very still.

"You said 'an unknown assailant.' What do you mean?" the older woman asked.

"We don't know as yet who is responsible."

"Oh, Ma," whispered Shirley.

Mrs. McHattie pulled her daughter in closer to her.

"Surely you're not telling us a Jerry landed here, went into our home, and shot two defenceless people?"

"At this point, Mrs. McHattie, I do not know who killed them. I will be conducting a full investigation."

Neither woman spoke for a moment. Tyler noticed Mrs. McHattie was looking at Sister Rebecca, not at him.

"Charlie is all right?"

The nun answered. "Yes, he is quite unharmed but in a state of shock. He's with Evan Hughes over in our quarters."

Mrs. McHattie faced Tyler. "I want to see him."

"Yes, of course," said Tyler. "I did have to question him already."

"And?"

"He said he was awakened by his brother, who appeared to have heard something suspicious and went to see what was happening. We found Ben's body in your bedroom. He had his cricket bat with him. He showed a lot of courage."

"Foolishness if you ask me," snapped Mrs. McHattie. "Thought he was all grown up, but he was still a bairn. What did he think he was going to do against a man with a gun?"

"Are you certain they're both dead?" asked Shirley.

"There is no doubt. I wish I could say otherwise."

Mrs. McHattie swayed, and for a moment, Tyler was afraid she would fall.

"Why don't you sit down, Mrs. McHattie?"

She ignored him. Her jaw was clamped tight. Again her eyes looked over at Sister Rebecca.

"Did he put up a fight, my Jock?"

"By the look of it, he was taken unawares," Tyler answered. "He was still lying in his bed."

"That doesna make sense," said Mrs. McHattie. "He would've done something, blind as he was."

Tyler didn't respond. McHattie definitely hadn't moved when the gun was put to his head.

"What about Charlie? Why was he spared?"

"I don't know. When the killer left, he hid under his bed until Hughes arrived."

It was Mrs. McHattie's turn to press her hand to her mouth. "My poor wee laddie. How long was he there?"

"We think the shootings happened between three and four o'clock this morning. Hughes went to the house at about twenty past seven."

"Hours, then. Wondering what had happened, what would become of him."

Shirley grasped her mother's hand. "Oh, Ma, try not to think on it. He's alive; that's what matters."

Mrs. McHattie brought her eyes back to Tyler. Her face was sheet white. "Who could've got in? We're locked up like jail-birds every night. Isn't that right, Sister?"

"Your front door was not locked, Mrs. McHattie," said Tyler.

"Jock was responsible for that. He did forget sometimes."

Again Tyler waited.

Shirley choked back a sob and Mrs. McHattie began to stroke her hair the way Hughes had stroked Charlie's.

"Did your husband have any enemies that you know of?" Tyler asked.

Mrs. McHattie bristled. "Jock was well respected, sir. He was blind and not a man to have enemies. You're barking up the wrong tree. I doubt it was a personal attack, if you understand me. There are some troubled young men in this hospital.

Ask the sister. Perhaps it was one of them. Reliving some battle he'd been through. Thought he'd nabbed a Jerry."

Tyler was of the opinion this murder had been carefully planned, but he supposed that didn't completely rule out madness and delusion.

"Now if you don't mind, I'd like to see my son," said Mrs. McHattie.

Tyler turned to the nun. "Sister, would you take Mrs. McHattie and Miss McHattie to Charlie? And would you make sure Hughes stays with them for the time being?" He added the last part quietly, but Mrs. McHattie still heard him.

"Don't fret, Inspector. We're not going to run off to reveal anything suspicious, if that's what you're afraid of."

"That was not on my mind, madam. I thought, as you know Mr. Hughes, he might be of some comfort to you."

"Comfort? I dinna think that's going to be possible." For the first time since she'd heard the news, Mrs. McHattie looked as if she were going to break down. But she sucked in her cheeks and didn't cry.

"When will we be able to go back to our house?"

"Not just yet, I'm afraid. First, we will have to remove the bodies to the mortuary."

"And when can we give them a decent burial?"

"You will be notified as soon as possible when they can be released."

"I see."

"We have a guest room in the sisters' quarters," said Sister Rebecca. "You can all stay there until things get sorted out."

"Thank you, Sister. That is kind . . . I couldn't bear to be too far away at the moment." She held out her hand to Shirley and helped her to heave herself out of the armchair. "Let's go and see our Charlie."

9.

Constable Mortimer had stationed herself in the hall outside the consulting room and Tyler beckoned to her to come in.

"Have the constables arrived?"

"Yes, sir. Constable Chase is in the common room. Constable Mady has gone down to the cottage."

"He's that little whippersnapper of a bloke, isn't he? Flat feet or something, so he couldn't go in the army."

"Yes, sir. I would say he fits that description."

Tyler sighed. She couldn't help her voice, at least he assumed she couldn't, but her way of speaking was getting his back up.

"What about the others?"

"Constables Eaves, Biggs, and Stanton are in the foyer awaiting orders. Constable Swinfell is on his way. Sergeant Rowell has sent word that four reservists should be here shortly after noon. He also wished you to know that he has reached Dr. Murnaghan and he will be arriving in about an hour's time."

"Good."

"What is the next step, sir?"

Valid enough question. She's not challenging you, just wants to know what to expect.

"I'm going to get my bearings first. Sister Rebecca will show me around the hospital. I want you to go tell the constables to start patrolling the grounds. As soon as we have our full complement, we'll organize a proper search, but they can at least have a look round now."

"Do you suspect a resident, sir?" Mortimer's expression was anxious. "My relatives were quite fearful of robbers. Hence the high wall and thicket. It would be difficult for an outsider to penetrate, I do believe."

"Yes, well, I tend to agree with you. We'll see what we find."

Tyler stepped out through the French doors. The almoner came towards him. She didn't need to say how painful it had been to witness the reunion of the McHattie women with Charlie; it was obvious from the haggard expression on her face.

"Where would you like to start, Inspector? I hope you won't mind if we move quickly. The residents have been waiting for quite a while now."

"I realize that." He was trying not to show how edgy he felt. "Is there a back door?"

"There is. Come this way."

She turned on her heel and he followed her around the side of the building to the rear, where a door opened onto a narrow hall. The day was already starting to heat up, but inside the main house it was pleasantly cool. The original oak panelling had been retained, and in spite of the linoleum floor covering, there was an immediate sense of a more luxurious, bygone age.

"The doors are closed," said the almoner. "The patients won't see us."

They went through to the main foyer, which was also panelled and spacious. An elegant staircase curved to the second storey.

A faint sound of BBC light music emanated from the room where the residents had been gathered. Tyler could feel himself grow tense. He'd be seeing them all soon enough.

Sister Rebecca proceeded up the staircase.

"The original bedrooms have been converted into wards. We have thirteen men on the second floor and our four women on the third. Their rooms were originally the servants' quarters. We would have preferred the women have nicer rooms, but it wasn't practical. We would also have liked more light on the ground floor, but obviously we can't take down the wall even though it blocks everything out. We are cramped, but as the house was donated for the duration, we're very grateful."

The stairs swept upward to a wide, gallery-style hall that opened to the left and stretched along the breadth of the second floor. Deeply inset windows looked out to the front of the house and the hall was currently splashed with bands of sunlight. The four bedrooms were on the opposite side and the doors to each were standing open. As with the downstairs, there was no carpeting, and here a dark wood floor gleamed with the patina of age.

It was impressive. Tyler thought Rowell's kitchen would have fitted in that hall a couple of times over.

Sister Rebecca gave him a bit of an impish grin. "Those Victorians knew how to waste space when they wanted to. The generosity of the design of this house is itself healing. It also makes it easier for our wheelchair-bound patients to get around."

She indicated an alcove a few feet to the right of the staircase. "We call this the nurses' station, although it barely deserves the name. There was originally a good-sized linen cupboard just there, and we were able to open it up sufficiently to make room for the desk." She pointed at two cabinets behind the desk. "We use these to store medications and medical utensils. And here—" she pulled open the lower drawer "—we have a spirit stove and kettle for the sister on night duty to make tea or cocoa when she has her break."

He could tell she was rather proud of their ingenuity.

Tyler went and sat in the wooden chair behind the desk. The desk was strictly functional, with a night lamp and a single drawer. Somebody had left a silver mug in which he could see the remains of cocoa.

"Who was on duty last night?"

"Sister Ivy Packwin."

"And presumably she hasn't reported anything untoward?"

"Nothing. She was as shocked as all of us when we heard the news."

From where he sat, there was a clear view down the hall as far as the side window where he'd seen the fire escape.

Tyler stood up. "I'd better take a look at that."

The sash window opened smoothly and the sill was low. He climbed out onto the iron steps. They were steep, dropping almost vertically to the path. He half-slid to the bottom and then turned and came back up as fast as he could. Once he had clambered back inside, he was panting. The fire escape would only be an easy exit for the agile.

The almoner waited.

"Sister, I'm going to need a list of all the residents, both patients and staff. I know I'll be meeting them shortly, but any information from you now would be helpful. For instance, how many of the patients are actually mobile and physically able?"

She hesitated. "I understand what you need to know, Inspector, but from our point of view the answer is not necessarily simple. All of our patients have a disability of some kind, whether it be mental or physical. Sometimes it is both."

He regarded her quizzically. "Details please."

"As I mentioned, we have seventeen patients in total: thirteen men and four women. I would say that eight of the men are clearly incapable, because they are either blind or unable to walk. In some cases, both."

Tyler took out his notebook and pencil. "What about the women?"

"One is blind. One has partial sight and is mobile. The other two are afflicted with severe psychosomatic troubles and are confined to wheelchairs."

"But physically there's nothing wrong with them?"

"I suppose you could say that."

Tyler chewed on his pencil for a moment. "If I've done my arithmetic properly, I count eight able-bodied people. Five of them are men."

"Technically speaking there are five, but as with our two female patients, two of the men have psychosomatic illnesses that incapacitate them."

"But there is no physical injury? They can see and they can walk if they have to?"

"Yes."

Sorry, Sister, I know you are being loyal and protective of your patients, but at the moment, they are all suspects. That's how it goes with a murder investigation.

"Other than the front and back doors, are there any other entrances to the hospital?"

"There is a door on the east side. It was originally reserved for the servants, who slept on the second floor. The stairs from those quarters lead into a passageway that can be accessed through here." She pointed to the door just a few feet behind where they were standing.

"Do you use that door?"

"Hardly ever. It's kept locked. We try to keep a close eye on the comings and goings of our residents and prefer that those who can walk make use of the main staircase."

"And if they can't walk?"

"We have a small lift. We were able to open the original dumb waiter in the kitchen. It's a bit inconvenient because it means the access is from there – and we weren't able to install it all the way up. The women patients have to be helped down to the second floor, but it's still a godsend."

Tyler made a note. "So I'm counting three common entrances and exits then? Front, rear, and side doors. If we include the French doors of the consulting room and this fire escape, we actually have five."

She inhaled sharply. "Yes, you're quite right. I wasn't thinking of the latter."

"Who has the side door key?"

"It is kept in the nurses' desk."

Tyler looked down the hall again. "I don't see how any of the
men on this floor could have got out without the night duty
sister seeing them."

"I agree."

Tyler stowed his notebook.

"Can I take a quick gander at the bedrooms?"

"Of course."

"Let's start with the one closest to the fire escape."

They walked to the end of the hall and she ushered him into
a large room. There were three beds, two mahogany wardrobes,
and a commodious matching dresser. The windows were long
and elegantly curtained, the wallpaper floral.

Tyler whistled through his teeth. "Are all the rooms this posh?"

"They are," she answered with a little smile. "As you can see,
we have retained the original plush wallcovering. It was in
good condition and we saw no reason to replace it. For obvious
reasons, we call this the purple room. All of the carpets have
been removed so that those who need wheelchairs can get
around more easily. I'm afraid the beds haven't been made yet."

"Understandable," Tyler murmured.

He walked over to the windows and pushed one open.
From here, he could see both the McHatties' cottage and
Mrs. Fuller's cottage. By leaning far forward he could even
glimpse the nuns' quarters. Between the two cottages was a
pigeon coop. Even as he watched, a bird flapped to a landing
on the protruding ledge.

He turned back to the almoner and took out his notebook
again.

"Who is in this room?"

"Do you want me to name each of them or only those who can get around unaided?"

He shrugged. "Might as well give me the lot."

"Eddie Prescott is by the window. A former gunner, who is blind, without nose or lips. The result of a crash and an exploding gasoline tank."

Tyler ran a line down the centre of his page, heading the left side NOT ABLE, the right, ABLE. He put Prescott in the left column.

Sister Rebecca continued. "The bed closest to the door is Victor Clark's. Also a pilot. He was on a training mission and his plane collided with an incoming Spitfire when he was taking off. He was badly hurt, and at the moment, the inside of his jaw is wired shut. The fingers of his left hand were also fractured. His spine was damaged and he uses a cane."

"Will he be able to fly again?"

"We're not sure. His jaw will mend and so should his fingers. We don't yet know about his spine."

She went to the third bed. There was a stack of playbills piled on the floor next to it.

"Over here is Nigel Melrose, our Olivier, as we call him. He's our oldest patient. He's fifty."

"Not a military casualty then?"

"He's actually an actor. Or at least he was. In fact, he was performing in a Shaftesbury Avenue theatre when there was a bombing raid. He was hit with shrapnel."

"Poor bloke. That can't be good for his career."

"Unfortunately, no. He is dreadfully disfigured and his sight was affected. But he is ambulatory and I'd say his morale is good." She smiled. "He was one of the patients you saw at the window. He always manages to give the impression he's about to step into a play by Noel Coward. All three of these men were students in Sergeant McHattie's class. We're certainly hoping it might provide a new career for them."

Tyler made a note. Nigel Melrose: ABLE; Victor Clark: questionable. He nodded to Sister Rebecca that they could move on.

The next room was indeed as posh as the first, with the same high ceiling and deep windows. The wallpaper pattern here was outsized ferns.

"Let me guess," Tyler said. "This is referred to as the Green Room?"

"Quite right."

This room also contained three beds, two wardrobes, and an antique dresser, in the same layout. Again Tyler went to the window and looked out. Another good view of the cottages.

The almoner continued. "The bed by the window is Jeremy Bancroft's. He's a Canadian and was flying with the RCAF."

"Another plane crash?"

"Yes. He was just returning from a mission over France. Ran into bad weather over Dover. He has lost his sight and he incurred serious burns. He's in a wheelchair for now." Again there was the involuntary sigh. "He is engaged to be married to an English girl. She hasn't seen him since the crash."

"You think she's in for a shock?" Tyler asked.

"Most definitely. Nothing prepares you for what burning gasoline can do to human tissue. But after a while you get used to it. If she can weather the initial shock, perhaps they'll be all right. Jeremy was also studying massage with Mr. McHattie."

Tyler put Bancroft's name in the left-hand column: NOT ABLE.

"The other two men in this room are Herb Mullin and Alekzander Bobik. Mr. Mullin is another colonial. An Aussie. Also with Bomber Command. You can definitely put him on the 'not able' list. He has no feet. They were shattered when his bomber crashed." She indicated the remaining bed. "Mr. Bobik's plane was downed in the Channel. He is physically able, but he remains in a state of shock from his ordeal and cannot stop shaking."

Tyler put Bobik's name on his ABLE list, also with a question mark.

They proceeded to the third room, not speaking.

Except for the colour scheme, the Blue Room was identical to the previous two. Sister Rebecca continued with her descriptions. Her voice was dry and matter of fact, but she was only human and her sympathies slipped through.

"Over here by the window sleeps Vadim Bhatti, our wonderful little Gurkha. I say 'little' not in any patronizing way, but he is quite small. He was injured by artillery shrapnel and cannot see. He also has lost his English. Apparently, he could speak impeccable English before the injury but now doesn't seem to understand it at all and will only speak Burmese." She flashed Tyler a brief smile. "You don't happen to know Burmese, do you?"

"'Fraid not, Sister. I never got farther than the trenches."

"We are hoping to get somebody to visit him soon from his old regiment. Someone who can talk to him."

Tyler added the Gurkha to the NOT ABLE list.

She moved on. "This bed belongs to Isaac Farber, another RAF pilot, whose Spitfire crashed in the Channel. He is Jewish." She frowned. "He says that the Nazis have imprisoned his entire family somewhere in Poland. They are specifically targeting Jewish civilians."

"It's not the first time I've heard this." Tyler shook his head. "If it's true, it gives us a darn good reason to win this war."

They headed for the last room.

"We have four men in here, as it is the largest. Be prepared. We refer to it as the Red Room for good reason. Lady Cooper seemed to like vibrant colours."

Tyler felt as if he had walked into the mind of an inebriated Impressionist painter. The flock wallcovering featured huge cabbage roses, the Victorian delight, splashed from floor to

ceiling. The white trim only served to accentuate the brightness of the wallpaper. The room was indeed large and managed to hold four beds, three massive black wardrobes, and two
dressers. When he checked the windows, he could see the
same view as the other rooms.

"Perhaps our most severe cases are in this room," continued
the almoner. "By the window is Ned Locke, who has no hands
and is badly disfigured."

"Another flier?"

"A navigator, actually. All of the rest of the crew were killed.
He is more tormented by that than by his own injuries. He
holds himself responsible because the plane went off course in
a fog."

Tyler marked him as NOT ABLE.

"Next to him is Donald Barnard, who is blind. He was
piloting a Lancaster that was hit by flak. The gas tank exploded
and burned off most of his face. Somehow or other he managed
to fly it home and save the lives of his crew."

NOT ABLE.

"In this bed is Sidney Hill, a civilian injured in a bombing
raid in Birmingham. Both legs were amputated and he is quite
deaf. The saddest thing is he has two young children."

NOT ABLE.

"Here is Graham Coates. He is our youngest patient, just
nineteen. He was working at a munitions factory when there
was an explosion. Five people died and he suffered severe burns
to most of his body."

"Was that at Bridgend?" Tyler asked.

She nodded. "That's the one . . . Graham has sight, albeit
poor, and he is mobile. But he is badly disfigured and unfortunately remains in a state of depression."

Tyler added Coates's name to his ABLE list, but again with a
question mark.

"You said earlier that some of the patients had been known to wander. Which ones?"

"We did have a case previously, but he went back to East Grinstead. He needed more help than we were able to provide. Of our current patients, we do have to keep an eye on Vadim. Even though he is blind, he still tries to get out."

Tyler made a note.

The final thing to inspect was a huge, marble-tiled bathroom and the separate toilet next to it. The entrance was from the hall just in front of the nurses' desk.

"We are given licence to use as much hot water as we wish," said Sister Rebecca. "Many patients find a saline bath to be soothing."

They went back into the hall. There was less sunlight now. Clouds were moving in – or maybe that was just his mood, Tyler thought. It wasn't easy to be given a tour like this.

Sister Rebecca had spoken without sentimentality but with much compassion. As for him, his policeman's mind was concentrating on ABLE, NOT ABLE. Possible assassin, not a possible assassin.

NOT ABLES were definitely predominating, and he felt a slightly irrational sense of relief. He didn't want his brutal killer to be a tormented patient.

"Those are all our male patients, Inspector. Shall we go to the third floor?"

At that moment, they heard rapid footsteps on the stairs and one of the sisters appeared.

The nun halted abruptly when she saw Tyler and the almoner. "Beg pardon. I realized I'd left me mug on me desk. It's me special one."

Sister Rebecca nodded at her. "Sister Ivy, I don't believe you've met Inspector Tyler yet. He's conducting the investigation into the . . . the, er, deaths."

The other nun was a husky woman, her broad cheekbones ruddy and sprinkled with freckles. Like Sister Rebecca, she wore a plain blue frock and a short black veil, but whereas the almoner was neat and composed, Sister Ivy was definitely rumpled. Tyler couldn't help but notice she had spilled what looked like some of her cocoa down her front.

She blinked nervously at Tyler. "What would 'ee like to know?" She was a Shropshire woman.

Tyler smiled reassuringly. "First off, the obvious. Did you hear anything at all last night?"

"Nowt. All quiet on the Western Front the whole time." Suddenly her eyes filled with tears and she ducked her head. "Who could have done such a dreadful wicked thing, Inspector? Young Ben McHattie was hardly out of short trousers. And Jock? A good man through and through. What on earth happened?"

"I can't give you an answer yet, Sister. Anything you can tell me could be of help. Anything at all."

Sister Ivy pointed at the sole chair. "Do 'ee mind if I sits meself down? I've been shaky on me pins all morning. Completely knackered is the truth."

"Allow me," said Tyler as he pulled out the chair. The nun plonked herself down with a sigh. "That's better," she said with a grin. She had big, widely spaced teeth, and her smile was infectious.

She was so unpretentious he couldn't help but smile in return. Sister Ivy was the kind of nurse who would always be described as jolly.

"Where were I?" she asked.

"I was just asking about last night. I'm sure you have your routine. Did anything out of the ordinary take place?"

He thought he saw fear flash across her eyes, but it was gone so fast he couldn't be sure.

"Well, I come on duty at eleven. Patients was all asleep by then. As they was supposed to be. We goes to bed early here 'cos we gets up with the dawn. Sister Rachel, who was on evening duty, handed me her report. All present and correct."

"Did you go to check in on the patients when you first arrived?"

"Not right then. I didn't want to disturb nobody. Some of them is light sleepers. As long as the previous sister says all is well, which Sister Rachel did say, I don't do me first round until midnight."

"Then did you go into each room?"

"Aye."

"Any problems?"

"None. What's I mean is, no unforeseen problems. I 'as to help Mr. Locke to the toilet at least once a night." She lowered her eyes. "'E's got no 'ands, see. 'E usually needs to go about one o'clock. Then I got 'im settled back in bed." She paused, and Tyler thought she was preparing her words. "Everybody was fast asleep. I checks to make sure they 'aven't kicked off their covers or they're not 'aving a nightmare. They whimpers and twitches if they is, so I might just wait to see if they're going to wake up and need another sleeping draught or if it will just pass. They was all peaceful last night, bless 'em."

"Did you do another round after that?" he asked.

"Oh yes. We go every hour. Then the last one is at half past five. They start getting up about six."

"Does your round include going to the third floor to check on the women patients?"

"It does. They aren't no trouble. There's only four of them."

"How long would that take you?"

"No more than ten minutes at the most. They each have a bell by theys bed, see. They can ring if they need anything. Never do."

"In between rounds, did you stay at your desk the entire time, Sister?"

She shot a glance at Sister Rebecca. "Course I did. Except for when I has me tea break at a quarter past two. I made some cocoa on the spirit stove and I also used the toilet. Otherwise I was sat right there without budging the whole night. As I'm supposed to."

"Could anybody have left their room while you were upstairs or in the toilet?"

"Not likely," she snorted. "Like I said, the upstairs round is only about ten minutes, and as for the toilet . . ." she dropped her eyes modestly. "Well, I was only in there a few minutes. Besides, if somebody did get out of bed, where would they have gone? Us don't encourage them to go wandering around on's own. You never know if they're going to trip over something. They're given strict instructions. 'Do not get out of bed to use the toilet without first calling the nurse on duty.' We say that all the time, don't we, Sister?"

Sister Rebecca nodded. "Yes, we do."

"Furthermore, when I have finished my ablutions," said Sister Ivy, "I always have another check of all rooms upstairs and down. Last night, as usual, all was present and asleep."

"It must get pretty dull on night duty," said Tyler. "Do you ever find yourself nodding off? Not that I'd blame you, mind."

Sister Ivy shook her head vigorously. "Not I. I does me reports and reads me Bible." But Sister Ivy had blushed and Tyler thought she wasn't telling the whole truth.

At this point, Sister Rebecca interceded. "We consider it safer to have a back-up plan. Our two orderlies rotate night duty. They can sleep if they want to, but they are on call if needed. There is a cot outside in the passageway."

"Who was there last night?"

"Dai Hughes. You met him at the cottage."

Tyler turned to Sister Ivy. "Did you see Mr. Hughes, Sister?"

Again she blushed. "Aye. He comes on duty same time as me. Eleven o'clock. We had a bit of a chinwag, then he went to his bed." She looked anxiously over at the almoner. "I don't mean chinwag exactly. Mr. Hughes wanted to ask something about the medications. We were expecting a new delivery from Boots, but it hadn't come yet. We didn't speak long. I didn't really break the Grand Silence, Sister."

"I'm sure you wouldn't talk unless it was necessary, Sister Ivy."

Sister Rebecca's tone of voice was neutral and Tyler didn't detect any covert sarcasm, but the other nun squirmed.

She scowled at Tyler.

"None of our patients would be a murderer, if that's what you're trying to find out. Isn't that right, Sister? Tell the inspector he's barking up the wrong tree."

Sister Rebecca let slip a barely audible sigh. "The inspector has to investigate every possibility."

"Well, I don't think it's right. Poor men have suffered enough."

Her loyalty was admirable even if her logic wasn't.

"I was just about to take the inspector to the third floor," said the almoner. "You must be tired, Sister. Why don't you get a rest. The inspector can call on you later if he has to."

Sister Ivy beamed her big smile again. "All right then. I could do with a bit of shut-eye."

"Just before you go, Sister, there is one more question," said Tyler. "A rather important one. At the moment, we have no idea if the murder of Jock McHattie was planned or random. If it was planned, the implication is that the murderer was familiar with the routine of the hospital. Perhaps he knew that Mrs. McHattie and her daughter would not be at home, for instance."

"They allus went to Wem on Tuesdays. Everybody here knows that."

"Precisely. In the same vein, then, how fixed a routine is there at night? You've described your rounds to me, but do you always take your tea break at the same time?"

She nodded and he could see how tense she had become. "Unless there was somebody needed tending to, I always have me cocoa after me two o'clock round. Just one cup and then it's back on duty."

"Thank you, Sister. You have been very helpful."

"I'll bid you good morning then."

She picked up her mug and left them.

Sister Rebecca turned to Tyler. "I apologize for Sister Ivy, Inspector. She is one of our longest-serving sisters, and she is not at all a worldly woman."

Maybe not, thought Tyler, but she was rather good at presenting herself as guileless. He'd have to question the orderly about the duration and content of the little chat they'd had. Was it just religious guilt that made her seem as if she was hiding something? Had they simply talked longer than they should have? Had she taken more time than she admitted for her tea break? Was it important if she had? From what she had said, there were short periods of time when patients were not under her direct supervision. But even if somebody had got out, they would hardly have had time to go to the McHattie cottage, commit murder, and return to their room.

Unless of course the murderer and Sister Ivy were, for some incomprehensible reason, in cahoots.

10.

SISTER REBECCA OPENED THE DOOR TO A NARROW passageway.

"We did our best to make it a little more presentable," said Sister Rebecca. "We gave it a new coat of paint and added wall sconces. Nonetheless, I do believe I can still feel the presence of those maids, going up to their bare attic rooms with their candlesticks, trying to make as little noise as possible so as not to disturb their betters."

Tyler raised his eyebrows. "Do I detect a whiff of socialism, Sister?"

"No particular politics, Inspector, just human sympathy."

At the far end of the passage was a flight of stairs that turned sharply up to the next level. Squeezed between these and the wall was a lift with an iron door. Tucked underneath the stairs was a cot.

"The orderly on night duty rests there," said the nun.

Tyler glimpsed a magazine partly hidden under the blanket. It was the kind familiar to young men, the kind his mother would have been shocked to see. He wondered if the nun was aware what one of her staff was reading.

The stairs to the third floor were steep.

They reached a tiny landing and Sister Rebecca switched on a low light. There were two doors and she opened one of them.

"Miss Susan Broadbent and Mrs. Caroline Bowman are in here."

Tyler made a note. Here again there had clearly been an attempt to make the room cheery, with fresh, buttercup-coloured paint, but there was only one small window, high up. The ceilings sloped and there was little space. It seemed dreary to him, especially after the spacious, light-filled rooms the men enjoyed.

"Miss Broadbent is confined to a wheelchair," said the almoner. "She was travelling home on leave from London when her train was strafed. We cannot determine the extent of her injuries. They seemed to be superficial, but she is unable to walk."

Tyler put her on the ABLE list, with a question mark.

"Mrs. Bowman is one of our saddest cases," said Sister Rebecca. "She is from Liverpool. Her house received a direct hit and she was buried in the rubble along with her two children. They had been sheltering in the pantry under the stairs. Both children were killed, and she herself was not rescued for three days. She has not uttered a word since."

"Is she mobile?"

"In a manner of speaking. She has her sight and the use of her limbs, but we can get no response from her. She doesn't move."

"Does she have any other family?"

"Her parents are deceased. Her husband is fighting in North Africa and we have not been able to contact him. The poor fellow has no idea what has happened."

Tyler added Mrs. Bowman to the ABLE column, with a double question mark.

"It must be difficult to get the women down those stairs if they can't walk."

"Very. We always need two people. But at least we do have the lift, tiny as it is."

They entered the second room. The walls were painted a soft pink, but otherwise it was the same as the first.

"Daisy Stevens is in here. She was a WREN. Still is, I suppose. She was injured by flying glass when an unexploded bomb went off near the restaurant where she was having lunch. She has lost most of her scalp and has no vision in her right eye. She was one of the group who were studying massage."

Tyler put Daisy in the ABLE column.

"Finally, we have Miss Barbara Oakshutt, who was a WAAF. She was injured during an attack on the airfield where she was stationed. Her fiancé, a mechanic, was killed in the same attack. She is blind."

NOT ABLE.

Tyler put away his notebook. "Thank you, Sister. I must say these are horrific tales."

"They are indeed. However, we do our level best to impart hope to these unfortunates. With the right attitude, there is a lot they can do. And mostly they are young people with all the resilience of youth."

The words could have sounded ridiculously optimistic, but Tyler already knew Sister Rebecca was not one to trivialize the terrible challenges her patients faced. She believed what she said and would stand by it.

"Perhaps I could take a closer look at their individual files sometime later."

"Of course. And my office is completely at your disposal."

"Right! The breakfast room."

"Exactly . . . Your constable seems very competent, by the way. I'm glad to see more openings for young women in the police force."

"I am too," said Tyler. "Although to be honest, I'm still sorting out how to respond to the changes."

She smiled. "As is the rest of the world, Inspector."

He plunged on. "I must say how much I admire the care you provide for your patients."

Her eyes met his in surprise. "I don't know how one could be other than caring. But as you know, St. Anne's is a drop in the bucket given the number of wounded men and women who need help . . . Madness has been unleashed upon the world. Here we are doing our best to help the victims of that insanity. Ultimately, I know it will not prevail."

He halted. "In my better moments, I agree with you, Sister. And at other times, I'm not so sure."

He half expected she would offer him some piety, some affirmation that God was looking after the righteous, but she didn't.

They went back down to the second floor.

Tyler indicated the lift. "Do you mind if we go that way to the ground floor?" he asked. "I'd like to check it."

She was right about the lift being tiny. It would barely fit a wheelchair, let alone two people. She and Tyler were forced into close proximity, shoulder to shoulder. She stood with her hands clasped, looking straight ahead. She was almost the same height as he was and she smelled faintly of antiseptic. Tyler's thoughts jumped to Clare, who loved expensive scent. What brand was it she liked so much? Something French, as he remembered. One bottle cost more than he made in a month. Sort of flowery . . .

The lift halted with a jolt and they exited into the empty kitchen. Sister Rebecca led the way into yet another passageway. She selected a key from the ring at her waist and unlocked the side door.

A trellis thick with climbing roses ran to a wooden gate in the wall, about a dozen feet away. It was identical to the one he'd entered through when he first arrived. The trellis ensured privacy, screening any comings and goings from the house itself.

"As you can see," said the almoner, "there are three bars on the gate – a holdover from the previous owners. They're probably rusted shut by now. I don't think we've used it since we arrived. It was a tradesmen's entrance."

"What's on the other side?"

"A public right of way. You can get to it by way of the road. It leads to the river."

Tyler walked to the gate, which was indeed barred with solid iron bolts. He tested the first one. It squeaked loudly but moved easily. Certainly not rusted. Neither were the other two. He pushed the gate open and it moved smoothly on its hinges.

On the other side was a grassy, tree-lined path.

He returned to Sister Rebecca.

"It does seem that the gate is usable, Sister."

"So I see. Obviously, the bolts were not rusted as I had presumed. Somebody has tended to them. But believe me, Inspector, we are very careful to keep all keys in safekeeping. This door is always locked. No one from the house would be using that gate. And I don't see how an outsider could have entered that way unless they were able to climb over the gate."

In fact, there was a strip of latticework on top of the gate making it even more difficult to climb over. With the high wall surrounding it, the locked doors and barred gates, St. Anne's appeared to be inviolable. Tyler could see the worry in the almoner's eyes. He wasn't the only one capable of drawing conclusions. Somebody had got to Jock McHattie. And if no one had got in from the outside, the killer must have come from within the hospital.

"I've seen enough for now," said Tyler. "I'd better talk to the residents. Patients and staff."

11.

"PLEASE, MA, I NEED TO STRETCH MY LEGS. I WON'T be long, I promise. I'll just go as far as the bridge and back." Shirley McHattie put on her most pleading expression. "Charlie needs you, Ma."

"All right. But only as far as the bridge, mind."

Shirley left quickly, before her mother could change her mind. The constable at the west gate studied her. She smiled at him but inwardly she cringed. She knew what he was thinking. *"Where's your husband, young lady?"*

But he let her through and she set off along the road in the direction of the Dinham Bridge until she got to the public right of way. She climbed clumsily over the style in the fence. The sun was peeping through the trees and she glimpsed her shadow on the ground as she walked. Monstrous swollen belly. She hated being pregnant. When they first became intimate, she'd been nervous, wanting to take precautions, but Rudy had whispered in her ear, overriding her objections. *"Oh, I know what to do, Shirle, my sweet. Don't worry."* But she'd got one in the oven regardless, so he didn't know what he was doing, did he? She wished they'd had a chance to marry and he was going through this with her. Polly said men who loved their women did nice things for them while they were expecting. *"Such as?"* Shirley'd asked. *"They rub your feet, get you a cuppa in the morning, cook supper on occasion."* Shirley knew her Pa couldn't do that but doubted he'd have the inclination anyway.

Polly was a few years older than Shirley and a hundred times more experienced in the ways of the world. Sometimes Polly scared her with that knowledge, but mostly Shirley found her new friend great fun to be with. Shirley craved fun. Ever since they had moved to Ludlow, her life had been completely dull. No dancing, only a few visits to the pictures. Nothing to do except get bigger and heavier every day. It was on one of her rare unaccompanied visits to the market square that she'd met Polly. Shirley thought she was so pretty and smart in her trim red costume and matching hat. She'd stood out among the dowdy housewives shopping for bargains at the stalls. Polly had been the one to strike up a conversation. "I see you're expecting. When are you due? I'm a midwife. I know a lot about babies if you want to ask me anything."

From somebody else that might have seemed intrusive, but Polly had grinned in her cheeky way and Shirley had felt immediately at ease.

"Do you want to walk down to the Wheatsheaf?" Polly had asked, and Shirley had happily agreed.

Polly said she was staying at the hotel. "But you must keep that to yourself. I'm not using my real name. My fellow is putting me up, see, but we can't tell anybody. He's already married."

Shirley was shocked, but Polly had linked arms in such a friendly way that she didn't want to get all uppity with her. Who was she to talk anyway? "I could do with a chum," said Polly. "It's bloody lonely being a kept woman." She laughed infectiously and Shirley was captivated.

"Me too. I could do with a chum."

"That's it then. We can be secret friends. We can leave each other messages."

"What sort of messages?"

"You know, 'Meet me at the pictures next Friday,' or 'at the butcher's tomorrow,' that sort of thing."

"I might not always be able to get away. My ma watches my every move." Shirley remembered she'd said that with some bitterness and her new friend noticed. "You're going to have to stand up for yourself sometime, Shirle. But if you can't get together, just leave a message, saying, 'Can't make it' and then give another time."

"Why do they have to be secret, Poll?"

"It's much more fun that way. We can pretend we're spies. Besides, you don't want your parents to know, do you? They might stop you from meeting me."

Polly was right, it was fun. The delicious excitement of finding a message in the hiding place; the nervous thrill of deceiving her mother and father when she went out. She adored her new friend and would have missed her terribly if she had not been able to see her regularly.

The only fly in the ointment was that, as the days passed, Polly became more and more interested in Shirley's pregnancy. She always wanted to know how she was feeling. Was she eating, was she resting? Shirley found this irksome. She wanted to talk about film stars and the pictures they'd both seen. Sometimes, she talked to her friend about her time with Rudy, brief as it was. To tell the truth, even though she went on about how handsome he was, his image was fading somewhat in her mind. She hadn't clapped eyes on him for months, after all.

Polly never reciprocated with her own confidences. "I daren't, Shirle. Nobody must know. All I can tell you is that my fella is a doctor of some renown."

"Is he going to get a divorce and marry you?"

Polly laughed. "He wants that – but not me. I like my freedom."

One hot afternoon when they were sitting by the river, Polly had winkled out of her the fact that her parents were insisting she give the baby up for adoption. Rudy might never come back, or at least not for years. Jock was adamant he didn't want a grandchild of his to be a bastard. *It will go to a good Christian home.* Shirley couldn't honestly say she was too upset about that.

She didn't really want to be encumbered by a child, especially if she was single. She'd poured all this into Polly's sympathetic ear.

"Don't worry, pet. I'll help you," said her friend. "I know lots of people who would be more than happy to take the babe. And you're right. You've seen nothing of life yet. A baby will hold you back." She gave her a big hug and Shirley felt comforted. Polly never uttered a word of criticism.

Shirley had reached the riverbank and she stood for a moment watching the sun as it made little butterfly shapes that danced on the water. It was another hot day and she felt sticky and uncomfortable. The river looked so cool and inviting. She giggled a little. Polly said once that she should swim in her birthday suit. Nobody would see her up here and it was such a marvellous experience. Maybe when she was thin again she'd give it a try. She sighed. Time to get back. She didn't want her mother sending a copper after her.

For the first time, she allowed her thoughts to dwell on what had happened to her father and brother. Her eyes filled with tears, but she brushed them away. Better not to think about things. Always better not to think about things. She started to trudge back along the path. She didn't expect to find a message from Polly, who usually dropped one off in the afternoon. But she might as well take a look. Shirley had been the one to find the hiding place. She'd noticed a loose brick in the wall just past the eastern gate. If you removed it, there was a little space, perfect for a note. So she and Polly started to exchange their messages.

Shirley pulled out the brick and let out a little cry. Glory be. There was a note. She took it out quickly and unfolded it. When she read the message, she actually felt as if she might faint. It hardly seemed possible that her deepest longings would be fulfilled.

HE'S HERE. HE WANTS TO SEE YOU. MEET AT THE RIVER TOMORROW NIGHT AT 11.

12.

TYLER STOOD OUTSIDE THE DOOR TO THE COMMON room, readying himself. It was eerily silent. The wireless had been switched off and nobody was talking. He'd known it was going to be hard delivering the news to Mrs. McHattie and her daughter, but in some ways he was dreading this meeting even more.

When he was serving in the Great War, Tyler had been witness to many horrendous injuries. Shrapnel slicing off the top of a man's head. An explosion removing a man's legs as neatly as a butcher might. But for the most part, they were discrete incidents; after an attack the injured were removed from the front line to the field hospital. He'd also known men to crack under the stress of the constant bombardments and do truly strange things. Curl up and whimper in the corner of the trench, unable to move, paralyzed by fear. Sometimes, he'd been impatient with these shell-shocked cases, sometimes he'd felt pity. He was a young man in his twenties back then, still imbued with a sense of invulnerability, fit and strong. Fear was something you pushed aside – and you got on with the job at hand. That was all there was to it.

He realized the almoner had been watching him.

"Let's get this over with, Sister."

Tyler had told himself he knew what to expect, but even so, the first impression of the patients was shocking. Perhaps it was the unnatural lack of response as he and the almoner entered the room. Few heads turned to watch them, no bodies shifted in their wheelchairs. Faces rendered immobile by scar tissue had no expression. They were silent.

The room had been set up to be as comfortable and homelike as possible for the patients. There was a large hearth, pictures on the walls, chintz-covered armchairs, and a couple of matching settees. The almoner led the way to a space that had been cleared in front of the fireplace. She waited while one of the sisters manoeuvred a woman in a wheelchair a little closer. Tyler glanced around. Seated a few feet away was a man whose face was a macabre death head. He had almost no hair and no lips, which exposed his teeth in a perpetual grin. His dark glasses made sockets of his eyes. Next to him was the young woman Tyler had seen earlier, standing at the window. Someone had drawn a white flower on her black eye patch, and a long purple scar puckered her cheek. This must be Daisy Stevens. Beside her was the man dressed in clownish attire. His face was brick red, as if he'd been scoured with a wire brush. There was a hole where his nose had been, and he had no ears. That would be Eddie Prescott. The older man next to him in the paisley cravat had to be the actor, Nigel Melrose. A scar ran across his face, obliterating his left eye. The most normal-looking one of this little group was a gaunt man with dark, intense eyes. He was leaning forward in his chair, supporting himself with a cane. Must be Victor Clark. His eyes were fixed on Tyler.

The almoner glanced over at him.

"Inspector?"

He nodded and she began.

"Ladies and gentlemen, I apologize for keeping you here like this. I know you must all be anxiously wondering what is happening. I'm afraid we have some bad news to impart to you. This is Detective Inspector Tyler. He will explain what has happened."

Tyler braced himself. "I am deeply sorry to have to tell you . . ."

13.

WHEN THE POLICEMAN TOLD THEM THE DREADFUL news, Daisy could hardly comprehend it. Jock, dead. And his son? Both killed. Murdered, in fact. The inspector said he could offer no explanation at this point, but he would have to talk to each of them and please not to go anywhere without letting him or Sister Rebecca know. Melly had seized on that of course. "What a jackass! As if we could?" he'd hissed. "Half of us are blind – or hasn't he noticed?"

Daisy squirmed. She thought the inspector might have heard him. He seemed a nice man, genuinely upset to have to tell them the news. You couldn't blame him for inadvertently touching on a raw nerve.

After fielding a few questions, the inspector had left, together with Sister Rebecca. The almoner, not surprisingly, looked tired and drawn, but as usual she managed to convey an air of calm competency. Daisy, more accustomed to her own highly strung mother, admired Sister Rebecca a lot.

A young policewoman had taken over. She moved to the front of the room and stood there, almost at attention. Daisy couldn't help but scrutinize her. Ugly uniform and too thin by far, but a pretty face really. When she was little, Daisy had expressed a desire to be a police officer, but her dad had laughed at her. There wasn't any such thing back then. The war had changed all that, and a few women were now being employed as auxiliary constables. Too late for Daisy, of course. Involuntarily, she touched her cheek, the deep scar tender beneath her fingers.

She was squashed between Jeremy and Eddie on the settee,

but what at first had felt uncomfortable now was reassuring. She could feel the warmth of both men's legs pressed against hers.

"I knew something serious had happened when the sarge didn't turn up for class," said Melrose. "But I confess I thought he'd had a heart attack or a stroke. He always seemed too tightly wound up for his own good."

"No he weren't," snapped Eddie Prescott. "Jock was a damned good bloke. Loved a joke same as anybody else. You two just didn't hit it off was the problem."

Daisy turned to Vic Clark. "Sorry you're not getting a chance to put in your tuppence worth, Vic. Do you want us to get some writing paper for you?"

Clark mumbled and gestured at them. His question was clear. Melrose answered, "He wants to know who did the deed. Any theories, comrades?"

"Don't be so ridiculous, Melly," said Bancroft. "How would we know?"

Melrose snorted. "I'm putting my money on one of the Itie POWS. They can get out of the camp easily enough if they want to. They're treated better than the locals if you ask me. Driven everywhere, easy work."

"But why Jock? What has he ever done to the Italians?" said Daisy.

"Besides, how would anybody get in the grounds?" asked Prescott. "The sisters are always nagging us about the night routine and how Hughes has to lock the doors and bolt the gate. Half past ten on the dot. We might as well be in a bloody prison."

"You'd know about that, I'm sure, Eddie," said Melrose. But before the other man could retaliate, Daisy jumped in.

"I don't think anybody could get over the wall either."

"I'm sure any able-bodied man could do it, my child," said Melrose. "How fortunate Chief Inspector Tyler doesn't have to worry about us chickens."

Daisy shivered and leaned into Bancroft. "I can't take it in, I really can't."

"What does the detective look like, Daisy?" the Canadian asked. "I'm always curious about checking my impressions against the reality."

"Does it matter, old chap?" interrupted Melrose. "I for one thought he had two heads, but I think that's a function of my new, improved eyesight."

"Ignore Melly," said Daisy. "If you want to know, I'll tell you. He's a redhead, for one thing. The carrot-top kind. He's above average height, rather on the muscular side, over forty, I'd say. Keen blue eyes."

Prescott snorted. "Good God, Daisy. You *were* paying attention. Fancy him, did you?"

Daisy glared at him. "It all comes down to that with you, doesn't it?"

"Come on, kids, sorry I asked," said Bancroft. "Except for the red hair and the blue eyes, keen or otherwise, that's pretty much how I envisioned him. His voice conveys authority. Now, let's not quarrel at a time like this. Like you, I am totally stunned."

"We all are," said Daisy.

They were silent for a moment, then Daisy continued, "I don't know about you blokes, but I'm famished. I only had a cup of tea for breakfast. If we're going to be stuck in here for who knows how long, why don't I see if Mrs. Fuller can rustle up some toast or biscuits?"

"What a little mother you always are, Daisy," purred Melrose. "Such an attractive quality in a woman, no matter what."

"What's that supposed to mean?" said Daisy with a flash of anger.

"Nothing at all, my dear. It meant nothing at all, except as a compliment."

Prescott turned himself in the direction of the other man's

voice. "You're a shite, do you know, Melrose, a complete, toffee-nosed shite."

"Hey, you two, cut it out!" exclaimed Bancroft. "We've got a lady here, don't forget. This isn't the place nor the time to fight the class war."

Prescott spluttered angrily. "Class war. It ain't hard to put on a posh accent, especially if you're an actor. I'd say Melrose ain't any better born than I am."

"Eddie, for heaven's sake. I don't give a darn if you were born within the sound of the Bow Bells or the dinner bells."

"That is rather well put, dear boy," murmured Melrose. "Do you mind if I use that on my next tour?"

"Be my guest."

Suddenly, a woman across the room burst into violent sobs.

"Oh dear, that's Babs," said Daisy. "I'd better see to her. She was just starting to come out of herself. This news could put her right back into the pit."

"See what I mean about your maternal instincts, Daisy, my dear," said Melrose. "But it appears that the luminous Sister Rachel is taking care of her, so you needn't worry."

"What the hell do you mean, 'luminous'?" asked Prescott. "Why don't you use ordinary words and stop showing off."

"What I mean is that the sister is quite beautiful in an exotic kind of way. What a pity to waste those looks on a life of celibacy."

Clark made an explosive noise in his throat.

"Vic is trying to tell us something," said Daisy. "What is it, Vic?"

The man tapped his watch and rubbed his stomach.

"You're hungry?" asked Daisy. "Me too. Why don't you come with me? Here, I'll help you up."

She offered him her hand and pulled him out of his chair. He took his cane and together they went slowly toward the table where the cook had set up a tea urn.

Daisy was having a hard time keeping a grip on her feelings. The truth was she was glad the nun had seen to Babs. She didn't think, in reality, that she would have been much help. She felt like crying herself. It was one thing to bend her mind around the fact of Jock's death, another to go the next step. Somebody had deliberately shot him and his son. Surely it couldn't be any of the residents? Please God it wasn't. Please God it would turn out to be a stranger, a foreigner, not anybody she knew.

As they went past Babs and the nun, Daisy took a fast peek. She hadn't thought of Sister Rachel as being attractive. She'd never got past the perception of her as a virgin, a woman dedicated to Christ. However, she could see Melrose was right. The nun was young, probably not that much older than Daisy herself. She had a good figure that the plain frock didn't totally hide. Whatever lumi . . . whatever that word was Melrose had used, she did have a sort of glow to her, dark eyes and smooth skin. Daisy kept moving. She already knew she was going to encounter a lot of young women whose looks hadn't been destroyed the way hers had. She'd better get used to it.

14.

SISTER REBECCA'S OFFICE WINDOWS WERE ALLOWING in as much sun as could conquer the wall. There was a large metal filing cabinet against one wall, a good-sized table with a typewriter and telephone, and a couple of wooden chairs. Apart from the simple wooden cross on the wall, it could have been any strictly functional business room.

Tyler sat down and took out his cigarette case. "Would you like a cigarette, Sister?"

She went to accept, then stopped. "Thank you, no. I've been trying to break the habit for the past two months. It got the better of me this morning, but I am determined to resist."

"Will it bother you if I smoke?"

"Yes. But that's my problem, not yours. Please." She waved her hand at him. It was Tyler's turn to hesitate. After all, he was supposed to be cutting back, wasn't he? He snapped the case shut. Virtue has its own reward.

"Will you give me a bit of history of the hospital, Sister? I've only been in Ludlow for three days. I don't completely know my jurisdiction yet."

She took the chair across from him and clasped her hands together in what was becoming a familiar gesture.

"We took over on April 19 and received our first patients on May 3. All of them have received initial treatment elsewhere, mostly at East Grinstead in Sussex, where Dr. McIndoe is doing pioneering work with such cases. Severe burns and facial injuries."

"So I've heard. The Guinea Pig Club."

"That's right. That's what they call themselves. Given the extent of their injuries, lots of experimenting with treatments is necessary," she said with a sigh. "Anyway, we, too, are a kind of experiment. A small number of patients, personal attention, emphasis on returning them to normal life."

Tyler couldn't help but raise his eyebrows at that, and she caught his expression.

"You'd be surprised at how adaptable our residents are, Inspector."

"I'll take your word for it, Sister. They've got a lot to overcome. I'd have a very hard time with that, if it were me."

"As would I. And some, of course, cope better than others. Fortunately, as I mentioned, we have the services of an experienced psychiatrist who is able to assess them and give us guidance. He comes up from London once a month."

"I'd like to talk to him. When is his next visit?"

"Unfortunately not until August. He was just here."

"What's his name?"

"Dr. Beck."

Tyler looked at her in surprise. "Bruno Beck? An Austrian chap."

"That's him. Have you met?"

"Yes, indeed. I was stationed out of Whitchurch when he was in the Prees Heath internment camp in '40. We . . . Our paths crossed." Tyler paused, wondering if she knew anything about the tragedy that had occurred there.

She gave no sign that she did. "Looking back on it, the wholesale internment of foreign nationals seems so draconian, but after Dunkirk, we expected England to be invaded at any moment, didn't we?"

Tyler nodded. That summer had proved to be one of the most painful of his life. He was suddenly inundated with memories of what had happened to him and his family. Maybe at a later date, he'd share them with the almoner. He thought he'd rather like to.

"I myself was in the Lake District all that summer," continued the almoner. "But even up there we were terrified of what might happen." Suddenly she held out her hand. "You know, if you don't mind, I'm going to give in and have that cigarette."

He opened his case, offered her a cigarette, and took one for himself. He lit hers with his lighter and did the same with his. They both drew in smoke with relief.

Tyler balanced his cigarette in the ashtray that she had produced from a drawer.

"Can you give me some idea of the daily routines, Sister? For instance, how do you as a religious community follow the rules of your order, as well as minister to your patients?"

"They remain our priority, of course. We have to accommodate ourselves to our work, not the other way around. If it is not feasible for a sister to break away from what she is doing to join in the saying of the office of the day, then she is permitted to make her observance on her own when she can."

So strictly speaking, Sister Ivy had no reason to feel guilty. Perhaps she had an especially tender conscience.

Tyler felt rather awkward questioning her about her nuns, but he couldn't rule them out as yet.

"Did all your community come here at the same time?"

"All except our novice, Sister Rachel. She joined us two weeks later. She was with the mother house in Ambleside."

"I'd like their names. How long they have been with your order and any particular expertise they might have."

"Why is that, Inspector? Are you concerned a member of our community has a knowledge of firearms?" Her voice was sharp.

Before he could reply, she said, "Forgive me. I apologize. That was quite uncalled for."

"This has been a shocking time for you, Sister. I can understand the strain it has put you under."

She smiled slightly. "Thank you. I am behaving like an utter idiot. These are things you need to know."

"They are, I'm afraid."

"First of all, our sisters are trained nurses. That is the mandate of our community. Because we are a small group, we rely on everyone to do other things as well. You've already met Sister Ivy Packwin. She is particularly good with hysterical patients. She's been with us for fifteen years. Sister Virginia Wren, always called Jenny, of course, is an accomplished piano player. She has started to give lessons to those patients who would like to learn. She entered the community five years ago. Sister Clarissa Cunningham is our oldest serving nun. She joined seventeen years ago. She teaches typewriting. Sister Rachel Hayden is our young novice. She has not yet taken her final vows. She is showing an aptitude for physiotherapy."

Tyler was writing all this down.

"And you, Sister? When did you join the community?"

"Ten years ago. I became the almoner of our chapter two years ago. Part of my work involves being the liaison between our patients and the outside world. I arrange for family visits, make sure pensions are correct. That sort of thing. When the patients are eventually discharged, I will make sure they are going into suitable situations where they will continue to make progress."

"Did anybody in the community or the staff have a prior acquaintance with the McHatties?"

"Not that I'm aware of. Nobody mentioned it."

Tyler finished his note. "All right. Tell me about the rest of the staff."

"Mrs. Fuller and Alfie are from Shrewsbury."

"And the Hughes brothers?"

"They're from Swansea."

"Reasons for moving to St. Anne's?"

"They all said we were offering better wages than where they were employed."

"I assume you have references?"

"Yes. They all checked out."

"I'll need to interview them as soon as possible."

"I'll arrange it."

"And the McHatties? What can you tell me about Jock?"

"As I said, he was a veteran of the Great War, gassed and rendered blind and scarred. But he adapted to normal life by teaching massage to others likewise damaged. He transferred here from Fort William in Scotland."

"What reason did he give for moving?"

The almoner shook her head. "Ironically, he said it was for a 'change of scene.'"

"Poor blighter. What was your opinion?"

She considered her answer for a moment. "Jock never struck me as the restless type, and I think the move had more to do with his daughter's pregnancy. I think he wanted to be in a place where they weren't known."

"But she still uses her maiden name. She hasn't pretended to be married, which she could easily have done."

"That's right. I think Jock was the kind of man whose integrity was uncompromising. He wouldn't have lied about the situation even though it left his daughter vulnerable to unkind gossip."

Tyler couldn't help but think of his own daughter. He hoped to God if anything like that happened to Janet, he'd be kinder, lying or not.

He sat back in the chair, eyed the cigarette, then took a puff.

"Who among the residents here would have had the most connection with McHattie?"

"Definitely the five massage students. The Rub-a-Dub Club, as they call themselves. Jock has been meeting them six or more hours a day for the past week. He has always tended to keep himself to himself, so I doubt if the other residents know much of him at all."

"Let's hope he wasn't killed because one of the students wasn't happy with their marks."

She looked at him uncertainly.

"Sorry, Sister. Bad joke."

He didn't want to alarm her any more than necessary, but Tyler was increasingly sure he was looking for an insider. Somebody who was familiar with both the routine and the layout of the hospital. The outside gates were bolted. The moon was waxing and the night had been dark. In his book, a person doesn't just stumble into somebody's house, in the pitch-dark, without, well, without stumbling. There was no sign of a disturbance. This person knew their way around.

"As soon as I can get my officers together, we'll conduct a search of the grounds. That might yield more information."

Sister Rebecca glanced down at her clasped hands. "Would it be possible for us to continue with our daily routines as much as possible? Today is when some of the residents go into town. We think it's important for all concerned, townspeople and patients, that they interact as normally as possible."

"I'm all for that, but . . ." He paused. His eyes met hers. "I don't see why most of the activities shouldn't continue. Just keep me informed."

"Of course."

There was a stubborn set to her jaw he hadn't noticed before. Sister Rebecca was no pushover where her charges were concerned.

"As I said, just let me know the comings and goings." Tyler took a drag on his cigarette. "My big stumbling block at the moment is that there is no apparent and understandable motivation for the crime."

"Are you suggesting Jock was the victim of somebody's troubled mind?"

"I didn't say that."

"It is the implication, isn't it? Which brings us back to our patients."

He shrugged. "They don't have a monopoly on madness, Sister. Sorry, but I've got to ask this: Could any of these people be malingering? Faking it? Pretending to be worse than they are?"

She frowned. "The ones with evident physical injuries obviously not, but those with more mental wounds . . . I suppose it's possible. I have to admit, though, the recompense for malingering, as you call it, is miniscule. Alekzander Bobik has no broken bones, no amputated limbs – he can see. But he spent five days in a dinghy in the North Atlantic when his plane crashed. Eventually, the only survivor of five. He shakes so badly, he can barely hold his knife and fork. Hard to keep up that act for weeks on end. I could say the same about Mrs. Bowman, who stares into space without blinking. So much so, we have to regularly apply lubrication to her eyes."

"Believe me, Sister, I have the utmost sympathy, but as a police officer, I have to ask the question."

"I realize that. I'm sorry if I again sounded sharp . . . It's just that these people have all suffered so. Perhaps you could speak with Dr. Beck. He has assessed most of them to date."

"I—"

They were interrupted by a sharp rap at the door and the nun Tyler had labelled in his mind as "the pretty one" popped her head around the door.

"Sorry to disturb you, Sister, but we can't settle Miss Broadbent down. She is quite hysterical. I think she needs an injection."

The almoner got to her feet quickly. "Thank you, Sister Rachel. I'll be right there. Excuse me, Inspector."

The two women hurried away.

Tyler made some notes. As well as the three in the Rub-a-Dub Club – the actor, the former WREN, and the mute – there were five other people in the ABLE column.

1. The Polish flyer. Bobik. Shell-shock case. Mental?
2. Isaac Farber. Doesn't move but no physical determining cause. Mental?
3. Graham Coates. Some sight. Mobile. Also depressed.
4. Mrs. Carol Bowman. No physical injuries. Mental?
5. Miss Susan Broadbent. No physical injuries. Could walk but doesn't?

Eight in total.

Add to this the two Welsh orderlies, the cook and her adult son, and the five members of the Community of Mary Magdalene. Tyler thought – that is, he hoped – he could exclude Jock's wife, daughter, and younger son. All together then, he had seventeen potential suspects. Not to mention a possibly suicidal pigeon. Wonderful.

He added, WHY? Then he underlined the word several times.

Sister Rebecca returned just then.

"Everything under control?" he asked.

"For the time being."

"All right then, Sister. I'm waiting for Dr. Murnaghan to arrive, and as soon as I've heard what he has to say, we can begin the interviews. Can I leave you to organize that? We'll meet in here, shall we? Assure them this is regular procedure. I'll start with the five massage students. As you say, they were the ones who had the most contact with McHattie. Then I'll go through the remaining residents in the ABLE group. I promise I shall take their mental states into consideration. And if it is possible I will ask you to sit in on the interviews when necessary."

"Of course, Inspector."

There was another brisk knock on the door and a man came in. "Breezed in" would be a good way to describe it. Brisk, moustached, formally dressed in a grey wool suit, everything about him said doctor, even without the telltale black bag he carried.

He stretched out his hand immediately.

"I was told I'd find you in here, Tyler. Came as soon as I could."

Tyler shook hands. "Dr. Murnaghan, this is Sister Rebecca Meade. She is the almoner of the hospital."

They, too, shook hands, then Murnaghan turned back to Tyler.

"Thanks for inviting me. Bit boring being retired, I must admit. Bit of excitement always welcome."

Tyler grinned. He knew the coroner well enough to know he wasn't being ghoulish. He was just a very capable man who loved his work.

15.

A NERVOUS-LOOKING YOUNG CONSTABLE GREETED them at the door to the cottage.

"Nothing happening, sir. Silent as the grave." Tyler and Murnaghan exchanged a look. The chap didn't seem to realize what an unfortunate choice of expression this was.

"Come on, Doctor," said Tyler as he led the way inside and up to the bedroom. With the curtains and windows closed, the house was heating up. He could hear the flies.

"Bodies are in here."

Dr. Murnaghan entered the room and stood for a moment. Then he went to Ben, knelt down, and placed his medical bag on the floor. Rigor mortis had advanced, and when Murnaghan attempted to move the boy's chin, he was unable to do so.

"I concur with your opinion, Tyler. I'd say death occurred about five or six hours ago." He squinted at the underside of one arm. "Lividity is intact. The body has not been moved." Dr. Murnaghan tended to talk as if he were addressing a class of aspiring medical students. He took a large magnifying glass from his bag and focused it on the bullet hole in the forehead.

"It's a large wound, and we can see from the sooty residue that the gun was fired at close range. Perhaps less than a foot away."

Carefully, he raised the boy's head enough to see underneath. "No exit wound, so the bullet is still in the skull. I'll examine the calibre and so on when I do the post. Have you found any casings?"

Tyler shook his head.

"Must have been a revolver then."

"A younger boy survived. According to him, the killer came to his door and the boy described a gun with a long barrel. He thought it was a rifle, but I'd guess he was looking at a silencer."

"All right. The bullet should tell us."

The doctor stood up. He tapped the cricket bat with his toe. "Poor chappie brought a weapon, I see."

He went over to the bed. Jock's corpse, too, was much stiffened, and his face was crawling with flies come to do their job. Shooing them away, Murnaghan scrutinized this wound too with his magnifying glass. "I'd say the gun was actually pressed against the man's temple. That's why there's a lot of powder burn." He checked the back of McHattie's head. "There is an exit wound here, Tyler. By the look of the pillow, the bullet will be lodged in there. I'll take the pillow with me and extract it. Do an examination of the brain tissue at the same time." He nodded in the direction of the dish with the glass eye balls. "Good fakes, aren't they. From the appearance of the eye sockets, I'd say the man suffered burns. Was that the case?"

"Apparently so. Sister Rebecca said McHattie was wounded in the Great War."

"What a shame to end his days like this." Murnaghan straightened up. "He was caught completely unawares. The assailant got right up to him without his waking up. But the boy came into the room."

"His brother said Ben heard something and went to investigate. That's why he's got a cricket bat."

"But what I'm puzzled about, Tyler, is why he didn't turn and run as soon as he realized what had happened?"

"I wondered the same thing. It was dark in here, but there's a night light in the hall that would have given off some light."

"The killer obviously reached him because he fired at close range. Perhaps he was already on his way out of the room."

"Let's try it," said Tyler.

He walked back towards the door and stood next to where Ben lay. The coroner was by the head of the bed, left side.

"Approach me, would you, Doctor. From where you are."

Murnaghan did as he asked, moving quickly. In a fraction of a second he was within a foot of Tyler. He raised an imaginary gun and pulled the trigger.

"You're quite right," said Tyler. "Unless he practically bumped into the killer, Ben would've had time to at least turn his head. In which case the bullet would have hit him much more to the side, near the temple. As it was, it hit him directly in the middle of his forehead. Let's do that move again."

Again the coroner did as he asked and went to the door, meeting Tyler more or less at the same spot.

"According to the account I've got from the younger boy, there was a short space of time between when Ben woke up, got his cricket bat, and went out to see what was happening. We don't know for sure what woke him. The stairs creak. Maybe it was that. It's also possible he heard the first shot. He enters his parents' room. He doesn't call out for his father – perhaps doesn't have time. The killer is on him right away. There is a soft *phuft* sound, then Ben falls to the floor. The assassin goes across the landing to Charlie's door, where he stands. If the boy's perception is to be trusted, it took him about twelve seconds to reach the boys' room. Why so long?"

Dr. Murnaghan blinked. "I'm sure you are making an important point, Inspector, but I don't quite follow you."

"It would take a matter of three or four seconds at the most to step over the body, exit the room, and cross the landing to the room opposite. Apparently, it took him almost twelve seconds. It suggests to me the murderer lingered after he shot

Ben and before he crossed the landing. Why? Did he stand and look down at the boy for a few moments? Contemplating the horror of what he had just done?"

Murnaghan frowned. "I suppose we can't rule out robbery. Perhaps the killer intended to go in search of loot, although God knows what he'd find in an ordinary household like this."

"I don't think so. There's absolutely no sign that he disturbed anything downstairs. He seems to have come in, gone directly upstairs to Jock's room, walked over to the bed, and shot him. Then he's surprised by the young lad and he shoots him too."

"Why do that?" said Murnaghan. "Ben wasn't big. Even with a bat, he couldn't have been much of a threat. Surely it would have been easy to knock him down and make a getaway? Do we know if our assassin was masked?"

"From Charlie's description, I'd say he most likely was."

"No real need to kill Ben then. He couldn't be a witness."

"He also didn't need to go and stand in the other boy's doorway, but he did."

Murnaghan shook his head. "I don't understand it."

Tyler looked at the two bodies again.

"Can we go back to Ben's entrance for a moment? Would you mind re-enacting the possible scenario? Mime firing down at the sleeping man. *Phuft.* Somewhere in here, Ben enters the room. You see me and come towards me."

Murnaghan came forward swiftly until there were only a few inches separating them.

"Why don't I turn?" asked Tyler. "I still have time to try to make a run for it."

He suited his actions to his words.

Suddenly Murnaghan hissed. "Tom!"

Instinctively, Tyler halted at the sound of his own name. It was a split second but quite long enough for the doctor to raise his imaginary gun and aim it straight into the middle of Tyler's forehead.

"Well, well," exclaimed Dr. Murnaghan. "Looks like the killer knew the boy."

"It's one possibility. Not conclusive, but a possibility."

16.

THE POLICE AMBULANCE, TOGETHER WITH FIVE MORE constables, had arrived by the time they emerged from the cottage. Dr. Murnaghan supervised the photographing of the crime scene before the bodies were removed to the morgue in Whitchurch, where he had all his paraphernalia "at the ready," as he put it.

Tyler made sure the carcass of the pigeon went with him. He dropped it into a brown bag he'd found in the McHattie kitchen and handed it to the coroner.

"Please find out everything you can about how this bird died, Doctor."

Dr. Murnaghan grimaced. "I've done post-mortems on cows and sheep and a number of dogs. A pigeon will be my first avian. I presume you will enlighten me later as to why you want this?"

"I will."

Each body had to be carried out to where the ambulance was parked. Ben's body went first, a small mound underneath the covering sheet.

Tyler walked with the doctor to his car.

Murnaghan cleared his throat. "Always sad when a young life is taken so cruelly. I, for one, never get used to it."

"Nor do I," said Tyler. "I hope for that matter I never do. Get used to it, I mean."

The doctor nodded. "You're right there, Tyler. Glad to see you're bearing up." He got into his car. "I'll get on the job right away."

Tyler set the constables to work in the cottage. They were all men past conscription age, but they seemed capable enough.

Not tottering anyway. There was a vampire-ish quality to the war. It was gobbling up all the young men.

"Eaves, do you think you can handle the fingerprinting kit?"

The grey-haired constable was close to retirement but looked spry and fit.

"I'm not sure, sir. Never had much call to use it, to tell the truth."

"Thieves just up and confessed, did they?"

"Summat like that, sir. They was turned in mostly. Everybody knows everybody else in these parts."

"Do what you can. Pay particular attention to the door jambs front and back and the outside of the windowsill of the downstairs bedroom. I'm highly doubtful you'll get anything, but we've got to rule it out. It's likely the killer didn't touch anything once he was inside the house, but you should give the door to the main bedroom a good going over. Constable Stanton, go with him and take photographs."

This constable was younger but rotund and red-faced. The man had better watch his pressure, thought Tyler. One of the only good things you could say about rationing was that it was forcing the Brits to cut back on beer and roasts and slim down.

"When you've done that, you'll have to get fingerprints from the residents. I warn you, some don't *have* fingers and there are several who are blind. Use common sense. The almoner or one of the sisters will help you."

The remaining four officers he directed to search the grounds.

"Are we looking for anything in particular, sir?" asked one of them whose name Tyler thought was Swindell. Or was it Swinfell? Another Shropshire man.

"Anything out of the ordinary that might give us a clue. Monogrammed hankies, foreign fag ends, an identity card."

By the expression on the men's faces, he thought his bit of sarcasm had gone completely over their heads. *We're still getting to know each other, don't forget. Serve him right if they did find something that obvious.*

"We're getting reinforcements soon. They'll join you."

He was heading back to the main house to see if he could start his questioning when he met Sister Rebecca coming towards him.

"I've set up the order of your interviews, Inspector. We can start whenever you're ready."

Before he could reply, there was a sudden horrendous screeching. A black cat came dashing from the direction of the pigeon coop. A man was close behind it, an air gun in his hands. He paused briefly to take aim at the unfortunate creature, which, Tyler could see, was spurting blood from one of its rear legs. The pellet hit the ground a few feet away, and with another yowl, the cat turned and dived into the vegetable plot, where it disappeared.

Tyler yelled at the shooter. "Hey! Stop that. Stop that at once."

Sister Rebecca called out as well.

"Alfie. What are you doing?"

Alfie swung the gun, and for a moment Tyler feared he was going to fire at him. He didn't wait to hear the answer. In one swift move, he snatched the gun out of Alfie's hands. The man staggered briefly, fell to the ground, and then began to wail. "He killed Prince. He killed my pigeon."

Tyler quickly unloaded the remaining pellets to the ground. The almoner crouched down beside the crying man.

"Calm down, Alfie. Please get hold of yourself."

Alfie continued to sob. "Prince has gone. Blackie killed him." He went to stand up. "I'll get him for that."

Tyler put his hand on his shoulder and shoved him back down. "No you won't. You will sit right there and tell me what's going on."

Alfie Fuller had a rather squashed face, as if the force of the explosion that had damaged his brain had squeezed everything together. Tufts of pale, downy hair sprang every which way on his head, giving the impression of an unformed chick. The rest of his body was normal, short and wiry. Before Alfie had a chance to respond, Mrs. Fuller came running out of the main house.

"Alfie, my Lord. What are you doing?"

"Ma, Blackie killed Prince." Alfie's cheek was deeply scratched and bleeding. He dabbed at it. "He hurt me."

Mrs. Fuller put her hand to her chest, gasping for breath. She addressed Tyler and Sister Rebecca.

"I tried to explain to him what happened to Jock and Ben. Why the policemen are here. I didn't know if he understood or not. Then the next thing I know he's taken off on me, saying he has to check on the pigeons." She swivelled to face her son. "Alfie Fuller, you are a bad boy. You know you're not supposed to have anything to do with those birds."

Alfie looked up at her, his eyes filled with tears. "But I had to, Ma. Mr. Mac has gone. Somebody has to tend to them. And Ma, Prince ain't in the coop and he should be. If Blackie didn't get to him, where is he?"

"I don't know, son." She noticed the pellet gun that Tyler was holding. "I hid it from him." She grimaced. "At least, I thought I'd hid it."

"He can't go firing off pellet guns at random," said Tyler. "They can be bloody dangerous. I'm going to have to confiscate it."

"Please do. You'd be doing us a favour," said Mrs. Fuller. "Mr. McHattie gave it to him to hunt rabbits, but he never should have." She looked back at her son. "Come on, Alfie. You're supposed to be helping me get the lunch ready."

"I'll have to have a talk with him," said Tyler.

Mrs. Fuller scowled. "He won't understand. He's not quite right in his head is our Alfie."

Tyler turned to the almoner. "Perhaps you could be present, Sister?"

The man got to his feet and his mother immediately grabbed him by the arm, giving him a little shake. "You'll be the death of me, Alfred Fuller. One more speck of trouble from you and you're going to the institution. Now come and get cleaned up."

Alfie looked chastened. "I'm sorry, Ma. I won't be any trouble again."

They went off and Tyler turned back to Sister Rebecca.

"You didn't tell me the whole story about Alfie."

"I was about to, but other things took over."

Tyler beckoned to the constable who was stationed at the front door of the McHattie cottage.

"Mady. There's an injured cat in the potato patch. See if you can lure it in. We'll have to get it seen to."

"There's a net in the pigeon shed," said the almoner. "I've seen Alfie use it with Jock's birds. That might help."

Tyler handed the constable the pellet gun and pellets. "Store these in a safe place, Constable."

"Take them to my office. I'll lock them in the cabinet later," said Sister Rebecca.

Mady hurried off.

Tyler indicated a wrought-iron bench between the Fuller cottage and the nuns' quarters.

"Why don't we sit there and talk for a minute, Sister. I think there's more I should know about Alfie Fuller."

17.

"HE'S A SAD CASE," SAID THE ALMONER AS THEY SAT down. "As I mentioned, he served in the Great War. He was one of the Lost Generation, just twenty years old when he was blown sky-high at the Somme. Shook his brain like a sponge in a bottle. He's all right most of the time, but every so often, he gets frustrated and he'll go off the deep end. Nothing serious. He throws a few pots and pans around the kitchen. Kicks at the bushes. His mother keeps a close eye on him and he's never done any harm to a person. Most of the time, he's cheerful and affectionate, works well as directed. His mother knows how to keep him within his limits."

Tyler leaned back against the bench. It was more ornamental than functional and not very comfortable, but in spite of that, and despite what had happened, there was a tranquility to the surroundings, a soft, sweet perfume on the air, a light breeze. This part of the grounds, too, was kept in shadow by the wall, and it was pleasantly cool.

"His social development is childlike, but the problem is that he's an adult physically," continued the almoner. She paused, and Tyler sensed she was choosing her words carefully. "He can get overly focused on women. This is mostly where his frustration comes from."

Tyler raised his eyebrows. "How does 'overly focused' manifest itself?"

"He just wants to be around them all the time."

"Did that happen with somebody here?"

"Yes. For a while Alfie was totally obsessed with Sister Rachel.

She is the youngest of our community and she is most attractive." She gave a bit of a smile. "As you have probably noticed."

She was right about that, thought Tyler. Even in her plain frock, Sister Rachel was a looker. He hoped he hadn't been gawking.

"Unfortunately, one day he behaved quite inappropriately." Another pause.

"How so?" Tyler prompted her.

"He exposed his genitals."

"Good Lord. What did she do?"

The almoner allowed herself a wan smile. "Sister Rachel is young but not unworldly. She was quite matter of fact. She told him in no uncertain terms that it wasn't good manners."

Tyler whistled. "That's one way to put it."

"His mother rides him hard, but needless to say she is very protective of him. She denies that he was exhibiting himself. Says he was caught short, as she put it, and was relieving himself in the bushes when the sister happened to come by."

"Do you think that's true?"

"It could be."

Again the almoner hesitated. Tyler sensed the real meat of the story was coming.

"Shortly afterwards there was a similar incident involving Shirley McHattie."

"Oh dear. What happened?"

"She was returning to their cottage and Alfie was in the garden. She claims he deliberately exposed himself. She told her parents and they were both incensed. Mrs. McHattie ordered Mrs. Fuller to keep Alfie on a leash as if he were a randy dog. Created very bad feelings between the two families."

"I'm not surprised. I wouldn't be too happy about a grown man showing himself to my daughter, mind of a child or not."

"Indeed so. But we don't know if it was deliberate or not."

"He was just 'caught short'?"

"That is not unlikely."

"But Jock didn't see it that way?"

"No. There is no father in the Fuller family. Hasn't been since Alfie was a boy. Desertion, according to Mrs. Fuller. Jock seemed to fill that role for Alfie. He had him help with the pigeons. Alfie kept all the records; he knows the name of each bird. But Jock sent him packing after the incident with Shirley."

"When was all this happening?" Tyler asked.

"Not long ago. About three weeks."

"Is he known to have done this before? Have there been other complaints?"

"Not that I am aware of."

Tyler wondered if Alfie's habits were the real reason behind his mother taking the job at St. Anne's.

"Please continue, Sister. What was the state of affairs with the McHatties as of yesterday?"

"Not good. No reconciliation, I'm afraid. Very sad, really. Alfie was skulking around like a kicked dog."

Tyler swivelled to look at her. "Let me get this straight, Sister. You're telling me about an adult man with the mind of a seven-year-old, who shows grossly inappropriate behaviour and is known to go off the deep end if frustrated. Yet unless I am mistaken, you do not seem unduly alarmed about him. Do you think he is capable of killing Jock McHattie, a man who had deeply hurt his feelings?"

She blinked. "No, I really don't. For one thing, he is quite clumsy. The brain injury has affected his balance. I don't see him walking about the McHattie cottage in the dark without knocking into something. And you saw the poor cat. He missed wildly."

"Not exactly, Sister. He hit it once. He handled the pellet gun quite comfortably."

"I realize that, but it's not a real gun. Where would he possibly get his hands on a real gun? None are allowed in the hospital, and his mother watches him like a hawk."

"Both good points, Sister. You know him better than I do, but in my book, he's a big question mark. I'd better have a chat with him." He got to his feet. "Shall we?"

She stood up. "I seem to be doing nothing but apologizing to you, Inspector. I'm sorry. It's just that we . . . we, er, seem to see things from quite different points of view."

He couldn't help but smile at her. "Probably a good thing too. The world needs more people who still look for the best in others."

18.

Tyler knocked on the door of the Fullers' cottage and Mrs. Fuller opened it at once.

"I suppose you want to arrest Alfie?" she said belligerently.

"Not at all, Mrs. Fuller. But I do need to talk to him."

She stepped back and let them in. Alfie was seated at the kitchen table. He was bare chested, and Tyler could see how muscular he was.

"Sister Rebecca's here. Put your shirt on, Alfie," said Mrs. Fuller. Grinning at them, he scrambled to do so.

The Fullers' cottage was identical to the McHatties' in layout, but whereas the other cottage was neat and Spartan, this one was cluttered with bric-a-brac and too much furniture. Every surface seemed to have a crocheted cover.

"We can talk in here," said Mrs. Fuller as she led the way to the sitting room. Alfie immediately went to the brocade Victorian loveseat and sat down, swinging his legs like a child.

"Why don't you have this chair, Sister," said his mother, leaving Tyler to take one of the straight-backed, velvet-covered chairs. Mrs. Fuller took up her position next to Alfie. The room was small and they were uncomfortably close to one another.

Tyler made his tone reassuring. "Alfie. I'm not going to scold you about your pellet rifle. I just want to ask you some questions about Mr. McHattie."

Alfie looked straight at him. His blue eyes had an odd, glazed look, like those of a broken doll. "Me ma said he's gone to heaven. Ben as well. She said a bad man did it and we've got to find him."

"That's right. Now, I understand you liked Mr. McHattie a lot."

"Yep. He let me feed the pigeons and write their messages." He frowned. "Sodding cat. Killing Prince like that."

Mrs. Fuller gave him a slap on his arm. "Oi. What have I told you about swearing, Alfie?"

Her son looked sullen and rubbed at his arm.

"I don't think Blackie killed the pigeon," said Tyler quietly. "We found Prince in the McHattie house. There was no sign that he'd been attacked by a cat."

Again Alfie looked straight at him. "He ain't dead then?"

"Yes, I'm afraid he is." Tyler paused. "Have you been in Mr. McHattie's house recently?"

Mrs. Fuller cut in. "Course he hasn't. Martha McHattie wouldn't let him cross the threshold after what he did." She halted abruptly and looked at the almoner. "I assume you've told the officer what happened?"

Sister Rebecca nodded. "Yes, I have."

Mrs. Fuller scowled. "Treated Alfie as if he was a criminal, not some poor soul who's not all there."

Tyler was about to point out to her that intentionally exposing yourself to young women was in fact a criminal offence when Alfie burst out.

"Mr. Mac was cross with me. He told me I couldn't go into his house anymore."

Tears welled up in his eyes and his nose started to run. He wiped off the mucus with the back of his hand.

This elicited another slap from his mother.

"What have I told you about that?" She fished a handkerchief out of her pocket and handed it to him. He blew his nose vigorously and scrubbed at his eyes.

Tyler waited until he'd finished. "I was wondering about the pigeons, Alfie. Do they carry messages back and forth?"

Alfie perked up. "They sure do. Lots of them. We have the

males shipped to Scotland on the train. That's right, to, er, to Scotland. When they get there, the man on that end gives the secretary a ring and tells him what the weather is like. If it's stormy or too windy, they won't let them go. It's not safe. Then when it's the right time, the man in Scotland lets them all out of their crates. All at once. Off they go into the air. It's called . . ." He frowned. "It's called what, Ma?"

"Liberating them. That's the proper word they use."

"Yes, that's right. Libering them. He rings again to say what time they've been let out. So at this end, we just have to wait. Can be a long time. Then we look up and see one or two who are circling around. We send out the lure bird to tell them where to come, and in they dive. They're tired out mostly. They've been flying for hours and hours without stopping. So one by one they land. I get hold of them. I'm the one takes the tube off. We've got a special clock that we put the band into. It stamps the time, see. But we only use the clock if it's a race. Otherwise, I just make a note in the book. Then I make sure the birds get something to drink and eat."

To Tyler's ears, Alfie sounded completely lucid.

His mother jumped in. "He's very good, he is. Just loves to do it. Why don't you show the inspector your record book, son."

Alfie got up eagerly and headed for the kitchen. He had to pass Sister Rebecca's chair and he turned sideways, wobbled a little, and slid by her shyly so there was no inadvertent contact. But he beamed at her.

"'Scuse me, madam."

"It broke his heart when Jock said he couldn't help him no more," said Mrs. Fuller. "Cruel, I thought. He had no evidence. It was a mistake. Alfie was having a wee in the open. He does that sometimes. He's a child in his mind."

Alfie returned, a red notebook in his hand. Same procedure getting by Sister Rebecca. He handed the book to Tyler, opening it to the last page. It was a book intended for keeping accounts and there were columns of tiny, neatly written numbers.

"See, I put in the date, the flyer's name, and the time it was let go from Scotland. See, Prince was released on July 14 at eight o'clock in the morning. It was on his band."

"Did you check him in, Alfie?"

A look of confusion came over the man's face. "No, I ain't allowed to be in the coop after hours. I have to be in bed by ten o'clock." He ducked his head. "Me ma don't like me to be out when it's dark." He cast a sly glance at his mother. "I went walking in me sleep once and she didn't know where the aitch I was."

"When was that, Alfie?"

Mrs. Fuller jumped in. "We'd just moved here. He was confused with the new surroundings. And sometimes he sleepwalks."

"Where had he got to?"

She shrugged. "Oh, I don't know. Just in the grounds somewhere. But I didn't want him near the river in the dark." Her eyes met Tyler's. "Now, I make sure he's in his room by ten o'clock . . . I lock the door."

"And that was the case last night? Alfie was in his room with the door locked from ten o'clock on?"

"That's right."

Tyler looked down at the accounting book. "According to this, Alfie has recorded Prince coming in at midnight."

"That must be a mistake," said his mother. "He makes mistakes sometimes. Doesn't know morning from night. Tell him, Alfie. Tell the inspector you got the time wrong for that bird."

Tyler handed over the book so Alfie could have a look. He stared at the page in bewilderment for several moments, then he smiled. "No, that's right. Spitfire was back by nine, but Prince didn't get in until twelve."

"Could you see them from your window, Alfie?" Tyler asked.

"That's it. They lands on the ledge and I can see them."

"Even in the dark?"

Alfie nodded.

At that moment, the clock on the mantle began to chime out eleven o'clock.

"Alfie, what comes next?" Tyler asked. "Would you say it's noon after this or midnight?"

Alfie told off each chime on his fingers. When the chimes had finished, he hesitated. "There were eleven. And it's daytime. So next is noon. Midnight means the middle of the night and it ain't that. The sun is shining."

"Quite right. And that's a good way to tell the difference. So did Prince come in at twelve midnight or twelve noon? Was it dark or light?"

Alfie shot a glance at his mother. "I forget."

Mrs. Fuller glared at Tyler. "He weren't out last night, I tell you. He checked in that bird at noon."

"That's right," said Alfie. "Spitfire was tired too. He come a long way. He was let go in Wales. That's far."

"Do you mind if I hang on to the book for a bit, Alfie?" Tyler asked.

"All right. But I'll need it back by tonight. There are two birds that haven't come in yet. I've got to keep records properly. Mr. Mac has trusted me." He looked over at his mother. "Would it be all right if I went into the coop, Ma? Mr. Mac is away in heaven and he won't get back in time to check on them himself."

"I don't see why not," his mother answered.

Tyler stashed the notebook in his jacket pocket.

"Alfie, I'm going to ask you something and I want you to swear on your honour that you will answer truthfully."

"We're not in a court of law," interjected Mrs. Fuller. "He don't know what that means."

"I do, Ma," said Alfie, and he raised his hand in a half scout, half military salute. "On my honour, sir."

"Did you put the pigeon in Shirley McHattie's room?"

Alfie stared at him. "Not me, sir. I'd never do that. Girls don't like dead things."

"Okay. Thanks." Tyler stood up. "I just have one more question. Like your mum told you, a bad person has hurt Mr. McHattie and his son. Do you have any idea who might want to do that?"

"Oh yes. I know who it was," said Alfie loudly.

"Who?"

"Bleeding Hitler, of course. I bet he dropped in on his parachute. I bet he come in and wrung their necks."

19.

"Would you mind if I took a look at Alfie's room?" Tyler asked Mrs. Fuller.

"Suit yourself," said Mrs. Fuller. "Do what you have to. Me, I've got to get over to the house. Those poor folks will be famished. Alfie helps me."

Her son beamed. "I peel the potatoes. There's always mounds and mounds."

"He sleeps in the back," said Mrs. Fuller. "He gets wobbly on the stairs, so it's better if he's on the ground floor."

She showed them the room and left them to it, her son docilely trotting after her.

Alfie's room, also off the kitchen, was a duplicate of Shirley McHattie's except that it looked more like a child's room than an adult's. A narrow bed over which hung a model of a Spitfire, a wall covered with pictures of fighter planes and bombers torn from magazines. The sash window was open, the blackout curtains were pulled well back, and the net curtain billowed in the breeze.

Tyler walked over to take a look. The rear of the house was taken up by a vegetable garden. Behind that, about twenty feet away, was the encircling wall.

"You can't see the pigeon coop from here," said Tyler to the almoner. "On the other hand, it would be very easy for Alfie to climb out of the window and walk around to it. And the McHattie cottage. What on earth made Mrs. Fuller think he was safely locked in his room?"

"Maybe she went to check on him periodically."

"At three in the morning? I doubt that," said Tyler. "I'm betting she closed and locked the door behind him, gave him a warning, and left it at that. She believes what she wanted to believe."

"Do you think he did go to the coop later?"

"Of course he did. It was his job to keep the records of the birds' flights. He's not confused about that. For sure, he was there at midnight. Question is, did he come back to his room, via this window, or hang about somewhere until three when he entered the McHattie cottage? He could have done both. Gone out and come back, then gone out again. Seems most unlikely, but I can't totally rule him out yet." Tyler turned to face the almoner. "All right. I'd better get on with the interviews. Perhaps we can do that right after they've had their meal."

They went outside and met Sister Rachel on the path, hurrying towards them.

"Inspector Tyler. There's a telephone call for you from Dr. Murnaghan. He's holding the line."

"That was fast," said Tyler as they headed towards the house.

Two residents in wheelchairs were on the gravel path. They both were wearing dark glasses and Tyler couldn't tell if they were asleep or not. Dai Hughes was seated on an apple box near them.

"I'll just have a word with Hughes," said the almoner, and Tyler continued on with the young nun.

Sister Rachel held the door open for him. She lowered her eyes as he brushed by, but not before he'd glimpsed an expression that he could only describe as worldly, as if the hint of sexuality was familiar. Not that a vocation in the church wasn't most commendable, but she was so attractive, it made him wonder what had brought her to it.

The telephone was waiting for him on the desk.

"Tyler here."

Dr. Murnaghan's voice came barrelling over the wire. "Goddamn it to hell, bloody car was in an accident. Nothing serious, just a stupid sheep wandering across the road. But I gave my noggin a hard knock. Saw stars, which is not a good sign. I probably have a concussion. I'm in the hospital wing right now. They've got to run a test. Bottom line is I won't be able to get your post-mortems done as quickly as I'd hoped."

"That's too bad, Doctor. When do you think you will be able to?"

"Can't say till I've been checked over. I've got a goddamn awful headache. You could try to get somebody else in, but the closest coroner is in Hereford. I wouldn't recommend him, to be frank."

"We'll wait then. Look after yourself."

"Sorry. I'll have to hang up before I pass out. Ring tomorrow."

The telephone clicked off abruptly.

Tyler sighed. An early post-mortem report would have been great, but he'd have to just continue with his own investigation until Murnaghan could get to it. And that meant first and foremost trying to unearth a motive for the killing.

20.

By the afternoon, Tyler could declare his interviews had been almost entirely unproductive. He'd started with the massage students and put the same set of questions to each person: "Did you hear anything during the night? Do you know of any reason why someone would want to kill Jock McHattie?"

Neither Prescott nor Bancroft was able to act alone, that was certain. Of the remaining three students, Melrose, now dressed in an elegant navy blazer with a cravat, had admitted to being, as he put it, "cool" towards Jock McHattie. His teacher had it in for him, he said, but he didn't come up with any convincing examples of Jock's malevolence. Not a powerful motive for a brutal killing. Daisy Stevens was the most upset. She had really admired Jock, she said. She didn't know who would have wanted him dead, and she had heard nothing last night. The mute chappie, Clark, wrote his replies on a piece of paper Tyler provided for him. NO and NO IDEA.

Daisy had asked on their behalf if they could go into town for a short while as previously planned, and Tyler agreed. At this moment, he had no good reason to suspect any of them.

The remaining interviews were also quite unproductive.

Unanimous answers. When any were provided, that is. Miss Bowman and Mrs. Broadbent didn't answer at all and seemed not to have even heard his questions. Graham Coates, obviously once blond and handsome, now no longer so, couldn't seem to understand the questions at all and lapsed into silence. Isaac Farber shook so badly, Tyler felt like a torturer and cut the interview short. Everybody else said no. Heard nothing and, no, couldn't imagine who would want to kill Jock.

The three nuns, Sisters Clarissa, Virginia, and Rachel, although obviously distressed, showed admirable self-control, each seeming to give a lot of thought to his questions. However, they had nothing new to offer. Their quarters were set apart from both the main house and the cottages. They had heard nothing. As for Jock McHattie, all agreed he was liked and respected and they couldn't imagine anybody wanting to kill him.

Of the resident staff, only the Hughes brothers tweaked Tyler's curiosity. The older brother, Evan, seemed cautious and wary, but the police often had that effect on people so Tyler didn't take it too seriously. However, the younger brother, Dai, was fidgety and uncomfortable.

"I was asleep the whole night, sir, truth be told. We're allowed to do that if we're not needed on the ward. I can wake at the drop of a hat, look you, so it isn't a problem."

"According to the sister on night duty, you and she had a bit of a chat when you came on."

Hughes's eyes widened. "Did we?"

"That's what she said."

"Oh. Oh, yes, I remember. Nothing much. Just about the weather. That sort of thing."

That wasn't what Sister Ivy had said, but Tyler let it ride for now.

"Then you went to spend the rest of the night on your cot, correct?"

"That's right. Didn't stir once. No need to, thank goodness."

Recollecting the magazine that Hughes had taken to bed with him, Tyler was surprised Dai had had any sleep at all. Perhaps it was merely his bedtime reading material that was giving Hughes such a guilty demeanour.

Tyler dismissed him, repeating what he'd said to the others. "If anything comes back to you, let me know at once."

Hughes gave a salute. "Yes, sir. I will, indeedy. Thank you, sir."

21.

Nigel Melrose was making his handkerchief into a sun protector by tying knots into the four corners.

"Well at least none of us has been arrested. I was in doubt for a bit, I can tell you. 'And where were you about four o'clock last night, Mr. Melrose?' Where the bloody hell do you think I was? Fast asleep dreaming sexy dreams in my hard, narrow bed, that's where. What a stupid question."

"Come on, Melly," protested Daisy. "He has to ask questions like that."

"Oh, you've got a pash for the man, Daisy. He could do anything and you wouldn't mind."

"Steady on, Melrose," said Bancroft. "She's quite right. I thought he was decent."

"I didn't know what to say when he asked if I had any ideas who might have killed poor old Jock," said Prescott.

"Some loony did it," said Melrose. "Present company excluded."

"Thank God for that," said Prescott. "Maybe Miss Oakshutt is faking being a live human being. Maybe she's a ghoul who prowls at night."

"Eddie!" snapped Daisy. "That is a very cruel thing to say."

He shrugged. "That's what I am, Daisy. Being blind as a bleeding bat has turned me into a monster."

Melrose stepped forward and slapped the handkerchief on top of his head. "I don't know about you lot, but I'm going into De Greys for a cream bun. Nothing like a cream bun for raising the spirits."

"You'll spoil your lunch," said Daisy.

"Nothing will do that, Daisy dear. A cream bun will only serve to improve my palate."

Daisy hesitated. "Do you want to go, Jeremy? I'll push the chair if you like."

"Sounds like a jolly good idea even coming from Melly. Anybody else? Who's here?"

"Me," chimed in Eddie. "Do you want to come, Vic?"

Clark made a noise indicating he did.

"Let's use one of the tandems," said Eddie. "It's faster. I'm not up to the walk in this heat."

"Do you want to come, Bhatti?" Daisy asked the Gurkha, who had followed them outside.

"It's useless trying to talk to him," said Melrose.

"I keep hoping he'll understand again," said Daisy. "We can't give up."

"Maybe you can't, but I can," said the actor. "We have a plethora of deserving cases to concentrate on. And they're all white."

"That's not a nice thing to say!" burst out Daisy. She stepped over to the little man and took him by the hand. "Cream bun? Yum." She patted his stomach, then touched her fingers to his lips. Bhatti smiled, said something incomprehensible, and nodded.

"See," said Daisy. "He understood that."

The Gurkha held out his arm, indicating he was ready for the lead they used for the blind patients.

"Good, he's coming."

"Hey, Daise, I said I want to go on the tandem," protested Eddie. "We can't both get on it. Somebody has to steer."

"Bhatti can walk with Jeremy and me. Vic can go with you."

"No offence, Vic, but you're not the steadiest of leaders. Last time we almost ended up in the river. Daisy, come on, be an angel and you ride."

"Sort it out, children," said Melrose. "I'll meet you at the shop."

He strode off, tipping his hat ostentatiously to the constable on guard at the gate.

Vic gestured that he was going to get the bicycle and limped slowly to a shed by the gate.

"Daisy, are we going or not?" asked Jeremy, shifting impatiently in his chair.

"Coming," she answered. "We're taking Bhatti."

"Jeez. Do we have to? I was hoping for a private conversation with you."

Daisy raised her eyebrows. "He won't understand what you say. It's as good as private." But she could see he was put out. Vic returned, leaning on the handlebars of the tandem for balance.

"Would it be possible to take Bhatti with you and Eddie?" Daisy asked him. "As long as you don't go too fast, he can trot alongside. He likes that."

Eddie heard her and called out. "Daisy, will you stop fussing over everybody. I want to go very fast, like the frigging wind. He won't be able to keep up."

More sounds from Vic, who was nodding his head at Daisy, making clear he would take charge and it was all right for Bhatti to go with them.

"Vic has said he can go with you, Eddie, so you'll have to put up with him."

Prescott swore under his breath. "Bloody hell. Let's go then."

Vic brought the tandem close so Eddie could get on. The bicycle had been made especially for the hospital by a local merchant, and the low frame was designed for a woman. Easier to get on. There was a short piece of leather with a loop at one end, dangling from the handlebars. Vic reached for Bhatti and pulled him over so he could fasten the lead to his wrist. The little man complied readily and stood waiting for the next signal. He was used to this method of getting around.

"Do you want help getting on the bike, Vic?" Daisy asked.

Clark shook his head, put his cane in the basket on the front handlebars, and with a groan swung one leg through and sat on the saddle. Eddie followed suit with the rear seat and clutched the rear handlebars.

"Fire the torpedoes, Vic," he called out. "Officer, open the gate if you please."

The constable addressed Daisy. "How long will you be gone, miss?"

"Only about forty minutes. Inspector Tyler has given us permission."

The constable swung open the gate.

Initially, the tandem wobbled violently, but Clark righted it and they rode out to the road. Bhatti trotted right beside the bicycle. He knew to keep a tension on the lead so he wouldn't bump into them.

"Whoopee," shouted Prescott.

The threesome turned onto the road.

Daisy returned to the wheelchair and took the handles. "Sorry, Jeremy. They're off now. We can talk."

Bancroft didn't respond immediately but waved her on. As the others had done, they passed through the west gate and turned onto the road heading for the bridge into town. There was a thin rope threaded among the hedges for the blind patients to follow if they felt like being more independent. On the other side of the river loomed the walls of the ruined castle. In spite of everything, Daisy could feel her mood lifting ever so slightly. The brightness of the light made it easier for her to see. Even the few roadside flowers were distinct enough for her to recognize them. Orange wood anemones and buttercups, a scatter of blue borage.

"I can hear the sound of the weir," said Bancroft. "Can we stop here?"

Daisy guided the wheelchair to the side of the road and put on the brake.

Bancroft reached for his shirt pocket.

"Daisy, will you read a letter for me? I just want to confirm something."

"Course I will."

He pulled out an envelope.

"It's from Lydia," he said. "She dabs eau de cologne all over her letters because she thinks that way I'll know they're from her." His shoulders sagged. "Some other guy might think that's cute. Not me. I feel like a dog having to sniff out the prize."

"Jeremy. Don't be silly. She doesn't mean that at all. A lot of girls do what Lydia does."

"Open it, please, Daisy."

"Are you sure? It's from your fiancée. Perhaps one of the orderlies should read it to you."

He burst out laughing. "Oh, Daisy, sweet innocent Daisy. Do you think my fiancée is writing me dirty letters so I'll get all hot and bothered and have wet dreams every night?"

Daisy didn't answer. He couldn't see that she had blushed at the crude language, so unlike him. She tore open the envelope. There was one piece of paper inside. The handwriting was large and sprawling.

Dearest Jeremy,
I can't believe that after all this time, I finally got a 48-hour pass and promise of a lift as far as Shrewsbury. I will take the first train from there to Ludlow. This means I should be at the hospital by early afternoon Tuesday. I can hardly wait to see you, my darling. I hope you get this letter in time, but if you don't I shall surprise you.
All my love, your own Lydia

"I didn't see any visitors yesterday," exclaimed Daisy. "Didn't she come?"

Bancroft banged his fist on the armrest of the chair. "Oh, she came all right. She arrived after lunch. Sister Clarissa is a great believer in the healing power of fresh air, as you know, so us wheelies and blindies were trundled out to various parts of the garden. You said you were going to help with Babs and you left me with Hughes. He took me to the front garden, then he buggered off to tend to some other helpless sod."

His voice was more bitter than Daisy had ever heard it, and she instinctively put her hand on his shoulder. He shrugged her off. "Don't pat me, Daisy. I might bite."

"Jeremy!"

"Sorry, it's just . . . Anyway, as I was saying, here I was in the fresh air with a nice breeze, sound of bees buzzing all around. I decided I need some sun so I took off my shirt to get a bit of a tan. It felt good and I must have dozed off, but I woke up suddenly to the sound of the gate opening. I could tell some-body was walking in my direction. There was the click of shoes. Woman's shoes. 'Hiya,' I calls. 'Who is it?' There was no answer. 'That you, Shirley?' says I, thinking she was the only one who would be wearing shoes like that. Still no answer. Whoever it was came closer, then stopped within a few feet of me. 'Identify yourself,' I said. 'Friend or foe?' Trying to be funny." Bancroft shifted again. "There was a bit of a snuffle, like the woman was blowing her nose. Then the footsteps retreated. Faster this time. In fact, I'd guess she was running. I heard the gate again as it opened and my visitor left."

"Jeremy, you're saying it was Lydia?"

"It was her all right. I caught a whiff of the scent she had drenched herself with. She reeked of eau de cologne, the same as the letter."

"But why didn't she speak to you?"

"Because, my dear girl, she had the opportunity to see what I looked like as I lay there in all my nakedness. She'd come to the hospital shortly after the crash, but at that time I was invisible in the bandages. White, clean bandages that give away nothing. She could have had no idea what has happened to me. What she would be saddled with if we were to marry. As Melly might put it, she came, she saw, but she couldn't conquer – her own revulsion. I'm sure that in the next few days, I shall receive another letter calling off our engagement. All very sorrowful and 'It's for the best' sort of thing. But the truth is, I'm too hideous to be married to."

Daisy rested her cheek on top of his head.

"Looks aren't everything. People have to get used to us, that's all."

This time it was his turn to pat her arm. "Keep thinking like that, little Daise. Keep thinking like that."

22.

Nigel Melrose was already waiting outside De Greys. The tandem riders and Bhatti were panting from the climb up the steep hill.

"Too late," Melrose called to them. "You chaps were too slow. They had only one cream bun left and I ate it."

"Greedy sod," said Prescott. "I fancied one of those, I did."

Melrose laughed and whipped out a brown paper bag from behind his back.

"Gotcha! In fact, chaps, I bought the last six. I thought given our ordeal we deserved them more than the local Luddites." He turned and pointed at the clock on St. Laurence's church. "Time moves apace. I suggest we all stroll up to the square and nab a bench. Eddie, you can stand us tea from the Castle Café. Okay?"

"I didn't bring any money with me."

"No matter; they are only too keen to give it to us for free. We're heroes in their eyes. If not, we can owe them. After all, we're not hard to find, are we? Follow me, you happy band."

They started towards the square. Eddie was walking beside the bicycle, holding on to the rear saddle, and Bhatti was still tethered to the handlebars. Vic was wheeling the machine, leaning on it for support. Nigel was slightly in front. All of them, even Bhatti, were wearing their dark glasses. As the group went by a seedy looking pub across from the church, two young men in farm dungarees and tweed caps emerged. Even at this hour and with war restrictions, they'd somehow got a good start on inebriation. One of them guffawed loudly.

"Hey, Bill. Look at this lot. You'd think they was film stars, wouldn't ya?"

His friend, who had more manners and knowledge, tried to hush him up. "They're from the hospital, Wilf. Them's pilots. They's blind."

That seemed to irk the young lout. "Gives 'em an easy crib, don't it? Get waited on hand and foot, I wouldn't wonder. Girls lie down for them. I wouldn't be surprised if they ain't just pretending."

The four St. Anne's residents were directly across from them now.

"Keep going, chaps. Don't get drawn," said Nigel.

Eddie turned his head. "How many are there, Melly?"

"Two. And that's one too many. Keep walking."

But Eddie stopped, holding on to the bike so that both Vic and Bhatti were forced to stop as well.

"Hey, fellas," Eddie called in the direction of the two men. "Do you wanna take on a blindie? I'll play fair. I'll take on the two of you at the same time. Give you an advantage."

Nigel put his hand on Prescott's arm. "Don't be an idiot, Eddie. They're arseholes. They'll step on you soon as spit. Ignore them."

It was too late. Perhaps the two farm boys didn't believe that Eddie was truly blind, perhaps they were too drunk to care.

The one called Wilf snickered. "That's a nice little black boy you've got there, mister. Keeps you warm at night, does he?"

"Don't be silly," said the other man. "You'd have trouble finding him in the blackout. I suppose they have to feel for each other."

Bhatti turned to the sound of the voices.

"Lookee, Bill. He's on a leash. I do that with my bitch when she's in heat. 'S that why he's tied up?"

What happened next took everybody by surprise. Eddie grabbed Vic's cane from the basket, took two steps forward, and held it double-handed in front of him, like a sword. Wilf didn't have time to jump back, and the stick caught him across the side of the throat. He dropped to the ground like a sack of potatoes, gasping and choking. Eddie continued to swing wildly, shouting.

"Sodding bastards. How'd you like these apples?"

The other man stepped back in alarm. Both Melrose and Clark grabbed Eddie and pulled him away.

"Calm down, Eddie. Calm down," said Melrose. "These pieces of shite aren't worth it."

Prescott was almost crying. "Let me at them. Sodding bastards. I'll show them, Melly. I'll show them."

"Sure you will, scout, but later. Leave it be for now."

Wilf was sitting up, still clutching at his neck. His pal helped him to his feet.

The proprietor of the tavern had run out at the sound of the skirmish. "You should be ashamed of yourselves," he shouted at the two farm boys. "These men have sacrificed a lot for their country."

"They're loonies, the lot of them," said his pal as they limped away.

The publican turned to address the four St. Anne's men. "My apologies, lads. And to think we're fighting a war for the likes of them lot. Look, why don't you come in and have a pint on me."

"Don't mind if we do," said an unfamiliar voice.

"Who's that?" Eddie asked.

"It's Bhatti," answered Melrose. "He seems to have got his English back."

Speaking in his finest plummy voice, he thanked the landlord but said they'd come back another day for their free pint when the company was more convivial. The landlord didn't press them.

With Vic and Eddie riding slowly, the group proceeded back to St. Anne's. Bhatti had been released from his tether and Melrose had linked arms to guide him. The little Gurkha had lapsed back into Burmese and was chattering away excitedly to his uncomprehending friends – as if the sudden return of his English had never happened.

Eddie didn't speak until they reached the bottom of the hill. Here he burst out laughing. "I'd say that was a jolly good show, wouldn't you, lads?"

"You certainly showed your killer instinct, Mr. Prescott. Which I always knew was there, seeing where you were spawned," said Melrose.

Eddie growled. "Sweet suffering Jesus, Melly. I thought for a minute you'd lost your fangs. Obviously not."

As they approached the gate at St. Anne's, Eddie reached out and felt for Vic's shoulder.

"Thanks, mate." He squeezed hard. "I have to tell you, I was ready to fight. Fight to the death, if truth be told. Being blind is driving me mad."

23.

TYLER GATHERED THE TEAM TOGETHER IN FRONT OF the McHattie cottage. Eaves and Stanton, the two constables on the fingerprint and photograph detail, had finished their tasks and he'd sent them back to the station to see what they'd come up with. He wasn't too optimistic and neither were they, but all possibilities had to be explored. The four reservists had joined them by now, but to his eyes, their force looked pitifully small.

"Anything, chaps?"

They all shook their heads.

"We've gone around the wall twice, sir," said Chase. "Both sides. Not the slightest sign that anybody got over from outside. No broken leaves, no depressions in the dirt from a ladder."

"Impressive, Constable," said Tyler. And he meant it. That was what he hoped they'd be looking out for.

"What's next, sir?" asked Mady. "Will we be doing a search of the hospital?"

"Right now, I'm postponing that as long as possible. We're dealing with severely traumatized individuals. I don't want to upset them any more than necessary. First, I'd like to get going with the house-to-house questioning. I want to know if anybody in the vicinity heard anything. An owl screeching, a rabbit farting – anything. Tell them there's been an accident at the hospital and you have to conduct an investigation. Our assailant had a weapon. See if you can winkle out any information. A lot of country folk keep guns. Keep questions simple. Find out how familiar they are with the hospital. Did any of them know the McHatties? They'll be curious, of course, but for God's sake don't start any rumours. Listen more than you talk. If anything significant comes up, come and get me at once. We'll reconvene in the foyer. Try to be done by three o'clock."

Mortimer looked at him. "Shall I participate in the enquiries as well, sir?"

"Absolutely. Some of the folks might open up more readily if a woman is present. If the opposite seems to be true, leave and get one of the men to take over. The afternoon shift will be here by four o'clock. They will relieve you and I want you all to go home and get some rest. I want three men back here for the night watch. Swinfell, you're excused as it is your rest day. You four reservists are also excused until tomorrow morning. You'll be on standby. Do I have some volunteers for night shift?"

"Me, sir," said Mady.

"I'll do it too," chimed in Biggs.

"Count me in," said Chase almost simultaneously.

He surveyed the group. Except for Mady and Mortimer they were all over conscription age. But he thought they looked keen and alert, happy to be needed again.

"Thanks, lads. And miss. This place should be locked and barred like the Royal Mint, so I doubt you'll encounter any intruders in or out, but I want one of you to be at the McHattie cottage at all times. Spell each other off. All right?"

The three constables nodded.

"Until the next shift arrives, I want you, Chase, and you, Biggs, to patrol the grounds. I'll be in the almoner's office if you need me."

24.

DAI HUGHES WAS IN THE ORDERLIES' SITTING ROOM about to light up when his brother burst in. Before the younger man could defend himself, Evan snatched away the cigarette, grabbed him by the shoulders, and shook him violently.

"What the fecking stupid game are you playing? You promised you wouldn't go back there. But you did, didn't you?"

Dai managed to slide out from his angry brother's grip, landing on the floor.

"What are you blathering about?"

"I heard you go out and I heard you come in. That sodding gate shrieks like a rutting Tom cat. Which is what you are, aren't you?"

He raised his hand, but Dai caught hold of it.

"I'm a big boy now, Evan. You can't knock me around just because you feel like it. I was here all night. Ask Sister Ivy. She'll vouch for me."

"Bollocks. You've got all those spinsters wrapped around your little finger. She'd swear she saw you walking on water if you asked her to."

"If I want to go for a bit of air, why shouldn't I?"

Evan glowered down at him. "Because you're supposed to be on fecking duty, that's why. If anybody found out, you'd be given the shoot in a minute. And me with you, most likely."

Dai glowered. "No, I wouldn't. We're priceless here. They couldn't fill our jobs. Not these days."

"Don't be too cocky about that. There's plenty more where we come from."

"In that case, why can't I sign up? I hate those blokes in town looking at me like I'm dirt. A shirker. And the women too. They despise me."

"That why you pay for it?"

Dai flushed. "It's not like that."

"Ha. Let me guess. She loves you. You're the best she's ever had. Is that the story she's been feeding you?"

"She's a nice girl."

Evan slapped his own forehead in exasperation. "Of course she's a nice girl. All tarts are. As long as you're opening your pockets, they're very nice."

"You sound like you're an expert," snapped Dai. "Can it be Ma's golden-haired boy has done his own share of prowling?"

This time Evan reached him with his palm and gave a hard slap. "I told Ma I'd look after you, and look after you I will if it kills both of us. Now get your sorry arse off that bed and go and help with the patients. Everybody's a fecking mess out there."

Dai reached for his cigarette packet, which had fallen on the floor, but Evan kicked it away.

"Now. I said, now. And if you come home with the clap, I swear I'll cut off your balls."

25.

WHEN SISTER REBECCA ENTERED THE NUNS' SITTING room, what she saw struck her like a blow. Perhaps it was the pathos of Charlie McHattie clinging to his mother like a primate might; perhaps it was Shirley McHattie, flipping through a women's magazine and greedily smoking a cigarette. Rebecca wasn't sure. Both things, probably. She felt like she could have marched over to the girl, snatched away both cigarette and magazine, and given her a good dressing down. *Don't you care about anything?* But Rebecca Meade had struggled all her life to master her temper and she wasn't going to succumb to it now. She also knew enough about human nature to not take Shirley's behaviour completely at face value. People often did odd or apparently inappropriate things when they were in shock.

Mrs. McHattie's eyes were dark with grief.

"I was wondering when the policeman is going to talk to me, Sister. I'd like to get it over with."

"I'll take you there now. He's using my office."

As Mrs. McHattie went to stand up, Charlie let out a howl and gripped her even more tightly. "No, Mummy, I don't want you to go. No, please."

"I won't be long," she said soothingly.

"No. You mustn't."

She addressed Rebecca over her son's shoulder. "I haven't even been able to go to the toilet without him going barmy."

Shirley hauled herself out of the chair. "Tell you what, why don't I go talk to the detective first? He's going to want to talk to me anyway. By the time we're finished, Charlie might be calmer. Maybe the sister can give him a sedative or something."

"I can do that if you like, Mrs. McHattie."

"Sedatives all round, I'd say," chirped in Shirley.

Rebecca ignored her and went over to the mother and boy. She crouched down in front of them.

"You know, Mrs. McHattie, some years ago my nephew went through a bad period in his life. He couldn't sleep and nothing seemed to help him. Then one night, when I was minding him, I started to tell a story in which he was the hero. I hardly remember what it was now, but it was something I took from a fairy tale. Andy was the noble prince who had to deal with trouble in his kingdom. He succeeded, of course. I told a different story night after night and gradually he calmed down. In his life, he had no control over what happened around him. But in the story, he became all-powerful and conquered all difficulties."

Mrs. McHattie was looking at her with some bewilderment. "I don't know if I'm up to telling stories at the moment."

Rebecca felt a wave of embarrassment. She had been too personal. The bad time she alluded to was when her younger sister had decided motherhood was too much for her. She filled her pockets with stones and walked into the river and drowned herself. The pithy note she left behind was addressed to her husband. *"Can't take it. Andy is all yours."*

There was definitely something about Shirley McHattie that reminded Rebecca of Paulina. The fear and desolation in the eyes of young Charlie also looked all too familiar.

Impulsively, she reached out and smoothed his hair. He made no response.

"I quite understand, Mrs. McHattie. Let me take your daughter to my office, then I'll come right back with something to help him sleep."

"Thank you, Sister."

Shirley was already waiting at the door. Her mother nodded at her. "Don't run off at the mouth, Shirle. Just answer the questions as he puts them."

"Of course. What do you take me for?"

26.

GIVEN THE CIRCUMSTANCES, TYLER WAS A LITTLE surprised at the care Shirley had taken with her appearance. Her smooth brown hair was curled into a fashionable pageboy, she had recently applied lipstick, and her pencilled-in eyebrows were well defined.

He indicated a chair that he'd pulled up to the desk. "Please sit down, Miss McHattie. I tell you frankly, at the moment we're stumped as to why your father was killed. I'm almost certain Ben was a secondary casualty, probably killed because he came in on the killer."

There was a sudden rush of tears into her eyes, and Tyler waited while she wiped them away.

"It would help us immensely if we had any understanding of why your father was a target."

Shirley shrugged. "Probably some crackpot. We've got enough of them in this place."

"Possibly. But if it was not a random act of insanity, is there any other reason that you can think of?"

"None."

Tyler tried to be tactful. "Miss McHattie, you are expecting a baby . . ."

"I'd say that was obvious, Inspector."

"You are not married."

"So what?" She looked at him defiantly.

"What I mean is . . . I wondered if your, er, your pregnancy might have anything to do with this case."

"Why would it?"

"I understand your parents were unhappy about the situation."

She shoved her hair back from her face. "They didn't approve, that's for certain. But then they never liked Rudy from the start. I should never have taken him to meet them." She turned her head away from him and stared at the floor. In spite of her swollen belly, she suddenly looked about fifteen.

"Why didn't you marry before he left?" Tyler asked. "Many couples have found themselves in the same predicament and got a special marriage licence."

She was fighting hard not to cry. "Rudy didn't want to. He was afraid he'd be kept back if he said his girl had a bun in the oven."

"That was his name, Rudy?"

"Yes."

"Surname?"

She ducked her head. "I don't know."

"You don't know? Excuse me, Miss McHattie, but am I to believe you have conceived a child with a man whose surname you don't even know?"

Her expression was sulky. "He was on a special mission. Very hush-hush. He wasn't allowed to tell me."

"Where was he stationed?"

"He couldn't say. But it was near us."

"When you were in Scotland, you mean?"

"That's right."

"Miss McHattie, I don't need to tell you there is a war on and many relationships are entered into on impulse. A man is away from his wife, for instance. He's lonely. He meets a pretty young woman. He makes up a story to ease her conscience."

"No!" she burst out. "It wasn't like that. Rudy wasn't married. I was the first true sweetheart he'd ever had. He told me that."

"And you believed him?"

"Of course I did."

Shirley looked so miserable that Tyler felt sorry for her.

"Have you heard from Rudy since he left?"

"I got a couple of postcards. He told me they had to write them before they left. Somebody else would post them, but as long as I kept getting them I'd know he was alive at least."

"When was the last time you received one?"

"The middle of May. It was postmarked somewhere in Sussex, but I know that's not where he is. He'd have come to see me if he was there, war or no war, I'm sure of it."

Tyler wished he could have offered her some comfort, but there was none he could give. "When is your baby due?" he asked.

"Not for three more weeks, but I feel like a whale. I think I could pop at any moment."

He smiled at her. "I've had two kiddies and that's what my wife said each time. Didn't happen though. They both came right when they were supposed to."

She shrugged.

"Just one more thing, Miss McHattie. Could you describe Rudy to me?"

"What do you mean?"

What Tyler meant was that in cases of desertion, the wronged lawful wife could file a charge with the police. This included some description of the missing man. He might be on a list. Also, if any of the locals had seen a man acting suspiciously the previous night, Tyler wanted to know if it might be the elusive and secretive Rudy.

"Just a general physical description."

"Well, he's medium height, brown hair and brown eyes. Dark. His eyes are dark brown. He's muscular."

"Anything distinctive? Scars? Moles?"

"No. He speaks English with a bit of an accent."

"Oh, does he? Where is he from?"

She looked away. "He couldn't tell me. Somewhere in Europe is all I know. He got out before Hitler invaded his country and came here to join the forces."

"RAF?"

"I think so, but he never talked about it." She wriggled on the chair. "I have to use the toilet. Are we finished?"

"Certainly." Tyler stood up. "You have been most helpful, Miss McHattie. If anything else comes to you, let me know."

She got out of the chair awkwardly.

"I know what you've been getting at, but you're wrong."

"In what way?"

"Rudy loves me, and when the war is over we're going to go back to his country and make a life for ourselves. I'm going to give the baby up for adoption when it's born, but we can have more. Be better when I'm older anyway."

Tyler had no response to that. He saw her to the door.

He returned to the desk. The case was like trying to put a puzzle together but with no idea what the picture on the box was – and the nagging feeling that several pieces had gone missing. He couldn't connect anything to anything else.

There was a knock on the door. It was Sister Rebecca, holding an envelope.

"Inspector, I thought I'd better bring this to you right away. It was in the post bag and it's addressed to you."

"How strange. Let me see."

She handed him the envelope. It was addressed INSPECTOR TYLER, c/o ST. ANNE'S HOSPITAL, LUDLOW, SHROPSHIRE. Across one corner was the word URGENT. What gave Tyler pause was the familiarity of the printing. Neat, tight block letters, black ink. He took the piece of paper he'd extricated from the pigeon's leg band and compared the two. The writing was identical. Cautiously, he felt the envelope, but he could detect no bulges or lumps. He sniffed at it. There was no unusual smell.

"There isn't a postmark," he said to the almoner, who was regarding him anxiously.

"I noticed that. Somebody from here must have personally dropped it into the hospital post bag."

"When could they have done that?"

"Anytime in the last hour or so. We have a delivery once a day. With so many residents, the postman finds it easier just to deposit the sack inside the front door. What with everything going on, I didn't have time to sort it until just now."

Tyler slit open the envelope and removed the sheet of paper. This was typed, not handwritten like the envelope. He read it through.

"What is it, Inspector?" asked Sister Rebecca.

Tyler handed her the letter. "Have a read yourself."

After the tenth line of executions the soldiers get a rest and a slug of schnapps for their nerves. The bodies remain where they have fallen, ten men in each line, seven more lines to come. The stench of blood, guts, and brains, all with a seasoning of cordite from the machine gun, is thick in the air. The soldiers have to move back from the carpet of bodies which is creeping slowly towards them.

The next group is led in from the barn. They are mostly silent, some from defiance, some from sheer shock. All of them in their working clothes, baggy pants, cotton shirts made by wives they will never see again.

There is a young boy who must have
officially turned sixteen but whose body
is still that of a child. He is small,
blond, and tanned from being outdoors. He
has put his hand in that of the man beside
him, his father probably, but when they line
up the captain yells at him to let go. It
would have made no difference to the killing,
but the captain is edgy, already half drunk.
The boy wraps his arms around himself for
comfort.

Mattresses have been leaned against the
stone wall of the barn so the bullets won't
ricochet. All of them are now splashed and
stained with blood. Around them apple trees
would have been fragrant with blossoms,
except no perfume can withstand the stench
of death. One of the men in the new line is
grey-haired and stooped. He leans on a stick.
In spite of his slowness he is dignified, a
man who will not give them the satisfaction
of dying a coward's death.

Earlier the captain has said that any
soldier who didn't want to continue could
step down without reprisal, but no one really
believes him. They know what punishment can
be meted out to the disloyal. Astonishingly,
in fact, three men put down their rifles.

They are excused. What has become of them, these ones who refused? Do they now weep?

At a command from one of the guards, the new line of villagers take their places in front of the wall. The NCO has already walked around and shot each previous victim in the head to make sure. The old priest comes over to give the men a blessing and comfort them. Most accept his attentions, but the captain becomes impatient. Hurry up, let's get on with this.

Does he know that he is now condemned for eternity? That they are all condemned?

Sister Rebecca put the sheet of paper down on the desk. Her hand was shaking.

"Inspector, what does it mean? Why has somebody sent you this?"

"I don't know."

Tyler held the sheet of paper up to the light. Nothing revealed itself. It was ordinary stationery.

"You said that anybody here at St. Anne's could have dropped it into the post bag?"

"That's right. The bag just stays in the foyer until I collect it. The delivery is usually about nine o'clock. Does the letter have to do with the murders?"

Tyler shrugged. "I don't know. Maybe."

The almoner sat down abruptly. "Do you think the letter is referring to a particular incident?"

"It could be," said Tyler. "Regrettably, I suspect it could also be a compilation of several incidents. An account of helpless victims being shot for some crime, not specified. The Nazis' favourite weapon of fear. Reprisal."

"Reprisal for what? Where?"

"The victims are referred to as villagers. It mentions schnapps, which suggests our Kraut friends. Could be anywhere in occupied Europe."

"And what does it have to do with the killing of Jock McHattie and his young son?"

"Maybe nothing. Maybe somebody is practising their school compositions." He shoved back his chair angrily.

"May I have a closer look?" Sister Rebecca asked.

"Go ahead."

She picked up the paper and studied it for a moment. "Inspector, forgive me if I sound like Sherlock Holmes, but I can tell you with some certainty that this letter was typed on one of the machines we have here at St. Anne's."

"Good Lord! Explain please, Sister," exclaimed Tyler.

"We have three typewriters that are available for those of our residents who can use them. They're not particularly new or well maintained. Sister Clarissa teaches a typewriting class and she complained to me just last week that the letter *w* on one of the machines was jamming all the time." She tapped the paper. "You can see where that has happened."

Tyler checked. She was right. "Anything else you can glean from the letter, Madame Holmes?"

"Only what you yourself would notice. The overall typing is even, with no errors or strikeovers. This suggests some expertise. The language is that of a well-educated person. The writer's English usage is perfect."

"Any such *literati* spring to mind?"

"I'm afraid not. Perhaps Nigel Melrose, but, frankly, it doesn't sound like him. Not florid enough."

"Do you know if he types?"

"No, I don't."

"Is there anybody at all in the hospital, staff or patient, male or female, who is a skilled typist?"

"Other than myself, Sister Clarissa is the only one I can think of. But it is not information that would necessarily be on their intake forms."

"What do you make of the religious overtone? The words 'condemned for eternity'?"

She gave a little shrug. "Christ taught us not to pass judgement on our fellows. What is described is, in my mind, utterly wicked and without reason, but it is only God who can save or damn, not we mortals."

She appeared uncomfortable about this profession of her faith. *If it were up to him, he'd be tempted to line up the soldiers against the bloody wall just as they had done to the innocents.*

Tyler returned the letter to the envelope.

"Thank you, Sister. I'll concentrate on the mechanics for now. I'd better have a talk with Sister Clarissa, your typing teacher."

"I'll fetch her." She hesitated. "I have instructed the sisters to go ahead and celebrate evening prayers. Some of the residents regularly join us and will be expecting it. I hope you don't mind."

"Not at all."

"Thank you."

Tyler sat a moment longer. He was growing to like the almoner more and more. She reminded him of a teacher he'd had when he was a boy. Miss Harrison was probably younger back then than the almoner was now, but of course to him, she'd seemed ancient. She tended to be strict and rather staid. That is until one unforgettable morning when she announced to the class she was engaged to be married and would be leaving the school at the end of term. Even to his young eyes, she looked different. Softer, happier. It wasn't until years later that he identified what had changed in his teacher. She was in love.

Clare, when are you ever coming back to me?

27.

HE WAS WRENCHED OUT OF THESE THOUGHTS BY THE return of Sister Rebecca. An older nun was trailing close behind her.

"If you don't need me to be here, I'll go back to the common room until Sister Clarissa can take over again."

"That's quite all right, Sister. We won't be long."

Tyler smiled reassuringly at the other nun.

"Please have a seat, Sister. I just wanted to ask you a few questions about your typing class."

"Oh dear. Why is that?" Her voice was high and shrill.

"Er . . . let's just say, I've received a rather peculiar letter today. Sister Rebecca is of the opinion that it was typed on one of the hospital's machines. I'd like to find out who sent it to me."

"Why do you say it's peculiar? What's in it?"

"I'm afraid I'm not at liberty to disclose the contents at the moment, Sister. But I'd like to find the letter writer if I can. It is quite well typed. No mistakes or errors."

He thought she looked relieved, but he wasn't sure.

"Who in your class would you consider a really good typist?"

"None of them," she said with a shrug. "They're useless, to tell the truth. Either can't see or can't use their fingers properly."

"Why are they taking a typing class in that case?"

"Gives them something to do. Mind you, we haven't been going at it for long. Only two weeks. I'm hoping they'll improve."

"So there isn't anyone among your students who you would call skilful?"

"Not a one. If it's a good typist you're looking for, you should speak to Shirley McHattie. She is quite accomplished. At least she is when she puts her mind to it. I asked her if she would help me mark the work, but she didn't want to. Most distracted, that girl. But that's not surprising, is it? Given the condition she's in. Good thing for her Our Lord forgives all sins."

Maybe the Lord was forgiving, but Tyler had the impression that was a virtue Sister Clarissa didn't come by easily.

"Could I have the names of the patients who are in your class, Sister?"

"They're all men at the moment. I'd like the women to come – a secretarial skill is more suitable for a woman – but none are up to it. So I have Graham Coates, Isaac Farber, and Sidney Hill. Daisy Stevens did start, but decided she'd rather do massage therapy."

"Can anybody use the machines?"

"Oh, yes, but as far as I know, they are not in high demand. They were donated, for which we are grateful, but they're really not very good. Some of the keys have a way of jamming."

"The letter *w*, for instance?"

"Definitely that one for sure."

"Have you noticed anybody else using the machines?"

"No. Not at all."

She was watching him expectantly, but she didn't offer any more information, and there didn't seem anything further to ask.

Tyler stood up. "Thank you so much, Sister."

She, too, got to her feet, but at the door she hesitated. "The letter you were sent. It wasn't what you'd call 'naughty,' was it?" Suddenly she turned bright pink. "You know what I mean. It didn't use dirty words, did it?"

"No, it didn't."

"And it was well typed?"

"Very."

"That's good," she said ambiguously.

She left and Tyler returned to his chair. What on earth did she mean by that? Who did this elderly nun know who wrote dirty letters?

28.

TYLER SPENT TIME READING THROUGH THE PATIENT files but once again drew a blank. There was nothing to connect any of the residents with the McHatties prior to their arrival at St. Anne's, nor, on the other hand, to suggest that one of them might be insane enough to commit an indiscriminate murder.

He sat back feeling tired and frustrated. Then he noticed a card propped up on the desk. It was a list of telephone numbers: the hospital in Shrewsbury, the police station in Ludlow, the community mother house, and a number for Dr. B. Beck.

Tyler picked up the receiver and dialled the operator.

"I'd like to place a trunk call. London." He gave the number.

While he was waiting, he lit up a cigarette. Only two left of his self-appointed ration. He'd better make this one last.

The telephone rang for a long time and Tyler was about to cancel the call when the doctor came on the line, sounding breathless.

"Beck here."

"I have a call from Inspector Tyler," said the operator. "I'll put you through, caller."

"Tom! What a surprise."

Tyler couldn't help but feel gratified at the evident pleasure in the other man's voice.

"I saw a notice in the Ludlow paper that you had taken on the job of inspector," continued Beck. "I was hoping to see you on my next visit to St. Anne's."

The doctor's English had improved a lot in the two years since Tyler had last seen him. His Austrian accent was now very slight.

"That's actually where I'm calling from, Doctor. I'm afraid I have bad news. I'll tell you what's happened – I'd be most appreciative of your opinion."

"Of course. Go ahead."

Tyler filled him in on the previous night's incidents. Dr. Beck didn't comment until he had finished.

"I am shocked to my core, Tom. I've only made two visits to the hospital so far, and I can't say I knew that family well. But I saw the two boys playing in the grounds. It is utterly incomprehensible that somebody would take such a young, innocent life."

"I believe Ben was only killed because he came into his parents' bedroom when he did; his father was shot first. The sister in charge here has been most helpful, but I thought I'd ask if you have any idea what might possibly have triggered this."

There was such a long pause on the other end of the line that Tyler wondered if they had been cut off.

"Doctor?"

"Yes, still here, Tom. I couldn't give you a quick answer to your question."

Tyler felt a frisson of impatience.

"What I mean is, did you have any sense when you were here that one of the patients might snap and go on a murderous rampage?"

"If I did, I'd have taken care to have them closely supervised."

"Yes, of course, I didn't mean to imply . . ." Tyler trailed off. He'd put his foot in his mouth for certain.

"Besides," continued Beck, "what you've described to me I would not call a rampage. There is no chaotic wild killing spree. The killer appears to have been highly organized."

"You're quite right," said Tyler. "I'll rephrase my question. Are there any of your patients who might decide to kill an unarmed man asleep in his bed? Also, more pertinent, might any have taken a scunner to Jock McHattie, whether rational or irrational?"

"Nobody. On the one or two occasions his name was mentioned, it was always with respect and admiration. I'd be much more worried about a patient hurting himself than attacking somebody else. Most of them are overwhelmed by trying to adjust to their new condition." Dr. Beck definitely sounded huffy. "Anyway, Tom, as you have no doubt learned, very few of my patients would be physically capable of the act."

"Some are." Tyler rhymed off the names he'd put on his ABLE list.

"Not Mrs. Bowman, Tom. She has not walked for months. Her muscles have atrophied. Nor Isaac Farber. He can't even hold a spoon."

"Easy to fake that."

"For days? Months? I doubt it . . . As for the others, I know Alekzander Bobik is mobile, but his sight is poor."

"So he claims."

"The doctor's report says there is damage to the optic nerves."

"Both Victor Clark and Graham Coates use canes, but it's not that hard to act as if you can't walk properly."

"Have you seen Coates's leg? It's mangled. And Clark's spine was damaged in the plane crash."

"Is that in the doctors' reports?"

"Yes. Both of them were transferred from East Grinstead. I have seen the medical records. They are both crippled."

"Permanently?"

"It is hard to tell at this point. We of course hope for the best, but in my opinion, neither Coates nor Clark is capable of walking normally, never mind running around in the darkness and climbing up and down stairs."

It was Tyler's turn to get a bit huffy. "I can understand you want to defend your patients, but I'm thinking from the point of view of a policeman. You've seen the wall. You know how high it is. The gates are barred at night. The murders must surely have been committed by somebody living at St. Anne's. And the assassin is not obvious. I'd say he – or, I suppose, she – is masquerading."

Beck made a tutting sound. "What if more than one person was involved? Could the killer have had an accomplice within the hospital who let him in?"

Tyler tapped his nail on the receiver in acknowledgement. "Now you're thinking like a copper."

He heard Beck sigh. "I'm not sure I like doubting everything and everybody."

"The main problem is that I can determine no discernible motive," continued Tyler. "Any ideas you'd like to throw my way about that, Doctor?"

"I'm afraid not. Don't forget, Tom, I subscribe to the theory that every criminal has an unconscious compulsion to confess. Primitive guilt. In fact, sometimes the desire to be caught and punished isn't even that unconscious."

"Ah, yes. We talked about that a few years ago when you were at the internment camp on Prees Heath."

"And I was right. Grant me that, Tom. I was right."

"Yes, you were. Speaking of the compulsion to confess . . . I have something quite outlandish to share with you. I want to read you a letter I received this afternoon. It's anonymous, but according to Sister Rebecca it was very likely typed on one of the typewriters here."

He removed the letter from the envelope and read it out loud.

When he had finished, there was another long silence on the other end of the telephone.

"Thoughts, Doctor? See any connections?"

"Not immediately. Except it has to do with victimization. The killing of innocents."

"Such as Jock and Ben McHattie?"

"Frankly, Tom, I am totally bewildered. It seems too bizarre a coincidence that somebody would send you such a letter shortly after two unarmed people have been killed, but why they have done so, I cannot tell."

"I'll pursue the physical aspects of the letter, typing and all that, but psychologically, any insights?"

"The general tone is quite anguished. And accusatory. 'Do they now weep,' for instance. And the reference to eternal damnation."

"Any thoughts as to what massacre is being described?"

But before Beck could reply, there was a loud knocking on the door and Constable Mortimer popped her head in.

"Inspector, can you come, quickly? Mrs. McHattie is demanding to see you."

"I'll ring you back, Doctor," said Tyler, and he hung up the telephone.

"What's happening, Constable?"

"Mrs. McHattie says that Alfie Fuller was spying on Shirley from the garden. She wants him to be arrested. I had the deuce of a difficult time getting her to stay where she was. She wanted to run after him."

"Where is Alfie?"

"I don't know. I thought I'd better fetch you right away. Constable Mady is with them. Mrs. McHattie won't stop shouting and carrying on."

Tyler groaned. "Is Charlie there?"

"No, thank goodness. I'd got him to stay with Hughes before this happened. His mother needed some time to herself. Shirley was taking a rest in one of the sisters' rooms."

"Let's go."

He followed Mortimer via the rear door to the nuns' quarters.

As soon as they entered, Mrs. McHattie whirled around. She looked as if she might run straight at him.

"If you don't do something about that pervert," she shouted, "I can't answer for what I'll do. This constable here is blocking the door. He's a young laddie and I don't want to hurt him, but I will if I have to. Somebody has to get to Alfie Fuller and cut his balls off."

"That sounds rather drastic, Mrs. McHattie. What has happened?"

"He's been up to his old tricks, that's what. And today of all days."

She was clearly on the verge of a complete hysterical collapse.

"Be a big help to me if you could say what you're referring to," said Tyler. "What sort of old tricks?"

She jerked her head in the direction of Constable Mady.

"He'll tell you."

The constable shuffled his feet. "Yes, sir. Well, you see, Mrs. McHattie thought she saw Alfie Fuller in the garden . . ."

She burst out angrily. "I didn't *think* I saw him, I *did* see him. He was skulking in the bushes over there. He wanted to spy on our Shirley. Expose himself like he did the last time. I swear I'll chop his parts off, I will. He won't be so quick to drop his trousers then."

She actually started to head for the door. Tyler moved to block her.

"Mrs. McHattie. If Alfie was doing what you say he was, it's a criminal offence. I'm a police officer. I'm responsible for charging those who break the law. I'd appreciate it if you would sit down and we can sort out what happened."

Reluctantly, she did so, perching on the edge of the chair, her hands curled into fists by her side.

"When did you see Alfie?" Tyler asked her.

"Just now. Out there." She pointed in the direction of the garden.

"Did you see anybody, Constable?" Tyler asked Mady.

He ducked his head. "I'm afraid not, sir. Mrs. McHattie started shouting. I came into the room and she, er, she said that there was somebody in the bushes spying on her."

"Did you go and have a look?"

"I didn't, sir. I called on Constable Mortimer to fetch you. I didn't want to leave Mrs. McHattie alone, and short of locking her in, I didn't see how I could stop her going in pursuit. And as I had not myself seen a man in the bushes, I had to assume she was mistaken."

Tyler thought Mrs. McHattie might explode at this, but she didn't. She simply muttered, "He'd run off by then."

"This has all been a dreadful ordeal for you, Mrs. McHattie," said Tyler. "And I am truly sorry I cannot let you go back to your own house just at present. We will move as quickly as we can to make an arrest."

"It's that village idiot you should be arresting. He's not right in the head. He was so upset when Jock said he had to stop helping with the birds." She tapped her finger to her temple. "Didn't connect. Didn't seem to realize how much he'd frightened our daughter. So Jock said no. No more coming in the house either. Alfie was beside himself. Crying and carrying on. I could see him going completely off the deep end and getting back at Jock."

"Mrs. McHattie, I'd like to go and talk to Mrs. Fuller and Alfie. Will you stay here with Constable Mortimer? I'll have Constable Mady patrol the grounds."

She nodded. "I'm just asking one thing from you, Inspector. No kid gloves. I know everybody feels sorry for Alfie Fuller, pathetic sod that he is – pardon my language. Well, I don't feel a bit sorry for him. He knows what he's doing. He frightens my

Shirley half to death the way he's been drooling around her. And that poor nun. He exposed himself to a nun, for Lord's sake! He doesn't deserve any pity."

"If he's guilty of a criminal act and knew what he was doing, he will be charged, Mrs. McHattie, I promise you."

29.

M RS. F ULLER WAS TIDYING UP THE DINING ROOM when Tyler came in. He explained his errand.

"Of course he wasn't in the garden," said Mrs. Fuller with indignation. "He was helping me prepare for tomorrow. You can ask the residents. Them that can see, at least. And the sisters. You've got half a dozen people who can vouch for him. That woman has it in for my Alfie is the problem. I told her and told her that he was caught short and he didn't mean anything. He's like a kiddie in that way. Her daughter, who is no better than she should be – no ring on that finger, you'll notice – anyway, she was the one who made a stink. It ripped Alfie apart when Jock said he couldn't help out with them pigeons. To my mind, they're dirty things – but he loves them."

Alfie came out of the kitchen.

"All done, Ma. I did a good job. Clean as a whistle."

"Good lad," said his mother. "Let's just finish those taties, then I'll set you up in the activity room and you can do a bit of practising on that typewriter."

"What?" exclaimed Tyler. "Does your son type?"

"He does that." She gave Tyler a conspiratorial wink. "He's fast, is Alf. He's just got to work on being accurate now. One of Sister Clarissa's prize pupils, aren't you, son?"

Alfie nodded vigorously. "I am. Only made five mistakes last time."

Tyler smiled at him. "How about if we go to the typing room and you show me, Alfie."

Mrs. Fuller frowned. "Why? Why'd you want to do that,

Inspector? He's not doing anything wrong. I give him a proper schoolbook to copy from. He only practises when there's a machine not being used. He enjoys himself. Keeps him occupied."

"Let's just say, it's part of our general investigation, Mrs. Fuller. You can come along if you want to."

Unexpectedly, Alfie spoke up. "No, Ma. You've got work to do. I can go by myself with Inspector. I'll go a bit slower and I won't make any mistakes."

It was clear he wanted to show off his skills and reluctantly his mother nodded.

"All right. But don't go blabbing about things you know nothing of, Alfie."

"I won't." He hesitated. "Can I talk about the pigeons?"

"He doesn't want to hear about no bloody birds, Alf."

"We won't be long, Mrs. Fuller," said Tyler. He thought it extremely unlikely that Alfie could have composed the letter unless he was capable of automatic writing, but he wanted to rule him out completely.

The so-called activity room was behind a low partition at the rear of the dining room. Three old typewriters sat on school desks along one side. Opposite was a table strewn with various bits of modelling clay, some shaped into recognizable sculptures, some just lumps, not yet born or already destroyed. There was a tray of paint jars, a tin of brushes, and beside them a pile of used sheets of paper. None of the residents were present.

Alfie went straight to the middle of the three machines. "This is my favourite. The keys go faster."

He sat down and rolled a sheet of paper into the carriage. He glanced over his shoulder at Tyler.

"What shall I type?"

"How about, 'The quick brown fox jumped over the lazy dogs'? Have you done that before?"

"Lots of times."

Alfie began to bang on the typewriter at great speed, not pausing for corrections or strikeovers. He stopped, rolled out the paper at the same brisk pace, and handed it to Tyler.

"How'd I do?"

Tyler looked at the sheet. The sentence was incomprehensible, but the typing was even except for where the letter *w* stuck. This was definitely the machine that had been used to type part of the strange letter, but Alfie was clearly not the typist.

"Well?" Alfie was staring at him, his face anxious. "Shall I do it again? I might have been going too fast."

"No, no, Alfie. You did a good job. You, er, you need to work a bit on your accuracy, that's all."

"I will. I want to get a job in an office when the war's over, and Ma says I've got to practise. I know that story about the fox. Sister said I should work on that a lot because it's got all the letters of the alphabet in it, so I do."

"Good. Tell me, Alfie. When you've been practising, have there been any of the residents in here? Maybe some of them want to work in an office."

Alfie didn't hesitate. "Nope. Just me. I usually come when they're having their dinner. It's the best time for Ma, see. When I've finished serving them I can come here and practise for a bit. After dinner, they all like to sit together in the common room. That means the room which they have in common. They listen to the wireless most of the time." He giggled. "Last week some of them got up and danced. Miss Stevens was pushing Mr. Bancroft around in his wheelchair in time to the music. Very funny it was." He looked at Tyler solemnly. "The nuns don't dance. God won't allow them to."

"So I understand. Did Shirley McHattie dance as well?"

Alfie ducked his head abruptly and muttered into his chest. "I ain't allowed to talk about her."

"Why not?"

"She told lies to her pa about me. He was very cross and wouldn't let me help with the pigeons anymore."

Alfie sniffed and wiped his nose on the back of his sleeve.

"What lies did Shirley tell?" Tyler asked him softly.

"She said she saw me showing my wee wee. But I wasn't. I was caught short and was just taking a leak against a tree when she went by."

Again Tyler kept his voice low. "Do you ever feel like showing your wee wee to girls, Alfie?"

Alfie didn't look up. "Girls get angry when you show your wee wee so I don't do that anymore."

"Did you used to?"

The man shrank farther into his own chest, looking like a whipped dog. "No, I never did. I'm just caught short sometimes."

The expression had clearly been drilled into him.

"What about today? Mrs. McHattie thought she saw you outside in the garden. Were you caught short again?"

"No," said Alfie emphatically. "I was in the kitchen with my ma since four o'clock. No, siree. I was working the entire time."

"So you didn't leave the kitchen? To get some vegetables, for instance?"

Alfie wrinkled his forehead. "I might have run out to pick a bit of fresh mint for the taties. I might have done that, but nothing else. You'd better ask Ma, she'd know."

"Okay. Thanks for your help, Alfie. Let's go back and see your mum, shall we?"

Alfie stayed in his chair. "Don't you want me to type another story? I'll go slower this time."

Tyler was about to refuse; then he saw what this meant to the man. "All right. You can do the same one if you like."

Alfie considered for a moment. "No, I have a better one." He sat down and inserted a fresh piece of paper into the machine.

The tip of his tongue protruded from the side of his mouth as he typed. Much slower this time. "Once upon a time somebody died. It was very, very sad." He glanced over his shoulder at Tyler. "Do you know this story, Inspector?"

30.

Tyler returned to the office and telephoned Dr. Beck a second time. He explained the interruption.

"Is Alfie a flasher, Doctor? Or a peeping Tom?"

"I'd say neither. At least consciously. He's got the mental age of a child, and we can't apply the same standards as we would to an adult. It's likely he didn't realize he should put his member promptly back in his trousers. By the same token, I could see him hanging around the women if he had a crush on them."

"Endearing in a small boy, disturbing in a grown man."

"True. I'm not saying he shouldn't be reined in. I'm just trying to put it in context."

"He says he popped out to pick some mint. He might have been out there longer than necessary."

"That is quite possible. Martha McHattie must be on the edge of her nerves by now and may have been overreacting." Beck sighed. "I wish I could come right away, but I'm afraid I have a crisis here as well. A suicidal patient I dare not leave. A delicate matter of trust. But I will try to get to Ludlow by Saturday at the latest."

"I think everybody would appreciate that."

He was about to end the conversation when Beck said, "Tom, I haven't had an opportunity to ask you about Mrs. Devereau. How is she? Is she still in Switzerland?"

"As far as I know."

"Will she be returning to England anytime soon?"

Tyler liked Dr. Beck, but he didn't want to fall into some

kind of doctor's "Here's my shoulder to cry on" conversation. He was sure Beck had enough of that to deal with in his work.

"Not that I know of."

"My wife is still interned on the Isle of Man," said Beck. "I don't know why exactly. She can hardly be considered a threat to national security. I can only get to visit her every couple of months. The time between visits seems endless. I completely sympathize with the wives and girlfriends of the fighting men who have to endure even longer separations."

Tyler hadn't clapped eyes on Clare for two years.

"I'm with you on that one, Doctor."

Both men fell into a silence, each lost in his own thoughts.

31.

THE NUNS HAD SET UP ONE OF THE END ROOMS AS THEIR sanctuary when they first arrived. It was barely adequate, but they made do. When Sister Rebecca entered, the other nuns were already kneeling on the old velvet prie-dieux they'd brought with them from the mother house. These were arranged in a semi-circle in front of the simple altar. Herb Mullin was in his wheelchair at the edge of the circle. He attended their services regularly even though, as he'd told Rebecca, he was a Baptist "through and through." At the moment, his body was slumped forward over his clasped hands. Jeremy Bancroft, also in a wheelchair, was on the other end, next to Daisy Stevens. Rebecca could see they were holding hands. Beside Daisy sat Vic Clark. Like Mullin, he was sitting with his hands clasped and his head lowered.

Rebecca walked straight to the altar, which was elevated on a polished table at the front of the room. She bowed her head, then turned to face the congregants.

"I apologize for being late. We will use the abbreviated service today."

"What a pity," muttered Sister Clarissa, "at a time like this."

She had spoken just loudly enough to be heard. The older nun had perfected the art of sly criticism. Clarissa professed to have no ambition, but ever since they had arrived at St. Anne's, Rebecca had felt the other woman's resentment. She knew Clarissa, being the senior nun, had expected to be put in charge.

Before she could take up the gauntlet, which she was unwisely about to do, the door opened and Nigel Melrose came in. Eddie Prescott was behind him, his hand on Nigel's shoulder. It was not in the actor's nature to resist making an entrance. Rebecca thought for a moment he might make a sweeping bow.

"So sorry, Sisters, everybody. We weren't going to come at first, but it's all for one and one for all, as they say. Where rub-a-dubs go, so go we all."

Daisy frowned at him. "You'll have to stand. All the chairs are taken."

At this, Vic struggled to his feet and indicated Eddie could take his chair.

"Thanks, old chap," said Melrose. "Come on, Prescott, Vic's sacrificing his seat and you can sit next to Daisy. I know you'd like that."

He led the blind man over to the chair, and with Daisy's help, Eddie sat down. Vic moved to the back of the room.

"Do carry on, Sister," said Melrose graciously. "If there's anything we all need today, it's a good dose of God-speak."

"Oi, show some respect," called out Herb Mullin. "To all intents and purposes, this is a house of the Lord. Right, Sister?"

Rebecca nodded. "I can't say I quite approve of your language, Mr. Melrose, but I do agree this has been a most troubling day and that turning to the words of the scriptures can give us comfort."

"Ridiculous," muttered Clarissa.

Exactly what she meant by that, Rebecca did not know.

"Let us start with a reading from Scripture. Psalm 139, verses eight to twelve. Sister Rachel, will you be so kind as to read them for us?"

The young nun stood up and opened her prayer book.

If I ascend up into heaven, thou art there: if I make my bed in hell, behold, thou art there. If I take the wings of the morning, and dwell in the uttermost parts of the sea; Even there shall thy hand lead me, and thy right hand shall hold me.

Sister Rachel closed the book and resumed her seat.

"Thank you, Sister," said Rebecca.

"Good reading for us lot, wouldn't you say?" chimed in the irrepressible Melrose. "I suppose you could take it to mean you can't hide from God no matter what you do."

"Show some respect," said Mullin loudly.

"But we are, old chap," said Melrose in his best stage voice. "Surely it is our right and prerogative to discuss the scriptures. Otherwise, what is the point?"

"That sounds sacrilegious to me," retorted the Australian.

If she'd had a gavel, Rebecca would have pounded it. "I'm happy you are all taking such an interest in the reading, but this is not the place to discuss it. We can do that later, if you wish. For now, let us bow our heads in prayer."

She waited until they all did so. All but Melrose, who just looked at her, a smirk at the corner of his mouth. She felt as if he was daring her to prove there was meaning, that there was a God who knew them all.

Rebecca had chosen a special collect for the evening, but now she almost regretted it. Perhaps it was too pertinent.

"Sister Clarissa, will you read us the Collect for Aid against Perils?"

"Is this a good choice, Sister Rebecca, considering the circumstances?"

"Perhaps especially given the circumstances."

The older nun took a while to leaf through her prayer book. She cleared her throat. "Collect for Aid against Perils."

Rebecca didn't miss the nudge that Melrose gave Eddie Prescott. Another cough from Sister Clarissa.

Lighten our darkness, we beseech thee, O Lord; and by thy great mercy defend us from all perils and dangers of the night; for the love of thy only son, our Saviour, Jesus Christ.

Melrose's "Amen" rang out above the others'.

Rebecca clasped her hands together. "I shall recite the Phos Hilaron, the prayer to light, and then we will conclude with the Lord's Prayer. After that we can all go along to the dining room, where I'm sure a welcome pot of tea will be ready for us."

"Good," said Eddie Prescott. "Daisy, will you take me in?"

"Love to, Eddie, but I promised Jeremy I'd go with him. You'll have to use Melly again, or Vic."

Rebecca could see the mutinous expression on Prescott's face and she hurried into the prayer.

"May the Lord bless us and keep us."

"Amen," chorused the group.

One by one they began to leave. Daisy was pushing Bancroft in his wheelchair, her head bent towards him in an attentive way.

Melrose took Prescott by the arm. "Come on, Eddie, I'm almost as good looking as Daisy, if only you could see me. Nothing to choose between us."

Prescott actually laughed. "Maybe you need a lesson on the birds and the bees, Melly. I'd say there's a lot of difference." And he allowed himself to be led out.

The nuns filed out, Sister Rachel pushing Herb Mullin.

"Praise the Lord," he said to Rebecca as he went. She was about to leave herself when she saw that Sister Ivy was still kneeling at her prie-dieu.

"I'm going to stay a little longer, Sister Rebecca."

Rebecca thought the other woman didn't look very well. Her eyes were puffy and darkly shadowed.

"Are you feeling all right, Sister?" Rebecca asked her.

"Oh, yes, thank you. Right as rain. I'm just a bit tired."

"Would you like me to get one of the other sisters to do the night shift?"

The nun shook her head. "No, no. That'd be too disruptive. I'll be all right."

"I'll see you in the dining room then."

She left and Sister Ivy started to murmur her prayers.

"Forgive me, Lord, I have done the things I ought not to have done . . ."

Rebecca closed the door.

32.

BLACKOUT WAS IN HALF AN HOUR AND THE EVENING was drifting into darkness. The new shift of constables had returned from the house-to-house detail but had nothing new to report. The nearby residents all said the same thing. Heard nothing. Saw nothing. Didn't know the man at all. Although several had expressed sympathy at the plight of the patients, it seemed apparent that they gave the hospital a wide berth.

He himself had gone back to the McHattie cottage and walked slowly from room to room, trying to see if there was a clue of any kind as to what had occurred. Something they may have missed. Nothing.

Finally, he decided to call it a day. He went out to the front entrance, where Constable Mortimer was stationed.

"I'm ready to leave, Constable. Frankly, I'm whacked. I think we both need some sleep. Are the guards in position?"

"Yes, sir."

"Good. You can fetch the motorcycle and we'll get back to the station. And, Constable, go a bit easier this time. My nerves can't take it."

"Yes, sir. Sorry about that. My mother complains constantly about the way I drive."

"Does she indeed?"

"Don't worry, sir. I'll get you home safely. The road is very familiar to me."

Despite his admonition, Constable Mortimer still drove too fast for his comfort, but they made the journey intact. She swept into the station car park and jolted to a halt. Tyler climbed stiffly out of the sidecar.

"Thank you, Constable. Get off now while there's still some daylight. Be back at the station at seven sharp."

"Yes, sir. Absolutely. I'll just lock up the motorbike and be on my way. Good night, sir."

"Good night," Tyler said. "And by the way, Mortimer, you've done a great job."

"Thank you, sir. And may I say that I think you, too, are doing splendidly."

Tyler smiled to himself. Constable Mortimer would never be described as subservient.

He walked the few yards to his house.

When he entered the kitchen, the curtains were drawn and the lights were on. To his surprise, he found Sergeant Rowell sitting at the table, his head resting in his arms. He woke immediately.

"You didn't have to wait up, Sergeant," said Tyler.

"It's been a long day, sir. I thought you might appreciate a nightcap. I've got some hot cocoa on the stove all ready."

"Thank you. Very thoughtful."

Rowell went to the stove and began to pour the cocoa into Tyler's cup.

"Anything new since we spoke last, sir?"

"Nothing. No helpful confessions. No accusations other than the one about Alfie that I told you about."

Rowell brought over the cup of cocoa. He'd placed a biscuit on the saucer.

"What a good dad you are," said Tyler.

Rowell blinked. "I would've liked to have had kiddies. But it was not to be. Won't happen now."

Tyler felt like an insensitive oaf. Once again, he'd put his foot in his mouth. He took a sip. The cocoa was too weak for his taste, and tepid to boot. A shot of brandy might liven it up, but he was too tired to fetch the bottle from his room.

"Delicious. Thank you."

Rowell sat down at the table. "Doctor Murnaghan telephoned about an hour ago. He wants you to ring him in the morning."

"That's all?"

"Yes, sir. He sounded a bit fuzzy, if you know what I mean. Said he had a headache."

"Nothing about any results?"

"No, sir."

"Pity."

"What's on the agenda for tomorrow, sir?"

"I'm planning to leave early for St. Anne's. I'll have the constables do more house-to-house calling. We'll just have to go further afield."

Rowell tried unsuccessfully to stifle a jaw-breaking yawn. "How did Constable Mortimer work out, sir?"

"Very well indeed. She's a capable young woman. I'll be just as glad to have the car back, but that's beside the point."

"I'll follow up with the garage. Put some ginger on their tails."

"Please do. Sergeant, you look as knackered as I feel. Get off to bed."

They said good night and Rowell went to leave but halted at the door.

"Goodness me, I almost forgot. I brought over the post for you. I put it in the hall."

He went to get it and returned right away with a bundle of envelopes. He hovered for a moment while Tyler riffled through them.

"Good night, Sergeant. Thanks for the cocoa."

"My pleasure, sir. I'll be off then."

At first glance there didn't seem to be anything that could be from Clare and he felt the usual sharp stab of disappointment. What the hell was she doing? He could only hope she was still alive and well. He knew that Grey at least would inform him if she wasn't – but that didn't stop him from worrying. He'd write again soon, but it was like tossing pieces of paper over a cliff for all the response he was getting.

There were two letters from local merchants complaining about rationing inequities on the part of other shopkeepers. Both would have to be followed up on. Tyler was determined to come down hard on profiteers and black marketers. A third letter was from somebody with an address on Broad Street who welcomed him to Ludlow and invited him to tea next week. The signature was spidery and indecipherable. He suspected the writer might be old Mrs. Yardley, who had already dropped in to the station to introduce herself. According to Rowell, her husband had been a chief of police in Warwickshire and she seemed to feel the need to stay connected with the police life. He put the letter aside. He had an excuse for not accepting for the moment. Then he picked up the last envelope.

DETECTIVE INSPECTOR THOMAS TYLER
c/o LUDLOW POLICE STATION

Goddamn it. He recognized the tidy black printing at once. The envelope had been franked yesterday at the Ludlow post office and must have been delivered in the afternoon post.

Gingerly, he took out the sheet of paper and started to read.

She and her husband have talked in whispers about what is going on. She was glad when she first heard that the Devil had died, but her husband, wiser in the ways of the world than she was, shook his head. "It will bring no good to us," he said.

A police officer had pounded on their door with the orders to stay inside and not look out. He is young, and she can smell his fear. All she says is, "Where are their men?" but he scowls at her. "Mind your own business, missus. If you know what's good for you, you'll not ask questions."

Today, she is very careful, lifting the curtain ever so slightly. In front of the schoolhouse there is a long line of canvas-topped lorries, the drivers standing at the ready beside them, smoking their cigarettes. There are even more soldiers than before. Nobody is talking. Then the women are led out. There are no children with them and all of them are weeping. No hysteria, just tears. Who are they? They are not from this village. All around them are soldiers, all weighed down with their weapons. What are they armed against? The withered old grandmother? The young woman holding her swollen belly?

The women are loaded into the lorries. The soldiers brook no dawdling and she can hear one of them shouting. None of the women resist. It is as if they are drugged. By despair, not anything else. One by one, the lorries are closed, doors snapping smartly. At a whistle from the sergeant,

they start to draw away, one a few feet
behind the other, moving slowly, like a
funeral procession.

She knows she should move from the
window, but she is powerless to break away.
The line of lorries has barely disappeared
from view when the two large coaches that
arrived earlier draw up in front of the
schoolhouse. The double doors open again
and this time two columns of children
emerge. They are quiet too, smaller ones
holding hands with older sisters or brothers.
Each clutches a brown paper parcel, the
little ones holding them close to their
chests the way children do if they have
something precious. One of the soldiers
directs them to the first coach. The windows
have been darkened, so she loses sight of
them once they are inside. There are about
forty or so in each coach.

Another whistle from the sergeant and the
coaches drive off. Faster than the lorries.
They leave swirls of dust behind them. Careful
not to attract attention, she lowers the
curtain.

Her body shudders as she weeps.

The world must weep also.

—

Tyler placed the sheet of paper on the table. Like the first letter, this suggested reprisal, again against innocent people, this time women and children. The narrator is female but also an observer. Directly so in this case. A woman who witnesses what is happening but is unable to act.

He read the piece again. What it was describing seemed even worse this time – children separated from their mothers. The narrator asks the police officer, "Where are their men?" She had to be referring to the men described in the first missive. The villagers who were being shot in cold blood. The tale appeared to be ongoing. A serial of sorts. Who was the Devil she referred to? He has died and she is glad, but her husband is worried. Is it his death that caused the reprisal? The last sentence was underlined. "The world must weep also." *Must* as in *should* or *must* as in *will*? Heaven knows there was enough tragedy occurring in the world right now that future tears were guaranteed. But to his eyes, the implication was more censorious. A wrong had been done and the world *ought* to respond.

33.

Sister Ivy liked the calm of night duty. Days could be busy, what with patients to tend to, prayers to say. Tonight the quiet was particularly welcome as it had taken a long time to settle everybody down. All of them were upset by what had happened. So far, nobody had stirred again, but she was jumpy. The slightest noise startled her. She heard the McHattie cat yowl in the back garden. Poor creature. They'd fixed it up as best they could. The wound from Alfie's pellet rifle was superficial, but the cat was still terrified.

She heard a floorboard creak somewhere deep in the old house and brought her silver cross to her lips and kissed it. *"Lord, keep me safe from harm,"* she whispered. She made a rather furtive sign of the cross on her chest. The community of Mary Magdalene had many practices in common with the Catholic Church, but crossing oneself could be a bone of contention for the purists. Sister Ivy herself liked the rituals of the older church.

Somebody spoke, sharp and anxious. She recognized the voice of Eddie Prescott, speaking in his sleep. Was he going to have a full-blown nightmare? No – he fell quiet again.

She took a sip of her cocoa. Darn it, the milk was on the turn. She reached into the cupboard behind the desk for the bowl of sugar, scooping a heaping spoonful into her cup. She promised herself she'd scrimp on sugar in tomorrow's drink. She tasted the cocoa. Hmm. Still off. She added another spoonful of sugar. Better. She took a sheet of paper out of the drawer, dipped her pen into the inkwell, and started her letter.

To Sister Rebecca and to Inspector Tyler. I am very sorry, but I . . .

Oh no. She'd made a blot on the paper. She was having a hard time keeping her thoughts straight. But it had to be done and she persisted to the end, writing slowly and carefully. Once she had finished, she read it over, sighed, hesitated, then signed her name. Sister Ivy Packwin, R.N.

At this point, she was overcome by a wave of fatigue and she rubbed hard at her forehead to make herself wake up. She could hardly keep her eyes open. Maybe just a short nap would set her to rights. Just a few minutes, that's all. She folded her arms on the desk and let her head sink forward. Within moments, she was fast asleep.

She didn't hear the soft footsteps in the hall, didn't see her death moving towards her.

34.

THE PERSISTENT RINGING BEGAN TO PENETRATE Tyler's unconscious and he stirred groggily. He'd set his alarm for six o'clock, and he was reaching over to switch it off before he realized it wasn't that making the din. It was the telephone. The clock showed ten past five. Suddenly fully awake, he jumped out of bed and raced downstairs.

He snatched up the receiver.

"Tyler here."

"Inspector, this is Sister Rebecca. There has been another death." Her voice was shaky and she sounded as if she had been running.

"What!"

"One of our sisters has died. Sister Ivy. Dai Hughes discovered her body this morning. She was at her desk on the ward. She has been dead for a while."

"How?"

Sister Rebecca paused. "It appears she took her own life. She had inhaled chloroform. There was a vial of it on the desk and a mask on her face."

"Did she leave a note?"

"Not that I found."

"I'll be there right away. Please don't let anybody touch anything."

"Hughes thought it best to cover the body, and he's put up a screen, but that is all." She took a deep breath, but he could tell she wasn't smoking this time – she was trying her utmost to compose herself.

"Good. We must take the same precautions as before. Nobody is to leave, and please don't discuss anything with the residents about what has happened."

"I don't *know* what has happened, Inspector. I have no information to impart. Sister Ivy is the last person I would ever think would take her own life."

Perhaps she didn't, thought Tyler.

"You've been a stalwart, Sister. Don't falter now. I'll be there as soon as I can."

They hung up and Tyler hurried back upstairs to get dressed. Sergeant Rowell opened his own door at that moment.

"What's up, sir? Sorry I didn't get to the telephone."

"There's been another death at St. Anne's. One of the nuns. Possible suicide."

"Good God."

"I'm getting right over there. Do you have a bicycle, Sergeant?"

"I do, sir. It's in the shed at the back of the house."

"I'll use that if you don't mind."

"Do you think the sister is the one who did for the others? Guilty conscience?"

"It's hard to believe," said Tyler. "She didn't seem either the murderous kind or suicidal to me. Sergeant, will you go and man the station? I'll ring you there once I get the lay of the land."

When he came back downstairs, Rowell was waiting with a plate in his hand.

"There wasn't time to make you a cup of tea, sir, but I thought you might do well to swallow down a slice of bread and jam at least."

Tyler took it gratefully. Then he picked up the letter from the night before, stuffed it into his pocket, and hurried out to the shed.

35.

THE SCENE AT ST. ANNE'S WAS EERILY SIMILAR TO that of the previous morning. Sister Rebecca was waiting on the front steps and she came to meet him as soon as he entered the gate. She was fully dressed and looked neat and tidy, but there were dark circles underneath her eyes. The young constable who had been on night duty was standing right behind her and looked as pale as she did.

"I'll take your bicycle, sir," said Constable Mady. He grabbed it from Tyler and went to wheel it to a place by the steps.

"Hold on a second, Constable. You know what has happened, I presume?"

"Yes, sir. Sister Rebecca has told me. I'm flabbergasted. Sister Ivy was a jolly person if ever there was one. It's so hard to believe. She did do it herself, did she?"

"We'll know soon enough. The almoner here believes Sister may have died in the middle of the night. Did you hear anything out of the ordinary then?"

"Nothing, sir. Not a thing. Well, that is, I heard Constable Biggs coughing now and again. He's got asthma and the sound carries in the night. He was on guard at the cottage." He stared with round eyes at Tyler. "I was sat here all night. Right there in the entrance. And it was black as Hades. I swear nobody could've come through the gate or over the wall without a light, in which case I would've seen them."

"What about the rear of the house?"

"Constable Chase is there. He's been apprised, but I told him to stay right where he was. We both patrolled the grounds every hour during the night and it was utterly quiet. We all three conferred throughout and nobody reported anything amiss."

"All right, Mady. Stay here for now. Don't let anybody in or out."

"Yes, sir."

Mady wheeled the bicycle away and Tyler turned to the almoner. "Tell me what you know, Sister."

"Our community rises early to say matins. We were all gathered in the sanctuary, except for Sister Ivy, when Dai Hughes came in. He beckoned me to come outside, which I did." She was speaking rather slowly and deliberately and Tyler could tell she was trying to anticipate the sort of things he might need to know, trying to put events that were without sense in order. "He told me that he had found Sister Ivy's body. Hughes acted very sensibly. He immediately put a screen around the desk and ran to fetch his brother. Evan Hughes remained on the ward while Dai came to get me." She glanced up at the brightening sky. "The residents will be getting up very soon." She clasped her hands together tightly. "Do you think we should evacuate everyone, Inspector? There seems to be one tragedy after another. Some of our patients are very fragile mentally."

"Let's hold off on that for now."

Sister Rebecca nodded. "With your permission, I will proceed with the breakfast routine and have them taken into the common room again. Shall I tell them what has happened or would you prefer it came from you?"

"I'd like to have a look at the body first. Have you informed the other sisters?"

She shook her head. "Frankly, I didn't know what to say. Obviously, they know something has happened. But they don't know what."

"And the McHatties?"

"They're still sleeping."

"Good. Let's leave them for the time being. What about Mrs. Fuller?"

"She was already in the kitchen. I simply said there had been an accident. Thank heavens she didn't press me."

Tyler inhaled. "Shall we go inside, Sister?"

She turned to lead the way.

"And of course, if there is anything you can tell me about Sister Ivy that might be relevant, I would appreciate it."

The almoner halted. "Relevant? Relevant to her taking her own life? I can think of nothing. She has been with our community for thirteen years. She was upset, as we all were, about the McHatties, but I never imagined she would do something like this."

"Thank you, Sister. I'll keep that in mind."

She flinched a little and her eyes met his. He immediately regretted being brusque with her.

As they entered the deserted foyer and headed for the stairs, Alfie Fuller burst through the swing door that led to the kitchen.

"What's all the carryings on? I was supposed take a cup of tea to Miss Oakshutt 'cos she's feeling poorly, but Ma says I mustn't. She says there's been an accident."

"That's right, Alfie," said the almoner. "I'd rather you stayed here with your mother for now."

"Somebody's died again, ain't they? Who is it, Sister? Please don't tell me it's Miss Shirley? Please don't say that."

Tyler interjected. "Why would it be Shirley, Alfie?"

"'Cos somebody is out to get all of them. Pa and kiddies. Her next and her ma. I just know it."

Mrs. Fuller emerged.

"Alfie! How many times must I tell you? You're to let me know when you go off somewhere. What are you doing?"

"I was going to the toilet, Ma, but the policeman and Sister was here and I had to asks him what was happening."

Mrs. Fuller frowned at him. "It's none of our business. They'll tell us soon as they're ready. Come on. Right now, do you hear?"

She held open the door so that her son had no choice but to do as she said. She rolled her eyes at Tyler but evinced no curiosity as to what had happened.

Tyler and Sister Rebecca continued up to the second floor.

The blackout curtains were still drawn and the ward was in darkness, except for the soft light from a lamp filtering through the screen around the desk. The orderly was seated a few feet away and stood up as soon as he saw Tyler. He looked frightened.

"Glad to see you, Inspector."

"Mr. Hughes. Will you make sure everybody stays in their rooms while I take a look at the body? I don't want anybody out here. Are they awake yet?"

"So far, only two are. Mr. Melrose and Mr. Mullin. My brother is tending to them. Miss Stevens did come down from the third floor to use the toilet but she can enter by way of the passageway, so I was able to make sure she went back upstairs without seeing anything."

"Good man."

Sister Rebecca stationed herself beside the screen and Tyler shifted it to one side. The body was covered with a sheet and he unfolded it carefully.

Sister Ivy, big, pink-cheeked country woman that she had been, was now grey-white as death claimed its territory. Her head was turned to one side, resting on her arm. The strings of a white, cone-shaped mask were hooked around her ears, pulling the mask tightly against her mouth and nose, and Tyler could smell the sweet, pungent odour of chloroform. A labelled vial was by her right hand.

He bent in a little closer. He could see that the inside of her right index finger was stained with ink. A pen lay on the desk.

He beckoned to the almoner. "She must have been writing something, Sister. But you say you didn't find a note?"

"No, I did not. The wastepaper basket is empty and there was nothing on the floor nearby. Perhaps she was writing her report."

A clipboard was balanced on the edge of the desk. Carefully, Tyler picked it up. It held the nurses' report sheet. WEDNESDAY, JULY 15.

"She signed in at eleven o'clock, taking over from Sister Rachel. She made her first round at midnight."

Sister Rebecca nodded as she said, "Yes, that is the routine."

"She reported that all patients were settled for the night except for Vadim Bhatti, who was in discomfort. She gave him two ASA powders. She made another round at one o'clock and then another one an hour later. Both included the women's rooms upstairs. Two o'clock is the final entry."

Tyler replaced the clipboard. Ironically, the last thing the nun had written was ALL WELL.

The desk itself was tidy. The blotter was straight, lightly used by the look of it. Tucked into the cubby hole with the inkwell and a container of drawing pins was the silver-plated mug Sister Ivy had claimed yesterday. He picked it up. She must have received the mug as a prize at some point because her name was engraved on it, together with the words FIRST PRIZE JUNE 1912. What exactly she had come first in was not specified.

"It looks as if she made cocoa and drank most of it. So we are to believe that after finishing her cocoa, at her usual time of a quarter past two, she then took out a vial of chloroform from the medicine cabinet, dripped the anaesthetic onto the mask, put it on, and inhaled enough to kill herself."

There was the sound of a woman's voice in the hall.

"Sister? Sister Ivy?"

Somebody was knocking on the door that led to the passageway.

"I'll deal with it," said Sister Rebecca.

Tyler turned to the alcove behind the desk. Nothing appeared to be disturbed. The kettle sitting on the spirit stove was cold, the lid was on the cocoa tin, the silver teaspoon was clean. The matching sugar bowl was almost empty. The key to the medicine cabinet was still in the lock, and so he opened it. The stock was neatly arranged and he could see the space where the chloroform must have been. He picked up the vial on the desk with his handkerchief. Only a drop was left. There was no leaving it to chance.

From the moment he'd clapped eyes on the dead woman, Tyler knew she hadn't committed suicide. He knew from experience that having a chloroform mask on your face was not pleasant. When he'd been injured two years ago and required anaesthetic prior to surgery, his every instinct was to fight against the mask that had been placed on his face. He felt as though it was suffocating him. But in an operating room, there were nurses and a doctor telling you to breathe normally, who had their hands on your arms just in case. If you were doing it yourself, it would require tremendous self-discipline not to rip off the mask that was impeding your breathing. He also knew that for the anaesthetic to work, the mask had to stay in place for at least five minutes.

Suicides frequently left people behind who were devastated by their death; who asked themselves how they could have missed the signs of utter despair. Because there were always signs; he'd been a copper long enough to know that. But here was a nurse, a woman of religion, who was performing her usual duties, who had made herself a hot drink. Nothing to indicate "the balance of her mind was disturbed," as the official language put it.

The majority of suicides left a note, some communication with those they were about to leave behind. If Sister Ivy had indeed written a farewell note, it had now vanished.

He pulled the sheet back over the body and came out from behind the screen. Dai Hughes was sitting a few feet away.

"I'd like you to stay here and make sure nobody touches anything. Keep the screen up, but you might as well open the blackout curtains. I'll have an officer relieve you as soon as possible."

"Yes, sir. And . . . sir?" The orderly gulped. "I'm terrible sorry about the sister. She was a good woman. To think she would do this . . ."

His voice trailed off.

Sister Rebecca returned. "It was Miss Stevens. She wanted some ASA powders. She's gone back to her room."

"Thank you, Sister."

"Shall I ring Dr. Murnaghan?"

"Yes, please."

"Unless you need me here, I'll go and speak to the sisters. We'll need to tend to the patients." Then she lowered her voice so Hughes couldn't hear her. "Sister Ivy didn't commit suicide, did she, Inspector?"

He shook his head. "I don't think so."

She left, and Tyler walked to the window at the end of the hall. It was half open. Was this to let in some air or had somebody entered the ward by way of the fire escape? He dismissed that notion immediately. Constable Mady might be flat-footed and short-sighted, but he was a conscientious lad. He'd been doing his job. Even if the killer had been moving swiftly and silently – as he seemed able to do – if he had climbed up and down the fire escape, Mady or Biggs would surely have detected him.

Ergo, the murderer was within the house. But how could a killer have got behind the nun and taken her so completely unawares that she didn't put up even the slightest struggle?

And we are back to "Why?"

36.

DAI HUGHES FELT AN OVERWHELMING URGE TO HAVE a cigarette. Sister Rebecca didn't like them to smoke on the ward, but he might be able to sneak in a few puffs before things got moving. He took out the single cigarette he kept tucked away in his top pocket. Matches? There'd be some for the spirit stove, but it meant he'd have to go around the other side of the screen, and he wasn't sure he was up to that. He'd been an orderly for a year now and he'd seen several dead bodies, but they were always nicely in their beds, not sprawled over a desk with a chloroform mask on their face. He was braced himself, just about to risk it, when Evan came striding out of the blue bedroom.

"We only have a minute. They're all waking up. Bancroft needs a bedpan."

His face was contorted with anger. Knowing his temper, Dai quailed.

"I've got to stay here until a constable arrives," he said.

Before Dai could move, Evan grabbed him by the arm and shoved him into the chair. He pulled a piece of paper out of his pocket and waved it under his brother's nose.

"Do you know what this is, laddie?"

"Looks like a letter."

"Aye. It is. The nun here was writing it to the inspector. No, don't start to make up a story, you sorry piece of shite. She says everything. She says how you were going out on a regular basis when you were supposed to be on duty. She was good enough to keep the side door unlocked for you. You went out again, didn't you, when I'd expressly told you not to?"

"Evan, I had to go. Polly's ill. She needed me."

"Got the clap, does she?"

"No, it's a touch of bronchitis."

Evan glared at him. "You're lying. Either she's telling you a story or you're telling me one."

"It came on sudden," said Dai sullenly.

Evan put the letter back into his pocket. "It's a bloody good thing I took a look at what the sister had been writing. Her farewell letter."

"What she did for me was a little thing – no reason to off yourself."

"Isn't it? How can you be so sure? She sounds pretty sorry."

"No, Evan. She didn't feel bad about helping me. She said I reminded her of her brother."

"I pity the poor woman, if that's the case."

"Evan, I just can't believe that the sister killed herself. She was so jolly."

Evan scrutinized Dai for a moment, then he stepped back. "Can I have faith that your little tom-catting in the night has nothing to do with what happened to Jock McHattie?"

Dai stared at him in horror. "How can you say a thing like that? Of course it didn't."

"I'm relieved to hear that. We'll let the copper sort it out. We won't say anything about the note for now. It's our business. Yours and mine."

"I don't know, Evan. We should probably tell. I'll take my lumps."

"Not yet. Let's see what happens. You say you don't think the sister did off herself. But she might have. Guilty conscience. She was religious, after all. In which case it don't matter what she wrote." He tapped his pocket. "I will keep this note to myself, but I warn you, if you so much as put a toe outside of these gates without permission, this little *billet* will find its way straight to the police. Is that clear?"

"I'm your brother. You wouldn't do that, would you?"

"Short answer? Yes."

"Everything all right, Mr. Hughes?" called a voice. Nigel Melrose was standing in the hall.

Evan turned to face him. "I'm afraid there's been an accident, Mr. Melrose. Sister Ivy." He walked towards the other man and his voice was soothing. "I'd appreciate it if you'd stay in your room for now. We're all going to meet after breakfast and you'll be told what has happened."

Melrose didn't move. He stared over Hughes's shoulder, where he could clearly see the screen.

"Is she dead?"

"Yes, I'm afraid so."

"Another one. Was it really an accident, or are you just saying that to keep me calm?"

"We'll know more when the doctor arrives. But we don't want to upset everybody more than we have to. When everybody's up, we'll proceed downstairs in an orderly fashion."

Melrose allowed himself to be directed back into his room as he declaimed:

"She should have died hereafter. There would have been a time for such a word."

Evan followed him and closed the bedroom door behind them.

Dai heard footsteps on the stairs, coming up to the ward, and then a police officer appeared. It was the young, skinny one.

"Good morning. I'm Constable Mady, and I've been sent to take over the watching."

Dai was too rattled from his conversation with his brother to be magnanimous.

"About time. I'll leave you to it. I've got to tend to the patients."

Mady looked around. "Could I just ask you something? Is it true there's maniacs in this place? One of them isn't likely to pop and start shooting, are they?"

"Wish I could guarantee that, but I can't," said Dai. "Let's just say it's not likely."

"But something has happened here – and people say that the patients are all crackers."

"People are ignorant then."

"So they're not loonies is what you're saying?"

"No. I said they wasn't likely to come out and shoot you. But let's put it this way, look you. If you suddenly had your legs shot off, your hands amputated, and you couldn't see but darkness, you'd be a bit off your rocker, wouldn't you, laddie?"

"I suppose I would."

"Not to mention you'd lost your good looks and the girls run away crying. Not to mention you couldn't be a man to her even if she wanted it. That'd send you around the bend, don't you think?"

"My God. Has that happened to some of these chaps?"

"It has indeed. Me, I'd rather be put out of me misery."

"So you do think it's one of them that did the murders?" whispered Mady.

Rather roughly, Dai tapped the young constable on the forehead.

"You're not using your noggin, my friend. How can you shoot anybody if you can't walk, can't see, and can't hold anything?"

"But they're not *all* that bad, are they?"

Before Dai could answer, Sister Clarissa appeared, puffing hard from the exertion of climbing the stairs.

"Mr. Hughes, Sister Rebecca wants to let you know that the patients should be brought down to the dining room as soon as possible. She wants them to have some breakfast before the inspector talks to them."

"We'll be right there, Sister." Dai nodded at the constable. "Chin up, laddie. The grave's where we all end up eventually."

The nun frowned at him. "Why're you saying that, Dai Hughes? It's nothing a young fellow like him should be thinking about."

"I disagree with you there, Sister," said Dai with a grimace. "None of us knows, do us? When we'll be called. We've got to be prepared, look you."

37.

A FTER A BRIEF CONSULTATION WITH SISTER REBECCA, Tyler decided not to include the McHattie family in the general meeting. He had no idea how they were going to react, and it seemed cruel to subject them to more tragedy. He'd have to talk to them afterwards. Once again, he found himself in the distressingly familiar position of delivering news of violent death to the gathered residents.

There had been a wide range of reactions: fear, disbelief, anger – the usual emotions people feel when presented with such a situation. Although he was beginning to fume at his own impotence, all Tyler could do at this juncture was say he didn't know exactly how Sister Ivy had died.

In terms of actual evidence or information, he got nothing new from the patients. He concluded the meeting by eight o'clock. He'd said all he could say, gone over the same ground a couple of times, reassured as best he could. Sister Rebecca said the other nuns would stay in the dining room and give the patients the opportunity to air their feelings if they wanted to. There was often a delayed reaction to these tragic incidents. In the meantime, she would go with him to talk to the McHatties.

First, Tyler had to organize the influx of constables. Rowell had done a good job. As well as the men from the morning roster and the reservists, he'd been able to contact the afternoon shift, and they were there as well. More than a dozen men all told. Tyler was gratified. Looked like an army to him.

The sergeant had come himself.

"This has priority, sir. I've left Constable Mortimer temporarily in charge of the station until Constable Pepper arrives from his rest day."

"The grounds were searched thoroughly yesterday, but we need to do it again," said Tyler. "Once we're satisfied with that, we'll continue to question the locals. We'll have to go further afield."

"When are you going to make the incidents public, sir?"

"Frankly, I'm delaying that as long as possible. People will be seeing Jerry parachutists under every tree."

Rowell looked at him. "I assume we are ruling out enemy infiltration, sir?"

Tyler sighed. "I'm not ruling out men from Mars, Sergeant. But first we'll keep looking closer to home. Have Eaves and Stanton made any progress with the fingerprint checks?"

"Not yet. They didn't get very clear impressions from the cottage, but they are studying everything they have."

Tyler turned back to Sister Rebecca. "Shall we go, Sister? The sooner I get this over with, the better."

She fell into step with him as they headed along the path for the nuns' quarters.

"I reached Dr. Murnaghan and he says he'll come as soon as he can."

"Good . . . You know, Sister, I've delivered news of death before. It never gets easier. In this case, I feel as if I'm piling on one more tragedy to people already devastated."

She glanced over at him. "Life doesn't necessarily parcel out grief like a fair-minded teacher. One for you, one for you. We have to deal with what we are given."

These words might have sounded pretentious and sanctimonious, but coming from her, they came across as matter of fact and real.

—

To Tyler's eyes, Shirley McHattie's belly seemed more swollen than it had yesterday. The cotton smock was tight. Perhaps she was close to delivering her baby. Her mother looked drawn and wretched. She didn't appear to have even combed her hair. They were finishing up their breakfast. They did not seem to be talking. When he and Sister Rebecca entered, he felt the tension seize both of them. Mrs. McHattie abruptly put down the cup of tea she was drinking.

"Something else has happened, hasn't it? The nuns have all disappeared and I can tell just by looking at you two, there's trouble."

There was no point in beating around the bush. Tyler told them.

"Sister Ivy! I can't believe it. She was always so cheerful," said Mrs. McHattie. "Killed herself?"

"That's what appears to have happened," said Tyler. He phrased his answer carefully.

Shirley had gone very pale. "I think I'm going to be sick, Ma. I need to go to the toilet."

"I'll take you, Miss McHattie," said Sister Rebecca. Too late. Shirley suddenly vomited onto her plate. Her mother and the nun both reached towards the table for a serviette to hand to her and Tyler waited for her to wipe her face. Sister Rebecca whipped away the plate and carried it to the sink, where she quickly rinsed it off. Then she poured a glass of water for the girl and brought it back.

Shirley gulped it down. "Sorry," she whispered to Tyler.

"No need to apologize. I regret I had to deliver such shocking news."

"Surely she didn't do it because of what happened to Jock?" asked Mrs. McHattie.

"So far we haven't discovered anything which might explain her reasons."

"Not that we knew each other, really. We all worked together to get the hospital in order when it opened," she continued. "But other than that, you might say we were only casual acquaintances. The sisters keep to themselves and so do we."

"I can let you go to Wem if you'd like," said Tyler. "Do you think you can stay with your relatives for a few days?"

He could ill spare the constables who would have to remain with them, but he couldn't bear to see their fear and misery.

"I'm sure Ethel will put us up," said Mrs. McHattie.

"No, I don't want to go to Auntie Ethel's." Shirley's tone was sharp. "For one thing, she's always looking down her nose at me. For another, I feel safer here with the sisters and the inspector."

Her mother stared at her doubtfully. "All right, suit yourself." She turned to Tyler. "What will I tell Charlie? He's still sleeping. I don't want to get him all upset again."

"I would recommend not saying anything for the moment. Keep him with Hughes or yourselves so he doesn't overhear anything accidentally."

"All right." Mrs. McHattie scowled at Tyler. "Is that all, Inspector? We wouldna mind finishing our breakfast in peace. Or do you have some other cheery news you want to tell us?"

Her tone was belligerent and Tyler almost snapped back at her. It wasn't exactly his fault that they had been interrupted.

Shirley put her hands on her big belly. "I still think I might be sick."

"Sip the water," said Sister Rebecca. "I'll go and fetch you something to settle your stomach."

For some reason, this offer irritated Mrs. McHattie. "The only bloody thing that'll settle her stomach is when the bebbie is out of it."

Tyler could see tears spring to Shirley's eyes, but she tightened her lips and didn't cry. He didn't miss the look of fury that she flashed at her mother.

"I'll come back later," he said, and left the two of them to their unhappiness. A sorrow he could not alleviate.

38.

DR. MURNAGHAN ARRIVED AT ABOUT TEN O'CLOCK. He was driving his own ramshackle Ford.

"The ambulance will be here in about half an hour," he said to Tyler. "Somebody forgot to get the petrol ration and we were almost on empty."

"How are you feeling?" Tyler asked. Murnaghan had a livid bruise on his cheek and bloodshot eyes.

"I've still got a headache, but I'll be all right. I was planning to do those other post-mortems this morning." He gave a rueful grin. "Never rains but it pours, eh, Tom. Let's have a look at what you've got for me today."

Tyler led the way upstairs to the men's ward. Dr. Murnaghan was moving slowly. "Banged my hip," he said in answer to Tyler's look.

Constable Mady was at the far end of the hall staring out of the window. Tyler had the impression he was keeping as far away as possible from the corpse.

"Go and get yourself a cup of tea, there's a good chap," said Tyler to him. "Come back in half an hour."

"Yes, sir." His relief palpable, Mady scuttled off.

Dr. Murnaghan removed the sheet.

The two men gazed down at the body. Then Murnaghan picked up the vial of chloroform.

"Assuming it was a full bottle, she's inhaled enough to kill a horse. But it's not an easy way to kill yourself."

"That's what I thought," said Tyler. "But there's no indication she struggled, so if somebody else put that mask on her face, she submitted passively, which doesn't make sense."

The coroner pushed at the left arm where her head was resting. It was already stiffening and the underside had turned purple with lividity.

"She's been dead about eight or nine hours. I'd estimate she died in the early hours of this morning."

Tyler pointed at the silver mug. "She was in the habit of making herself a nightcap at a quarter past two. It was her tea time. From her position she looks as if she was asleep or resting. Whether naturally or unnaturally, it'd be good to find out. I'd like you to analyze the contents of the cocoa mug."

Dr. Murnaghan pursed his lips. "Would you believe I knew Ivy Packwin many years ago? I was a G.P. in Hereford at the time. She always struck me as a sensible woman. Salt of the earth type. She didn't leave a note or anything, I gather?"

Tyler indicated the ink stain on the nun's finger. "She was writing something before she died. It may have been her report – I'm not sure. But we found no note."

"I'll just wait here until the ambulance boys arrive," said Murnaghan. "I'll need to supervise them. They're both totally green at the job."

"Do you want me to have a cup of tea sent up?"

"That would be grand." Murnaghan went over to the empty chair and sat down wearily. "Don't get me wrong, I've always loved my work. Still do when it comes along. But when I see something like this, it brings me down." He flapped his hand in Tyler's direction. "Don't mind me, Tom. I'm getting old is the problem. A nice hot cup of tea will fix me up."

Tyler sighed to himself. He wished it were that simple.

39.

Daisy Stevens could see sufficiently well to report to the others of the Rub-a-Dub Club what was happening outside the window.

"They're taking out the stretcher."

"I hope the damn things aren't rationed," said Melrose. "At the rate we're using them, they'll run out."

Prescott burst out with a snort of laughter.

"I do wish you wouldn't make jokes like that, Melly," Daisy scolded. "It's not funny. I'm scared to death. I think we should be moved as soon as possible."

"That won't do us any good if the killer is one of the residents," said Melrose. "Don't forget the story of the Trojan horse."

Prescott's mood turned immediately. "What's that? A posh pub in Soho? Overrun with cockroaches, was it?"

"Come on, Eddie," said Daisy. "I know what he's talking about. We studied it in school. The Greeks built a wooden horse and sent it as a gift to their enemies, the Trojans, who took it inside the walls of Troy. During the night, the Greeks who were hidden inside the horse jumped out and let in the rest of the army. They won the war."

Melrose clapped his hands. "Well done, Miss Stevens. And the lesson is? Never trust a Greek? I knew some Greeks who lived on my street. Two brothers, both queer as frogs and would steal your trousers out of the privy if you were taking a shite."

"Hey! Watch it." Jeremy was jolted out of his distraction. "Don't use language like that around Daisy. I've told you before."

"And what word did you object to, pray tell?" said Melrose.

"Trousers? Privy? Oh, I know, I should have said something more refined, like 'if you were in the middle of defecating.'"

Daisy actually laughed. "For some reason that sounds worse."

Jeremy reached up his hand so she could hold it. "I get your point, Melly, but I don't think it fits. Nobody's a traitor here and there's no war among us."

Nobody said anything.

"Well there isn't, is there?" continued Jeremy. "Eddie? I know you are always fighting the battle of the subjugated peasants but you wouldn't shoot Jock for some imagined slight, I hope. He was hardly upper class anyway."

"Of course it wasn't one of us," exclaimed Daisy. "Somebody got into the grounds. That's what frightens me. I want to go somewhere else, where we can be safe."

Clark had taken the chair next to Melrose, who reached out to him.

"Anything you want to say, Vic? You can write it down if you like and I'll utter the words for you."

Clark shook his head and mimed wiping at his eyes.

"Sad? I'll agree with you on that score," said Melrose.

There was the sound of a thud from the hall.

"What was that?" asked Bancroft.

Daisy went and looked out. She returned to stand beside Bancroft. "It was the ambulance men negotiating the stairs. They've just taken out Sister's body."

Melrose sat down in an armchair abruptly. "I liked her. She never seemed prissy like some religious can get. I don't understand why she would commit suicide . . . if she did, that is."

Daisy eyed him. "Melly, don't say that."

Melrose slapped his hands on the arms of his chair. "I'm going in search of some alcohol to drown my sorrows. Anybody else want to come? Sister Rebecca might take pity on us and take out some medicinal brandy."

"I'll come with you," said Eddie. "I'd rather have a Guinness, but brandy'll do if that's all they've got."

"Daisy? Jeremy? Coming?"

"Too early for me," said Bancroft. "I was hoping you could wheel me to the river, Daisy."

"Of course I will. Let me get my hat." She stopped in front of Melrose. "Don't get too drunk, Melly. It's not worth it."

"Fat chance of that with the amount Sister's going to dole out. We'll see you when you get back. You're coming for a drink, aren't you, Vic?"

Clark made one of his gurgling noises. Prescott got to his feet. "So that's where you are. Lead on, will you, chum."

Clark turned so that Prescott could put his hand on his shoulder and they lurched off, Melrose behind them.

"Have a good cool off, you two," he called to Bancroft and Daisy.

There was a little silence, then Bancroft said, "Daisy, have they gone?"

"Yes."

"There's nobody within earshot?"

"No, there isn't."

"Come close so I can whisper in your ear."

She giggled, leaned forward, and blew lightly on his cheek so he would know. "What do you want to say?"

"Daisy, will you let me make love to you?"

Involuntarily, she jumped away.

"Jeremy! We can't do that."

"Why not?"

"For one thing, you're engaged."

"Lydia doesn't want me. I'm doing her a favour. I'm disengaging myself."

"I—"

"We were never intimate. She wanted to wait until we were married."

"So what makes you think I don't feel the same way?" asked Daisy.

"Daisy, dear, don't be insulted. I don't mean that you're easy. It's just that . . . Well, with what's happened here, I thought, my God, I don't want to die without knowing what it's like to be with a woman."

"Jeremy! Why are you talking like this? You're not going to die."

"All I'm saying, Daisy, my love, is that we never know, do we? A bomb? A crash? A maniac stalking the halls?" He managed to grasp hold of her hand. "I'm sorry, Daisy. You're cold. I don't want to scare you any more than you're already scared. Forget what I just said."

"All of it?"

"Yes. Just go and get your hat and we'll simply go into town. I apologize for being out of line."

Daisy didn't move for a moment, then bent over again and put her cheek next to his. "You don't have to apologize. I'm glad that you even, er, desire me. I'm not much to look at anymore."

"What?" He chuckled. "Can't say that bothers me. It's you who should be put off. I can tell I'm pretty ugly."

Soft as new love itself, her kiss touched his lips. "Good thing everything is blurry then, isn't it? You look handsome to me."

He caught her chin and held it so he could kiss her again. His hand moved up to caress her neck and moved down to her breast. When he let her go, they were both breathing hard.

"Didn't you have a question?" she asked softly.

"So I did," he whispered. "Can I make love to you?"

"I'd rather like that, Mr. Bancroft. But where in heck are we going to do it?"

Daisy seized the wheelchair handles and pushed Jeremy out of the house. She turned rather sharply at the bottom of the ramp, bumping him onto the driveway.

"I'm glad you're eager, Daisy, my darling, but I don't mind if you go a little slower."

"Sorry."

She made herself slow down.

"Have a good walk," said the constable who swung the gate open for them. Daisy glanced over her shoulder. Inspector Tyler was standing at the front window of the common room, watching them. He waved in a friendly fashion. When she'd asked his permission to go into town, he hadn't demurred. He said he understood their need to escape the confines of the hospital. Daisy thought he couldn't possibly know what they were planning, but she had a rather uncomfortable feeling he suspected.

Suddenly, Daisy felt a sharp spasm of alarm. In spite of everything, the hospital was a place of security and she shrank from leaving it, however briefly.

Jeremy reached his hand up. "What's going on, Daisy mine? You can change your mind if you want to."

She grasped his clawlike fingers. "I don't want to. It's just that you're a lump to push and I'm not even going to try getting up the hill. We'll have to settle for the Wheatsheaf."

"That's okay with me. I haven't been in it, but if it was good enough for Catherine of Aragon, it's good enough for me."

Daisy spluttered with laughter. "Catherine of Aragon? Where did you hear that?"

"She did reside at the castle. She must have gone somewhere for a quiet pint while she was waiting for her fate to be decided. I'm guessing it was the Wheatsheaf."

Daisy shivered. She couldn't help herself. Perhaps it was the words he used, *waiting for her fate to be decided*. She knew that Henry VIII's first wife had spent time in the castle when she'd been married to Henry's older brother, Prince Arthur. Legend had it that she had walked around the grounds of the keep. But Daisy hated the idea of always waiting for somebody else to make decisions for you. Before the accident, she had been fiercely independent, choosing to leave home when she was just eighteen, much against her mother's objections.

"Daisy?"

"Yes?"

"I can hear the weir."

"That's right. We're just going past it."

"Will you stop a minute?"

She pushed the wheelchair to the side of the road and into the shade of the trees.

"Daisy, do you realize I will be dependent for the remainder of my life? I won't be able to make the decision that I'd like to go for a swim, or a walk up to the castle on my own."

"Don't be silly, course you will be able to. What do you think the rope's for? You just follow it and it will take you to the river."

"That's just here in Ludlow. At some point, I'll be shipped back to Canada. I live in a big city. There won't be any handy ropes guiding me to the lake."

She wanted to brush off what he was really saying, but she couldn't. She'd been having identical thoughts.

"I understand. I don't like to need people either, but there's not much we can do about it, is there? No more fine sewing for me or for you.",

"What? What on earth are you talking about? Fine sewing?"

"You know what I mean. Don't pretend you don't."

He chuckled and his frozen grimace widened. "I liked to make model boats when I was a kid. My mother still keeps them stored in my room. I guess I won't be adding to the collection."

"Nope."

He turned his head in her direction. The bright light accentuated the raw scars of his ravaged face.

"Sometimes the thought of what lies ahead is almost unbearable, Daisy. If I could figure out a way to do it, I'd throw myself off the bridge."

"That wouldn't work. You'd probably just hit the riverbank. Then you'd likely be crippled and that would be worse. Blind and crippled."

"May I remind you, I *am* blind and crippled."

"No, you're not! You've been making progress. Your legs are getting stronger every day. You'll be walking by the end of the summer, I guarantee."

"But I will still be blind. And hideous."

"Good thing you won't be able to see yourself then, isn't it?"

There was a spasm across Bancroft's mouth that was the closest he could get to a smile.

"Daisy, will you marry me?"

She tapped him playfully on the top of his head. "I thought I'd already said yes to that. If you think I'm going to sully my virtue and not get something out of it, you've got another think coming. You're going to have to make an honest woman of me."

"Done."

She bent over and kissed him.

40.

Daisy halted outside the Wheatsheaf.

In fact, she was losing some of her courage. Somehow the brightness of the day made the idea of a tryst seem even more wicked. No cover of darkness; everybody would know what they were taking a room for. They hadn't thought this through. Neither of them could stay away from the hospital for long. They were being ridiculous.

Jeremy bent his clawed fingers in a sort of beckoning motion. Daisy leaned over him.

"Daisy, your breast was as soft as a pillow."

She burst out laughing. "Not a very romantic description. Makes me sound fat. You've got to do better than that, Mr. Bancroft."

"Words fail me, but I hope the same won't be true of my actions."

She tapped him on the head. "Were you having me on when you said you'd never had relations with a girl before?"

"No. I swear. I'm as untried as a schoolboy."

"Ha. These days that isn't saying much."

"Would you prefer me to be experienced, Daisy? Come on, tell the truth."

She hesitated. "I suppose so. I don't have a clue myself."

"We'll learn together."

"I did read a book once when I was fourteen. My two friends and I sent for it from *Women's Weekly*. It was intended for "the new bride.""

"And?"

"Useless. Said that marriage would have its ups and downs and it was important to maintain a sense of humour and always be cheerful when your husband came home."

"Nothing about the other kind of ups and downs?"

"Don't be cheeky," Daisy said, laughing.

Bancroft shifted in the wheelchair. "All right. Properly speaking, I should be the one to get the room, but it should probably be you, Daisy. They might think I have something catching, like the bubonic plague."

"Stop it. You don't look that bad, honest. If anything, you look like you've got some rare strain of measles."

"Thanks. That's most reassuring."

"Why don't you stay outside? I'll feel better lying through my teeth if you're not listening."

Suddenly he caught hold of her arm. "Daisy, you won't run away, will you? You won't leave me here, bellowing like an unweaned calf for its mother? I won't know where you are."

This time, it was she who planted a kiss on his lips. "I'll be right back, I promise."

She pushed the wheelchair into a patch of sunlight, facing him down towards the river. Both sides of the wide, cobbled street were lined with narrow-fronted houses. House-proud women kept the windows sparkling clean, and the curtains were lace. Probably none of the doors or trim had been painted since before the war, but you wouldn't know it today. The sun bathed everything in a warm, golden light. Even in these austere times, the window boxes were filled with brightly coloured flowers. Except for a black wreath on one of the doors, the ravages of war seemed far away.

With a sharp intake of breath, Daisy opened the door of the hotel and went inside. The lobby was dim after the brightness of the sunlight, warm and fusty-smelling; beer and tobacco odours lingered in the air. The woodwork was dark, weathered by time and smoke. The bar was off to the right, empty now, closed until the evening opening time. The tiny reception area was tucked beside a flight of stairs. A sign proclaimed, PRIVATE. GUESTS ONLY. There was a big red ledger on the counter and a neat plaque that read, M. ALLTHORPE, PROP. Daisy dinged the bell on the counter and waited. Nobody appeared. She dinged it again. Still nobody. She was tempted to rush outside and tell Jeremy there was no room available when the door beside the counter opened and a woman emerged. She was wearing a pair of blue overalls and was in the act of removing heavy leather gloves.

"Beg pardon, madam. I was out in the back garden tending to my bees. You can't rush bees, so you'll have to forgive me being slow."

It was hard to determine how old the woman was. Her skin was tanned and her body wiry, but when she pulled off her straw hat, she revealed iron grey hair, cropped short. As she lifted the counter flap and squeezed into the cubicle, she gave Daisy a friendly smile. If she was shocked by her disfigurement, she hid it well.

"Dearie me, I do hope you're not wanting accommodation. What with all the workers coming in for the factories, I'm completely full."

Daisy could feel her resolve melting away. How on earth could she say to this brisk, respectable woman that she was hoping to get a room for the afternoon so she could have illicit sex?

"Well, as a matter of fact, I was hoping . . ." Her voice trailed off. Stalling, she pointed at the plaque. "I'm speaking to Mrs. Allthorpe, I presume?"

"Not *missus*. I'm Maud Allthorpe, *Miss*."

"I beg your pardon," said Daisy.

Miss Allthorpe nodded an acceptance of the apology. "What sort of time were you thinking of?"

"Er, anytime really. Now, I suppose."

The proprietor opened the large ledger and ran her finger down the page. Her hands looked strong and capable, the nails cut short.

"I'm totally booked until at least the end of next week. I might have something then." She looked up and her keen blue eyes met Daisy's.

"Booking for you and your husband, are you?"

Daisy nodded, trying not to be too emphatic. "Er, yes. As a matter of fact, he's outside at the moment. He has a bit of leave and, well, we were hoping – such short notice, I know . . ."

Miss Allthorpe raised her eyebrows. "He's outside?"

"Yes, he's disabled. Plane crash."

"He's in a wheelchair, you mean?"

"Yes, that's right."

Miss Allthorpe closed the ledger. "I'm terribly sorry, my dear, but all my rooms are upstairs. We have no way to accommodate people if they can't walk. No lift, you see."

This wasn't a problem that either Daisy or Jeremy had foreseen. The woman was being perfectly polite and kind, but Daisy felt a spurt of anger.

"He was a pilot in the RAF. His plane was shot down. He's lost his sight and most of his hands. For now he can't use his legs."

Again the blue eyes stared into hers. Appraising.

"That must be very hard for both of you. You've been in the wars yourself, I see. What was it? A bombing raid?"

"An unexploded bomb decided to go off."

Miss Allthorpe made tutting noises of sympathy and shook her head. But she gave Daisy the same shrewd look.

"I didn't think the WRENs accepted married women."

"No, they don't. We've only just tied the knot. I'm going to have to sort all that out later. Frankly, we're keeping it quiet for now. We haven't even had a honeymoon."

Daisy was amazed how easily the fibs slipped from her lips. But she'd caught the quick glance Miss Allthorpe had thrown down at her left hand. Another thing she and Jeremy had not thought about, the lack of a wedding ring.

"Where have you come from?" Miss Allthorpe asked.

"We're both convalescing over at St. Anne's."

"That's where you met, was it?"

"Yes, as a matter of fact."

At least that part was true, thought Daisy.

"I see. No privacy for married couples, is that the problem?"

"That's right."

Miss Allthorpe smiled. "I have a very nice couple booked in here from that hospital. At least, I should say, the wife stays here. Her husband works long hours and can't always get away. But he likes to come as often as he can." She smiled slightly. "I don't think they've been married very long either. All lovey-dovey when they're together."

Daisy was puzzled. St Anne's was small and she hadn't heard of any wife stashed away in Ludlow.

"You say the husband works at the hospital?"

"That's right. He's a doctor. Young fellow, good-looking." Miss Allthorpe positively beamed. "He reminds me of a younger Walter Pidgeon, you know, the movie star, with his dark hair and brown eyes."

"Really? What's his name?"

"I'm not supposed to say. He wants to keep his private life private. You know how people gossip. The market's a terrible place for people talking. Even today, with all the warnings about loose lips sinking ships, you can't stop them. It's been going on for generations. Hard habit to break, if you ask me. Mind you, I think it's only harmless stuff . . . Who's having a baby, who's just had one." She winked. "Whose husband's away at sea and how long has he been gone? That sort of thing."

Daisy wasn't sure that kind of gossip was entirely harmless, but she didn't want to antagonize the woman by contradicting her.

"I can understand the need for discretion," she said. "I feel the same way."

"Dr. Sargent said he—" Miss Allthorpe's hand flew to her mouth. "Oops, I let his name slip out. Don't tell anybody, will you?"

"I won't. Besides, I don't think I know him."

Miss Allthorpe leaned her elbows on the counter and looked from side to side in a conspiratorial fashion.

"He's very good. About a fortnight ago, he comes up to me and says, 'You're looking a bit peaked. Are you getting enough shut-eye, Miss A?' That's how he refers to me, *Miss A*. Well I admitted that I'd been having some bad nights. Sometimes I get terrible migraines. 'We jolly well can't have that, can we?' says he in his posh voice. He's very well educated."

She hardly paused to get her breath. Daisy nodded politely. She was still puzzled as to who this paragon might be.

"So next time he comes, doesn't he bring me a bottle of something to help me sleep. Vile-tasting stuff, it was. Bitter. He poured a splash into a cup and had me toss it back as if it was a whisky. He says, 'My wife suffers from headaches and this always helps her. Take it before bed and you'll sleep like a baby.' And I did. Never charged me a penny. 'Just keep my little secret, Miss A,' says he."

Miss Allthorpe reached under the counter and took out a piece of chamois. She began to rub at the brass bell. "I like things tidy, I do. I always have their room clean as a new pin. She can be a bit messy, I'm afraid. I make sure I put something nice in there. A bunch of my dahlias. A bit of savoury pie when I can."

For a moment, Daisy watched mesmerized as the polishing extended itself to the trim along the counter.

"They're lucky to have you for a landlady," she said, not quite sincerely.

Miss Allthorpe continued what she was doing. "Thank you, my dear. I know I am a bit of a chatterbox, always have been. You wouldn't think running a hotel would be lonely, but it can be. Everybody's got their own lives to live."

"Yes, of course."

Daisy thought she might try to steer the conversation back to the matter on hand. "How long do you think the doctor and his wife will stay with you?"

"It's hard to tell. They've been here three weeks altogether. He only just graduated, he told me. St. Anne's is his first appointment." She lowered her voice. One woman to another. "Frankly, it's dull for her with nothing to do during the day. I mean, I do all the housework and when he does come, they eat in the dining room, so there's none of that to worry about."

Daisy couldn't help but smile. "Goodness me, how *does* she occupy her time?"

"I encouraged her to join the wvs, and she has been getting out more regularly lately. I think she's made a friend in town." More vigorous rubbing. "She's a pretty young thing, very fashionable. Not what you'd expect for a doctor's wife. She's not got much education, by the sound of it. Not like him." Miss Allthorpe shrugged. "But it takes all sorts. Probably it was a love match, and you know how love is blind." Again her hand flew to cover her mouth. "I hope what I said wasn't offensive, my dear. You did say your poor husband had lost his sight, didn't you?"

"Yes, he has."

Miss Allthorpe lowered her eyes. "I myself lost my chance at marriage in the Great War, when my fiancé died in the Dardanelles."

"I'm sorry," said Daisy.

"The letter from his captain was ever so nice. 'Donald succumbed to his wounds,' he said. Perhaps it was a blessing. I saw so many young men come back with dreadful injuries. Both of the mind and the body. I saw women crushed under the burden of taking care of them. I admire you, my dear."

Miss Allthorpe stopped her polishing and gazed at Daisy. "Just because you've got some scars doesn't mean you're not still an attractive young woman, my dear. Don't throw your life away."

Daisy didn't know how to respond, but just then a young woman came down the stairs. She was smartly dressed in a tailored, cherry red outfit with a matching, saucer-shaped hat.

Miss Allthorpe turned to greet her. "Good day, Mrs. Sargent."

The young woman nodded coolly. "I'm going out for a few hours, Miss Allthorpe. I'll be back for dinner."

She was busy buttoning on her gloves and didn't seem to take in Daisy, who did her own appraisal. If Dr. Sargent was the medical profession's answer to Walter Pidgeon, his wife seemed to have modelled herself after Jean Harlow. Or maybe Veronica Lake. Her pale blond hair fell in a smooth pageboy, drooping over one eye to her shoulders. Her lips were crimson, her brows plucked and reshaped into thin arches.

Not Daisy's idea of a doctor's wife, either.

Then the woman saw Daisy and immediately averted her eyes. She'd seen this type of reaction many times before, but Daisy still wasn't indifferent to it. She instinctively ducked her head and shrank down into her shoulders.

"Are we to expect Dr. Sargent tonight?" asked Miss Allthorpe.

"I don't think so. It'll just be myself." The other woman kept fiddling with her glove buttons. Daisy knew she was avoiding looking at her.

Suddenly there was a loud thumping on the front door and Daisy heard Jeremy's voice.

"Daisy. What's happening?"

"Thank you, Miss Allthorpe," muttered Daisy, and she shot off to open the door. Jeremy had wheeled himself up closer and she almost bumped into the wheelchair. He must have been kicking at the door.

"Daisy, is that you?"

"Of course it is. Who were you expecting, Vera Lynn?"

"What kept you so long? Do we have a room or not?"

Daisy grabbed hold of the arms to the wheelchair and turned him around.

"No, we do not. Ludlow is as full as Bethlehem on the night of Christ's birth."

He laughed. "Never thought I'd identify with St. Joseph, but you know what, if you can find us a manger, I'm all for it."

"Well, I'm not. Too itchy, all that straw. We'll have to try again."

Jeremy uttered an exaggerated groan. "Forgive me for being crude, Daise, but I don't know how much longer I can hold up."

"These days, things can change fast. Somebody could be called away to work somewhere else. We can come back tomorrow. Maybe try the Feathers."

"If we live that long."

Daisy stopped the wheelchair, pushed on the wheel brake and came around to stand in front of Jeremy. "Don't say that."

He threw up his hands. "I'm just joking."

"Well, I'm not. I promise we're going to be together and that's all there is to it."

"I'm so happy to hear your confidence," said Jeremy. "Give us a kiss to seal the promise."

She did, and it was a long and lingering kiss.

He sighed. "I'd say that was well and truly sealed."

41.

THE SMALL OFFICE FELT TOO HOT AND STUFFY AND the long day was getting to Tyler. He'd been going through all of the patient files with a fine-tooth comb, but nothing had yet thrown any new light on the investigation. He stood up. Maybe another walk around the grounds would yield something.

He stubbed out his cigarette, stowing the butt in a flat tin, which he returned to his jacket pocket.

Outside, the sun felt hot on his face. He'd have to watch it. His fair skin burned easily. As he rounded the corner, he saw Alfie Fuller seated on the bench directly in front of the pigeon coop. His stance, stiff and straight, suggested he was on high alert. He was holding a bicycle horn in one hand.

"Hello, Alfie. What are you doing over here?" Tyler asked.

"I'm keeping guard of the pigeons. I seen a hawk around and he'll come in for the kill if I'm not careful." He squeezed the horn, and it gave off a harsh blast. "You took me gun, so I'm going to use this. 'S not as good, mind you. They's still alive even if they fly off."

"Do you mind if I join you for a bit?"

"S'pose so. I've got to go and help me ma soon though."

Tyler sat down next to him.

"Grand day, isn't it?"

"S'pose so. Me ma don't like me to get too much sun. She says it can turn your head funny." Alfie glanced sideways at him. "Not as bad as the moon though."

"What do you mean?"

"Somebody told me that all the patients here go funny in the head when it's a full moon."

Startled, Tyler looked at him. "Who told you that, Alfie?"

"I can't remember. I think it was Miss McHattie."

"Shirley?"

"Yep. She don't like living here. Mind you, she said living in Scotland was like living in hell, so it must have bin worse." He turned to gaze into Tyler's face. "Did you know she has a bun in the oven?"

"She's having a baby, you mean?"

"Yep. But you might have noticed she doesn't have a ring on her finger."

Tyler could guess where Alfie had heard that expression.

"Nobody's supposed to know who put the baby in her, but I do," continued Alfie with a grin. "I know who it was. Do you want to know?"

"Okay."

"It was Himmler. That's why she won't tell anybody. Her pa wouldn't like it."

"Why do you think the baby's father is Herr Himmler, Alfie? He lives in Germany for one thing, and for another, he's our enemy."

"I know that. But he likes English women. All foreigners do. It was him all right." Alfie wriggled his rear end on the bench. "My privates itch something terrible, but me ma says that I must never *ever* scratch them, not even when I'm by myself. And never even so much as touch them in public. Ladies don't like to see men touching their privates. Is that true, sir?"

"Hmm. I think your mum's right about that, Alfie. It's not good manners."

"Right."

"You know what," said Tyler, "it would be a big help to me if I saw how things operated with the birds. Would you show me?"

"Is it okay?"

He looked anxious. Clearly he was still afraid of entering the place he'd been banished from.

"I think Mr. McHattie would be proud of you if you could help the police, Alfie," said Tyler. "We want to find whoever it was that hurt him and Ben."

"All right. Come on."

Tyler followed him to a lean-to shed attached to the coop and they went inside. Like Jock's house, the shed was neat and spare. One desk, one chair. On the desk were several trophies.

"I see Jock had some good racers," Tyler said.

Alfie promptly trotted over to the desk, picked up one of the cups, and thrust it at Tyler.

"This was the best. He was up against the top flyers in the country."

Tyler examined the inscription. AWARDED TO JOCK MCHATTIE, WINNER OF THE CALAIS TO EDINBURGH RACE, AUGUST 9, 1939.

"That's a heck of a long way!" exclaimed Tyler.

"It most certainly is. Hundreds of miles. Won by two seconds. There ain't been no more races like that because of the war. We can only do ones in the country."

Tyler returned the trophy to its place.

"Will you show me how the time stamp works?"

Alfie nodded and took down a wooden box from the shelf and placed it on the desk.

"As soon as the flyer comes into the loft, you nabs him and you remove the band. It's got the time on it when he was set free." He pointed to a hole on the top of the box. "You puts it in there. Then you takes this key." He removed a large key from a drawer in the box. "You've already set the clock, see. Big Ben time. You gives the key a turn and it stamps the time on the piece of paper that you took out of the band. Like so."

He gave the key a hard twist, then he pulled out a strip of

paper. "You takes this to the club meeting and everybody compares notes. No cheating allowed."

"How was Jock able to use the clock stamp?"

"Oh, easy as pie. I'd read out the times to him, but we didn't know if we had a good un until we got to meet the others."

"Does every bird that comes in get stamped?"

The man looked at Tyler slyly. "Not all of them. No point unless there's a race. Like I said before, sometimes I just writes down the time myself in the book. But I get mixed up sometimes."

Tyler nodded reassuringly. "We all do, Alfie. Don't worry about it."

Next to the stamp machine was an open box of tissue-thin papers.

"Was the shed door kept locked?" he asked Alfie.

"Never. Cats don't eat seed, so there's nothing to steal, is there?"

But obviously there was. The paper that had been used for the cryptic message on the dead pigeon.

"One more thing," said Tyler. "Prince had a message in the band on his leg. But it wasn't the time when he had returned home."

"What was it then? There's not supposed to be anything else."

"The message said, 'They have no known grave.'"

"That's a queer sort of thing to send on a pigeon."

"I thought so too. Do you know what it might mean?"

Alfie nodded emphatically. "Course I do. All sorts of things can happen to the pigeons when they're trying to get home. Mr. Mac says they're the same as soldiers. We can lose at least two birds every flight if it's a long one. We can't bury them properly like we want to because we don't know where they fell. I asks Mr. Mac if we could go and find them so I could put up a white cross like they do for soldiers, but he said it was impossible. He said they have no grave that we know of. He said that lots of dead soldiers don't have white crosses." Alfie ducked his head and scuffed his feet in the dirt. "But Mr. Mac will have a white cross, won't he, sir? He and Ben and Prince?" He pointed to the flowerbed in front of the McHattie cottage. "We can bury them there. There's room."

Before Tyler could answer, there was a light tap on the shed door. Constable Mortimer had joined them.

"Dr. Murnaghan just rang, sir. He'd like you to telephone him right away."

Tyler turned to Alfie. "Thanks, son. You've been really helpful."

The other man frowned. "I wonder who's going to run the pigeons now that Mr. Mac's gone. Mrs. Mac don't like them at all." He shook his head, his distress obvious.

"You know what, Alfie," said Tyler, "as a police officer, I'm allowed to assign tasks like that. I officially appoint you guardian of the pigeons until further notice."

Alfie beamed. "Thank you, sir. Thank you so much. I won't let you down."

Tyler followed Mortimer back to the house.

"Bearing up, Constable?" Tyler asked her.

"Yes, sir. If it doesn't sound strange to say, I am finding this experience a very rewarding one."

Was she indeed? A detective in the making?

The patients seemed to have remained indoors except for Herb Mullin, the Aussie. Dai Hughes was seated across from him, tucked in at one of the wrought-iron picnic tables. Tyler halted in mid-stride. Hughes was using a typewriter. His fingers were fast and proficient.

Tyler strode over to the table.

"Gentlemen. May I have a word?"

Hughes stopped what he was doing and Tyler didn't miss the expression of apprehension that raced across his face. Mullin turned his sightless eyes in Tyler's direction.

"Inspector Tyler, is it?"

"That's right, sir. I noticed you were dictating a letter to Mr. Hughes."

"I'm not saying anything about the case, Inspector. I understand the need for utter discretion at this stage of your investigation."

"It's imperative, in fact."

"To tell you the truth, it's not a letter. I'm writing a novel," said Mullin. "I thought it would take my mind off everything if I continued. Mr. Hughes is kindly taking dictation."

"Do you mind if I take a look?"

"Go ahead, but I warn you, it's only in a rough draft."

It wasn't the literary merit that Tyler was interested in, but he didn't say that. He leaned over Hughes's shoulder so he could see the type. There it was, the jamming letter *w*.

"Is this a typewriter from the craft room?"

"I couldn't tell you," answered Mullin. "Is it, Hughes?"

"Yes, sir. You said you wanted to be outdoors, so I borrowed it to work on."

"You're very efficient by the look of it, Hughes," said Tyler.

The orderly was regarding Tyler warily. "I took two years of typing school before I switched to medical work."

"You've retained your skill," said Tyler. He was deliberately keeping his tone neutral and non-committal. If someone had a guilty conscience, it was often an effective approach. Got the criminals squirming trying to figure out how much he knew and wasn't revealing.

"Are you reading my novel, Inspector?" Mullin called out. "I'm always open to feedback."

Tyler hadn't been paying attention to the content, but now he did.

The noble knight's doublet was besmirched with blood and mud, but his eyes gleamed with the inner fire of the pure of heart such that his lady saw not the dirt but only the beauty of his soul and he won her heart as easily as if he was playing at bowls on the village green.

"It's a medieval romance," said Mullin. "More or less based on the tales of King Arthur. I loved those stories when I was a child, so I thought I'd do my own version. What do you think?"

"It's not quite my field, sir. But I commend you for trying. These days, stories of love and honour are always welcome."

The Australian guffawed. "An extremely diplomatic answer, Inspector. Thank you. As I said, this is my first draft. I'll polish it up later. Is it all right if we continue? I haven't finished Chapter 1 yet."

"Of course." Tyler didn't know if he'd learned anything useful or not. Hughes was definitely to be added to his list of those who could type well. Mullin was blind, but that didn't mean he hadn't composed the anonymous letters. Not the same prose style, but, like an accent, style could be faked.

He beckoned to the orderly to follow him out of earshot.

"Be right back, Mr. Mullin," said Hughes.

"Has Mr. Mullin dictated anything else to you?" asked Tyler. "Any letters, for instance?"

"No, sir. Nothing like that." Hughes squinted against the sun.

"You're telling me the truth, I hope. He didn't pay you to type some letters?"

"No, sir. I swear. It's only been his novel. I haven't neglected my duties. Sister Rebecca suggested I help Mr. Mullin. Keep up his spirits."

"And you haven't done typing for anybody else in the last little while?"

"No, sir. Nobody. Is there a problem, sir?"

Tyler studied the Welshman for a few moments and Hughes's gaze shifted away.

"Have you noticed anybody else using that particular typewriter?"

Hughes's expression was bewildered. "No, sir. I believe one of the sisters teaches a typewriting class. She might be able to help more than me."

"All right. Better get back to work. Literature awaits."

Hughes returned to the table.

"Righty-o, Mr. Mullin. Where were we?"

Tyler saw Hughes's fingers start to fly over the keys as the Aussie's deep voice dictated.

"Whither now, my love? Praise the Lord almighty, there is much work that lies before us."

Indeed, thought Tyler.

42.

SISTER REBECCA KNELT ON A PRIE-DIEU AND BEGAN to pray. The sanctuary was empty; everybody was busy with the patients over at the main house. Rebecca couldn't spare much time herself, but she felt the need to have a moment, however brief, to reflect.

She looked up at the cross with the suffering Christ. As Anglicans, the community of Mary Magdalene followed many practices that others might consider papist. The daily prayers, the confessional, the vows the nuns took, which were the traditional ones of poverty, chastity, and obedience. When Rebecca had first applied to join the order, the mistress of novices had been stern about questioning her vocation. "You must be sure you are making the right choice. The religious life is not suitable for everyone. It requires dedication, of course, but more important, sacrifice. You will not have the life most women have – a husband, intimacy, children. There may be times when you will sorely miss the fulfillment these things can bring."

And the truth was she hadn't always been completely sure she *had* made the right choice. Over the past fifteen years she had sometimes doubted.

This was one of those times.

Sister Rebecca was too honest not to acknowledge to herself the reason for these stirrings. Inspector Tom Tyler, with his copper-coloured hair and intelligent blue eyes; Tyler with the burden of sorrow on his shoulders that she ached to lift; Tom Tyler whose good opinion she desired. She said the Our Father.

"Thy will be done . . ."

Then she said her own prayer asking God for guidance. Her knees were aching and she got up stiffly. She couldn't honestly say she felt calmer, but at least she had confronted those errant longings. Time to get back to work.

43.

Dr. Murnaghan answered the call right away.

"Sorry to keep you waiting, Doctor."

"That's all right, Tom. Gave me a chance to sit still." Murnaghan still didn't sound like his usual hearty self. "Can you get over here right away? I've done all three P.M.s. Some discoveries that I'd like to show you." He paused. "I won't go into it on the telephone. Makes my head ache. How soon can you be here?"

"I'll leave at once, sir."

"Good. Very interesting stuff. Rather disturbing." On that tantalizing note the doctor hung up.

Daisy Stevens appeared in the doorway.

"Can I have a word, Inspector?"

"Of course." He pulled out a chair. She moved the chair slightly so that she could sit with her back to the window, leaving her face in shadow.

"I wouldn't have come to you about such a small matter if it wasn't for what has happened here. I know people do all sorts of things in wartime, Inspector. Perhaps he's a married man and the so-called wife is his mistress."

"Whoa, Miss Stevens. Start at the beginning. What are you referring to?"

Shyly at first, but with gathering animation, Daisy poured out the story of her encounter at the Wheatsheaf and what Miss Allthorpe had told her about her guests.

"There certainly isn't a young doctor named Sargent practising out of St. Anne's. There's only Dr. Beck, our psychiatrist, who comes in from London once a month. He's handsome enough, but you wouldn't call him Walter Pidgeon. And he's at least fifty."

Tyler winced inwardly. Only a girl of twenty-two could speak so cavalierly about being fifty years old. He'd be there himself soon as shouting.

"You were absolutely right to come and tell me, Miss Stevens. As you say, it could be a married man making up fibs to cover his sins, but it's worth checking into. People who tell elaborate lies always are."

"You don't think they're spies, do you?"

Prior to the murders, Tyler would have dismissed the notion out of hand. Now he wasn't ruling anything out.

"I will follow up on that possibility as well."

Daisy hesitated. "Miss Allthorpe said he gave her something to help her sleep. It was in liquid form and tasted awful. Sounded like it could be morphine. I've had it myself when I was first injured."

"If it is morphine he gave her, it would have come from a legitimate source. A nurse would have access, or a dentist. Even a chemist. Perhaps he's actually a chemist. There's a Boots at the top of Broad Street."

"The wife didn't look like a nurse to me," Daisy said. "Besides, anybody can say they're a doctor. Who's going to check up on you if you're just renting a room? It's not as if you're taking out tonsils on the kitchen table, is it?"

Tyler smiled. "Quite right."

Daisy leaned forward and her livid scar became visible. "I don't want to sound catty, Inspector, but I don't think that's the only bit of fibbing going on. The woman I saw wasn't the sort to be a genuine doctor's wife. For one thing, that hair colour wasn't what she was born with. For another that outfit she was wearing left nothing to the imagination, if you know what I mean." Daisy shrugged. "Miss Allthorpe said they were in love. It takes all sorts, as they say, but in my experience, nobby folks don't marry the peasants. They might dally with them, but they don't marry."

Tyler felt himself wince again. That had been the burning issue between him and Clare all those years ago. They were in love, yes, but she was born into the landed gentry. Poor as any slum child, but that didn't matter. Blue blood was blue blood. His was definitely the normal red kind.

He realized that Daisy was scrutinizing him. Her one good eye was hazel.

"Maybe the man isn't nobby either, Miss Stevens. Just as anybody can say they're a doctor, anybody can put on a fake posh accent. I can do it myself, don't you know, pip-pip and tally ho."

Daisy giggled. "I suppose you're right. I was just taking Miss Allthorpe's word for it." She got to her feet. "You don't have to tell anybody that I was at the Wheatsheaf with Jeremy Bancroft, do you?"

"If it isn't necessary, I won't say a word."

"Thanks. I don't want to look cheap. We really care for each other, but I want to make sure it's true love and not just a war-time infatuation."

"Whatever it is, my dear, enjoy it to the hilt. Love is precious."

He showed her out.

He was intrigued by Daisy's report. He couldn't yet see if it was relevant to his investigation, but right now he was ready to follow up on anything. It was probably just a case of the old story, a man having a little affair on the side, but lies were lies and the truth was always worth uncovering.

He went to get Constable Mortimer. The coroner had sounded most mysterious. Perhaps this was the breakthrough he needed.

44.

THE JOURNEY TO WHITCHURCH ALONG NARROW, twisting roads was as hair-raising as the previous day's ride through Ludlow but of much longer duration. Tyler crouched in the sidecar, holding on to the sides for dear life as they raced around the sharp bends. If another vehicle had been coming towards them they wouldn't have seen it until the last minute, and *if* Mortimer had been able to get out of the way in time, they would have ended up crashing through the thorny hedgerows.

The trip, which usually took an hour, was over in forty-five minutes.

Mortimer slowed down as they turned onto the main street.

"Go left at the traffic light," said Tyler. "And Constable . . . no need to speed. The dead don't care if we're on time or not. We can join them at a later date."

"Yes, sir. Sorry, sir."

They came to a halt as the light turned red.

And there was Vera.

She was crossing directly in front of them, her arm linked through that of a man Tyler presumed was her new fellow. He was chunky and round-faced, wearing a cloth cap, tweed jacket. Tyler recognized him as one of the tradesmen who delivered bread to the restaurants in the town.

If Tyler could have stuffed himself in the sidecar's footwell, out of sight, he would have. The red light seemed to take an interminably long time to change, but luckily Vera and the other man were too absorbed in each other to notice him. She looked pretty in a light, flowered summer frock and white hat.

He hadn't seen her look that happy for years, and Tyler felt a mixture of relief and guilt. It had weighed heavily on his conscience that his marriage was so miserable.

The light switched to amber, then to green. With a roar of gears, the motorcycle lurched forward. For once, Tyler was glad Constable Mortimer was a maniacal driver. Out of the corner of his eye, he caught Vera glancing over her shoulder, but they shot off and he didn't have to acknowledge her.

Constable Mortimer guided the motorcycle into the driveway of the hospital and came to a halt. Tyler undid the latch of the sidecar and started to extricate himself.

"I don't know how long I will be. They probably have a canteen inside. Get yourself a cup of tea while you wait."

"Thank you, sir."

He left her to manoeuvre the motorcycle into a parking space beside the hospital ambulance. The place was deserted, no patients or visitors that he could see. There was nobody at the reception desk; a handwritten sign proclaimed, BACK IN TEN MINUTES. He headed for the basement, where the morgue was located.

He went down the stairs, uncarpeted as they'd been since the turn of the century. The hospital had begun life as the county poorhouse and there was no concession to comfort. The large, cold room seemed empty at first. Then he realized with a start that Dr. Murnaghan was lying on one of the gurneys.

"Doctor?"

Murnaghan lifted a languid hand. "I'm just taking a rest, Tom."

He sat up slowly, his face pale and shiny with perspiration.

"I've still got an infernal headache," he said.

"Shouldn't you see somebody?" Tyler asked.

Murnaghan grimaced. "Nothing you can do for a concussion except take it easy. I'll be all right in a couple of days."

He swung his legs cautiously over the edge of the gurney. He was wearing a colourful Fair Isle jersey against the chill.

He got to his feet and stood for a moment, swaying slightly.

"I'm just waiting for the room to stop spinning," he said. "All right. Good. Now then."

He went over to one of the recesses where the bodies were kept in special compartments.

"What did you find that was so disturbing?"

Murnaghan held up his finger. "Patience. Let me have my moment of drama."

There were three stretchers in the recess, all with ominous-looking mounds beneath the sheets.

"Let's start with the female," said Murnaghan. "I've done some of the preliminary. I'll have to run a few more tests, but basically she was a healthy, well-nourished individual at the time of her death."

He pulled back the sheet on the closest gurney. "There was a significant amount of phenobarbitone in her stomach. Your intuition was right, Tom. I found traces of the drug in the cocoa."

"You say a significant amount? Was it a lethal dose?"

"No. She would just have woken up the next day feeling very groggy. But the drug takes effect quickly and I'd say she'd have been almost comatose when she inhaled the chloroform."

"I wonder if she took the barbiturate thinking it would do the trick, then did the chloroform to make sure."

Murnaghan shook his head. "Very unlikely, I'd say. She was a nurse. She knew what constituted a lethal dose. She also knew the body fights against what it sees as foreign intrusions. She would know that there was a possibility she would vomit and, even more likely, that she would tear off the mask unless restrained."

"Maybe she took the drug to keep herself calm?"

"Or maybe somebody else doped her nightcap for that very reason."

"You're thinking she was murdered?"

"That's the way I'm leaning. Aren't you?"

"Yes, but I needed to go through the possibilities with you."

"Besides, you know as well as I do, the cases of suicides who don't leave notes are few and far between. They all want to tell the world what's on their minds. *Forgive me, I can't take it anymore,* and they leave behind a crushing weight of guilt and sorrow on the backs of the unfortunate people who cared about them."

The coroner conveyed such feeling that Tyler wondered if he was speaking from personal experience.

Murnaghan gazed at the dead woman. "I don't think she had an easy life growing up in such a poor family as she did, but she was always so optimistic and cheerful. I suppose you'd call her a sunny person. I expected she'd marry some sturdy farmer's son and have lots of children, but she didn't. She became a nun. Pity really. And now it's come to this."

Again he made the gesture of wiping his forehead, but Tyler thought it might be a way of disguising the fact that his eyes had filled with tears.

"All right, let's move on. I'm saving the best till last. First come and look at this." He pulled Jock's flaccid arm from under the sheet and rotated it so that the inner arm was uppermost. "Can you see the marks?"

The tracks left by the needle injections were hard to discern against the discoloration of the skin, but Tyler could make them out.

"What is it? Morphine?"

"Years of use I'd say. Given the state of his lungs and the extent of his scars, I'm not surprised. He was probably in constant pain from that early gas poisoning."

"Do you think it was prescribed for him?"

"Most likely. It was in his system. That also might account

for his not hearing his killer creep up on him. He'd be in a pretty deep sleep."

He pulled back the sheet completely, exposing McHattie's face. The skin was grey, the blood at his shattered temple dark brown; the empty eye sockets had turned black.

Dr. Murnaghan took a magnifying glass from a nearby shelf and handed it to Tyler.

"Get ready for this, Tom. Take a close look at the wound."

Tyler did so.

Murnaghan plonked himself down in the chair by the wall.

Tyler straightened up. "Okay."

The coroner held up his forefinger. "Before you say anything, take a look at the boy."

Tyler uncovered Ben's body. He was accustomed to the appearance of death, the way it erased the etchings of time, but it was hard to gaze at the masklike face of such a child. Ben looked about six years old. He studied the blasted forehead.

"Well? What do you see?" asked Murnaghan.

"There are actually two bullet entries, one right on top of the other."

"Exactly. What at first appeared to be one wound with a large-calibre bullet is in fact two."

"Jock's wound is the same."

"Quite so. Both of them were killed the same way. The gun was a .22-calibre. All firings were placed with utter accuracy. I tell you, Tom, I've never come across anything quite like it."

Tyler sighed. "I have. I wish I could say I hadn't."

"And?"

"It's known as the double tap."

"What the hell does that mean?"

"It means our killer has been trained as a commando."

45.

MURNAGHAN WAS LEANING FORWARD, HIS HANDS ON his knees. Tyler waited and finally the coroner looked up at him.

"Sorry, a bit of a spell for a minute. Where were we? Right. You said the wounds indicated the work of a commando. Aren't they special troops that Mr. Churchill commissioned? Men of the hunter class, he called them. Got the term from his own hijinks against the Boers."

"That's them."

"Dangerous stuff to play around with," said Murnaghan ambiguously. "What the heck is a trained killer doing wandering around a convalescent hospital full of the maimed and the destroyed? They couldn't possibly be considered combatants."

"I don't have the foggiest. Not yet. But there's no mistaking that method of killing. Last year, the Shropshire chief constable sent some of us senior officers to attend a special course concerning what was called the Auxiliary Units. All very hush-hush and ultra top secret."

Murnaghan held up his finger. "Hold on, Tom. Get me a drink of water, there's a good chap. You can use that beaker on the shelf. It's clean."

Tyler did so and the coroner sipped some water gratefully.

"Would you rather I tell you all this at a later time?" Tyler asked. "Maybe you should get some rest."

"Absolutely not. Go ahead."

"We were sent up to the Lake District for a week." Tyler grimaced. "Glorious views, terrible digs. Before the war it was a youth hostel. Even the Spartans would have complained, never mind us old geezers. However, we knew we had to be prepared if England were invaded."

"That was our big fear after Dunkirk," interjected Dr. Murnaghan. "Realistic too. Doesn't look as if Jerry is going to do it now, but I suppose it is still possible."

"Let's hope not, but the big brass wanted us coppers to know what they were planning in the case of invasion." Tyler paused. "I just have to remind you, doctor, that what I am telling you comes under the *Official Secrets Act.*"

Murnaghan waved his hand dismissively. "I'm one of the most tight-lipped fellows you can ever hope to meet. Comes with working with corpses for years."

Tyler didn't quite see the connection, but he trusted the doctor completely.

"They were forming Auxiliary Units, four or five men strong, whose job would be to act as saboteurs. Like any resistance group in occupied Europe, they were to harass the enemy, create as much trouble as possible, kill if need be. They were being trained the same way they were training the commandos. There was a camp not too far away and they sent over an instructor and a group of said fellows to demonstrate some of their methods. I tell you, doctor, I was impressed by these men. Not to mention what they might be called upon to do," Tyler said, frowning. "They referred to it as silent killing, or unarmed combat, although they are all handy with a knife."

"I never did understand that aspect of soldier training," said Murnaghan. "Nothing prepares you for the real experience. It's one thing to shove your bayonet into a bag of sand, all jolly and shouting, it's another to thrust same bayonet through the guts of another living human being. I'm glad I never had to do it."

Tyler nodded. "They're all volunteers from other branches of the service. Tremendous esprit de corps. I've never seen such fit men. The commando won't take any pub brawlers or bulging biceps, as they put it. They take only the best. One in seven qualifies. The instructor that led the demos was a tough Scot by the name of Douglas." Here Tyler drew himself up and puffed out his chest. *"If you're going to kill your enemy, which is no doot your intention, you have to make bloody sure of it. No puir wee laddie to give away your position because he's howling on the ground for his mammy. You shoot twice.* Bam, bam. *Right into the head. Noo possibility of doot.'* That's the double tap."

"What was the gun of choice to do the *bam, bam*?"

"A .22-calibre Colt automatic that could be equipped with a silencer."

"I'd say that's what did these shootings, Tom. I've put the bullets in that jar for you, by the way."

Tyler continued. "They particularly emphasized being able to move about stealthily in the dark. *'Ye should move like you're a spirit come back from the daid. Not even an owl will blink. You get so close to your enemy you're like another pair of socks. Then you do your deed. You grasp him like so. His head goes in one direction and his body in the other. One quick snap and Robbie's your uncle. Ye musnae forget to let him down lightly so his gun dosnae clatter.'"*

Murnaghan sniffed. "Think of everything, don't they. Make it sound easy."

"As easy as killing a pigeon," Tyler added.

"Ha. The avian. I did examine it, and the neck was twisted. It wasn't broken because it flew into a window." The coroner shook his head. "But surely some benighted renegade commando didn't wander into St. Anne's?"

"I don't know. The main camp is way up in the wilds of Scotland."

"If it is one of them, they're blown a bit off course, wouldn't you say?" Murnaghan chewed on his inner lip, then he got unsteadily to his feet. "I'm fading fast. I'll clean up the corpses and I should be able to release them sometime tomorrow."

"I'll inform Sister Rebecca. She'll know what to do about Sister Ivy's burial. I assume Mrs. McHattie will claim her husband and son."

Tyler pulled the sheet back over Ben's face and helped the doctor to push the gurneys back to the recess.

46.

GIVEN THIS NEW INFORMATION, TYLER KNEW WHO HE had to talk to – and face to face. He said his goodbyes to the pallid doctor and went to get Constable Mortimer. He found her sitting outside by the motorcycle, reading some kind of pamphlet. When she saw him approaching, she quickly stuffed it in her pocket and stood up, offering no explanation. He wondered if she was studying how to permanently silence an enemy in the field, but then thought he was being morbid. It was probably one of those Cooking for Victory books that all the women were reading.

"I've got to make one more stop, Constable, then we can call it a day here. Did you get some tea?"

"Yes, sir. Thank you. I'm quite refreshed."

"Good. It's on the way out of town. I'll direct you."

He climbed back into the sidecar, a task that didn't seem to get any easier. Constable Mortimer revved the motorbike into a roar and, with a jerk severe enough to induce whiplash, got to top speed in a split second. They raced out of the hospital grounds and onto the main road, avoiding by the skin of their teeth a flock of sheep wending its innocent way to the other side of the road. If it hadn't been for the fact that he had to tell her what route to follow, Tyler would have closed his eyes.

"Turn left at the top of the hill and proceed along to the end of the lane, where there is a large building and grounds. Anything you see or hear from this point on must not be talked about. I need hardly remind you that we are at war."

Although it was officially an army laundry, the Old Rectory

was indeed an unlikely looking one. Lorries came and went at strange hours, there were an awful lot of people living in special huts on the grounds, and the entrance gate was guarded by men in army uniform. What you don't know won't hurt you was the credo by which people were learning to live these days. The rectory was, in fact, now being used as a radio receiving station and employed dozens of people whose job it was to intercept any messages from occupied Europe and forward them to Bletchley Park for decoding. Two years ago, circumstances had made Tyler acquainted with Mr. Grey, the man in charge of these special operations, the man with a pipeline to MI5, the intelligence-gathering department of the War Office. Grey by name, grey by nature, was how Tyler thought of him, but sometimes he suspected the colourlessness was a kind of camouflage meant to lull people into dismissing him.

As they approached the entrance to the rectory grounds, Mortimer was forced to come to a halt. A wooden barrier prevented them from going any farther. A soldier stepped out of the side lodge.

"What is the nature of your business, sir?" he asked, directing his question at Tyler.

"I'm Detective Inspector Tyler of the Shropshire constabulary. I'd like to speak to Mr. Grey."

"Do you have an appointment?"

"No, but please inform him it's urgent. He knows who I am."

"May I see your identification, sir?"

Tyler handed it over and the soldier studied it carefully. Nothing perfunctory about this man.

"And yours, Miss?"

She gave him her card.

"Cut your engine and wait here, please."

Still holding both cards, he went back to the lodge. There was another soldier inside and the first fellow handed over the identity cards and said something Tyler couldn't hear. The other man picked up a telephone. Mortimer in the meantime was sitting still and quiet. If she was curious about all this heavy security, she didn't express any of it. After a few moments, the inside man replaced the receiver and handed the cards back to the first soldier, who returned to the motorcycle.

"You can go to Mr. Grey's office. Do you know where it is?"

"Third floor through third door."

"That's it." The soldier was looking more relaxed. He smiled at Mortimer. "We don't allow any motorized bikes on the grounds proper, Miss. They tend to make too much noise. You can park it around the corner while you wait."

She dismounted and Tyler had no choice but to make the usual awkward clamber out of the sidecar.

"I shouldn't be long."

Except for some wooden huts at the far side, the inner court-yard of the rectory seemed hardly touched by the war. Trees and flowering bushes surrounded a lush green lawn, not yet commandeered for vegetables. Three or four peacocks strutted around, dragging their gorgeous tails behind them. Two women in summer frocks were sitting on one of the benches lining the edge of the grass, their faces upturned to the sun as if they craved it.

Tyler was walking across to the main building when a door opened and a young man emerged. He was in the formal "uni-form" of the civil servant, a grey three-piece suit, close-cropped hair, spectacles. Except for the fact that he was short and a decade or more younger, Tyler thought he might have been looking at Grey's twin. The man hurried over, his hand out-stretched in greeting. Well that was different anyway.

"Inspector, Bill Nesbitt here. I'm afraid Mr. Grey has had to go down to London unexpectedly. I'm his assistant. The guard said your business was urgent. How can I help?"

Tyler shook the proffered hand. Mr. Nesbitt seemed to have better public relations skills than his boss. He was actually smiling.

He glanced around the quiet quadrangle. The young women were gathering up their handbags and getting up from the bench.

"I don't mind talking out here, if you don't."

"What?" Nesbitt also looked around as if he were seeing it for the first time. "Good idea, actually. It's always nice to have some fresh air, wouldn't you say?" He gestured to the now-vacant bench. "Why don't we nab that one. It'll be quite private."

The young man pulled out a pristine, large handkerchief and flicked away crumbs from the seat. They sat down and Nesbitt waited politely for Tyler to begin. He was a good listener. Maybe that was a prerequisite for an intelligence officer. When Tyler had finished relating the events that had occurred at St. Anne's, Nesbitt was quiet for a few moments.

"And you think that the assassin had received commando training?"

"There's not much doubt about that. I was hoping you folks could furnish me with a list of the men who have gone through Ariscraig. There has to be a connection to the hospital."

Nesbitt removed his glasses and started to rub vigorously at one of the lenses, as if that would help him clarify things.

"This will have to go in front of Mr. Grey, of course. I have no authority to reveal that information."

"I understand. Do you know when he's expected to return? I'd like to make this a priority."

Nesbitt replaced his spectacles. "And so it will be. We can't have murder and mayhem running wild in the countryside." He frowned. "It's such a rum go, isn't it? No rhyme or reason that you can see as to why these unfortunate people were killed?"

"None. I have yet to find a motive."

Nesbitt was silent for a moment. "Could the killer have been an accomplice, do you think? A sort of hired gun, so to speak."

"I don't know that either."

"You do realize, sir, that the training and development of the commando force is highly secret? It is possible that we might not be able to release the names of the individuals in the programme."

"Even when there are three murders to be investigated?"

"Even then. Not quite cricket from your point of view, but alas, in times of war, ordinary justice doesn't always get the first look in. Longer-term goals and all that."

"In other words, the government will protect even a vicious criminal if they deem it necessary."

Nesbitt winced. "Quite. Now I do know that for the most part, the recruits for the commando units are thoroughly decent chaps. Want to do their bit and so on. But sometimes a bad apple does slip through. The training requires a certain amount of toughness."

"Isn't that another word for ruthlessness?"

"I suppose it is really. Couldn't do it myself, don't you know. Faint at the mere sight of blood." He turned and his eyes met Tyler's. "To tell the truth, sir, I'm damn grateful that there are blokes willing to do the dirty work for us."

Tyler knew what Nesbitt was getting at, but in his own mind there was no moral ambiguity to the murder of a blind man, a boy, and a woman. All defenceless. He stood up.

"I'd appreciate it if you could bring this to Mr. Grey as soon as possible, Mr. Nesbitt. In the meantime, I'm going to do my job as a copper and follow up a couple of clues, faint as they may be."

The young man also got to his feet and again offered his hand.

"Good for you, sir. I personally shall make sure Mr. Grey gets all this information first thing."

They shook hands and Nesbitt bounded off back to his lair at the top of the stairs. A different pair of women came out of one of the huts and went to a bench, where they sat down and stretched out their legs, discreetly hitching up their skirts to catch the sun.

47.

TYLER MADE MORTIMER SWEAR SHE WOULD NOT DRIVE beyond thirty miles an hour, and he was more able to collect his thoughts as they headed back to Ludlow. Dusk was falling as they approached the town, the ragged battlements of the castle turning red in the setting sun. More sedately than he would have thought possible, the constable brought the motorcycle to a halt in front of the hospital entrance.

"Good job, Constable," said Tyler as he got out.

"Thank you, sir. Is there anything else I can do to be of assistance? I feel a bit like a fifth wheel so far. Just fetching and carrying, as it were."

"Thought you were going to say fifth columnist for a moment there. You'll have to wait for me, I'm afraid. I don't know how long I'll be."

"That's all right, sir. I'll wait for you in the common room."

Tyler went in search of the almoner. She was in her office writing at her desk. She greeted him warmly.

"Good evening, Inspector. Please sit down. You look tired."

He took the chair opposite her and he could feel his shoulders sag.

"What did Dr. Murnaghan have to impart?" she asked. "I can see from your face that it was distressing news."

"It was. Dr. Murnaghan was able to do all the postmortems, and I'd say there are three major things for us to consider. First, he found a large amount of barbiturates in Sister's stomach. Was she in the habit of taking sleeping pills?"

"Not at all," answered the almoner. "Quite the opposite. She was fond of boasting that she could sleep on a bed of nails if called upon to do so."

"She was certainly drugged last night. The barbiturate was put into her cocoa. Dr. Murnaghan believes she would have become unconscious quite rapidly. Which would have made inhaling the chloroform of her own volition highly unlikely."

Sister Rebecca drew in her breath. "Not a suicide. Another murder then?"

"I'd say so."

For a moment, the almoner fell silent, lost in thought. Tyler waited until he had her attention again.

"Sister, I presume you are in charge of overseeing all drugs and medications."

She nodded in confirmation.

"Could anybody other than yourself and the nurses or the orderlies have gained access to them?"

Sister Rebecca pointed at the cupboard behind her desk.

"All medications are locked in there. Every shift I give the nurse what she needs. She, in turn, locks them in the cupboard that is on the ward. You saw it. I check that I am giving her the correct dosage as has been prescribed. She always reads it back to me as a double check." Sister Rebecca frowned. "I quite understand the direction of your questions, Inspector, but I cannot see how anybody who was not authorized could have taken medication without my being aware of it. I go through my stock twice a day."

Tyler believed her. Even if somebody had broken into the medicine cabinet, she would have detected that some of the drugs were missing.

"I'd like to have a look at your patient records. I want to see who is receiving sleeping pills at night."

She went to the filing cabinet and took out a folder. "I should say that we don't believe in giving pills as a matter of routine.

We tend to leave that choice up to the individual patient. If they are having trouble sleeping, medication is available to them. Otherwise we do not administer it."

He opened the file. According to the list more than three-quarters of the patients had taken medication for sleep over the past week. The amount varied, but the variation was minimal. Three to five milligrams, and that was not consistent with every patient every night.

"How is the sleeping pill administered?"

"The tablet dissolves better in hot liquid, so it is usually stirred into a nightcap such as cocoa, hot milk, or Horlicks."

"Does the nurse put the pill into the drink or does the patient?"

"That depends on the individual physical ability. As I said, we do encourage independence as much as possible. They do it themselves if they are able. But the evening round is busy. Usually, the nurse puts the pill in a paper cup. If it's not there when she returns, she would naturally assume the patient has taken it."

Her tone was a touch defensive.

"So in fact, it would be easy for somebody to ask for medication, pretend to take it, keep it aside, and use it later."

There was silence between them. When she spoke the almoner's voice was low.

"The implication is that one of the patients might have drugged Sister Ivy . . . and then killed her."

"I'm afraid that is a likely possibility."

She swallowed hard. "It is almost impossible to contemplate." Then she continued, "You said earlier there were three major things the coroner told you about. You've told me one. What are the other two?"

"Were you aware that Jock McHattie was taking morphine?"

She blinked. "Yes. I was. He experienced a lot of pain from his war injuries and the morphine had been prescribed for some time. Our local doctor simply renewed the prescription when necessary."

"Who gave him the injections? I presume he couldn't do that himself?"

"His wife knew how, but when they came here from Scotland, he asked one of our orderlies to do it. He said Mrs. McHattie was too nervous."

Something struck Tyler. "Which orderly?"

"Dai, the younger one."

Dai, dark-haired and handsome. Not that Tyler would compare him to Walter Pidgeon, exactly, and he certainly wasn't English gentry – but everything else fitted. The description, the proximity to the hotel, and especially the potential access to the morphine that the admirable Dr. Sargent had given to Miss Allthorpe for her migraine.

Tyler filled the almoner in on what Daisy had told him. Miss Allthorpe and the wonderful doctor from St. Anne's who had cured her migraine with what sounded very much like a dose of morphine.

Again Sister Rebecca was quiet for a few moments. "I regret to say it, but that is plausible. A couple of weeks ago, Jock complained to me that his morphine injection didn't seem to be as effective as usual. I know that patients can build up a tolerance to the drug and I assumed that was the reason. I asked his doctor to increase the dosage and he did so."

"Could Hughes have siphoned off some of the morphine when he was giving Jock his injections?"

"It would not be hard to do, as it's soluble in water. But for what purpose?"

"I don't know for certain. It's useful coinage on the black market," Tyler said with a shrug. "Perhaps that's what he was doing."

"Even if Hughes has been stealing morphine, that does not

explain the barbiturate given to Sister Ivy. I told you how the medication is monitored. And why on earth would Dai Hughes want to kill Sister Ivy?"

"Again, I have no answer I can give you, Sister. I'm going to have a talk with him shortly, but before I do, there is that third thing I learned from Dr. Murnaghan."

He described what they had discovered about the wounds to Jock and Ben. The double tap.

She stared at him. "You're telling me that the assailant was trained as a commando?"

"There's no doubt."

"But who could it be? You've gone through the files. The only man close to being a commando is Vadim Bhatti. He was trained as a Gurkha. But he is most definitely on your NOT ABLE list. He's completely blind."

Tyler pursed his lips. "There's absolutely no evidence of outside entry."

"You said the killer would have been highly trained."

"True. But where is he then? He has to live somewhere. And of course we keep circling back to the so far unanswered question. Why target Jock McHattie?"

Sister Rebecca shuddered. "We're at a complete impasse, aren't we? If the killer was a commando as you claim and not from outside the hospital, somebody has well and truly pulled the wool over our eyes."

"I'd say that is the case, Sister."

Again the silence was heavy between them. Then she said, "What now? Are you planning to arrest Dai Hughes?"

"Not at the moment. Frankly, he doesn't strike me as the cold-blooded type. I don't seriously suspect him of murder."

"I'm relieved to hear it. Neither do I. To the best of my knowledge he has not had any military training. He and his brother are considered to be in reserved occupations. I always thought this was something of a sore point for Dai. He would like to have the respect that soldiers get."

"Nevertheless, I am most certainly going to have a talk with him."

"Shall I fetch him?"

"If you would." Tyler got to his feet. "While you do that, I'm going to have one of my constables pop in at the Wheatsheaf and bring the mysterious Mrs. Sargent down here. We can arrange a little confrontation."

Constable Mortimer was leaning back with her eyes closed in one of the armchairs. The common room was deserted except for Alfie Fuller, who was mopping the floor. He beamed at Tyler as if they were the best of friends.

Mortimer woke up as soon as he approached.

"Sorry, sir. Having a bit of shut-eye."

"I've got a job for you, Constable." He told her what he wanted her to do. "You might as well use the motorcycle."

"Yes, sir. What if the lady in question refuses to come with me?"

"Persuade her, Constable. That's part of your job."

"Is it? I didn't realize that, sir, but I'll do my best."

There was that tone again.

"The young woman could be most important to our investigation, and I want to talk to her. So in this instance, perhaps you could surpass even your best."

"Yes, sir. Of course."

She looked rattled, but Tyler left her to get herself sorted out and returned to the office to wait for Dai Hughes.

48.

TYLER GAVE THE ORDERLY PERMISSION TO SMOKE AND the young man's face was almost obliterated by the fog from the cigarette that he drew on as if it were oxygen itself.

Tyler let him stew for a bit longer, then said, "Mr. Hughes, do you know a woman by the name of Miss Allthorpe?"

Hughes clearly wasn't expecting that question and he actually flinched. "Allthorpe? No, can't say I do."

"What about a doctor by the name of Sargent?"

"No. Never heard of him either."

Tyler leaned forward until he was very close to the young man's face.

"Begging your pardon, Mr. Hughes, but I'd say you're not a very good liar."

"I don't know what you mean."

Tyler shoved aside the ashtray, plucked the cigarette end from Hughes's fingers and stubbed it out.

"I think you do. Miss Allthorpe is the proprietor of the Wheatsheaf, and according to her she has guests, a doctor and his wife. The doctor says his name is Sargent and that he works here at the hospital."

Hughes didn't speak.

Tyler continued. "Now we both know there is no such person working here. Registering at a hotel under a false name in time of war is an offence. I could charge you."

"That has nothing to do with me," said Hughes sullenly.

"I think it does. However, what I'm more concerned about, Mr. Hughes, is the morphine you have been pilfering from the hospital. Now that is a worse crime. And unless you convince me otherwise, it *is* something I'm going to charge you with."

That did get a response.

"What? I don't know what the hell you're talking about."

"Let me elucidate. I believe you were siphoning off liquid morphine from Jock McHattie's nightly injections. You administered some of the drug to one Maud Allthorpe, the proprietor of the Wheatsheaf, where you have been visiting on a regular basis, using the alias Dr. Sargent."

Hughes had obviously decided to bluster his way out of this pickle.

"This is all a pile of shite, look you."

"The almoner says that Mr. McHattie was complaining about his morphine being less effective. Was that because you were giving him a less potent dose?"

"No."

"I need hardly remind you that Jock McHattie has been murdered," said Tyler. "Did you shoot him to make sure he didn't reveal what you'd been doing?"

Hughes met Tyler's eyes directly this time. He had gone white. "Good Lord. Of course I didn't."

Before they could go any further, there was a rap on the door.

Tyler went to answer. Constable Mortimer was standing outside with an older woman beside her. She was grey-haired, suntanned, and sturdy-looking.

"Sir, this is Miss Allthorpe," Mortimer said quietly. "She kindly agreed to accompany me. Apparently, Mrs. Sargent has had to deal with a family emergency and she checked out of the hotel this afternoon. I thought perhaps Miss Allthorpe would be able to make an identification for us equally as well."

The other woman shuffled her feet. "I don't understand what's happening. Why are the police involved? Dr. Sargent is an absolute gentleman. He's only one week in arrears and I trust him to make good the bill when he can."

Tyler nodded at her reassuringly. "Thank you for coming, Miss Allthorpe. I'm not at liberty to explain everything at this moment. I would ask you to come into the room with me. If you recognize the man in the chair, I'd like you to tell me his name."

"Very well."

Tyler stepped back into the room and Miss Allthorpe followed. When she saw Dai Hughes, she beamed.

"Hello, Doctor."

Dai looked at her in dismay and didn't respond.

"Miss Allthorpe," said Tyler, "is this gentleman sitting here the person you know as Dr. Sargent?"

"That's correct." She glanced anxiously at Hughes. "Is everything all right, Doctor? It's not about the medicine, is it?"

The orderly had the grace to duck his head. "No, it's not. Thank you, Miss Allthorpe."

Tyler pulled out a chair for the proprietor to sit in. She perched on the edge.

"Miss Allthorpe, I understand that this gentleman has a wife who has been residing at your hotel?"

"Yes."

"Do you know if the gentleman visited his wife on Tuesday night?"

"Yes, he did. I am a light sleeper and I heard him come in shortly before midnight. I leave the door on the latch if I know guests will be late."

"Do you know what time he left?"

"It was just getting light. I . . . er, I felt sorry that he had to work so early."

"And you are certain it was this gentleman and not another of your guests?"

"Certain. Dr. Sargent's room is down the hall from my own. I heard him go past on the way to the stairs."

Hughes was leaning forward in his chair, his head in his hands.

"What about last night?" asked Tyler. "Did the gentleman spend the night at the Wheatsheaf?"

"Yes, he did. I had left out a bit of supper for him and the empty tray was on the counter when I got up."

Tyler smiled at her reassuringly. "He brought you some medicine for your migraine, did he not?"

"He did. My headache vanished right away."

"But he didn't say what this medicine was?"

"No." Miss Allthorpe blinked. "I do hope he's not in trouble because of that. It was only one occasion."

Tyler got to his feet. "Thank you, Miss Allthorpe. You have been most helpful."

She, too, stood up. She addressed the orderly. "I'm so sorry to hear about your mother-in-law, Doctor. I hope she soon recovers."

Hughes's head jerked up. "What? What do you mean?"

"Mrs. Sargent said she had an urgent telegram this morning to say that her mother is seriously ill. She had to leave at once for Manchester."

Hughes gaped at her. "Polly has gone?"

"Yes, Doctor. This afternoon . . . She took her things."

"Did you see the telegram yourself?" Hughes asked.

"No, Doctor. I was out at the shops when it arrived."

He turned away. "How could she?" he whispered.

Tyler noticed he was not speaking with the slightest trace of a posh English accent.

As he walked her over to the door, Tyler said, "Thank you for coming in, Miss Allthorpe. I'll have Constable Mortimer drive you back to the hotel."

She beckoned to him. "May I have a word, Inspector?"

He followed her out of the room and closed the door behind him.

"He deceived me, didn't he? They both did. He's not a doctor at all, is he?"

"No, he's not, Miss Allthorpe. He's one of the orderlies here."

Tears welled up in her eyes. "He must have taken me for a right old fool. Why would he concoct such a story?"

"Perhaps he thought it was the only way he could get a place where he could install his mistress. You might not have accepted him if he didn't pretend to be a married doctor."

"No, I wouldn't have. I run a respectable establishment." She wiped at her eyes. "Nevertheless, he did cure my migraine. I suppose I can be grateful about that."

Tyler delivered her back into the care of Constable Mortimer and returned to the office.

Hughes hadn't moved. Tyler sat down in front of him.

"Shall we start again, Mr. Hughes? With the truth this time."

49.

DAISY STEVENS WAS UNABLE TO SLEEP. SHE'D GONE to bed at ten, but she felt wide awake. Was it the passionate, deep kiss she had exchanged with Jeremy when they said good night?

He'd called her into the shadow of the hall. "Can anybody see us, Daisy?"

"No. Not at the moment," she replied.

"Kiss me then, my love. Kiss me as if we are never going to meet each other again."

"Stop talking like that. Tomorrow we'll go into town and find a hotel or a room."

He shook his head. "No, you were right, Daisy. We should get properly married and we can go anywhere we want. We don't have to be sneaking around. Let's get a special licence right away."

Daisy hesitated. "Are you sure?"

"Sure as Niagara Falls is sure. Look, I'm saying it formally. Daisy Stevens, will you do me the honour to be my wife, till death us do part?"

Daisy giggled. "I do."

"Sooner the better then."

"Sooner the better, you impatient man, you."

They had kissed again and again he caressed her tenderly. Daisy heard somebody coming up the stairs and she broke away breathlessly.

"Tomorrow then. I'll go straight off and get us a licence."

"Let's hope nobody gets themselves killed in the meantime. We might all be quarantined."

It was Sister Rachel who had come up the stairs.

"Now then, you two, time for beddy-byes. Mr. Bancroft, I'll wheel you in. Miss Stevens, you'll be all right on your own steam, I presume?"

"Yes, Sister. Good night."

Daisy had made her way upstairs. Babs had already been put to bed and seemed to be asleep. There was a glass of water and a sleeping pill for Daisy to take if she wanted them. She was tempted but decided against it. She would only be groggy in the morning, and she didn't want that.

Did she really want to marry Jeremy Bancroft? She found him immensely attractive and was quite prepared to have intimate connections with him. Why not? But marriage was a lifetime commitment. And he was Canadian. Presumably he would want to return to that country when he was sufficiently recovered. She heard it got very cold there, and she didn't like cold weather. If she still had her good looks, the prospect might have been exciting, an adventure. But she was disfigured. Here people were getting used to maimed and disfigured people walking around, but probably not in Canada. Would she have to explain all the time? Cover her face? Cover Jeremy's face? And what did she know about him? Other than that he was charming and funny and very sweet to her, she knew nothing. Not even what he'd done before the war. Did he have brothers and sisters? He hadn't said. Daisy was close to her younger sister and she would miss her if she had to go and live in Canada. She'd be all right without their mother, but being without Pam was a different story.

She sat up in bed, turned her pillow over and thumped at it, then lay down again.

Maybe getting married was too impulsive. Maybe they should just make love to each other without benefit of clergy. She felt no guilt about the idea, even though her mother had drilled into her ever since she could remember that good girls didn't behave like that. Only tarts and tramps. And if she ever got herself into trouble, don't come crying to her; she'd get no sympathy from her.

That was another thing. Daisy had only a hazy idea of what having sex meant. She read a pamphlet once that spoke about the necessity to take precautions if you weren't ready for pregnancy, but she didn't know what that meant. What precautions? Perhaps Jeremy would know. He said he was inexperienced, but men seemed to know these things. But would that entail Daisy having to help him? She didn't fancy that. She wanted the fade out, the way Anna Neagle and Michael Wilding had faded out in each other's embrace when she saw them in the pictures.

She was glad she'd told the inspector about Miss Allthorpe and her guests. The young woman was so smart-looking, but it did seem that she and her so-called husband weren't genuine. Daisy shivered. She had no desire to be a kept woman. And neither did she want to end up like Shirley McHattie, with a baby on the way and no husband in sight. No thank you. She tried out the sound of what would be her new name, *Daisy Bancroft*. She liked it.

She turned over and finally fell asleep.

50.

It was almost eleven o'clock when Tyler finally headed home, and the town was almost in darkness as the blackout came into effect. He'd sent Constable Mortimer home to bed, but he had to bring back Rowell's bicycle. The front lamp, shaded as per requirements, didn't give off much light, but the river was silvery and he was able to see well enough not to go crashing off the bridge. He pedalled slowly from sheer fatigue but rather enjoying the brief respite of trees and river and birds settling down for the night.

He stowed the bicycle in the station shed and walked across to the house. When Tyler stepped inside the front door, Rowell was there, his demeanour so much like that of a solicitous wife that Tyler almost expected to be handed his slippers, nicely warmed.

"My goodness, sir, you look bushed. Can I get you something? A cup of tea? Cocoa? A bite to eat?"

"No, thanks, Oliver. I'm tea'd out and I ate at the hospital." Tyler would have loved to pour himself a quiet nightcap and turn in, but the sergeant looked so glad to have company, he didn't have the heart to abandon him immediately.

"Tell you what, I've been keeping a bottle of whisky for special circumstances. This feels like one of them. Will you join me for a shot?"

Rowell hesitated. "I'm not much of a drinker, sir. But you're right, I think we could call this an emergency. A sip or two would cheer us both up."

Tyler intended to have more than a sip or two, but he didn't quibble and followed the sergeant into the kitchen.

Rowell went to the cupboard. "I had a little spare time this evening so I was actually able to bake up an apple pie. When Evelyn was so ill I took over the cooking, and if I say so myself I got to be rather good at pies. My roasts leave something to be desired, so I've been told, but the pies always get good reviews."

Tyler wasn't hungry but again didn't have the heart to disappoint Rowell.

"I'll get the whisky. It's in my room."

When he returned with the bottle, the sergeant had put the glasses and plates out, and an admittedly delicious-looking pie sat in the middle of the table. Without asking, Rowell began to cut a large piece. Tyler poured them both generous measures of whisky and took a big gulp of his. The warmth hit his stomach with a wallop.

"Evelyn and I liked nothing better than to talk over the events of the day when we sat down for tea," said Rowell. "On the few occasions when we didn't do that, I found it hard to go to sleep. Chatting together lifted away all kinds of worry, you might say." He handed Tyler a plate with the pie. "Is that something you've done with your wife, sir?"

"No. We never have. Maybe if we'd followed your lead we'd be better off."

But Tyler knew that no amount of talking over the day would have saved his marriage. Not when from the beginning his heart had belonged to another woman and Vera knew it. He took another drink of whisky, slower this time. Rowell did likewise, cautiously. No, definitely not a drinker, this man. Tyler took a bite of the pie.

"Very good, Oliver, very good."

"I thought my crust could have been a bit lighter, but you have to go so easy on the lard these days, it's hard to keep the pastry flaky."

They sat in silence for a few moments, companionably enjoying the pie.

Tyler thought this was a good time to fill in the sergeant about what had been happening. He told him about the visit to Dr. Murnaghan and the discoveries the coroner had made in the post-mortems. The double tap in particular, with its connection to the commandos.

Rowell sat back in his chair in astonishment. "Well, I never. Surely it's not some sort of blood lust?"

Tyler shrugged. "There are a lot of other people the assassin could have targeted more easily if that's all it was. I'm still thinking it has to be personal; I've just not put the pieces together yet." He poured himself another shot of whisky. "I keep feeling Shirley McHattie is at the centre, but I can't begin to tell you how. Her mother wouldn't let me question her again. She's afraid Shirley will deliver before her time."

To his surprise the sergeant let out a long sigh. "My wife and I had two miscarriages. Evelyn wasn't as advanced as the young woman in question, but they're right to be cautious."

Tyler felt at a loss for words and muttered awkwardly, "Sorry to hear it, Sergeant." He shifted uncomfortably. He and Vera had married in haste when she'd discovered she was pregnant. Perhaps his ambivalence had affected the way he'd related to his son. He'd been too disengaged, leaving Vera to be responsible for most of the parenting. Something Tyler deeply regretted now that it was too late to make amends – and would regret to his dying day.

"Please go on, sir," said Rowell. "I didn't mean to load my personal history onto your shoulders."

"Not at all, Sergeant."

He went on to relate his interview with the young orderly.

"Well, I never," exclaimed Rowell again. "Quite a fabrication. I know Maud Allthorpe quite well. Good woman. Salt of the earth but a bit of a typical spinster. I can see her being smitten by some good-looking chap and believing everything he said."

"Miss Allthorpe took the wind out of his sails when she said Mrs. Sargent had flown the coop. Ill mother, my eye. He realized she'd run off."

Rowell grinned. "I bet that was a bit of a shock."

"It was indeed. His bravado vanished almost instantaneously. He admitted to everything."

"Good Lord, sir. Not the murders, surely?"

"No, not that. But the whole fabrication."

"Did he admit to stealing morphine?"

"Not exactly. He claims that Jock was trying to wean himself off the drug. His wife thought he already had come off it, but that wasn't the case. Hughes says that Jock asked him to dilute his medications. Which he did. He admitted he kept the unwanted morphine, as he put it, because Polly suffered from headaches. Jock isn't here to deny this and Sister Rebecca has a different version."

"Are you treating him as a suspect in the murder, sir?"

Tyler shook his head. "No, I'm not. What saves the man's bacon is that Miss Allthorpe gives him an alibi for both the nights. His mistress, if we ever track her down, might confirm that."

"Why do you think she abandoned him now?"

"I got the impression Hughes wasn't that surprised. She might be a hard girl to keep under wraps."

"How did he manage to come and go so freely? I thought the hospital was locked up tight as a drum at night. And last night we had constables on watch."

Tyler took another swallow of the whisky. "Sad really, Sergeant, but Hughes admitted he sweet-talked Sister Ivy into unlocking the side door for him so he could exit by way of the east gate. He'd slip out at midnight and come back at sunup. He says last night he managed to elude the constables who were patrolling the grounds, and I believe it. It's secluded and black as Hades over on that side. Frankly, I don't think he's really a bad lad. Just got his balls snared by a floozy."

"Won't be the first or the last. Are you going to charge him, sir?"

"Other than giving a false name out to Miss Allthorpe, I don't have much to charge him with. I can't prove he stole the morphine although he should have reported Jock's request to wean off. If it's true, that is. The almoner will have to decide whether or not she fires him." Tyler yawned. "I'd better get up the wooden hill. God forbid we have another dawn crisis."

Rowell suddenly slapped his hand to his forehead. "Good heavens, I almost forgot. There's some post for you. I brought it over from the station. I'll get it."

He scuttled off and Tyler snuck a second, small slice of pie. Rowell could have a second career as a pastry chef if he wanted one.

The sergeant returned with a small bundle of papers in his hand.

"This all came in the second post, sir. Seeing as you're up for a bit longer, I'll sit and read the newspaper, if you don't mind. What with one thing and another, I've got behind on the latest war news."

Tyler gestured in the direction of the table. "Help yourself."

Rowell sat down and opened his newspaper. Once again Tyler experienced an odd sense of domesticity. It was not unpleasant. He opened the bundle of letters the sergeant had given him.

One was a postcard from his daughter, Janet. An old, tinted view of Blackpool that looked as if it had been taken in the '20s.

Dear Dad,
Just here for a couple of days with some of the girls. Strong sea breezes. You wouldn't like it. Love, Janet.

Tyler scowled. What sort of message was that? Since Janet had joined the Land Army he hadn't seen much of her. He missed her a lot. She didn't write that often and he hadn't even known she was going to Blackpool. He couldn't imagine it would be much fun these days. But then he wasn't a lively young woman who he hoped could find fun anywhere. Strong sea breezes, indeed. Why did she think he wouldn't like them? He loved the seaside and often wished he'd been able to live somewhere on the coast.

He put the card down and picked up a long, narrow envelope. The return address was that of Laine and Clutterbuck, his wife's solicitors. His now–former wife's solicitors. He put it aside. He couldn't face reading it right now. Vera was probably asking for more alimony. Even though she had actually initiated their separation and left him, she was bitter about the end of the marriage and her anger was coming out in unreasonable demands for money. He thought about the glimpse of her he'd had in Whitchurch. Perhaps her new-found happiness would soften her.

The third envelope was addressed to THE INSPECTOR, LUDLOW POLICE. Spidery handwriting. Dated yesterday. It was from a Mrs. Valentine. She said that somebody had come into her front garden, pulled up half of her fence, and taken off with it. She had a dog who had got out because of this and she was putting in a complaint. Even with a war on, the police had to do their job. Theft was theft. She hoped he would pursue the matter at once and find out what had happened to her fence. She'd only just paid to have it spruced up.

Tyler frowned. Mrs. Valentine was right. Police still had a job to do.

"Sergeant, take a read of this. I'm handing it over to you."

Rowell scanned the letter. "Some delinquent probably. He'll sell it on the black market for scrap. Pity. It probably dates back to the 1800s. Most of the wrought-iron railings do. History wiped out in a minute."

Tyler got up. "I really am off to bed, Oliver, before I fall asleep at this table."

Suddenly, startling both of them, the telephone rang shrill and demanding in the quiet night.

They exchanged dismayed looks.

"Shall I answer it?" Rowell asked.

"I'll do it," said Tyler.

Please don't let it be more bad news.

Unfortunately, it was.

51.

SISTER REBECCA WAS ON THE OTHER END OF THE LINE.

"Inspector. I'm sorry to disturb you, but I thought I should let you know right away. Shirley McHattie has disappeared."

Tyler heard a woman's voice shout from the background, "Kidnapped. Tell him she's been kidnapped."

"I gather that was Mrs. McHattie," he said to the almoner. "What's happened?"

"Perhaps I should let her tell you herself."

Mrs. McHattie's voice came over the wire. She was breathless, her voice high-pitched.

"Somebody's kidnapped my girl. What's going on, Inspector? I feel like I'm being driven mad."

"Mrs. McHattie. Try as best you can to tell me what has happened. Why do you think Shirley has been kidnapped?"

"I don't just think it. I know it. She's been taken. Somebody came into her room and took her."

Tyler could hear that the woman was on the verge of hysteria.

"When did you discover she was missing?"

"Just now. She went to bed ages ago. She'd said she wasn't feeling well." The woman's words were pouring out. "I stayed in the sitting room so as not to disturb her, until I couldn't keep my eyes open. When I did go into the room, she wasn't there." Tyler could hear her gulp back her panic. "The light was still on. Her handbag was on the chair, and her nightie was on the bed. She hadn't even got undressed."

Mrs. McHattie struggled for control and Tyler waited. He could hear that Sister Rebecca was trying to comfort her.

Tyler kept his voice neutral. "Mrs. McHattie? Did you check to see if she is anywhere else in the hospital? With her brother, for instance?"

"She's not. I went there straight away. He was fast asleep." Again she made the impatient snorting noise. "You've got to come, Inspector. We've got to find her."

Tyler braced himself, trying not to be pushed by Mrs. McHattie's fear.

"You say you think she has been ab—"

She interrupted him. "The bedroom window was wide open. She was took that way. If she went out the front door, I'd have seen her."

"Mrs. McHattie, could Shirley have gone out by way of the window just so you *wouldn't* see her?"

"Why? Why would she do that? Where would she go?"

"Is there anybody in the town she might want to be with?"

"No. We hardly know anybody. I tell you, Inspector, she's been kidnapped."

She broke into sobs, all the more heart-rending because she was trying so hard to hold them back.

"Mrs. McHattie, will you put Sister Rebecca on the line, please?"

The almoner was there immediately.

"Is it at all possible the girl has just gone out of her own volition?" Tyler asked.

"Not out of the question."

He sighed. He felt like a wrung-out dishcloth already and he didn't fancy racing back to St. Anne's only to discover a sulky young woman had been trying to escape her mother's over-zealous attention. On the other hand, a pitch-black night was not particularly inviting for a heavily pregnant girl to be out in.

"I'll come over."

"Thank you, Inspector. I know you don't have a proper vehicle, so perhaps I can fetch you myself in our car. We still have some petrol ration."

"Sounds like a good offer."

She hung up.

Rowell had been hovering anxiously and Tyler filled him in.

"I understand that women can get very restless before they're due," said the sergeant. "Go for walks at the oddest of times. That sort of thing. Perhaps that's all it is."

What the sergeant said rang true. Shortly before giving birth to each of their children, Vera had begun to rise early, and sometimes she'd go out for a stroll around the town. He never accompanied her. She didn't ask and he didn't offer. Tyler felt a pang of guilt at the memory.

"I pray that's what it is, Oliver. I truly pray." He hesitated briefly. "You know what, Sergeant, I think given all these occurrences, it might be good to have a firearm."

"Funny thing. I was thinking that myself, sir. The killer is certainly armed."

"What have we got?"

"There are two Webleys with holsters over in the station."

"Are they in working order?"

"Yes, sir. I make a point of maintaining them myself. Shall I fetch one for you?"

"Yes, please."

52.

TYLER WENT OUT TO THE STREET TO WAIT FOR SISTER Rebecca, who soon arrived.

"I checked the room myself," she said as they drove off. "I could see no evidence that Shirley has been taken unwillingly. I sleep right next door, and the walls are paper thin. I went to bed shortly after you left. Just before ten o'clock. I did fall asleep right away, but if somebody did get in via Shirley's window and overpowered her, he would have to have been awfully quiet about it or I would have heard something. As it was, I was woken by Mrs. McHattie calling out. Before I rang you, I checked with the constables on duty, and they both said they saw no one. I simply cannot fathom how Shirley got out of the grounds."

"And you're sure she's not inside the hospital somewhere?"

"Positive. There's nowhere she could be."

"Is everybody else accounted for?"

She bit her lip. "Yes. I went straight to Sister Virginia, who is on ward duty. The wards, both men's and women's, have been completely quiet. We checked each room. All the patients are present." She glanced over at Tyler. "I'm just keeping my fingers crossed Shirley will be waiting for us when we get there, wondering what all the fuss is about when all she's done is go for some fresh air."

The sliver of the waxing moon came out from behind a cloud and briefly lit the river as it rippled over the shoals near to the bridge.

"Stay out, moon, we might need you," said Tyler, but the

moon did not oblige and the night was plunged once again into darkness.

Within moments, they were at the hospital. Sister Rebecca parked the car and Constable Mady stepped forward from the shadow of the gate.

"Has the girl returned, Constable?" Tyler asked.

"No, sir. No sign of her."

Tyler's heart sank. He'd been hoping Shirley might indeed have gone for a bit of a stroll and was now safely back home having a cuppa.

They went through the gate and, guided by the meagre light from the almoner's torch, walked around the side of the house to the nuns' quarters. All was dark, the blackout rigorously obeyed. As they drew close, a figure emerged from the darkness. He had a shaded torch of his own.

"Sir. Constable Biggs here."

Tyler thought he sounded nervous.

"Keep a good eye out, Constable. Sound the alarm if so much as a bird tweets out of turn. Who's on watch at the cottage?"

"Constable Eaves, sir. He has not reported anything amiss."

"I asked Mrs. McHattie to wait in the sitting room," whispered Sister Rebecca as she unlocked the front door. "Sister Clarissa is with her."

Martha McHattie was in the same chair as before, her face white and agonized. Sister Clarissa was in her nightclothes, a grey flannel dressing gown and, rather incongruously, an old-fashioned white bonnet that tied under her chin.

Mrs. McHattie looked up at once. "Any news?"

"No, I'm afraid not."

"She's been kidnapped, I told you."

"Perhaps I could take a look at the bedroom."

"I'll come with you," Mrs. McHattie said.

The older nun reached out and placed a hand on her arm.

"Maybe you should wait, my dear."

Without a word, Mrs. McHattie shook her off.

Tyler followed Sister Rebecca down the dimly lit hall, Mrs. McHattie right behind him. The doors to the nuns' individual rooms were closed. No light showed. Nobody else was stirring.

The room the McHatties had been using was at the far end. Tyler opened the door.

There were two single cots close together, a dark mahogany wardrobe and dresser, a wooden chair, a crucifix on the wall. On one of the beds was laid out a pink nightdress, pretty and feminine. The single window was open, the sash pushed up as far as it would go.

Tyler went over to have a closer look. The sill was quite low and it was feasible that Shirley climbed out that way, although it would have been awkward. Had she? If so, why? She wasn't being held captive here. If she wanted to go for a walk, she was entitled to. But seeing the narrowness of the window, Tyler could not imagine a heavily pregnant woman being removed through it against her will. And there was no evidence of a struggle. A rag wool rug lay straight and tidy on the floor. Nightdress undisturbed. The cot was still made, the cover smooth.

He leaned out of the window and flashed his torch, but there was nothing obvious. No visible footprints. He swung his legs over the sill and climbed out. Easy for him. The surrounding wall was only a few feet away and he walked towards it, aiming his torch at the ground. Again, no sign of footprints. He put out his hand to guide himself, keeping his torch low, and followed the wall to where it curved. The nuns' quarters completely blocked the view from the main house. Tyler rounded the corner and found himself close to the east gate and the trellis. The gate was not bolted. It seemed very likely that Shirley had exited the grounds this way.

He retraced his steps to the window and climbed back in.

"Well?" said Mrs. McHattie.

"I think she must have exited through the east gate."

"Was taken, you mean."

"I don't know that yet."

"Where were the guards? Sitting on their duffs?"

"They didn't hear anything," interjected the almoner. "It's very dark. Somebody moving quietly would not have been noticed."

Mrs. McHattie glared at the almoner. Tyler jumped in to intercept the harangue he knew was about to erupt.

"Mrs. McHattie, you said that Shirley left behind her handbag. Do you mind if I take a look in it?"

"It's over there."

The handbag was of newish-looking red leather with a jewelled clasp. He snapped it open, took out a dainty silver compact and an eyebrow pencil, and placed both items on the dresser. There was also a handkerchief and a couple of shillings. Other than Shirley's identity card, that was it.

"Did she have a lipstick? It doesn't seem to be in here."

Mrs. McHattie snatched the handbag and scrabbled inside it, then upended it and shook it hard. Nothing.

Her eyes met Tyler's. "It's not here."

"She had it last night," interjected Sister Rebecca. "I saw her use it."

Mrs. McHattie's voice went to an even higher pitch. "I know what you're getting at, but Shirle wouldna just go off like that. Not at a time like this. She'd know I'd worry myself sick."

"Perhaps she left a note. It might have slipped off the dresser. Do you mind if I take a look?"

"Help yourself."

Tyler bent down and looked underneath the beds. Nothing. No note, no lipstick.

"What was she wearing?"

"What she's been wearing for the past two days, seeing as how we can't get into our cottage. She was in her pink maternity smock." Mrs. McHattie went over to the wardrobe and jerked open the door. She paused. "Her cardie's not here." She turned around to face Tyler. "That doesna mean anything. She probably felt a bit chilly. Are you going to get up a search party or not?"

"Let's put it this way, Mrs. McHattie. I have limited resources. It's pitch-black outside, and I cannot use lights without violating the blackout. But more to the point, I'm not convinced your daughter has, in fact, been abducted."

"So, you're saying you're going to do bugger all."

Sister Rebecca attempted to intercede. "Mrs. McHattie. We can understand your worry, but we have to be sensible. Please listen to what the inspector is saying."

Mrs. McHattie whirled around. "I'll look for her myself then. If she's dead, you lot can have it on your conscience for the rest of your lives."

She rushed for the door, but Sister Rebecca held out her arm to block her.

"I think we can do much more good if we sit down calmly and go over the situation."

Tyler wasn't sure which way the struggle would resolve itself until, abruptly, Mrs. McHattie sat down on the edge of the cot. She held her head in her hands and said in a low voice, "I can't take much more."

Sister Rebecca knelt beside her.

"I do think the best thing to do right now is to talk to Inspector Tyler. Why don't I go and make us some tea while you do that?"

The other woman nodded.

"I won't be long," said Sister Rebecca, and she left.

Tyler waited for a moment. "Mrs. McHattie, when we spoke on the telephone you said that you knew no one in Ludlow itself. But are you absolutely certain that Shirley wasn't in contact with somebody in town?"

"Like who? She never said so. Besides, she hardly ever went out beyond the grounds. Just a walk down to the bridge and back to stretch her legs. When we did go to the pictures in the town hall, she went with me or her brothers."

"If she left of her own volition, and without letting you know, I can only assume that she had a compelling reason."

Mrs. McHattie turned her head away from him. "Perhaps somebody got in and put a gun to her head. That's a compelling reason."

"True. But then I'd have to ask, why? Why risk coming in the room, obviously by way of a narrow window, to forcibly abduct a pregnant woman? One would expect protest, struggle, noise. None of that seems to have occurred."

"Somebody killed my husband and my son. Now my daughter's disappeared. What in God's name is going on?"

"I wish I had an answer for you, but I don't."

Finally, her eyes met his. "Do you have children, Inspector?"

He paused, choosing his words carefully. "I have a daughter. She's about Shirley's age."

"So you've got some idea what it's like. The girls are the ones you worry about. Jock and me – well, especially Jock – were very protective of our Shirley. But she was a handful from day one. Oo, she could be so defiant. When he could catch her, Jock would wallop her, but it didn't make no difference. She'd stand up to him till he knocked her down. She took advantage of him being blind and she'd stay just out of reach, taunting him. Terrible scenes we had. He was ready to disown her more than once. Not that he would have, of course, but she did drive him to the brink."

She halted, lost in her own unhappy thoughts.

"You're saying that in spite of the situation it's not out of character for Shirley to disregard your feelings and take off on some adventure of her own?" Tyler spoke quietly.

Mrs. McHattie sighed. "No, I suppose it's not out of character, as you put it. I knew when she told me she was pregnant there would be nothing but tragedy ahead of us, and that's what happened. Jock was livid. Forbade Shirle to have anything to do with the man. Ha. Too late. The horse was out of the barn by then."

"Do you think this lover might be in some way implicated in what has happened?"

"I don't see how. He's gone overseas."

"Shirley told me she didn't even know his surname. He couldn't tell her because he was on a highly secret mission."

"That's what he said." Again Mrs. McHattie scowled. "Could have been a pile of horse manure what he was dropping us in. Fact is, he got her up the stump and left her in the lurch."

"And your daughter has had no contact with this man since he left?"

"Couple of postcards with no return address. Nothing recently. I'm the one who sees the post first, so I make sure. She hasn't received anything. Maybe he's dead. Good riddance to bad rubbish, I say."

53.

SHIRLEY MCHATTIE WAS FEELING DECIDEDLY UNDER the weather. Her back was aching something awful and her stomach felt queasy. The pain had begun when she was in the boat, but now it was getting worse.

Polly had been waiting for her at the riverbank. She was chipper as could be and gave her a big hug as she helped her get into the rowing boat. *Don't worry. One of my many undisclosed talents, Shirle dear, is that I can row awfully well.* And so she could, although it had been hard going against the current. Soon they disembarked at a derelict dock and Polly led her to this church. *The perfect hiding place, and I've made it all cosy.* Shirley couldn't help but get into the spirit of adventure and her heart was beginning to pound in anticipation of seeing Rudy. She'd caught hold of Polly's hand. *Oh, Pol, I can hardly stand it. Do you think he will have changed? Do you think he'll be put off because I've lost my figure?* Polly had pinched her cheek. *Silly goose, of course not. Things will be just the same, you'll see. It's his baby after all.*

But the sense of excitement was fading fast. Even Polly seemed subdued. She'd lit a couple of candles, but they didn't give off much light and the church was dark all around them. Shirley hadn't been in a Catholic church before and the shadowy statues and stained glass windows were vaguely disturbing. She knew how her own minister felt about papists, as he called them.

Worse, however, was the man who'd arrived shortly after them. Polly said he was a friend of Rudy's, a soldier pal from training school. He'd agreed to act as a go-between as an act of friendship. She couldn't reveal his name, "for security reasons." He didn't say a word – no greeting, no acknowledgement of Shirley, nothing. He was wearing dark clothes and a balaclava that covered his face. He sat in one of the pews outside the circle of light. He was so silent and still, he was almost invisible, but Shirley could feel his presence behind her.

She yearned to engage him, hungry for news of her love.

"How is Rudy? Was the mission successful? Is he on leave now? He hasn't been hurt, has he?"

The last question elicited a shake of the head. Exasperated, Shirley turned to Polly. "Cat got his tongue, has it?"

"Nothing like that," Polly answered. "He'd be in trouble if it came out he was helping you and Rudy to get together. They're having to break the rules for him to come."

"Well, I can't stay any longer. My mum will be frantic enough as it is."

She got to her feet and the man jumped up, fast as a cat, grabbed her arm, and shoved her back into the pew.

"Oi! Stop that," she said, but she was now truly frightened. "Polly, what's going on? Where's Rudy? Who is this bloke? I don't like him."

"Don't worry," said Polly. "He's all right, just the nervous type. Rudy will be here soon. And don't worry about your mum. I rang the hospital and told them to give her a message. Said you'd decided to take a few days' holiday with a friend."

Shirley looked at her in dismay. "Why did you say that? She knows I don't have any friends in the area."

"Except me, silly goose."

"Yes, but she doesn't know about you."

"Stop being such a worrywart. Remember, I said you had to learn to stand on your own feet? Your mum will sing a different tune when you come home a married woman."

Polly's voice was bright, but Shirley didn't feel reassured and she felt a sharp stab of guilt at her own actions. This was a terrible time to be adding to her mother's worries. She also had a nagging feeling that Polly was fibbing. That she hadn't left a message at the hospital. What game was she playing?

"What time is it? If Rudy isn't here soon, I'm going to go back."

Polly smiled. "Tell you what, I brought us some cocoa. It'll warm you up until he comes. I'm sure he won't be long now."

She reached into a black doctor's bag she had with her and took out a large Thermos, unscrewed the top, poured out a cup, and handed it to Shirley.

"You first."

Shirley shook her head. "No, thanks. My tummy's upset."

"It's got a splash of whisky in it," said Polly. "It'll settle you right down."

"I don't know if I should. The doctor said that whatever goes into my mouth will end up in the baby's system."

Polly chuckled. "No fear of that. One drink won't do anything. It's not like you're a regular tippler. Here."

She shoved the cup of cocoa at Shirley.

"All right then. Thanks. It is nippy in here."

Shirley jerked her head in the direction of the silent man. "Aren't you going to offer him some?"

"Nope. It's only for us girls."

Shirley took a sip and quickly lowered the cup. "I don't mean to be rude, but this cocoa leaves a bit to be desired. Is the milk off, do you think?"

"Hope not," said Polly. "Here." She went into her bag again and took out a small tin. "I brought along extra sugar just in case. I like mine sweet." She handed the tin to Shirley. "Help yourself. Here's a spoon."

"As long as I'm not taking all your ration, I don't mind if I do."

"I've got lots left. Don't worry," said Polly.

Shirley spooned two heaping spoonfuls of the sugar into the cup and stirred. She could tell the man was watching her. Well phooey to him. Nothing wrong with sugar for a pregnant woman. Truth was she got fed up with her ma watching her all the time. *Eat this, Shirle, don't eat that, Shirle.*

The cocoa tasted much better now, so she drank it down. Polly took the empty cup from her and poured herself some cocoa. She blew on it. "Bit hot yet."

Shirley yawned, engulfed by a sudden wave of tiredness. "You know what, I could do with a kip. It's past my bedtime. I'll just put my head down for a minute. Just a minute, mind. Wake me up as soon as Rudy comes."

"Why don't you stretch out," said Polly. "Better to put your feet up."

"Oo, I don't want to be disrespectful. This is a church after all."

The other woman flapped her hand. "I wouldn't worry about it. Come on, I'll help you."

She lifted Shirley's legs and swung them around so that she was lying on the pew.

"Ten minutes only . . ." Shirley's voice tailed off.

Polly looked down at her for a moment or two. "Silly little bint. I thought she wasn't going to drink it for a minute."

The man pulled off the balaclava.

"Bloody thing is scratchy," he said.

"I've got the feeling she's going to pop soon," said Polly.

"She'd better. I can't wait forever."

Polly scowled. "What do we do now?"

He stood up. "I'm going back before I'm missed."

"Hold on. What if she goes into labour?"

He gave her a half grin. "I'm sure you know what to do."

"I can handle the birth, that's not the problem. I just don't fancy spending the night in this bloody place."

"It'll be worth it. I told you that, Polly. One night, that's all. I'll be back tomorrow and it will all be over."

"Then what? What do we do then?"

54.

TYLER HADN'T STAYED MUCH LONGER WITH MRS. McHATTIE. She had looked so exhausted, he didn't have the heart to keep at her. Like an arrow scratched in the sand, faint as it was, he thought he at least had *something* to follow. Who and where was Rudy, the putative father of Shirley's child? Clearly, the lover himself couldn't be hiding out in the hospital. Was it somebody in cahoots with him? *Hey, pal, my gal's pa is against us marrying. Off him for me, will you? Remove the obstacle. Sure. Happy to oblige. Oops, sorry. There were two potential witnesses I had to dispose of.*

Well, if Shirley had done a bunk to meet her lover, they'd soon find them. One of the very few good results of wartime, as far as the police were concerned, was that the people couldn't really travel about the countryside undetected.

Sister Rebecca and Tyler returned to the sitting room.

"I'd like to suggest you stay here for the night, Inspector," she said. "We have a spare room that we keep ready for our spiritual adviser, Reverend Jervis. It's basic but adequate, and you would be right on the spot if . . . if anything happens."

Tyler felt as if his eyes were filled with sand. A bed, however basic, sounded like heaven to him.

"I accept, Sister. With thanks."

She smiled. "We even have a pair of pyjamas you can use."

She led the way down the passageway to a room at the far end, next to the sanctuary.

She switched on the light. A narrow bed, a chair, a washstand. Very monklike. But a bedroom nonetheless.

"We say matins at five o'clock. Would you like me to call you?"

Tyler rubbed at his jaw. "Does everybody get up at that hour?"

"Just our community initially, but now some of the patients like to join us."

"I think I'll join. And of course, if Shirley does reappear, fetch me immediately. Pregnant or not pregnant, I will personally give her a chewing out for worrying the heck out of everybody."

Sister Rebecca grimaced. "I'll be next in the queue." She indicated the dresser. "The pyjamas are in there. Reverend Jervis is rather a stout man, so they may be a bit big for you."

"That's quite all right. Thank you." He stopped. "Darn, Sister. My brain's turning to blancmange. I should let my sergeant know I won't be back tonight."

"I'll ring him if you'd like."

"Thanks, much appreciated."

For a moment, Tyler thought the almoner was lingering, but she turned away.

"I'll say good night then."

"Good night, Sister."

Tyler took out the pyjamas, blue hospital issue, and definitely on the large side. He got undressed, switched off the light, and climbed into the bed, which was as it had looked, hard and uncomfortable.

How long was it since he had lain with a woman in his arms? It was almost two years ago that he'd last been with Clare, and the thought of her was an ache. They'd had such a brief time together, and the joy he'd experienced at their reunion was so tempered by the sorrow of his son's death he could hardly separate the two. He rolled onto his back trying to bring back the memory of his time with Clare, but he was too tired. All he could remember was her softness; the feeling of the love that had encompassed him, comforting him in his anguish. If he were a praying man, he'd offer up a prayer. *Dear God, send her back to me soon.*

Finally he fell into a restless sleep, tormented by unhappy dreams. He was only too happy to be awakened by Sister Virginia, who was standing at his bedside holding a tea tray.

55.

"SISTER REBECCA SAID YOU WANTED TO BE AWAKENED at five, sir."

Tyler pushed himself up in the bed. As well as a china cup and saucer, there was a brass candleholder with a lit candle on the tray that the nun placed on the bedside table.

"Shall I draw the curtains, sir? It is looking like a pleasant morning."

"Please do. Has there been any word of Shirley McHattie?" Tyler asked.

"Nothing, I'm afraid, sir."

She returned to the bedside.

"I'll extinguish the candle if you don't mind, sir."

"Of course."

The soft light of early dawn was bathing the room. The sweet fresh air coming through the open window was momentarily tainted by the acrid odour of the snuffed candle.

"Do you take milk and sugar, sir?"

He could see she was managing to focus her gaze somewhere in the space over his head.

"Yes, please," answered Tyler, feeling rather lordlike at being waited on in bed. Nobody had done that for him since Vera, in the early days of his marriage. Very early days.

"Will you be joining us at matins, sir?"

"Er . . . Maybe not this morning. Perhaps some other time." Tyler took a sip of tea. "Perfect. Thank you, Sister."

There was a burst of singing from the sanctuary. Something hymnal, male voices mixed in with the sopranos.

"Will you be taking breakfast in the dining room, sir, or would you like to have it in here?" Sister Virginia asked. "We start serving at half past six."

"As long as my presence doesn't put people off their food, I'll eat with everybody else, in the dining room."

The nun smiled shyly. "Naturally we are dreadfully upset about what's happened, but I have every faith you'll get to the bottom of things soon."

Tyler wasn't sure he was as confident.

"The bathroom is next door," she said, her eyes again averted. "I've placed a fresh towel on the rack, and the toothbrush is for your use. I should warn you – the water tends to be a bit scanty and tepid. I can bring you a jug of hot water if you'd like."

"I'll be fine. No special treatment please."

"I'll leave you then. I should join in matins." She gave a little curtsy and, quiet as a mouse, slipped away. Tyler would swear Sister Virginia had been in service prior to joining the community.

He drank the tea, put the dainty cup and saucer back on the tray, and swung his legs out of bed. He pulled off the reverend's ample pyjamas, folded them neatly, and placed them on the chair. His own shirt could have done with an iron, but there was no opportunity to do that now, so it would have to do. He got dressed quickly and went in search of the wc. The singing got louder as he went past the sanctuary. Even to his ears, the music was unusually harmonious and professional sounding. He might have been tempted to join them if he hadn't felt so dragged out by his night.

As Sister Virginia had warned, the water in the bathroom was meagre, sputtering out reluctantly from the taps. He splashed what little there was into his face. He needed a shave, but he felt he wanted some fresh air and a walk even more.

He went outside.

The sunlight was sparkling on the strip of grass. Even the vegetables looked more sprightly. The birds were putting up their usual frenetic twitter. He turned to have a look at them. And froze. What the hell was that?

Along the grass verge in front of the Fuller cottage were thrust four white wooden crosses.

56.

He waved over the constable who was stationed in front of the McHattie cottage.

"Biggs. Where the hell did these come from?"

The officer hurried over. "The chap who works in the kitchen, sir. The one who's a bit . . ." He twirled his forefinger by his temple.

"When did he put them in?"

"About half an hour ago. He said that you had given him permission to commemorate the poor dead folks."

"I did no such thing. You should have checked with me first."

Tyler knew he was being testy, but he couldn't help himself. The sight of the white crosses had given him a shock.

"I'm sorry, sir. Didn't seem any good reason to wake you up. I couldn't see the harm to it."

Tyler leaned over to take a closer look at the crosses. They looked as if they came from a fence of some kind. The edges of the cross pieces were jagged, as if they had been sawn off from larger pieces.

Shite. Mrs. Valentine's letter. *"Somebody stole half of my fence."*

Rowell had assumed the aforementioned fence was a fancy wrought-iron one that would fetch money, but this must be it. A plain white, wooden fence.

Tyler straightened up. "Go and fetch Alfie Fuller for me. Tell him to get out here right away."

"Yes, sir."

Biggs started off.

"Hold on a minute, Constable. Have you had breakfast?"

"Not yet, sir."

"Neither have I. Tell you what, when you get Alfie, see if you can filch us both a couple of slices of toast. I tend not to think clearly on an empty stomach."

"Yes, sir. Right away. Thank you, sir."

He hurried away and Tyler stared down at the white crosses. Why four? Jock, Ben, and Sister Ivy were the three who had died. What was going on in Alfie Fuller's addled brain?

The rear door that led to the kitchen opened and Alfie came out. He started to walk purposefully towards the verge, but when he saw Tyler, he stopped in his tracks. Tyler called to him.

"Hey, Alfie, come over here for a sec. I want to ask you something."

Alfie didn't move. "What do you want? I've to get on with breakfast."

"Won't take a minute."

Again Alfie didn't move, but the constable had appeared right behind him and Alfie couldn't retreat without knocking him over. Biggs seemed to size up the situation immediately and took a step closer. Alfie glanced over his shoulder, flashed him a broad smile, thrust his hands into his pockets, and sauntered towards Tyler, the constable close behind.

Alfie's expression was wary. Tyler stared at him. His face seemed unnaturally flushed.

"What do you think of these?" Tyler asked, indicating the white crosses.

"They looks like grave markers."

"They do, don't they. The constable said you put them here. You told him I gave you permission, which is a fib."

"No it's not. We talked about graves just last week."

"Last week?"

"Well, recently anyway."

"Nobody's buried here that I know of."

Alfie eyed him solemnly. "A marker don't have to mean there's a body there. It can mean somebody died and we don't know where."

"That is true."

"In fact," said Alfie, "I put them there for Mr. McHattie and his son. And Sister Ivy of blessed memory."

"But we know where they died, Alfie. Their graves will not be unknown."

"That is correct, sir. But they are in memoriam."

"Who is the fourth cross for?"

"Could be anybody. Millions and millions of soldiers have already died. And pigeons, for that matter."

"Is this one for Prince then?"

"It could be."

"Where did you get the crosses from, Alfie? One of the ladies in town says somebody stole her fence. These crosses all look like they were once part of a fence."

Alfie bent down and studied the crosses ostentatiously.

"I'd say you are quite correct in that regard, sir."

"Alfie, look at me. Did you cut up Mrs. Valentine's fence?"

"Did somebody see me do that, sir?"

"Did you or didn't you?" Tyler asked in exasperation.

"No. I found them just behind our cottage."

Tyler didn't believe him for a minute, but he doubted Alfie was going to confess to the theft. If he even remembered that's what he'd done.

Alfie gave him a disarming smile. "In my opinion, those markers are a good thing."

"I tend to agree with you, Alfie, but I think we have to remove them for the time being. People might get upset if they see them."

Alfie thought for a moment. "You are probably correct about that, sir. Shall I pull them out?"

Before he could do that, the constable stepped forward. "May I interject for a moment, sir?"

"Be my guest, interject away."

Biggs looked at Alfie. "Perhaps you should show the inspector what you have in your pocket."

"Don't have nothing," said Alfie. He opened up his palms. "See. Empty." He took a couple of steps back. "Can I go now? I've got to be in the kitchen or my ma will give me an earful."

The constable blocked the way. "I think you should turn your pockets inside out. Just to make sure."

"Why're you going on at me?" asked Alfie with a scowl. "I don't have nothing, I told you."

Tyler spoke in a stern voice. "Alfie, this gentleman is a constable of the law, just like I am. If he wants to see your pockets turned inside out, he has the right. If you have nothing to hide, you have nothing to worry about."

Alfie started to scuff his feet in the dirt. "I found it, I didn't steal it."

"Found what?"

Reluctantly, Alfie reached into his right pocket. He held out his palm, revealing a tube of lipstick.

Tyler took it from him and checked the end of the tube. CHERRY RED. Made by Coty.

"Where did you get this, Alfie?"

"I told you, I found it. Finders, keepers, that's what my ma says."

"But where was it, specifically?"

Alfie waved vaguely in the direction of the east gate. "Out there. It was lying by the river."

"When did you find it?"

Tyler saw Alfie flinch. He must have allowed his own worry to sharpen his voice.

"I saw it first thing this morning."

"Do you know who it belongs to?"

Alfie pursed his lips. "Not one of the nuns, that's for sure. They're not allowed to wear war paint. Might be Daisy Stevens. She really needs it. Or maybe Miss Shirley. They's the only two I can think of."

Suddenly, Tyler realized that Alfie's pink cheeks owed a debt to the lipstick. He'd put some on his lips as well.

"I saw Alfie with the lipstick, sir," said Biggs. "He, er, he was applying it."

Alfie ducked his head. "My lips are chapped."

Tyler made himself take a deep breath. "Alfie, I want you and me to go to the place where you found the lipstick. Do you think you can do that?"

"I dunno. I should get back to the kitchen. Ma will be needing me."

"Tell you what, I'll have the constable go and tell your mum you're doing important police business."

"All right. But I can't be long."

Tyler nodded at Biggs. "Remove those crosses. Put them behind the cottage for now."

The constable pulled a napkin from his pocket and unwrapped it. "I did manage to procure you a piece of toast, sir."

Tyler grabbed the slice of bread and took a bite. "Lead on," he said to Alfie.

"My ma says it's rude to talk with your mouth full."

Tyler swallowed. "She's right about that, Alfie."

57.

ALFIE WENT DIRECTLY TO THE GATE AND SHOVED aside the bolts. He immediately set off along the path, and Tyler had to scramble to keep up with him.

"Follow me," said Alfie over his shoulder as he trotted ahead. "We'll walk like red Indians."

Overhanging trees leaned into the path. They were damp with dew, and as he brushed past, Tyler received a chilly shower. He kept a close eye out for any sign that Shirley had come this way last night, but he saw nothing. The woods on either side weren't deep or extensive, but they were lush with summer and hid the surrounding fields from view.

They continued along the path for several minutes as far as the river, and here Alfie stopped so suddenly, Tyler almost collided with him.

"I think it was about there," he said, pointing to a spot close to the water's edge.

Tyler shifted his position so he was facing Alfie.

"Now, son, I am going to ask you an important question."

"Fire away."

"Are you positive you found the lipstick this morning? That it wasn't here when you came some other day?"

Alfie nodded. "That is quite correct. I'm always on the lookout for things, sir. I've found two sixpences before. And a half a crown from the time of Charles I." He eyed Tyler. "You don't want those as well, do you?"

"No, son. You can keep them."

Tyler hoped that one old coin wasn't valuable enough to be considered government property.

He looked over at the river sparkling in the sunlight. The current was moving fast.

"Have you ever got across the river, Alfie?"

"No, sir. For one thing I can't swim. For another thing, my Ma says it's deeper than you might think in the middle. In my opinion it's not safe."

Tyler gazed down at the bank, which sloped gently to the water. There was a long gouge in the grass, as if a boat had been pulled up onto the shore.

"Alfie, Miss Shirley has disappeared. She hasn't been seen since last night. Do you have any idea where she might be?"

Alfie gaped at him. "She has a baby in her tummy. Perhaps she went to the hospital."

"I don't think she did. I think she came here sometime last night."

Alfie gazed around the clearing, his expression bewildered. "Where would she sleep?"

"That's a good question, son. I believe she went in a boat." Tyler pointed. "See that? Somebody pulled a boat up the bank."

Alfie crouched down and examined the earth. "I'd say you were correct about that, sir."

"Who has a boat that you know of?"

"Nobody." Alfie wrinkled his forehead. "The police will know. They know everything like that."

"Quite right, Alfie. I'll make enquiries."

Tyler experienced a wave of what he could only call desperation. What the hell had induced a girl weighed down with advanced pregnancy to slip away in the dark and trek down here? Who had she met? Where had they gone?

He nodded at Alfie. "Let's go back now."

The other man didn't move. He was staring at his feet.

"Sir, I told a bit of a fib just now."

"Yes?"

"I told you my lips was chapped, but that's not true. I rubbed the lipstick on because I was pretending that Miss Shirley – Miss McHattie, that is – I was pretending she had given me a big smacker on the lips."

"Did she ever do that, Alfie?"

"No. Not to me. I'm not right in the head, you see, so the girls don't fancy me."

Tyler was taken aback by this honesty, but he had the feeling the poor bugger was simply repeating what he'd heard too many times.

"You know what, Alfie, if Miss Shirley is in trouble and we find her, I would be willing to bet she'll be giving out big smackers right and left."

Alfie grinned. "Let's go on searching then."

Tyler turned, about to retrace their steps, but suddenly Alfie slapped himself on the forehead. "Lord help us, what's wrong with me? For a minute, I forgot." He stood stock-still.

"Okay, Alfie. What did you forget?"

"I know why Miss Shirley has taken off. She must have got a letter."

58.

ALFIE REMOVED A BRICK IN THE WALL JUST BEYOND the east gate.

"I came down here one morning for my walk, like usual, and I sees Miss Shirley. She had a note in her hand and I could see the brick had been removed." He pouted. "She was very cross with me. 'Are you spying on me, Alfie Fuller?' says she. 'No,' says I. 'I'm just going for my walk.' 'Well don't tell a living soul that you saw me here.' 'I won't,' says I. Then she says, 'If you tell, I'll say you tried to rape me. You know what that means, don't you?'" Alfie rubbed his head. "Now I've told you, sir. I hope she doesn't go and say I hurt her."

"Don't worry, son. I'm a policeman. You were right to tell me. Now, when was it you saw Miss Shirley with that note?"

Alfie ducked his head. "I can't remember exactly, but I'd say it was weeks and weeks ago. But there was messages all the time."

"Ah. Did you take a look then, Alfie?"

"I confess I did, sir."

"Did you read the notes?"

"That is correct, sir. They weren't mushy or anything like that. Just said, 'Meet me tomorrow, market, afternoon.' That sort of thing."

"Were they signed?"

"No. No kisses or anything either. Miss Shirley put her notes in the same spot, but I didn't always see those. Usually she just wrote 'yes' or 'no,' or 'can't.'"

"Did you ever see anybody else pick up the messages?"

Alfie shook his head. "No, sir. And I only saw Miss Shirley that once. I didn't want her to get the wrong idea. I stayed out of her way but good."

"I have another important question, Alfie. Can you tell me the last time there was a message behind the brick?"

The man clicked his tongue. "Hmm. I'm not so good with days, sir. It's hard to say."

"Yesterday, for instance. Did you find one yesterday?"

"I would say not. I don't think I came for a walk yesterday. Ma didn't want me out of her sight. So she said."

59.

Sister Clarissa ushered Tyler into the nuns' sitting room. Martha McHattie was still in her dressing gown, her untouched breakfast on the table in front of her.

"No news, I presume?"

"Not exactly, but we found this." Tyler showed her the lipstick tube. "Is this Shirley's?"

Mrs. McHattie took it from him and examined it carefully. Her face turned even whiter. "Could be. Coty's CHERRY RED. She did use that sometimes. Where was it?"

"Near the riverbank, at the end of the public footpath."

"I see." She held the lipstick in her palm. She knew what the implication was. "You think she went to meet someone, don't you?"

He paused and looked into the fear in the woman's eyes. "If she went freely, there's much more likelihood she isn't harmed."

"What if she fell into the river in the dark? Or got pushed in?"

"There's no indication of that. My guess is that she got into a boat. There were marks on the riverbank."

"A boat! What bloody boat?"

"I don't know. I'm going to have my officers search the river."

He waited for Mrs. McHattie to digest this information, then continued.

"As you know we don't have much manpower in the police force these days. If we are going to treat this as a missing persons case – or an abduction – I'm going to have to use what men I do have as efficiently as possible. If Shirley went to meet somebody, she took nothing with her. No extra clothes, for instance. She must have intended to return last night and . . ." He paused, reluctant to voice the thought. "For some reason she's not able to. So I must ask you again, do you know why Shirley would have gone off the way she appears to have gone off? She was secretive about it and she took her lipstick, as if she were meeting somebody. Somebody she wanted to look good for."

Mrs. McHattie didn't answer.

"Alfie Fuller says that Shirley was hiding messages in the wall," said Tyler quietly. "She was in contact with somebody on a regular basis."

"What? Alfie Fuller told you that? He's a loony. You can't believe a word he says."

"He showed me the hiding place and he claims the messages had to do with assignations. I must ask you again, do you have any idea who your daughter might have been communicating with?"

Mrs. McHattie had collapsed back into her chair. "No, I don't."

"Could she have made contact with her lover, the father of her baby?"

She looked up, startled. "What? Of course not."

"Why are you so certain?"

"I told you, he was sent overseas months ago."

"He might just have been stringing you all a line. Maybe he's a cook in an army canteen."

She actually smiled wanly at that. "No, that's one thing I did believe about him. He was definitely a fighting man."

"How did the two of them meet?" Tyler asked.

"A dance, where else? She fell for him right away. Hook, line, and sinker. I've never seen a girl so mad for a bloke. She brought him home to see us the very next weekend. She'd never done that with any of her fellas before."

She halted, remembering.

"And you didn't like him?" Tyler prompted her.

"Neither of us did. Jock kept insisting he wasn't who he said he was."

"What did he mean?"

"He couldn't really explain, but Jock, being blind, was sensitive to people's voices and how they talked. He picked up things all the time that went right past me. He was dead against the bloke."

"I understand Shirley is planning to give her baby up for adoption?"

"Yes. It's better that way. She's far too young to take proper care of a babe all on her own. The almoner has said she'll find us somebody suitable."

"What if the baby's father does return and wants to marry your daughter?"

"He should have done that before he got her pregnant, shouldn't he? Besides, he's a foreigner. We didn't fancy her getting married to a foreigner."

"Where was he from?"

"He wouldna say. Another secret, according to him. Spoke good English and was very polite. Too polite, in my opinion. You know the type. Butter wouldna melt in his mouth."

"Shirley told me she didn't know his surname."

Mrs. McHattie scowled. "It probably suited him that Shirley would have a hard time tracing him. He's most likely got an entire harem scattered around Britain."

"You mentioned that he was training at a special camp. Did you meet any of the others? Any of his friends?"

"No, just him. He kept saying they was all hand-picked, cream de la cream, bloody brothers. He never said what they was picked for and I never met any of them. Why?"

"I'm wondering if maybe one of his chums was hiding the

messages in the wall for him. According to Alfie, they weren't love letters. They were only to do with making arrangements for meetings. Did you notice any change in your daughter's behaviour over the past while?"

Mrs. McHattie thought for a moment. "She seemed happier, a bit less mardy. I put it down to the fact that she knew the pregnancy was almost over. But I tell you, Inspector, I doubt very much she was meeting Mr. Rudy. That I would have known. She couldn't have hidden that from me."

Tyler paused. Then he said quietly, "I'm starting to think that Shirley got a message that caused her to slip away without being seen. But that she did intend to come back."

"A message from Rudy?"

"Yes. Either he's in the area or she believes he is."

Mrs. McHattie's eyes filled with tears. "I can't believe she'd do that to me. Go off like that. Even with all our troubles, she wouldna. Not after what's happened."

Again Tyler waited. Mrs. McHattie had taken a handkerchief from her pocket and she was twisting it between her fingers.

"What do we do now?" she asked finally.

"There is an RAF camp in Ludlow," said Tyler. "I'll get in touch with the commandant and see if he can help us. Rudy might be stationed here."

"You know what? Much as I didn't like the fellow, I'd feel better if I knew she was with him. At least I'd know she was safe."

She spoke so softly Tyler could hardly hear her.

60.

TYLER WENT IMMEDIATELY TO THE ALMONER'S OFFICE. Sister Rebecca, matins over, was already seated at her desk. She got to her feet as soon as he entered. Her face was full of alarm and his heart sank. More bad news, obviously.

"The post arrived early. I'm afraid you've got another of those letters."

The neat handwriting was unpleasantly familiar. He tore open the envelope. Sure enough, it contained a single sheet of paper with a typewritten message.

She has been having labour pains for the last several hours. She and two other women, also close to their term, have been taken to the city, where she has been put in a bare and cheerless room by herself. There is nobody with her, except a hard-featured nurse who has checked for dilation. The examination is painful, but the nurse does not apologize. The woman asks for water, pointing at her mouth and making drinking gestures. The nurse either does not understand or chooses not to speak. She shakes her head. A doctor enters, old, grey-haired, bowed. His hands shake as if he is palsied or perhaps drunk.

He examines her a little more gently than
the nurse has. He holds up three fingers.
"Soon," he says. "Soon." She wants to catch
hold of his hand and keep him beside her
because he treats her as if she is a human
being. But he leaves hurriedly and a second
nurse, cap and body stiff and starched, comes
into the room. Then the overwhelming tide of
pain seizes her and nothing else matters.
She groans. She wants to shout out but is
too proud in front of these haughty women.
Finally, the first nurse signs at her to push
and she does, until the baby comes out into
the world in a rush of blood and fluid. She
half sits up in the bed, and holds out her
arms for her infant. It is a boy, her first.
The nurse ignores her, wraps the newborn in
a blanket, and walks away. "Wait," she cries,
trying to struggle out of the bed. The other
nurse's eyes flicker at her. "Later," she
says. She knows this is a lie and she
screams. The doctor comes hurrying back.
While the nurse holds her down, he jams a
hypodermic needle into her arm. From outside
of the room, she can hear the thin wail of
her newborn. She shrieks again but the drug
is taking effect and she sinks into oblivion.

     The baby will continue to cry.

——

"Inspector, what is the matter?" Sister Rebecca asked in alarm.

"Take a look."

Sister Rebecca read it quickly. "Lord have mercy on us all." She crossed herself.

Tyler thumped one fist into his hand. "What are these letters about, goddamn it? Oh, sorry, Sister. Whose story are they telling?" Suddenly he grabbed at the envelope. "Shite. When was the darn thing franked?"

In opening the letter he'd barely missed tearing off the corner, but the stamp was clear enough. Ludlow post office. Two thirty. Wed. July 15, 1942. It had been posted a day before Shirley vanished, but after Jock and Ben McHattie were shot.

"I'd say the letters are following a definite chronology, wouldn't you, Sister? First, the killing of the men, second the removing of the mothers and children. This third one describes a woman being taken to a hostile place to deliver her baby, which is then taken from her."

"Shirley McHattie?"

"I'd say so. The parallels are too close not to be significant. But this letter was intended to reach me after she disappeared. It smacks of careful planning."

He told the almoner about Alfie and the revelation of the secret letters in the wall.

"It certainly sounds as if her lover has been in contact with her," she said. "Perhaps he is stationed at the Ludford RAF camp. It certainly is close by."

"Mrs. McHattie insists he's gone overseas, but he could have returned. If the family is so hostile to him, he might think it prudent to lie low for the time being."

The almoner was already reaching for the telephone. "I know the commandant of the camp. Shall I ring him for you?"

"That would be grand. Rudy might not be his real name, but there can't be that many men on the base who are foreigners and trained as commandos in Scotland."

Sister Rebecca looked at him. "I am probably being impossibly naive, but do you think we could be dealing with a simple elopement?"

"Unfortunately, I'd say there's very little chance of that being the case."

61.

THE MORNING SUN HAD VANISHED, AND IN TYPICAL English fashion, the weather had changed. A louring cloud was coming in fast over the trees, and it was threatening rain. The common room was dim, electricity always used sparingly.

For the third time in two days, Tyler found himself addressing the residents of the hospital. Faces with unseeing eyes, horrible scars and mutilations; ordinary faces like those of the two orderlies and the four nuns in their plain habits. Mrs. Fuller with her work-stained apron. Alfie fidgeting mightily on his chair.

It was hard to believe one of these people had been trained as a killer and, presumably, had acted as such. But it had to be somebody among them. It *had* to be.

"Ladies and gentlemen. I'm sorry to inform you that Shirley McHattie is missing. She left her room in the nuns' quarters late last night and has not returned. Frankly, we don't know if she is staying away of her own free will or if she has, in fact, been abducted. In either case, given her condition, we need to find her as soon as possible."

A gasp rippled through the group, followed by silent, intense attention.

"The reason I have asked you here," continued Tyler, "is because I want you to search your memories and see if there is anything, even the smallest thing, that you can tell me that might help us find her. For instance, did Shirley ever speak to you about the father of her child? A hint, a casual word she let slip about his identity. Some of you know this area far better than I do. Is there anywhere she might be? Perhaps hidden.

Did you hear anything at all last night? An owl cry? A dog bark? Allow me to decide if it is relevant or not."

Nobody spoke. Nobody jumped up and said, *I did. I heard Shirley McHattie being dragged away screaming. Not only that, I know who abducted her.*

Those who could look back at Tyler simply appeared frightened or confused. He went on.

"To date, I have received three anonymous letters that may have a bearing on this case. They were all typed on one of the machines in the hospital common room. If you know anything about that, please let me know at once."

It was me, Inspector. I typed those grief-sodden pieces. I confess.

No such luck. More blank stares, confused expressions.

Daisy raised her hand as if she were in school. "What sort of letters are you referring to?"

"As the bishop said to the Pope," muttered Melrose.

"I'm not at liberty to disclose the contents at this point, Miss Stevens."

"As the Pope replied," said the irrepressible Melrose.

Tyler was getting nowhere fast. "Three people have died on these premises. A young woman, about to deliver a child, has disappeared. She could be hurt and unable to seek help. She could be trapped somewhere by a malicious person or people. She is at risk. Her unborn child is at risk."

Again he was met with silence, but he could sense that he'd got his message across. To most of them anyway.

Daisy again raised her hand. "Inspector, would it possible for us to take a little time to ponder? I think we are all shocked by what you've said. Perhaps if we got together in small groups, those who are more, er, capacitated can help those who aren't. It might be easier that way, less intimidating."

Tyler could have kissed her. "Miss Stevens, that is a brilliant idea. Of course, you can have some time."

Daisy seized the handles of Bancroft's wheelchair and swung him around.

"Come on, touch and thumpers. Let's gather over in the corner."

Slowly the rest of the assembly began to disperse, the nuns and the two orderlies assisting those who needed help.

Tyler watched them. Somewhere stuck in his brain were the final words of the letter. *The baby will continue to cry.* Across the room his eyes met those of the almoner and he saw reflected back at him the same fear.

They had to find Shirley McHattie soon.

62.

HE WENT BACK TO THE OFFICE. HOWEVER, HE'D barely sat down when there was a sharp rap at the door and without waiting for permission, Dai Hughes entered.

"Inspector, there's something I must tell you," he burst out.

The orderly was actually sweating with emotion. He wiped his face with the back of his sleeve like a boy might. His words came out in a rush.

"I've done something terrible . . ."

"Pipe up, lad. I'm all ears."

The orderly scrubbed at his eyes. "I've committed a sacrilegious act."

Hughes broke into sobs. His behaviour certainly didn't seem to be that of a callous murderer, nor that of a tough commando.

"I don't have the foggiest notion what you're blathering on about. Now, why don't you have a seat and stop crying. What do you mean by a sacrilegious act?"

Hughes gulped hard a few times but appeared to be regaining some control. Sister Rebecca had left a carafe of water on the desk for Tyler's use and he poured out a glass.

"Here, have a few sips of this."

Hughes did so and with a hiccup his sobs subsided.

"Okay now? Do continue."

"As you discovered," said Hughes, "I've had a girl who I said was my wife."

"Surely you're not twisting yourself inside out because you lied about that, are you, lad? I'd hardly call that an act of sacrilege."

"No, it's not that. You see, Polly . . . Well, she's from Manchester and she's used to a more exciting life than she's been getting here in Ludlow. She said she wanted more adventure." He shot a glance at Tyler. "We couldn't really go out much because of my work, and we didn't want to be seen in public. Then last week, Polly said she'd come across this old church that's down in a field by the river. She thought it might be exciting to go there at night. It's quite isolated. She said there were bodies buried in the crypt and if we went there at night we might see a ghost. So I thought, why not? Anything to keep her happy." Hughes stopped. "The church wasn't locked up or anything. It's not very big, only a few wooden pews. Polly went over to a book that was on a stand. Not a bible, a register of some sort. *Look at this,* says she. *This dates back to Norman times; the priests have got French names.* That didn't impress me that much to tell you the truth, but she seemed quite chuffed. *I bet they'll turn in their graves if we do it in here,* says she."

Tyler held up his hand. "Just to be clear. By 'do it,' you mean have sexual intercourse?"

Dai squirmed. "Polly was brought up a Catholic, but she hates the church. Says the priests ruined her mother's life . . . She never explained how, but I think she was born out of wedlock and they made her mother pay for her sins. *I want you to have me on that altar,* says she. *That'll show them.* Well now that we were in there, I didn't want to really. I was raised chapel, but a church is a church. It seemed sort of holy in there. What we were planning to do didn't seem right. But she got at me the way she usually did. She found some sort of priest's robe in the vestry and she made me put it on. Then she climbed onto the altar table and I got on top of her." He flashed Tyler a wan smile. "Tell the truth, it wasn't very successful, but Polly was thrilled. *Good thing I don't believe in Hell,* she says, *because we'd go there for certain.*" Hughes paused.

"When did all this happen?" Tyler asked.

"Last week. Tuesday."

"I'm a police inspector, Dai, not a man of the cloth. Why are you telling me all this? I can't absolve you of your sins. I can't even charge you with trespassing, as you're telling me the church wasn't locked. If I look it up, I'll probably find sacrilege is still on the statutes as a criminal offence. I could charge you if that would make you feel better."

"No, please don't. My brother will skin me alive." He lowered his head and stared at the floor.

"What else?" prompted Tyler. "There's more you've not told me."

Hughes's voice dropped to a whisper. "I'm scared that Polly might have something to do with Shirley's disappearance."

"What!"

"There's a part of Polly that's a bit off, if you get my meaning. She tells everybody she's a nurse, but she's not. She admitted to me she got chucked out of nursing school ages ago. She was bitter about it. Anyway, she has a thing about babies. She told me she often felt tempted to make off with the infants. She usually considered the woman who'd given birth would be a dreadful mother and she would do better."

Tyler could feel himself growing cold. "Did she know Shirley McHattie?"

Hughes nodded. "Polly met her one day at the market. She struck up an acquaintance with her. Shirley was lonely I think, and Polly didn't know anybody here except me. They were like a couple of kids, writing secret letters to each other, having little rendezvous whenever they could."

"How did they get letters to each other?" Tyler asked, although he thought he already knew the answer.

"They had a hiding place in the east wall. Polly would put a note behind the brick and Shirley would pick it up and then leave one for her."

So he'd been wrong about Shirley getting a message from her lover. It was Polly all along.

"Do you think Polly has truly gone to Manchester to take care of her mother?"

"She doesn't have a mother in Manchester. Her ma died years ago."

"Where do you think Polly has gone?"

Hughes bit his lip. "I'm afraid she might have lured Shirley to the church."

"She wants to take the baby?"

"I think so."

"Good God. Where is this church?"

"I'm not completely sure, look you. I borrowed the tandem, but it was so dark, and Polly was the one leading the way. All I can tell you is that it's to the west of here. Maybe a quarter of a mile. It's set back from the river in a field."

Tyler jumped to his feet. "Come on. We've got to find it. Now."

Hughes said softly, "I'm sorry, Inspector."

"Me too, lad. Let's hope we're not too late."

63.

THE ORDERLY AT HIS HEELS, TYLER HURRIED OUT TO the front entrance to look for Constable Mortimer. She'd know where this church was if anybody would. She was standing at the west gate chatting with Constable Mady. Tyler gave them a quick précis of Hughes's sordid story.

"Do you know what church this might be? Old. Small. Norman probably."

"Yes, sir, I believe I do," answered Mortimer. "It has to be St. Clement's. I attended services there when I was a child, but it's hardly used at all these days."

"I think Shirley got into a boat. There were gouge marks on the bank at the end of the footpath. Is it possible to access the church by way of the river?"

"People did sometimes come in by boat when the road was impassable. There's a private dock for that purpose."

Before Tyler could proceed further, Sister Rebecca came out of the house.

"A Mr. Grey is on the telephone, Inspector. He says you have been trying to reach him."

"Damnation. Please tell him to hold on. I'll be right there." Tyler turned to the constables. "I've got to talk to this bloke. It's urgent. Mortimer, I want you and Mady to proceed to the church. Use the motorcycle. For God's sake, be careful. For now, I just want to know what's going on. Don't take any action unless you consider it a matter of life or death. Understood?"

They both stared at him with round eyes. "Yes, sir," said Constable Mortimer.

"As soon as I've taken this call, I'll follow. Constable Mortimer, give me directions."

"The church is about a quarter of a mile west of here. Go across Dinham Bridge and follow the road that runs beside the river on the castle side. You'll pass a red barn, and about a hundred yards farther on, you'll see a lane veering off to the right. There's an old faded signpost that says, Church Lane. You can just make it out. The lane bends twice. You'll see the church on your left as soon as you take the second bend. It's in a little dip surrounded by a copse of trees; there's a gravel lane leading up to it."

Tyler turned to the orderly. "Does that sound familiar, Hughes?"

"Yes, sir. I do remember the river and the little lane. It was bumpy."

"Okay. Get back to the patients. I'm sure you're needed. Keep your mouth closed. I don't want anybody told anything at this point. Understood?"

Hughes's face was utterly miserable.

"Yes, sir. Understood."

Tyler turned to the two constables. "Okay, go! When you get there, keep out of sight. This is strictly a scouting mission. Got that?"

"Yes, sir," said Mortimer. "I should say, however, that the church stands in the middle of a clearing, and it might be a problem to approach without being seen."

"Suggestions?"

"It will be best to park at the bottom of the lane and walk up."

"Okay. Do that."

She set off towards the motorcycle with Mady trotting at her side. Tyler called after them, "Be careful."

He hurried to the office, Sister Rebecca behind him.

"Sister, I'll need to commandeer your car," he said over his shoulder.

"Of course. I'll bring you the key."

She'd rested the receiver on the desk and he picked it up.

"Hello, Tyler here."

Grey's familiar mumble greeted him.

"Tyler? 'Bout to hang up."

"Sorry, sir. I was outside."

"Yes, well, I apologize that I wasn't available when you rang before. Business in London, don't you know. Most disagreeable."

He didn't elaborate as to whether it was London or the business that was the problem and Tyler had to bite his lip not to burst out impatiently. Grey continued.

"You asked my assistant, Nesbitt, about the special training unit that is up in Scotland. You said you wanted names of the men who were based there since December last."

"That's right, sir. There definitely seems to be a connection with the commando unit in Ariscraig and my case."

"Does there, indeed? Well, I followed up as best I could, but they're a closed-mouthed bunch at the War Office." Tyler heard him drawing on his ubiquitous pipe. "The first two chaps I got refused to open up until they'd consulted with another higher-up muckety-muck. Good thing probably, these days, but it can be aggravating. When I emphasized blind man, child, and nun, all killed, they got a move on. Finally I was connected with a chap by the name of Hubbins. Turns out we knew each other at Oxford, so I got clearance and we didn't have to go through tiresome identity checks. I said I was trying to track down a commando, first name possibly Rudy, who had gone overseas in December on a special mission. He was a foreigner, but I didn't know what sort. With me so far, Tyler?"

"Yes, sir. With you." *And for God's sake, hurry up.*

"I know I'm rambling, but I want you to get the whole story."

"Yes, sir. The rigmarole in high places is always fascinating."

"Don't get sarcastic with me, Tyler, I'm not in the mood. I'm surprised I got that much information, with Göring's boys interrupting us constantly."

"Sorry, sir. Didn't mean to sound sarcastic. It's just that I'm very concerned about the whereabouts of a young girl from here. She's the daughter of the murdered man and she's about to give birth. I think she's been lured away."

"Good Lord. I'll get to the point then."

"Thank you, sir. That would be helpful."

"Tyler! Well, anyway, Hubbie was as helpful as he was able. There was a special mission into occupied Europe right around the time you mentioned. Codename Operation Anthropoid. Where they come up with these names, beats me. Anyway, a handful of commandos were sent over, all trained at Ariscraig. They were Czech, and part of the manifest was to show Mr. Churchill the Czechs were onside and not eating out of Herr Heydrich's paw. They were parachuted into Moravia in December for the express purpose of assassinating the blond butcher himself."

It was Tyler's turn to draw in his breath. "Bloody hell. They succeeded. Big brouhaha in Nazi circles. Heydrich was buried with hero's honours and all that."

"That's right. Herr Hitler was most ticked off and ordered severe reprisals. As is his wont. Apparently, the Gestapo thought they had tracked down the assassins' collaborators. Wrongly as it turned out, but they're never too fussy about evidence. They descended on a nearby village and ordered every male over the age of sixteen to be shot."

This had to be the incident the letters referred to. The villagers being stood against a wall and shot. The devil referred to in the second letter, the one whose death might be worse than his reign, must be Heydrich.

Tyler gritted his teeth, waiting for Grey to go on. He was not a man to be rushed.

"After this bit of brutality, the local police, who were helping out, loaded the remaining women and children into lorries and took them off. The story we've got from one of our operatives in Prague is that the mothers and children were separated." Grey paused to draw on his pipe. "Very nasty business, Tyler. Very nasty. According to our source, all but four of the children were gassed."

"My God."

"Quite so. The four who were spared, presumably because they have an Aryan appearance, have been taken to the Fatherland for Germanization."

"And the mothers?"

"They have been sent to concentration camps; the Nazis' idea of inflicting a slow, miserable death on innocents." Grey paused again. "There were some pregnant women in the village and they were taken off to Prague. We don't have the complete story yet, but rumour has it that the newborns have also been removed, probably to Germany as well."

Letter number three.

Tyler rubbed his head hard. He felt icy cold.

"I read that the commandos were caught."

"Oh, yes. They were tracked down to a church where they'd taken up hiding. They held out, but eventually they were all killed. Brave men, Tyler. Worst thing is, they might have escaped, but they were betrayed by one of their own. Turned in by a commando who was on the mission."

Tyler bit his lips, holding back his impatience. "Do we know who it was?"

"We do. The traitor was a chap called Rudy. Rudy Pesek. There was only one man named Rudy who went on that mission. I'd say it's the man you're looking for."

Tyler whistled. This was an unexpected turn of events. "Could he be back in England?"

"No. He's received a handsome reward and is being feted by the Nazis."

"And all the other commandos died?"

"Those who went over with the operation did. However, given the situation you're dealing with, Tyler, I thought I should follow up on any man who was connected with Operation Anthropoid, no matter how peripherally."

Thank you, Mr. Grey. You hold the position you do for good reason.

"Hubbie did a check for me," continued Grey. "There was another fellow who went through the training with the group, but at the last minute he didn't go on the mission. He was injured."

Tyler could hear Grey tapping the pipe bowl on his desk following a bout of coughing.

"Did you get the name of this particular bloke?"

"Well now, and here's the disagreeable side of my trip that I mentioned earlier. Hubbie and I had barely concluded our conversation when we were interrupted by an air raid warning. He had to get off the telephone. And I had a train to catch, which was itself delayed for an hour."

Suddenly, Grey's voice faded away completely.

The telephone had gone dead.

Tyler bellowed into the receiver. "Sir? Mr. Grey?"

Damn. He jiggled on the cradle and abruptly Grey's voice came back on.

"Tyler. Sorry about the damn telephone. There's a loose wire somewhere. Anyway, as I was saying, the chappie who didn't go on the mission ended up in East Grinstead with serious injuries. Got treated there but apparently he healed fast and recently he asked to be transferred to, guess where?"

"St. Anne's?"

"Bang on, Tyler! Said he had a girlfriend who lived in the area. He was released just over three weeks ago."

"What's his name? Do you know what his injuries were?"

The line went dead. Tyler jiggled the cradle desperately but with no luck. He slammed down the receiver and raced out.

64.

WITHOUT A WORD, THE ALMONER HANDED TYLER THE car key. He hurried to the west gate, where one of the officers was standing guard.

"Constable, I've just obtained information that may lead us to our killer. Until we locate him, absolutely nobody must leave the grounds. No one."

The constable looked alarmed. "Somebody already did, sir. One of the patients. He said that the sister had given him permission to go for a bit of exercise. He took the tandem."

Sister Rebecca overheard this. "I gave no one such permission, Inspector."

"Shite!"

"Sorry, sir, if I should have stopped him," said the constable. "I saw no reason to mistrust him. Especially as he was crippled. He said that bicycling was helping him get back the use of his legs."

"What did he look like?"

"Dark-haired. Bit on the thin side."

Tyler stared at the constable. "He actually spoke to you?"

"Yes, sir. He seemed a polite young chap."

"Was he walking?"

"He did come out at first with a cane, but he said he needed to practise walking without it. He left it over there by the shed."

Tyler turned. A cane was propped against the wall. The last time he'd seen it, a supposed mute and supposed cripple had been leaning on it.

Victor Clark.

—

"He's been faking," said Sister Rebecca, aghast.

"Seems that way. Constable, did you see which way this man went?"

"He turned right as he went out of the gate."

West. In the direction of St. Clement's Church.

Tyler felt as if he'd swallowed ice. Three of the reservists were standing by the front steps and he hurried over to them.

"Flynn and Jordan, you stay here. Constable McNab, go to the almoner's office and ring Sergeant Rowell. Tell him to get over to St. Clement's Church right away. Tell him to come armed and to bring as many reinforcements as he can. I'm not sure what I'm going to encounter, so please stay on high alert."

He beckoned to the remaining constables. "Chase, Biggs, Swinfell, come with me."

The almoner caught him by the sleeve. "I'd like to come as well. I'm a nurse. Shirley might need me."

"Absolutely not, Sister. The situation is potentially highly dangerous. I'll send a runner to you immediately if necessary."

She let him go. "Please take care. God be with you."

Tyler drove as fast as he could, following the river road as Mortimer had directed.

There was the red barn.

And there was the entrance to a laneway. A weathered sign-post tilted on the corner. He could just make out the words CHURCH LANE. He could see the motorcycle and sidecar tucked off to one side. He pulled up behind.

"All out, lads. Maintain silence."

He loosened the revolver in its holster.

The lane was narrow, and trees lined the edges. They set off at a fast jog. Around one bend, then they approached another. A gravel lane branched off to the left: this presumably led to the church. He signalled to the others to stop, and as he did so Mortimer emerged from the trees, Mady behind her.

"Here we are, sir," Mortimer said softly.

"Thank God," panted Tyler. "Give me a minute." He bent over, struggling to get his breath. "All right, listen. The man I believe to be our murderer left the hospital about twenty-five minutes ago. He was riding on a tandem."

"There is a tandem lying on the ground on the other side of the church, sir," said Mortimer. "I noticed it when I was scouting out the situation."

"We have to exercise extreme caution. He's most likely armed and he's a trained killer. He's been masquerading as a mute and a cripple. He's neither. He's somehow tied in to the abduction of Shirley McHattie. Our first priority is to get her out. Unharmed."

Tyler was breathing more normally now. He addressed Constable Mortimer.

"Did you see any signs of life?"

"Yes, sir. I went by way of the woods until I had a clear view of the church. While I was there a woman came out of the vestibule door."

"Shirley McHattie?"

"No, sir. I didn't recognize this person. She is dark-haired, perhaps mid-twenties. She was wearing a white nurse's uniform."

Had to be Polly.

"What did she do?"

"Nothing. She just stood and smoked a cigarette. She spoke to somebody inside the church over her shoulder, but I didn't hear what she said. When she finished her cigarette, she went back inside and closed the door."

"And you're sure she didn't see you?"

"Positive, sir. She gave no indication of alarm."

Tyler stared at the church. "I've got to determine what's going on."

"We could use the lepers' window," said Constable Mortimer eagerly.

"What the hell is that?"

"It was intended for those who could not be allowed into the church itself. Through the opening, the lepers were able to gaze upon the altar, where they could see the Elevation of the Host. This is the moment when—"

Tyler interrupted her impatiently. "I know what the Elevation of the Host means, Constable. I just want to know how this window might help us."

"Sorry, sir. The window isn't glazed, and we might be able to hear anybody talking inside the church."

"And where is it?"

"On the far side, sir."

Tyler looked at her. Her pupils were dilated with excitement, but she seemed steady enough.

"Let's go take a look. Are you up to it?"

"Yes, sir. Absolutely. I'm a Girl Guide captain, sir."

"Well these aren't little girls we're dealing with. They could be extremely dangerous. All I want to know is who's in there and what they're doing. And if Shirley is safe."

"Yes, sir."

"Let's go." He turned to the waiting constables. "We're going to take a gander, but if you hear anything that sounds like trouble, come on the run. Try to look like a battalion."

Tyler undid his jacket so that the revolver was easily accessible and nodded to Mortimer to start.

"We can proceed through the woods," she said quietly. "There is a strip of grass between the trees and the church wall which has become quite overgrown. It can give us cover."

"Lead on."

She stepped back into the dense stand of trees and he followed. It was raining heavily by now and water started to drip down the back of his collar as he brushed against the leaves of the trees.

In spite of the foliage, they moved quickly, Tyler close behind Mortimer. He hadn't even realized they'd been circling, but she signalled she was about to stop. Cautiously, she pushed aside a branch and he saw that they were now about fifty feet away from the church. In between them and the church was the graveyard, with a scattering of old, worn markers, many tilting at angles, many crumbling.

St. Clement's wasn't big, but it had an imposing presence, the stark simplicity of the grey stone walls emanating an ancient authority. The windows were narrow and high up in the walls. Nobody was going to see them from inside the church.

"All right, let's gaze upon the altar," Tyler whispered.

Mortimer in the lead, they scurried around the gravestones to the shelter of the overgrown verge. They waited, but nothing stirred. She indicated the lepers' window was just to her left. There was a large, smooth rock directly underneath, presumably a stepping stone to enable the outcasts to get a better view. Tyler climbed up and peered into the opening.

It was like looking through a periscope without the magnification. The slit in the thick wall sloped down and widened as it went inward. As was the original intention centuries ago, a section of the altar was clearly visible.

Ah, that was something nobody from a previous era would have seen. Sitting on top of the altar table was a black doctor's bag. Next to it, a pair of women's shoes. And he could hear voices. A man's and a woman's. Unfortunately, the reverberation of the stone church muffled the words. He couldn't make out what they were saying or even the tone. The voices ceased abruptly.

Then he heard a moan, increasingly loud, followed by an even louder cry that was cut off suddenly. He knew what it was, he'd heard it before. It was the age-old wail of a woman in labour. Shirley McHattie *was* in there.

He stepped down and gesticulated to Mortimer that they should return to the trees.

"Did you hear that, Constable?" he whispered. "I believe Shirley's gone into labour. We need to get her to a hospital."

He signalled to Agnes again and she turned and led the way back to where they'd left the constables. He didn't speak until they were there.

"Draw in, lads. Shirley McHattie is definitely inside that church and I'd say she's close to delivering her baby. We need to get her out and to a proper hospital. She might have gone in there voluntarily, but I doubt that's where she would want to give birth."

"Are we going to break in?" asked Mady, his eyes wide.

Tyler hesitated. "Right now, I'm the only one armed. You can bet our man has a weapon as well." He addressed Mortimer. "Sergeant Rowell should be on his way. Take the motorcycle and meet him. Tell him what's going on. Then get back to St. Anne's. Fast. Have every available constable get over here immediately. Two to a bike if necessary."

"Is Shirley in danger, sir?" asked Constable Biggs.

Tyler nodded. "Probably."

Constable Mortimer looked at him. "Can we afford to wait, sir?"

Tyler's anxiety made him short-tempered. "I'm not God, Constable Mortimer," he snapped. "I don't know. If we try to break in now, it might make matters worse. If we don't, Shirley's life may be endangered. I'm trying for a compromise. We move in as soon as we can secure the situation. Now go. Hurry."

Mortimer ran to get the motorcycle from the bushes.

Tyler faced the others. "I'm going to try to get a better sense of what is happening. Don't make a move unless you hear a command from me."

"Yes, sir. Shall we have truncheons at the ready?" asked Mady.

"Yes."

The man in there has been trained in war tactics you've never even heard of. Truncheons won't be of much use.

But he was glad to have these men with him. He knew they would do their best for the innocents.

"All right, let's go. Single file. Keep to the side of the road. We'll go as far as the second bend, where we can see the gravel path to the church. I'll go on alone from there. You will wait."

They set off. Tyler could feel his heart beating faster. Hearing that cry of pain from young Shirley McHattie had made his desire to catch this man implacable.

Victor Clark. Trained killer. Triple murderer.

65.

SHIRLEY WAS DRIFTING IN AND OUT OF CONSCIOUSNESS. When she surfaced sufficiently to grasp where she was and what was happening, she cried out. A woman in a white uniform was leaning over her. It was Polly. Her friend. Shirley, through the fog of her mind, could just make out what she was saying.

"I'm going to give you something to ease the pain, pet. Baby's coming fast."

Suddenly a man's face appeared next to Polly. Puzzled, Shirley tried to make sense of what was happening. She recognized him from the hospital. He used a cane and he'd had his jaw wired so that he couldn't talk. But he was speaking now.

"How much longer?" he asked Polly.

"Soon. The baby's crowning."

Shirley managed to catch hold of Polly's hand. "Where's Rudy? You said Rudy would be here."

The man's face came in very close and he gripped her chin so she couldn't turn her head. There was spittle on his lips; he smelled bad.

"This is Victor Clark. I was here last night."

Shirley was momentarily overcome by a wave of pain and she moaned, trying to turn away.

"Rudy," she said again.

Clark held her fast.

"Your sweetheart will not be coming. We told you that so you would come willingly, but alas, the truth is he's dead. I should say, more precisely, that to all intents and purposes he is dead.

Did you know the man who impregnated you is a traitor? And a murderer? Responsible for the cruel deaths of many, many people. Ah, I see you did not know. How could you?"

Polly's face appeared again. "She is ready to start pushing. Do you have to do this now? Can you have some pity for the poor girl?"

The man's voice was harsh. "Who had pity on my father? My brother? Who pitied my mother?" He actually gave Shirley's head a bit of a shake. "All are dead, Miss McHattie. All have died because of him. Because of your dear Rudy."

She wanted to get up and run, but she couldn't. He let go of her chin, but suddenly there was something being pressed on her nose and mouth, choking her. She tried to shove at the hand holding the mask but she couldn't. She heard Polly say, "Breathe normally, there's a good girl. This will all soon be over."

66.

Tyler surveyed the scene in front of him. The church looked forlorn in the slanting rain; the graves didn't suggest peace so much as desolation. He could not detect any movement or sound.

He ran across the grass to the lepers' window. Once there, he removed his revolver from the holster. He stood up on the rock beneath the window and, steadying himself, pointed the gun into the slit and cocked the hammer.

Polly had put a sheet on the pew where Shirley was lying. It was soaked with blood and fluid. Her legs were propped up on an upended prayer stool, but Shirley had no sense of the indignity. She was unconscious.

"It's coming, baby's coming," cried Polly.

She cupped her hands underneath the infant's head as it crowned and helped it to slide out of the womb. A boy child. It was bluish and showed no signs of life.

"Is it alive?" Clark asked.

Polly grabbed the infant by the legs and upended it. She slapped its scrawny buttocks hard. It made no sound.

"The anaesthetic has doped him, is all. Get me my medical bag."

Tyler could hear the voices but again could not make out what they were saying. He thought there was a new urgency in the tone.

Then the man came into his sights. It was Clark all right and he was moving quite normally. He was also holding a gun by his side. He reached for the doctor's bag that was on the altar, giving Tyler a full view of his upper back.

Tyler fired.

67.

SOLDIERS OFTEN HAVE AMNESIA ABOUT WHAT HAS taken place in battle, but for Tyler the ensuing events remained crystal clear.

The bullet smashed into Clark's shoulder, spinning him around and knocking him to the ground. Somehow he maintained his grip on his revolver and he rolled over and lifted it, aiming up towards the window. Tyler fired again but the bullet ricocheted off the altar, slicing off a piece of wood.

He fired a third time and this shot hit Clark in the wrist, knocking the gun from his hand. What felt like seconds later, the door to the front vestibule crashed open and Tyler could hear Sergeant Rowell shouting at top volume.

"Don't move. Don't move or I'll shoot."

The sergeant came into view. Clark was struggling to get to his feet, but Rowell shoved him down, grabbed his arm, and twisted it so he could snap a pair of handcuffs on his wrists. This elicited a yell of pain from the injured man. Two other officers who were right behind the sergeant grabbed Clark by the feet and immobilized him. Somewhere in the background, Polly was yelling.

Tyler had stayed where he was, on his rock. Rowell turned and looked up to the lepers' window.

"Sir, are you all right?"

"I'm fine, Sergeant," Tyler shouted back at him. "I'll be right there."

When he stepped down from the rock, he almost fell. His legs felt decidedly wobbly.

—

It was almost midnight by the time things had got sorted out, and Tyler, Sergeant Rowell, and Sister Rebecca were all three sitting in her office.

Rowell was drinking whisky, "given the special circumstances." Tyler sipped on a glass of brandy that the almoner had produced. She herself had settled for hot milk.

"I didn't recognize myself," said Rowell. "I'd never have thought my blood would get up like that. But I swear if he'd moved a muscle, I would have shot him. I could see that poor girl lying in the pew, you see. She looked dead. And that other woman holding what looked like a dead baby in her arms." He looked over at Tyler. "There was no sign of you. There had been three shots. I didn't know if you were alive or dead." He grinned. "Imagine what a relief I felt when I saw your mug – excuse the expression, sir – peering through that window." He turned to the almoner. "How are the baby and Miss McHattie, Sister?"

"It's still touch and go for the infant. Polly gave Shirley too much chloroform and his respiratory tract was seriously compromised. We'll know more within the next couple of days. It's a little boy, by the way. Shirley herself has recovered consciousness, but that's all I've heard. We sent them to the general hospital. Her mother says she'll telephone us when she gets a report from the doctor."

"And Mr. whatever-his-name-is? What has he got to say for himself?"

"Inspector Tyler, you took his statement," said the almoner. "What did he say?"

"He mumbles slightly because of the jaw injury, but he is most articulate. He learned English as a child from his grandmother and he speaks it better than I do. His real name is Vaclav Kozik. He is Czech."

Rowell shook his head. "Is he insane? Why did he do what he did?"

68.

Kozik had been transported to the general hospital at Ludlow, where a brusque, unsympathetic doctor had treated his wounds. Tyler's first bullet had passed through the right shoulder without hitting bone. Even though the third shot had blasted his revolver from his hand, he had suffered no serious injury, only bruising. At the hospital, the doctor stitched up the shoulder wound without using a general anaesthetic, and after a couple of hours, Tyler was able to question the prisoner.

He was offered morphine but refused. He said he wanted a clear mind.

Suit yourself. If you want to be a tough man, be my guest.

Actually, Kozik didn't look tough. His emaciated face was drawn and grey and he had deep circles around his eyes.

"Unlike most men you deal with, Inspector, I want to tell you what I did and why. I don't wish to hide anything or hold anything back."

"It might surprise you, lad, but an awful lot of criminals are keen to present their side of the story."

Tyler sat across from him at the table they'd set up in the hospital room. Constable Mortimer had revealed yet another talent. She knew shorthand and she volunteered to take notes if Tyler wished. He did wish and she was seated slightly behind him. If she was distressed by what Kozik had to say, she kept it to herself.

Tyler had brought the three letters with him, and he put them on the table.

"I'm assuming you wrote these?"

Kozik nodded.

"I gather they are referring to what happened when Reinhard Heydrich was assassinated? A village was the object of Nazi reprisal."

"That's right. The village of Lidice. One hundred and ninety-seven inhabitants, four babies due to arrive any day. The village was burned and razed to the ground. The villagers had nothing to do with the death of Heydrich, but the Gestapo didn't mind about that. They'd been told that one of the assassins was from Lidice and that many of the villagers had been complicit in the assassination. That was all they needed. You don't have to have evidence if you're the Gestapo. You can always get evidence by torture and brutality."

Kozik had a slight London accent, courtesy of his English grandmother and his summers in England.

He drank some of the water that Tyler had provided for him.

"Was it true?" Tyler asked.

"Was what true?"

"That one of the assassins was from Lidice?"

"Lidice was the village where I was born. Where my family lived."

"I see."

"See what, Inspector?"

"I understand you were one of the original commandos from Operation Anthropoid. The object of your training was, in fact, to kill Heydrich."

Kozik nodded. "I would have been on the mission except that I was injured in a freak crash. A training flight, not even the glory of combat."

"That must have been disappointing."

A flash of fury leaped into Kozik's eyes. "Don't patronize me, Inspector. It might be difficult for you, a civilian, to understand, but for months that is all we had lived for. For the day when we would accomplish our mission. It is not for nothing that Herr Heydrich was called the blond butcher. And he practised his trade in my homeland."

"Rudy Pesek was part of Operation Anthropoid, wasn't he?"

"You are well informed, Inspector. Yes, he was one of the group. We all trained together." Kozik halted. He looked on the verge of passing out, so Tyler handed him the glass of water. Finally he continued. "We were like brothers, we knew everything about each other. Pesek knew I was betrothed to a girl in Lidice. He knew my parents lived there. He knew my young brother was about to turn sixteen. All of it. He is from Prague and has no family. No family that he cared for at least. He often said he envied me. Then, shortly before we were to embark, he met Shirley McHattie. He talked a lot about her."

"He knew he'd got her pregnant?"

Another pause. "I've never seen Pesek so happy. He said it was what he always wanted. But it was time to launch the operation, so off they go, brave men and true, not knowing they took with them the asp itself." Kozik lowered his head into his hands. There were beads of perspiration on his forehead. "The operation did not go smoothly. Initially, Heydrich was only wounded. But seven days later, he died. In great agony, I am happy to say. So the hunt was on for the perpetrators of this hideous crime. Herr Hitler would have wiped Czechoslovakia off the map if he'd had his way. He was persuaded that a more sensible way was to kill just a few hundred or so." Kozik's tone was ironic. "They began to search for the assassins, killing and torturing innocents in the hope of discovering them. However, they had no success for two entire weeks, until finally the comrades were discovered to be hiding out in a church. Rudy Pesek was not with them; it was he who had revealed their whereabouts to the Gestapo. He claimed he wanted the bloodshed to stop. That's why he betrayed them." Kozik chuckled. No mirth in it. "The reward was handsome. Far from stopping, the bloodshed increased. The Gestapo got out of Pesek that one of the original commandos, me, had been from Lidice and there they focused their revenge." Kozik had to stop again and drank more water. "My father, my brother were destroyed, as were two uncles. My mother and my dearest Anna have been sent off to what they call their 'camps.' They will not live."

"So you wanted revenge on Pesek yourself?"

Both Tyler and Kozik were speaking quietly. They might have been seated at a dying man's bedside, which, to all intents and purposes, they were. Agnes Mortimer didn't move a muscle.

"Of course I wanted revenge. Who would not? But more than that . . . I also want the world to know what happened. What Hitler and his henchmen are capable of."

"Jock McHattie and his son cannot be held responsible for the massacre. They committed no crime. Nor did Sister Ivy."

"Neither did the villagers of Lidice commit a crime," snapped Kozik. "Surely, Inspector, you don't believe that only the guilty suffer in a time of war?"

Tyler felt a rush of anger. He knew all too well that the innocent suffer. Kozik must have sensed he'd hit a nerve because he waited for a moment before continuing.

"The only person Pesek has shown any real love for is Shirley McHattie. He wanted her family to be his." Again the ironic tone. "He would've had a hard time persuading them he was a suitable husband for their daughter, but that is not my affair. I wanted him to experience even a fraction of what I experienced. So I chose to kill the father. As mine had been killed."

"Ben was a witness?"

"That was not why I shot him. He would never have known it was me."

"Why then?"

"He was just sixteen. Like my brother. All the boys of Lidice died who were that age. The other boy, the younger one, I spared."

Tyler took a deep breath. He would have liked a cigarette but wasn't about to break up the flow of Kozik's narrative. He glanced at Constable Mortimer. Her eyes met his and he saw her deep distress. But there was nothing to do but press on.

"You didn't spare an innocent nun," said Tyler. "Did she guess you were the killer?"

"Not at all. She suspected nothing. But she was a nurse. The women who came to take the children away were nurses. The children of Lidice were gassed. I gassed a nurse to settle the score."

Kozik needed another drink. Tyler thought the man was experiencing a great deal of pain, but he asked for no relief.

"I see. You would have taken any of the sisters?"

"Sister Ivy was on duty. It was easier to get to her."

"You drugged her first, I assume?"

"Yes. I drugged her both nights. As you have surmised, I needed her to be asleep while I got out. She was a creature of habit. Cocoa at a quarter past two on the dot. I doctored her sugar with a little sleeping dust. I had plenty of time to exit and return while she slept. The fire escape made it easy for me. I stored my gun in the bottom of the pigeon seed bin, by the way. I'm sure nobody thought of looking in there."

No, they hadn't, thought Tyler ruefully.

"Did you know Sister Ivy was letting Dai Hughes in and out?"

"Of course I knew. I am an observer. We commandos are trained to observe and note the comings and goings of the local population. It is now ingrained in me. Sister Ivy was up to silly shenanigans with the orderly. Unlocking the door so he could tom-cat around with a certain Polly Hutchins when he was supposed to be on duty. She is a girl who, you might say, lacks a sense of morality. She is amenable to most things if you pay her."

"Sounds like you know her well."

"Let's say we became acquainted when I took a short leave in Manchester before I was injured. After the massacre, when I decided what I was going to do, I got in touch with her. She agreed to come to Ludlow, to make certain liaisons as I directed. Polly can be most charming when necessary."

Tyler was stunned to realize how carefully Kozik had planned everything. Again the man seemed to pick up on Tyler's thoughts. He smiled. "Human nature, Inspector. One of the best tools in our arsenal as commandos is to understand human nature. Surely this is something both you and I share. You are a shrewd man, I know that about you. And I sense that you, too, feel things deeply."

Tyler had no desire to be linked to this man and he made no comment.

"You certainly managed to fool some good people."

"I made myself above suspicion by presenting myself as a man who couldn't walk properly and couldn't talk. I was really quite recovered when I arrived at St. Anne's, but because I didn't complain or make a fuss, nobody bothered to question the earlier records. People will accept what they perceive as the truth if you are convincing enough."

Tyler couldn't help himself. "I don't know whether to think the world has lost a great psychiatrist in you or a great actor."

Kozik actually smiled. "Let's say both professions have been studies of mine."

"You were the matchmaker for Dai Hughes and your friend, I presume?"

"Quite so. Mr. Hughes was fooled into believing Polly loved him. By the same token, Shirley McHattie thought she had found a best friend. Lonely people are so susceptible. As for Polly, she is eager to have a child. Alas for her, she herself is unable to procreate. Therefore, like the German women who took our children, she needed to take somebody else's. I introduced her to my scheme. She was only too happy to go along with it if she got what she wanted. Plus a nice sum of money, of course."

"So you conspired to abduct Shirley McHattie?"

"Precisely. The penultimate act. She is such a gullible young girl. She thought she was going to meet Rudy. Polly knew of a good hiding place – and of course a church was a perfect parallel. My best friends, my comrades, all died in a church."

"What were you planning to do with the baby?"

"Polly was going to disappear and raise the child as her own."

"Which meant you would have to kill Shirley, its rightful mother."

Kozik looked away. "That's what happened to the mothers of Lidice. They have gone to their deaths."

The insanity of the words spoken so calmly was unutterably chilling. Tyler tried to keep his own voice under control, but he didn't succeed. He found himself shouting.

"What happened to your village, to the people in it, was wicked. Nobody denies that! Do you think it helped any of them that you, too, took reprisals? Do you? You have also killed innocent people."

"I realize that and I have remorse." Kozik spoke solemnly.

"I don't believe you," yelled Tyler. "You're no better than the Gestapo."

For the first time Kozik appeared rattled. "That isn't true. I weep for those I have killed. But I weep more for the men who were stood against the wall and shot in cold blood. I weep for the children who were taken away and gassed. For the mothers whose infants have been stolen from them."

"You are insane," cried Tyler. "You try to sound magnanimous, but you are no better than a petty thug who is full of spite."

Kozik stared at him. "Perhaps it does seem that way. I admit I did what I did so that Rudolph Pesek would know what would never be his and he would suffer. But I also did what I did so that the world would know and also weep."

He reached beside him for the box containing the contents of his pockets. He removed an envelope. "I was going to give you this last letter, Inspector. The ultimate act. Frankly, I was contemplating imitating the final razing of my village."

"What! You mean you were going to set St. Anne's on fire?"

"Precisely. But to tell you the truth, I am bone tired. I could not do it."

"Thank God for small mercies," said Tyler sarcastically.

He took the envelope. Kozik leaned back and closed his eyes.

"You've got all of it, Inspector. I'm not going to say any more. In your eyes, my crimes are heinous. Do with me what you will. I care not. My heart has been destroyed already."

69.

Sister Rebecca and Rowell had listened without comment to Tyler's recital.

"May God have mercy on his soul," said the nun.

"What is going to happen to him?" asked Rowell.

"He is now in the custody of the soe. The Special Operations Executive. We will have to work together to see how we are going to prosecute. If we get that far, which I doubt, given the man's state of mind."

"And Polly Hutchins?"

"She has been charged with kidnapping and forcible confinement. She will go to jail."

"What was the final letter about?" Sister Rebecca asked.

Tyler handed her the envelope. "You can read it yourself. In some ways it is the worst."

She took out the sheet of paper. "I'll read it out loud, shall I?"

They have been brought from the camp to bury the dead. The trampled grass is slippery with blood and the bodies still lie where they have fallen. The soldiers regard the workers sullenly, ready to pounce at the slightest indication of awareness. Not protest, forget such a thing as protest. Nobody would dare to do so, but the guards are alert for the slightest glance, the mere

flicker of an expression that might be
construed as judgement.

"Who are you looking at, Juden?" yells
one, but he is too drunk to follow up on his
question.

All around the killing ground, tossed
among the sweet-smelling apple trees, as far
as the eye can see, are empty bottles. Rum,
cognac, much wine.

Behind them the houses are already on fire
and the air is speckled with bits of flaming
wood blown on the wind.

The place is razed.

Who will remember what it once was?

Sister Rebecca put down the paper. She reached over and
touched Tyler's arm. "We will remember."

He clasped her hand in both of his.

"We will. We will indeed."

EPILOGUE

THE RESIDENTS OF ST. ANNE'S HAD BEEN PROFOUNDLY shocked when they learned the man they had known as Victor Clark had deceived them, and what he had done. It was especially hard on the remaining rub-a-dubs, but in the end it had brought them closer together. When Daisy and Jeremy announced they were getting a special licence so they could marry immediately, even Eddie Prescott approved. "Good idea, kiddies," Melly had exclaimed. "*Carpe diem.* Eddie, that means seize the day, in case you're wondering."

Jeremy asked Melrose to be his best man. "Somebody has to be able to sign the registry."

The sisters offered their sanctuary for the ceremony. The invited guests were crammed together, but nobody seemed to mind. Shirley McHattie was seated near the back, holding her infant son close to her chest. Mrs. McHattie had declined to come. Daisy was pleased to recognize Inspector Tyler among the guests. He was next to Dr. Beck. Both had beamed at her as she went to take her place at the altar. She thought the inspector might even have winked.

The ceremony was performed by the Reverend Jervis. A bespectacled, rotund, and rather unprepossessing man, he nevertheless conducted the service in a sincere, unhurried way. His voice was resonant.

"Does anyone here present know of any reason or just impediment why this couple may not be joined together in holy marriage, let you now declare it or forever hold your peace."

Nobody did.

Everybody who could had donated their sugar rations, and Mrs. Fuller had baked a cake that was big enough to ensure everybody had a slice, albeit a tiny one.

Daisy had been intending to wear her WREN uniform, but Constable Mortimer took her aside and told her that she could have the loan of the Mortimer family wedding gown if she so wished. Apparently, her mother was only too happy to lend it to deserving but impoverished young women who were in one of the services.

"My mother is shorter than I am," said Agnes Mortimer with a shy smile. "I don't think it will have to be much altered."

The wedding gown turned out to be a beautiful full-length dress of white organdie lace over taffeta.

Jeremy whispered to her afterwards that the taffeta swishing around her body was one of the most sublime sounds he'd ever heard.

AUTHOR'S NOTE

This is a work of fiction. St. Anne's Convalescent Hospital is a figment of my imagination, as are the people who inhabit it. However, the town of Ludlow is real and has been for centuries. The events that are described in the letters that Tyler receives really happened, and I have rendered them as faithfully as I could. If in this small way I have created interest in that tragic event, I am glad. We must never forget.